A MOTHER'S DELIGHT

A mother's tender love for her family is a wonderful gift and what better way to celebrate than with these six charming Regency stories in honor of Mother's Day. Share in one mother's special day as she enjoys some much-welcomed rest, experience the delightful intrigue of a matchmaking mama who falls in love with her daughter's fiancé, and revel in the wondrous excitement of a newborn babe whose birth reawakens a magical first love.

Stories of love and magic, passion and romance — Sara Blayne, Teresa DesJardien, Melissa Lynn Jones, Valerie King, Mary Kingsley, and Nina Porter recreate the world of Regency England and remind us all that the enduring love of a mother is the most beautiful treasure of all.

A Mother's Love

SARA BLAYNE   **TERESA DESJARDIEN**
MELISSA LYNN JONES   **VALERIE KING**
NINA PORTER   **MARY KINGSLEY**

ZEBRA BOOKS
KENSINGTON PUBLISHING CORP.

ZEBRA BOOKS

are published by

Kensington Publishing Corp.
475 Park Avenue South
New York, NY 10016

First Printing: April, 1993

Printed in the United States of America

CONTENTS

The Singular Miss Marsh

by Sara Blayne

Chapter One

"Here we be, miss," announced the farmer, pulling the gray cob to a halt in front of the great house. "Cedars, jest as I promised 'ee."

Rebecca Marsh stepped down out of the pony cart on to the gravel drive bordered on either side by stately cedars. "Thank you, Mister Talbot, for a most pleasant journey," she said, tendering the farmer a coin. Then turning, she gazed with frank curiosity at the Tudor house with its twin towers and sprawling wings. Perched on the brow of a low hill, it overlooked sweeping lawns and cozy walled gardens, and a sparkling stream that vanished into a deer park thick with trees. The Duke of Ratherton's country house was even more lovely than Eleanore had described it, Rebecca decided. Why, then, should it affect her so strangely? she wondered, aware that for some time she had been experiencing the oddest sensation that her life was about to be altered forever. Perhaps it was only the result of the thickening of storm clouds overhead, she mused with a wry crinkle of her lightly freckled nose. Or perhaps her impressions were colored by the disturbing contents of the letter that had reached her in Portugal a fortnight ago practically commanding her presence here in the wilds of New Forest.

Her cousin Eleanore, who had been more like an older sister to her, had succumbed to complications resulting from a difficult childbirth. The news was no less shocking to Rebecca because it was over a year since the actual event. She felt her throat tighten at the thought that Eleanore was gone. Somehow it had never occurred to her that her cousin could ever be touched by misfortune — not Eleanore, who had al-

9

ways seemed blessed in all things. Beautiful, vivacious, and possessed of a sizable fortune, she had captured the heart of the most sought-after man in London and wed him. It had been, from all accounts, one of those rarities — a happy marriage, yielding two daughters and the heir, who had been the inadvertent cause of his mother's demise.

Rebecca had been in the Americas at the time of her cousin's wedding, and, afterward, she had followed her father and the drum to India and finally Portugal, so she had never actually had the pleasure of meeting Ratherton. What she knew of the duke she had gleaned from her correspondence with Eleanore. And yet, in the wake of his loss, Ratherton had sent for her. Why? she wondered, not for the first time.

Well, she would not find out standing here in the drive, she told herself with characteristic practicality, and bending down to pick up her leather valise and band box, both of which, though of excellent quality, had obviously seen much use, she squared her slender shoulders and climbed the steps to the Duke of Ratherton's front door.

"If only you'd let us know you were coming, miss," exclaimed the housekeeper who, upon being summoned by an ancient and exceedingly toplofty butler to tend to the unexpected visitor, had introduced herself as Mrs. Mason. "I'm sure his grace would have made arrangements to have you met in Christchurch. You would have been spared the inconvenience of the mail coach and, heaven forbid, a farm cart. Neither one is fit for a lady of quality like yourself."

"Perhaps not, Mrs. Mason," replied the young lady, smiling to reveal the flash of a dimple at the corner of her mouth. "However, the mail coach was almost luxurious compared to some of the modes of travel I have experienced following the drum. And at least the pony cart gave me the opportunity to view the countryside at my leisure. I quite enjoyed it."

"Er — indeed, miss." With an effort, Mrs. Mason schooled her plump features to reveal nothing of her startled reaction to that frank admission. Oh, she was a rare one was Miss Marsh. Old Stemming, the butler, was plainly scandalized at the notion of receiving a young woman who arrived unaccompanied by a female companion. But then, what could one expect? It was bad enough that the child had been rendered motherless when she was hardly out of leading strings,

10

but then to be reared alone from the age of ten by a father who was a colonel in the Royal Horse Guards? Why, it would be marvelous indeed if the girl was not a trifle odd. Not that there was anything to fault in either her dress or her bearing, reflected the housekeeper, observing the slender figure impeccably attired in a green velvet carriage dress trimmed in gold braid *à la militaire*. The curls peeking out beneath the smart beaver with the curly brim and green ostrich feather were decidedly red, and the eyes, heavily lashed and having the hint of an exotic slant upward, were a deep emerald green. She had the creamy complexion of a true redhead, which was marred by a sprinkling of freckles. Her cheekbones were fine and high, her nose long and straight, and her chin pleasingly pointed if somewhat stubborn. Were it not for her mouth, which was wide and demonstrated a strong tendency toward levity, she would have been judged a beauty of the first water. As it was, she was striking rather than beautiful and a mite tall for most tastes. But she carried herself with an easy, unconscious grace that made her appear elegant rather than gawky. Indeed, in spite of the fact that she could not be above three and twenty, she yet had about her an air of self-composure that made a person feel that Miss Marsh was up to every rig.

"I'm afraid his grace is away at present," said the housekeeper, taking up the girl's valise and band box. "The duke is at Windhaven, a guest at Mrs. Wendover's house party. He didn't say as to when he might return."

"Mrs. Wendover?" queried Rebecca, not having failed to detect the faint note of disapproval in the housekeeper's voice.

"Mrs. Caroline Wendover," confided Mrs. Mason, "the widow of old Mister Percival Wendover, who passed on hardly a year after the wedding. Like as not he wore himself out trying to stay up with his young bride. At any rate he never lived to see the birth of the heir that he set such store by. And a good thing, too. For if he had, he'd have—"

"I believe, Mrs. Mason," pronounced an imperious voice from the landing at the top of the stairs, "that Miss Marsh has heard enough of our neighbors for the present. Be pleased to bring her here to me this instant and then see if you can find something more constructive to do with your time than to indulge yourself in idle gossip."

"As you wish, Your Grace," gulped Mrs. Mason, dipping a hasty curtsy.

Rebecca was given only the briefest glimpse of a spare form, garbed in funereal black and held rigidly straight, before the Dowager Duchess of Ratherton turned with a rustle of silk skirts and retreated from sight down the hallway.

"If you'll follow me, miss," urged the housekeeper, her round, pleasant face suddenly and conspicuously wooden.

"It would seem I am given little choice in the matter," Rebecca observed with a wry quirk of an eyebrow. "Odd," she added, as Mrs. Mason preceded her toward the gracefully curving stairway, "but I was given to understand from my cousin that her grace made it a practice never to leave London."

"No, nor did she, until she arrived here better than four months ago." Mrs. Mason's mouth straightened to a grim line. "Now it's beginning to look as if she plans to take up permanent residence."

Clearly Mrs. Mason did not view the duke's mother as a welcome addition to the household, observed Rebecca in no little amusement. She was quite sure, in fact, that she heard the woman mutter something about "the old dragon" as she began to mount the stairs. Then she forgot Mrs. Mason as she took stock of her surroundings.

It was easy to detect her cousin's hand in the warmth of colors that permeated the house—sunny yellows and vibrant greens, muted lavenders and pale blues. What a perfect setting they must have been for the fair-haired duchess with her pale skin and blue-violet eyes, Rebecca thought with a pang. And the rich profusion of *objets d'art*, which might so easily have given the impression of mere opulence, even garishness, by one less discriminating, under Eleanore's careful eye had been made to reflect the tasteful elegance that had been so very much a part of the woman herself. More than anything else, however, it was the vases filled with freshly cut flowers that evoked images of the beautiful Eleanore. But then, there was hardly anything strange in that. Eleanore had always loved flowers. She would have made sure her home was filled with their bright colors and delicate scents. The thing was, everything brought her cousin to mind so strongly that Re-

12

becca found herself half expecting Eleanore to appear suddenly around every corner.

It was not a comfortable sensation. It had been over a year since her cousin's death, and it was as if Eleanore had only stepped out of the house for a time or, indeed, as if she had never left it. Surely if the duke's affections for his duchess were as strong as Rebecca had been led to believe, he must find the constant reminders of Eleanore unbearably painful. It was hardly a marvel that he had chosen to attend Mrs. Wendover's house party, Rebecca reflected. Indeed, she shouldn't wonder if he took advantage of every opportunity to absent himself from the house.

Sternly Rebecca shook off the melancholy feeling that the house seemed to evoke and instead straightened her shoulders in preparation of meeting the dragon in her lair.

"You've the look of your father," pronounced Lady Zenoria Dameron, Dowager Duchess of Ratherton, a single pale blue eye grotesquely enlarged as she surveyed Rebecca through an ivory-handled quizzing glass. "You're no beauty, not like your cousin was, but you've an air about you that must attract attention wherever you go. That is a deal better than fair looks without substance, as you've no doubt discovered for yourself.

"I am glad that you approve, Your Grace," Rebecca replied coolly, refusing to be intimidated either by the dowager's protracted scrutiny or her less than complimentary assessment of her guest's appearance.

"You're not in the least glad of it," snapped the dowager. "In fact, I daresay you do not care in the least what I might or might not think. Which is precisely why I sent for you. From all accounts you've a mind of your own."

"*You* sent for me!" Rebecca blurted before she could stop herself. But immediately she recovered. Folding her hands demurely before her, she calmly met the dowager, glance for glance. "I beg you will forgive me, Your Grace, for my unseemly outburst. I was given, however, to believe it was your son, the duke, who had requested my presence."

"As well you might, since that was my intention. Oh, spare me any pretense of outraged sensibilities, I beg you," continued the dowager, leaning heavily on a gold-crowned cane as she lowered herself into a tapestry-covered chair. "You know as well as I that you would not have come had you known it was an old woman, practically on her deathbed, who had summoned you. Curiosity brought you, admit it."

The corners of Rebecca's mouth twitched ever so slightly. The dowager duchess might indeed be every bit of sixty, and her hair was undeniably white, her spare frame utterly devoid of excess flesh and her face fine-lined with age, but if she was anywhere near her deathbed, Rebecca would have been surprised indeed.

"I do not deny that I was curious," she admitted easily, "but you are mistaken did you think I should not come — no matter who asked me — if I thought I was needed by the children. Or was that all a hum, too, Your Grace?"

"Do not be impertinent," snapped the dowager. "They have lost their mother." To Rebecca's surprise, a flash of pain twisted across the dowager's austere visage. "And their father as well, for all intents and purposes." The thin white hand with protruding blue veins opened and closed on the handle of the cane. "Of course they need you. Did you honestly imagine they would not?"

Carefully, Rebecca schooled her features to reveal nothing of the bestartlement that that little speech had engendered. "I cannot take the place of their mother, Your Grace," she answered quietly after a moment. "And I have not the inclination to serve as their governess. Just exactly what did you have in mind for me to do for them that you or their father cannot?"

"I shall leave that for you to discover," replied the dowager, in tones that indicated the interview was fast coming to an end. "Your father has written his consent for you to stay for the two months until his return to England. Time enough for you to get to know your cousins. As for me, I shall be returning to London in the morning."

"Indeed?" murmured Rebecca mildly. "Will not his grace find such an arrangement just a trifle inconvenient?"

A wry gleam flickered in the keen blue eyes, quickly masked. "I may be old, but I am not such a fool. I am leaving my companion, Miss Annabel Twickum, to give you countenance. No doubt I shall rub along well enough without her."

14

"How very generous, to be sure," Rebecca applauded without the flicker of an eyelid, though she did not doubt for a moment the companion was a dried-up old spinster with more hair than wit whom the dowager was more than pleased to foist off on someone else for a few weeks. "I am sure Miss Twickum and I shall get on famously. And, now, if you have nothing further to add, I shall beg leave to withdraw, Your Grace. I should like to unpack and freshen up before meeting the children."

"I doubt not you will do exactly as you wish, Miss Marsh," observed the dowager shrewdly. "As I never come down for dinner and since I plan to make an early start in the morning, I shall bid you goodbye here and now."

And that was that, thought Rebecca, as she let herself out of the dowager's sitting room and followed the upstairs maid down the hallway to the chambers which were to be hers for the next eight weeks.

"May I help you unpack, miss?" queried the maid, as they entered a sitting room, bright with yellow rose wall hangings and a blue silk-covered settee and chairs.

Rebecca, leaning over to inhale the sweet fragrance of yellow roses in a Meissen porcelain vase, paused ever so slightly as she caught sight of a flash of movement out of the corner of her eye.

"No, thank you — er — Lottie, isn't it?" she replied, turning to smile at the maid. "But perhaps you would see that my trunks are brought up as soon as they arrive. I doubt that they are more than half an hour behind me."

Rebecca waited until the maid had departed, closing the door carefully behind her. Then, dropping her reticule on a cherrywood occasional table, she gazed casually at her reflection in the oval looking glass hung on the wall.

"She is gone," she announced apparently to the room in general and calmly reached up to remove from its jaunty perch atop her head the curly brimmed beaver with the ostrich feather. "You may be pleased to come out now and show yourself."

In the ensuing moment of silence, Rebecca patted her short curls into place, brushed a smudge of dust from the sleeve of her dress, and shook the creases from her skirt before turning expectantly toward the door to

15

the bedroom, standing slightly ajar.

"Well?" she demanded pointedly. "Since I am not accustomed to carrying on conversations through keyholes, I suggest you come out into the open and face me. Unless, of course, you are a footpad or a burglar, in which case I shall have no choice but to shoot you," she added as though she were perfectly accustomed to dispatching any number of unsavory persons without bothering to ascertain their identities beforehand.

That startling announcement was greeted with a sharp gasp, quickly stifled, followed by a low exchange of whispers.

"Please don't shoot us!" came a frightened plea couched in a childish treble. "We're coming out."

"Oh, don't be such a gudgeon, Nobie, I pray you," chided a second voice in no little disgust as the door swung open. Dark eyes framed in a heart-shaped face and openly defiant coolly took Rebecca's measure. "She's only roasting us. I daresay she would faint at the mere sight of a firearm."

"Then you would be mistaken, Alexandra," Rebecca answered with a gravity no less than that of her accuser, a girl with the long limbs and lanky build of a preadolescent. "The colonel, I assure you, would never have tolerated a swooning female. Why, at the first sign of vaporish behavior, I should have been packed off to a boarding school for young ladies, and that, I should have found a dead bore."

"She knows your name, Alex," piped up the second of the two young intruders, peeping out from behind her sister's skirts. Blond-haired and blue-eyed, she could not have been above seven.

"Hush, Nobie," Alexandra scolded, distrust vying with a sudden spark of interest in her sober young face. "Grandmama must have told her."

"On the contrary," Rebecca countered. "Her Grace did not tell me. She did not have to. I am, after all, your Cousin Rebecca, and I was very close to your mama. She wrote me about you both on numerous occasions. I know that your papa gave you a puppy on your fifth birthday, Zenobia, and that you snuck her into your room at night so that she would not be lonely away from her brothers and sisters. What a very kind heart you must have. And I know that your mama was very proud of your accomplishments in music, Alexan-

16

dra, and how much you hate to practice, preferring, as you do, to steal out for a ride on your pony—let me see—Castor is it not?"

"You're wrong," Alexandra uttered harshly. "I hate ponies, and I shall never play the pianoforte again!"

"Castor is dead," offered the smaller of the two girls, her eyes so very like her mother's suddenly huge in her face. "Papa had to shoot him."

There was an instant of silence in which the ticking of the ormolu clock on the mantelpiece sounded inordinately loud. Then Rebecca said quietly, "I'm sorry, Alexandra. I didn't know. It must have been very hard on you to lose a friend like Castor. And on your papa . . ."

"*He* didn't care! He doesn't care about anything anymore since Mama . . ." Alexandra broke off in the middle of her outburst, her face having gone deathly pale. Rebecca stood perfectly still as she saw the child catch her lip between her teeth to stop its trembling. Then Alexandra's head came up. "*I* killed Castor," she declared, her youthful features hard with defiance. "I didn't care that he was too old or that he would never have refused to do anything I asked of him. I was thinking only of myself. I ran him at a stone fence, and both of his front legs were broken. Now tell me that you're sorry for me."

"I shan't, if you don't wish me to, Alexandra," Rebecca answered gravely, wondering with a swift surge of anger who was responsible for having placed such a terrible burden of guilt on the child, for she did not doubt for a moment that such foolish notions had come from someone other than Alexandra herself. "There is nothing more tiresome, after all, than having people force their sympathy on one when that is the very last thing one wants them to do. I am curious to know, however, why you were hiding in my bedroom. Somehow I cannot think it was to welcome me, since you had not the least idea who I was or that I was to arrive here today."

"We were changing the roses," Nobie declared with childish simplicity and wrinkled her nose at her older sister's vain attempt to silence her. "We change them every Tuesday and Saturday, just like Mama used to do. Only Grandmama said we should very likely break something and that we must leave it for the servants to do from now on." The little girl's eyes grew round with apprehension. "You won't tell her, will you?"

"I really don't see how I can," Rebecca said, appearing to consider the ramifications of such an action, "since your grandmama has made it plain that she will not emerge from her room for the rest of the day and, further, plans to depart for London early on the morrow. Besides, it would be such a dreadful bother — having to listen to a certain lecture. Personally, I should much rather go fishing."

"Fishing!" exclaimed little Nobie, her face lighting up. "Oh, I know I should adore fishing. Alex says Papa used to take us all the time. But that was ever so long ago. I can't remember it anymore."

Rebecca's heart gave a little lurch at the note of longing contained in that final utterance.

"Then of course we must go," she declared emphatically. "No doubt Stemmings can fix us up with the proper gear. And I shouldn't be at all surprised if Mrs. Mason would pack us a lunch, since of course we must miss afternoon tea. I don't know about you, but I find being outdoors always makes me positively famished."

"Oh, please, Alex. May we?" pleaded Nobie, gazing hopefully at her older sister. "It would be such fun."

"Now see what you have done," Alexandra said accusingly to Rebecca. "You must know very well we can do no such thing. Just look outside. It's going to rain at any moment."

"Yes, I shouldn't wonder at all if it does," agreed Rebecca complacently. "However, it is my experience that fish bite more readily in the rain. And there is nothing like a sudden downpour to make an adventure out of what might otherwise be a very dull outing."

Little Nobie giggled at such an idea. Clearly Cousin Rebecca was not in the usual style of grown-ups.

"No, it's quite impossible," declared Alexandra, after the barest hesitation, her expression one of determined self-abnegation. "We have our geography lessons, Nobie. You know I promised Papa. Besides, who would tell Miss Blydesdale?"

It soon transpired that Miss Blydesdale was the governess, and from the dread in the girls' faces, Rebecca suspected that she ruled the schoolroom with the hand of a petit tyrant. "Of course you must keep your promise to your papa," was Re-

18

becca's pronouncement. "We shall simply have to contrive to combine geography with fishing. A not very difficult task, since I know a great deal about the subject from firsthand experience. As for Miss Blydesdale, I shall be only too happy to tell her for you. In fact, I should like very much to make her acquaintance."

The girls exchanged startled glances, and just as it seemed that they would be unable to overcome their very real awe of Miss Blydesdale, Alexandra gave a defiant toss of her black curls. "I'll take you, Cousin Rebecca," she stated, the pallor in her cheeks giving mute evidence of the effort the decision had cost her.

Travers Anthony William Dameron, the ninth duke of Ratherton, lifted a jaundiced eye to study the heavy mass of clouds overhead. Good God, he thought acidly, as a spatter of raindrops splattered obligingly against his face, it needed only a cloudburst to crown the less than gratifying events of the past two weeks.

He had succumbed against his better judgment to Caroline Wendover's blandishments to attend a house party which he knew beforehand would be fraught with the sort of tedious annoyances he had hitherto made a practice to avoid. His expectations had been more than realized. He had been thrust into the sort of company whose excesses he found not only unappealing, but utterly boring. He had been forced to tolerate the sycophancy of aging dandies, the cajolery of full-blown females on the lookout for a fortune to support their various acquired vices, and the incipience of such pursuits as a mock hunt through the house with one of the ladies in the role of the fox. But even those provocations paled before Caroline's blatantly renewed attempts to start up a liaison that, far from being appealing, had left him utterly cold.

Perfectly capable of giving his would-be inamorata the snub direct, he had instead restrained himself sufficiently to employ a subterfuge to extricate himself from what was becoming an increasingly intolerable situation. He had, in short, pleaded the necessity of returning to Cedars to ascertain the well-being of his ailing mother. Egad, he mused sardonically to himself. He shuddered to think what use his

19

redoubtable parent would make of *that* if ever she learned of it. Then, tugging his curly brimmed beaver firmly down over his forehead, he touched spurs to his restive mount and set off at a ground-eating canter cross-country for Cedars.

Thirty minutes later it began to rain in earnest. Ratherton, caught in the deer park, uttered an oath and urged his mount to greater efforts. Nearly blinded from the pelting raindrops and thinking only to reach Cedars as quickly as possible, he burst from the trees into a secluded meadow little more than a mile from home. He was as little prepared to find the clearing occupied by a herd of wild ponies as he was to have a slender figure rear up suddenly out of a stand of gorse almost beneath his horse's nose.

A shrill cry of "Papa!" rent the air.

Cursing, he pulled back hard on the reins.

All in an instant, his mount reared, the wild ponies made a mad dash for the woods, and he glimpsed his two daughters, disreputably clad in an odd assortment of oilskins and canvas, staring, horror-stricken, up at him.

With an arm of steel, Ratherton brought his frantic stallion under control. Then, in a single, swift movement, he had dismounted and turned to face the creature who had precipitated what might very well have proved an utter disaster.

"That was magnificently done, Your Grace," exclaimed the miscreant, apparently unmoved by the hard glitter of a pair of remarkably black piercing orbs. "Though I daresay that is the last thing you wish to hear at this moment," she added with frank candor. "You are probably more interested to know why your daughters are out in the middle of a cloudburst with a female you have never had the pleasure of meeting before."

The duke discovered, to his amazement, a young woman, unfashionably tall and rendered vaguely absurd in a yellow oilskin raincoat and hat of the sort used by mariners. Furthermore, she was unabashedly appraising him. Ratherton, blessed with good looks, a title and a fortune, was used to being ogled by females. This time, however, he had the uncanny feeling that with *this* female, he had come very close to being found wanting. While the novelty of such a suspicion did indeed serve to spark his interest, it did nothing at all to improve his temper.

"Indeed, ma'am," he drawled with icy intensity. "And you, I trust, are about to satisfy my curiosity on both points."

If he had thought by that to put her in her place, he had blatantly misjudged the object of his rancor.

"On the contrary," she had the unmitigated gall to answer him, "I'm afraid that would be quite impossible without a lengthy explanation, and these, you must agree, are hardly favorable conditions for a calm and rational discussion. Suffice it to say that I am Miss Marsh, Eleanore's cousin, and that in spite of the fact that every care has been taken to insure the well-being of your daughters, I suggest it is time we returned to the house. We, after all, have caught enough trout for our dinner, and since *you* have frightened away all the wild ponies, there would seem little point in remaining further."

Ratherton's eyes narrowed to hard glittering points. It was on his lips to retort that there was never any point in being there at all, but since he could not deny the practicality of her observations, he was forced to reserve such comments for later. As for the accusation implied in her last remark, he was startled to discover a reluctant sympathy for the sentiments that lay behind it. A single glance at his daughters' crestfallen expressions left little doubt that his arrival had been inopportune in the extreme. They had been enjoying their little adventure, and he had spoiled it. The knowledge left him with a bitter taste in his mouth and an unreasoning anger at the meddling Miss Marsh.

"I am afraid, ma'am," he informed her coldly, "that we find ourselves in something of an impasse. I am the only one who can be trusted to handle Apollo. And while he may be persuaded to carry Alexandra and Zenobia, he cannot be depended upon to carry all of us."

"But I should not dream of asking him to," exclaimed the unsettling Miss Marsh, reaching up to run her hand over the stallion's sleek neck. "He is a perfect gentleman, I doubt not, without a mean bone in his body, and I am no stranger to spirited animals. But be that as it may, you, naturally, must ride ahead with the girls. I shall follow on foot."

There was a chorus of objections to that, both of the girls swearing that they would rather accompany Cousin Rebecca on foot than leave her to battle the elements alone. Unaccustomed to open rebellion from his daughters, Ratherton's lean countenance took on a forbidding expression. At that point, however, Miss Marsh smoothly intervened.

"Well of course you may walk with me if you wish, Zenobia," she said, appearing to give the matter the consideration it deserved. "But if I were you, I should think things over very carefully. After all, it is not every day that you get an invitation to ride with your papa on a steed like Apollo. Just think how very exciting it would be. And I was depending on you, Alexandra, to make sure Cook has our trout in time to prepare them for dinner. It would not be at all the same if you left it for your papa to do. There is, after all, the matter of the special recipe we discussed. But naturally the decision is yours. If you really prefer to walk—"

"No," Alexandra spoke up, noticeably squaring her thin shoulders, "you are quite right, Cousin Rebecca. I should be the one to discuss the menu with Cook. After all, I shall be mistress of my own house one day."

Ratherton, who had just witnessed his eldest offspring demonstrate a maturity he had thought beyond her years, was next brought to awareness by a small tug on his coat sleeve.

He glanced down into the upturned face of his younger daughter. His mouth thinned to a grim line as he saw the child visibly shrink beneath his scrutiny. Good God, he thought, had things changed so greatly that his own daughter was frightened of him? He experienced an almost forgotten urge to swoop the child up in his arms and sling her playfully over his shoulder as he had been used to do before Eleanore had insisted that while it might be all right for little boys to be tossed about, it certainly was no way to treat delicately bred little girls. Why, they would grow up to be tomboys or at the very least unruly little hoydens. Unconsciously, his eyes hardened and his handsome features assumed the cynical mask that had become habitual over the past few years. "Well, Zenobia?" he demanded, perhaps more sternly than he had intended. "Was there something you wished to say?"

Zenobia swallowed and nodded. "Yes, Papa. If you still want me to, I think I should be pleased to ride with you."

"Oh, you think so, do you," returned his grace, a spark of startled amusement flickering briefly behind his eyes. "I am no doubt gratified by this sudden change of mind and shall endeavor to make your ride as exciting as your heart may desire."

The child glanced doubtfully at the prime bit of blood snorting its displeasure at the delay. "Well, sir, as to that," she ventured in a small voice, "I don't think my heart is wishful of too great an excitement. He's a very tall horse, isn't he, and I don't think he likes me very much. He might be pleased if I fell off."

"Well, *I* should not be pleased. You may be sure that I shall let nothing of the sort happen to you." Mounting easily, Ratherton lowered a lean strong hand first to Alexandra. "Up with you," he said, helping the girl to swing up behind him. "And now, Miss Marsh, if you would be so kind as to lift Zenobia?"

In short order, Zenobia was snuggled cozily in the secure circle of her father's arms. Ratherton, feeling the small body relax trustingly against him, experienced an unfamiliar pang in the vicinity of his breast bone.

He glanced down at Rebecca as she handed Alexandra the basket of fish. "This won't take long. I shall be back for you in under twenty minutes."

"If you are, I shall be very disappointed in you," she flung back at him. "I shall, in fact, have a very poor opinion of your powers of comprehension, my lord duke. Now begone with you. And do not, I pray you, worry your head over me. I witnessed the march to Talavera and explored the tributaries of Hudson Bay in a canoe. I assure you a short walk in the rain will not discommode me in the least."

Somehow Ratherton, pausing long enough to observe the redoubtable Miss Marsh bend down to gather up the various fishing poles, tackle box, and lunch basket that she and the girls had brought on the outing with them, did not doubt for a moment that she was indeed perfectly capable of coping with any number of more difficult conditions than was offered by a mere spring shower in New Forest. The knowledge, however, did little to alleviate his own feelings of what was due a gently born female, and abandoning one to make her own way in the rain, while he rode, was in blatant violation of every gentleman's code.

At last muttering an oath at having been placed in an untenable position by a meddlesome female, he irritably sent the stallion plunging down the steep bank into the stream and up the other side. Immediately, he heard Zenobia gasp and felt her small hands tighten spasmodically on the fabric of his coat. Cursing himself for a witless fool, he slowed the horse to a gentler pace.

"You know, there is really nothing to be afraid of, Zenobia," he said quietly after a moment. "Apollo is very sure-footed, and I have a very good hold on you. You must know that I'd never let anything happen to you."

"Y-yes, Papa," came the hesitant reply, couched in a small voice. "Only —"

"Only what?" the duke gently prodded, when it seemed nothing else was forthcoming.

"Only she remembers what happened to Castor," supplied Alexandra in low, vibrant tones. "And Mama. Sometimes she has bad dreams about Mama and then she's afraid to go back to sleep until I climb in bed with her. But you mustn't think bad of her," she added defensively. "It took a lot of pluck for Nobie to put the worm on the hook. Cousin Rebecca said so. And Nobie didn't complain at all when she slipped and scraped her knee on a rock. It's just that she's very young and sometimes she misses Mama dreadfully."

"I see," murmured Ratherton, acutely aware that this was the first he had heard anything about any bloody nightmares. "And you, who are so much older, have been looking after your sister all this time, have you. Did you ever think to tell Nanny Slade, Alexandra?"

"I-I didn't wish to bother Nanny," Alexandra reluctantly admitted. "She isn't as young as she used to be, you know, and, well, she has enough to do looking after Anthony. He's been so terribly fretful of late that she hardly gets any sleep at night."

"Does she not?" murmured Ratherton, experiencing an unfamiliar stab of conscience that he was so little informed of the state of his youngest offspring. "And Miss Blydesdale? Surely your governess was not similarly engaged with Anthony?"

He felt a tremor of apprehension shudder through Zenobia's small frame even as he sensed Alexandra withdraw behind an invisible barrier.

24

"No, sir," answered the older girl in a peculiarly guarded voice.

Ratherton silently cursed. He was keenly aware that until that moment he had been sharing in something singularly special. The rapport created by the storm and their physical closeness on horseback was hardly what he was used to enjoying with his daughters. The fact that the mere mention of the governess had been enough to spoil the moment spoke volumes. He did not have to ask Alexandra why she had not confided in Miss Blydesdale. Obviously his daughters' relationship with their governess was not one conducive to confidences.

"Tell me about your outing with Cousin Rebecca," he said after a moment, deliberately changing the subject in the hopes of salvaging something from the remainder of their time together. "Did you use only live bait? Or did you try some of the flies we tied—summer before last, was it?"

"It was *four* summers ago, when I was eight," corrected Alexandra, noticeably brightening. "And, no, we used some marvelous specimens Cousin Rebecca brought back from America. Cousin Rebecca says no trout worth its name can resist them. We only switched over to worms after the water became too murky from the runoff upstream. You should have seen Cousin Rebecca cast, Papa. She's ever so good at it."

It soon came to the duke to wonder if there was nothing that Cousin Rebecca was *not* good at or did not know from firsthand experience, as the girls eagerly related the day's events. Nearly every other sentence seemed to ring with "Cousin Rebecca says" or "Cousin Rebecca did this or that," until he was quite convinced Miss Marsh must be the most singular female of his experience.

Perhaps almost as singular, however, was the sudden awareness that he had been proceeding for some time at a slow walk and that, furthermore, a full twenty minutes had elapsed since he had left Miss Marsh stranded in the rain. He was conscious of a twinge of conscience at his dereliction, which was only slightly less strong than his regret that the episode had so quickly come to an end. Oddly enough, he had quite enjoyed the novelty of finding himself the recipient of his daughters' confidences.

25

He lowered the girls to the ground and, ordering them to go in immediately and change into fresh gowns, he was preparing to go back for Miss Marsh, when Alexandra cried out in glee. "Look, Nobie. It's Cousin Rebecca. She's already at the foot of the hill."

Miss Marsh definitely was *not* in the usual style of gently bred females, decided Ratherton, arrested by the sight of Rebecca coming toward them with a long, swinging stride. Meddlesome, inordinately sure of herself, obviously stubborn and very likely opinionated—if he did not know the truth of it, he would have had difficulty in believing she was in any way related to Eleanore. She was, in fact, just the opposite of the sort of conformable woman he had always looked to for female companionship. Having been reared in a household with four elder sisters, he had early on learned an abhorrence of managing females. And yet suddenly he could not help thinking that if Eleanore had been just a little less persuadable and a trifle more sure of her position as his wife, perhaps things might have turned out differently.

The thought wrenched at old, never healed wounds. All in an instant the softened mood that had taken hold of him during the ride home with his daughters gave way before a bitter flood of memories.

Chiding himself for a bloody fool, he set spurs to the stallion and rode down the hill to meet his troublesome guest.

Chapter Two

Rebecca, perched across the saddle in front of the duke, her waist encompassed by a pair of strong, masculine arms, could not but reflect that his grace was going to prove a trifle more difficult than she had first anticipated.

Her initial impressions of a lean, powerful figure on horseback had been thrilling, to say the least. After all, with his coal black hair, pale complexion, and hard, glittery eyes, he had loomed out of the mist like some dark and brooding character from a Gothic novel. Nor had she been disappointed on closer inspection to discover that, while his undeniably handsome features gave every evidence of an arrogant, strong-willed nature, there was a certain sensitivity about the stern lips that hinted at a capacity for passion and tenderness. Which he, no doubt, was at great pains to conceal behind that habitually cynical mask, she mused, gazing up at the strong profile out of the corner of her eye. Furthermore, there was a high degree of intelligence reflected in those marvelously black, piercing orbs, which no amount of studied pretense at ennui could camouflage. Anymore than it could hide the bitterness etched in fine lines at the corners of his mouth, she reflected, a thoughtful frown puckering her brow.

Apparently she had been rather too optimistic to believe that a few minutes alone with his daughters would be enough to breach the wall he had built up around him. The poor man had been positively grim when he rode up to her a few moments before and dismounted.

A gleam of amusement sprang to her eyes at the memory. It had been obviously pointless to suggest that he need not have come back for her at all. She had seen at a glance that he was already aware of it *and* the fact that it was going to be absurdly awkward trying to transport two riders, three unwieldy poles, a basket, and a tackle box on a single, high-spirited mount. He had quickly resolved the problem of the fishing gear, ordering her to leave the blasted things behind for a servant to retrieve later; and, with a demureness he had obviously found suspect, she had complied with his demands. After all, there was little point in offending his masculine sense of pride merely to demonstrate that she was perfectly capable of taking care of herself.

"I cannot but wonder, Miss Marsh," drawled his grace, breaking into her train of thought, "do you always make it a practice to go fishing in the rain, or had you something else in mind when you gave into the impulse to expose my daughters to conditions a rational being would normally take care to avoid?"

"I had in mind becoming acquainted with my cousins, Your Grace," she answered, smiling humorously at his pointed sarcasm. "And you must admit there is nothing like a small adversity or two to break down the usual barriers between strangers. The girls will come to no harm from this afternoon's adventure, I assure you, and they enjoyed themselves immensely. Surely you cannot be angry over so small a breach of what might be considered behavior acceptable for delicately bred females."

"On the contrary, Miss Marsh," rejoined the duke in accents calculated to put her in her place. "I have never, since Miss Blydesdale came to Cedars, been in the least doubt that my daughters would be made to conform to the accepted mode of behavior. How *did* you persuade the paragon of governesses to give her consent to such an outing?"

Rebecca smiled, a demure smile belied, Ratherton noted grimly, by the flash of a roguish dimple at the corner of her mouth.

"I did not ask her consent," confessed the reprehensible Miss Marsh. "I simply informed her that, as I was taking the girls out, she might enjoy the afternoon off."

Ratherton quelled the urge to give vent to a low whistle. "And doubtless she was *pleased* at her unlooked for freedom?" he inquired with the sardonic arch of an eyebrow.

"Not at all, Your Grace," she answered, lifting her eyes to

28

reveal unmistakable imps of laughter in their emerald depths. "She was uncommonly put out by it. I believe she expressed the opinion that when you were informed of my irresponsible action, I should soon be made to learn the error of my ways."

"The devil she did," growled Ratherton, finding nothing amusing in the governess's impertinence to a guest in his house. "It seems I owe you an apology, Miss Marsh. Though perhaps Miss Blydesdale may be excused in part. She was naturally concerned for the well-being of her charges."

"Oh, naturally," agreed Rebecca without batting an eyelid. "Miss Blydesdale did not hesitate to make herself quite clear on that point."

Ratherton glanced sharply down at her, quite certain that her comment had had a double-edged meaning. But as they had by then reached the house and the girls had come running out to meet them, he was not given the chance to question her further.

A few moments later, as she and the girls hurried, giggling, upstairs, Rebecca was quick to deduce from Alexandra's eager, whispered comments that his grace had been almost human on the short ride home. He had, in fact, quite captivated Zenobia's trusting heart as was evidenced by the rapt manner in which she described her first time on horseback. Rebecca would have given a great deal to know what had happened to change him in the short interval between the time he dropped off the girls at the house and rode back to pick her up. But whatever it was, the fact remained that she had not entirely failed in her efforts to bring his grace to a closer understanding of his offspring. What they needed was more time together, and the sooner the better.

Dinner that night was to be a novel experience for his grace, who found himself invited to the schoolroom to share in a dinner hosted by his daughters. He did not doubt for a moment that Miss Marsh was behind it or that she had had a hand in persuading Mrs. Mason, Cook, and Lottie, the upstairs maid, along with John Trumbull, the underfootman, to abet them in this undertaking. Considering the fact that the schoolroom was on the third story, it was no mean feat to prepare a table sufficiently large to seat five people, let alone to convey the third best plates, silverware, glasses, and all the other accoutrements necessary for a formal dinner, for so the written invitation had informed him it was to be. At least the presence of a dumbwaiter facilitated the transport of the covered dishes, with the result that the trout fillets, sautéed in butter and topped with almonds and a garnish of lemon wedges, would be served hot, as would the English peas and steamed potatoes.

He was not quite sure what to expect when he arrived at the schoolroom at precisely eight o'clock, but certainly it was not to discover his older daughter garbed in a red silk sari, her thick curls subdued in a knot at the back of her head and gold earrings dangling from her ears in the manner of an East Indian princess. He was stunned, not by her exotic garb, but by the realization that his gawky, long-legged daughter was actually a strikingly lovely female on the verge of budding into womanhood.

He was rudely jarred from his moment of enlightenment by a loud sniff at his back.

"Shocking, is it not, Your Grace," commented a voice, filled with triumphant self-righteousness. "To think that I should ever see one of my girls dressed in a manner wholly unbefitting a female of refinement. I feel it is my duty to inform you that *I* had nothing to do with this disgraceful display. And, furthermore, to warn you that your daughters are in danger of being subverted by an unwholesome influence. Not that I entirely blame Miss Marsh for what she obviously cannot help. One must take into account that she was reared in foreign places where I doubt not she lacked the advantage of a proper English governess."

"You are mistaken, Miss Blydesdale," drawled the duke, grimly observing the stricken look in his daughter's eyes. "Miss Marsh had the advantage of my late wife's English governess. Nor do I find anything in the least shocking in my daughter's attire." Giving Alexandra a long look, he lightly saluted her knuckles before straightening to turn a cold eye on the visibly wilting governess. "On the contrary, I have never been welcomed by a lovelier hostess."

Miss Blydesdale's pinched features, framed in steel gray hair done in rigid waves from a center part, took on a peculiarly frozen look. "Indeed, Your Grace," she uttered in a strangled voice. "I only meant that . . ."

She was interrupted in what she had been about to say by Miss Marsh, who, fashionably elegant in a cream-colored silk evening dress, came sweeping into the room with Zenobia in tow.

"Good evening, Your Grace," said Rebecca, a trifle out of breath. "I am sorry if we are late. I'm afraid I had some difficulty locating the finishing touch to Zenobia's costume. We decided at the last moment to adopt a theme for tonight's dinner, and, since the girls are studying geography, we thought . . ." She broke off at sight of the governess, who gave every appearance of having been immersed in starch. "Miss Blydesdale," she exclaimed instantly, going forward to take the elderly spinster's arm, "how kind of you to join us. I see you found the invitation Alexandra slipped under your door while you were out. We were afraid you would miss the girls' presentation tonight, and that would never do, now would it. Here, you shall have the seat at the foot of the table. And, Your Grace, if you would be so kind as to take the seat of honor at the head. Alexandra, you and Zenobia are on either side of your father. And I shall sit here next to Miss Blydesdale. Now, John," she said to the underfootman, standing at attention next to the dumbwaiter, "you may ring for the first course to be sent up."

Dinner was, in spite of Miss Blydesdale's grim presence, a merry affair. Rebecca had not served as hostess for the colonel on three continents without acquiring considerable skill at it, though perhaps Ratherton was the only one of the company who fully appreciated the ease with which she kept the conversation flowing or the flawless sense of timing required to keep the courses coming and going with such consummate smoothness.

More than once his eye strayed to the far end of the table where Rebecca sat. He could not but note the subtlety with which she made the younger members of the party forget that they had never before dined with grown-ups, let alone with so august a personage as their very own father. It was not long before the room rang with their laughter or that the duke found himself being regaled with a lively account of his daughters' encounter with the wild ponies of New Forest. Even Miss Blydesdale was not immune to Miss Marsh's remarkable knack for drawing people out. Upon discovering that the governess had spent her youth in the Lake Country, Rebecca led

31

her into a description of the gray stone houses of Kendal and the old castle on the hill overlooking the town. The duke, glancing up, was more than a little surprised to behold the hard-bitten governess in the act of noisily blowing her nose. Then swiping at her eyes with her linen handkerchief, she remarked in a noticeably gruff voice that she had not thought of the old town in years.

Rebecca, leaning forward to squeeze Miss Blydesdale's hand, failed to see Ratherton watching her, a peculiarly arrested expression in his compelling eyes.

When the last dish had been taken away, Rebecca rose to announce that the young ladies of the house had prepared a short entertainment. Zenobia, looking to Rebecca for encouragement and more than an occasional prompting, gave an account of the origins of her American costume, which consisted of a fringed elkskin dress, decorated with colorful beads, leather leggings, and beaded moccasins. The dress was the traditional garb of a girl child of the Blackfoot tribe, and Cousin Rebecca had brought it all the way from Hudson Bay for her, she announced proudly.

Alexandra's recitation included a description of the various ways in which a sari was draped around the body according to differing customs, religious beliefs, or geographical adaptations and ended with a discussion of the Greek influence on the short bodice worn beneath the sari.

Applauding as she rose from her place at the table, Rebecca went quickly forward to hug first one and then the other of the two girls. "That was wonderfully done," she exclaimed softly in Alexandra's ear.

It *was* an amazing presentation, considering that it was unrehearsed and owed its source to the hurried remarks Rebecca had made as she helped the girls dress. Alexandra, it seemed, had absorbed every word.

Alexandra flushed with pleasure, then visibly started as she became aware of the tall form of her father coming toward her.

Suddenly shy, the child dipped a flustered curtsy. "Father," she blurted, dropping her eyes.

Consequently, she did not see the slight break in the duke's stride, or the sudden hardening of the handsome features into an impregnable mask. But Rebecca did. Indeed, she was almost sure his grace had been about to sweep the child up in a warm embrace, until Alexandra's unfortunate retreat into formality had squelched the impulse.

"You and the girls are to be congratulated, Miss Marsh," he remarked, his gaze unfathomable as it rested on his daughter before lifting to Rebecca. "Dinner was excellent. And the entertainment both interesting and informative."

"It is kind of you to say so, Your Grace," murmured Rebecca, wishing she could shake the man. Surely he must see what his cold words of approval were doing to his daughter. Alexandra was aching for his affection, not his congratulations.

Unexpectedly, it was little Nobie who retrieved the day.

"Did you really like it, Papa?" she exclaimed innocently, reaching up to take his hand. "I think Alexandra is beautiful, don't you? She was afraid you might not like her in her sari. But you do, don't you. I can see that you do. I think I'm pretty, too."

Inexplicably, Rebecca found herself holding her breath, as she sensed the struggle of emotions behind the duke's impassive features. Then suddenly he had bent down to pick the little girl up in his arms.

"I think," he said with mock severity, "that it is time you both went to bed. Even very pretty girls, like you, need their beauty sleep."

"Will *you* take us, Papa?" asked Zenobia, who had found it quite natural in the circumstances to wrap a dimpled arm around her father's neck.

"Pray don't be absurd, child," interposed Miss Blydesdale. "Your father cannot be bothered with such a triviality."

Rebecca stifled a groan at the governess's untimely intervention. Then Alexandra's clear voice bridged the awkwardness of the moment.

"Please do, Papa," she said, the expression on her sensitive face one of grave determination. "Cousin Rebecca promised to tell us a story about her encounter with river pirates in India. You could stay and listen, too."

For a breathless moment the duke's black eyes met those of his older daughter.

"As it happens, Miss Blydesdale," murmured the duke, breaking the silence, "I do not find it a bother. On the contrary, I am quite looking forward to hearing Miss Marsh's account of her exploits. If, that is, my presence would not be an intrusion."

Unaccountably, Rebecca felt her heart behave in a most erratic manner as she found herself the next object of those black, piercing orbs. Then, to her further dismay, her low gurgle of laughter sounded suspiciously breathless. "I hardly think *exploits* is the word I should use to describe my little misadventures," she quipped, wondering if she was on the brink of coming down with something. "And of course you are welcome to join us, Your Grace."

Ratherton himself helped Nobie into her night things, while, in the privacy of the girls' dressing room, Rebecca performed a like service for Alexandra. Then, with the girls tucked into bed, Rebecca told her story in the muted glow of an oil lamp.

It had been a long and exciting day for the children, and Rebecca was hardly surprised when she saw, first Nobie, and then finally Alexandra drift reluctantly off to sleep. Leaning over the bed, she tucked Alexandra's hand beneath the blankets and kissed her lightly on the cheek. At last, smoothing a lock of hair from Nobie's forehead, she turned to find the duke watching her.

She smiled and, pressing a finger to her lips, led the way to the door.

"I think," Ratherton remarked as he carefully closed the door behind them, "that little Nobie will not be troubled by dreams tonight." He looked at Rebecca, a penetrating look that made her suddenly and acutely aware that she was quite alone with this man, who had been wed to her cousin. "Thanks to you, Miss Marsh. Tell me, do you take every place you visit by storm? If so, I wonder that the colonel has not been induced to enlist you in the Portuguese campaign."

Rebecca laughed, grateful for the distraction.

"The colonel and I have an agreement," she answered. "I do not interfere with his military operations, and he does not interfere with me. Otherwise, I daresay we should never have got along so well together."

Ratherton's sudden smile served to transform his face so that he appeared younger, less the brooding duke and more the man who must have charmed Eleanore some thirteen years ago, mused Rebecca, as she let him take her arm and lead her leisurely toward the stairs.

"He sounds a singular parent," commented Ratherton. "I

34

doubt that I should have chosen to rear a daughter under similar circumstances. Why did he send for you? I should have thought it would have been better for you to continue with your aunt."

"Oh, but you are quite right," Rebecca answered, the dimple peeping forth at the corner of her mouth. "He *is* a singular parent – singularly selfish. He sent for me because Aunt threatened to turn me into a proper English miss, and *that* he could never have tolerated. It was arranged from the very beginning that I should go to him as soon as Cousin Eleanore was of an age to make her come-out." She paused as they came to the second-story landing and glanced mischievously up at him. "Next you are going to ask me if I never missed having a mother or a female companion other than Fanny, my dearest governess. And the answer is no, because Fanny, for all intents and purposes, was everything I should ever have needed in a mother. You see, she was my mother's governess, too, and so she always thought of me as her own." Suddenly she was quite serious. "A woman does not have to bear a child to love it as dearly as if it had come from her own body. Motherhood, after all, is a thing of the heart."

"Is it," murmured Ratherton, staring at her with a peculiar intensity. Unwittingly, a slow flush began to mount in Rebecca's cheeks as it came to her that he might have mistaken her motives. She had spoken on impulse, thinking perhaps to open his mind to the possibility of marrying again in order to give the children the mother they so obviously needed. But she had certainly not had herself in mind as a candidate to step into her cousin's shoes. Indeed, she found the notion more than a little disturbing.

"I think, Your Grace," she murmured, "that it is time I bid you good night. I am persuaded it is quite late, and it has been a rather long day."

"Quite so," replied the duke, his gaze unfathomable as he watched her turn away. "Good night, Miss Marsh."

Rebecca paused before the door to her rooms, her hand on the door handle. "I'm glad you enjoyed the evening," she said, glancing back at the tall figure of the duke. "It meant a great deal to the girls."

Opening the door, then, she went in, leaving Ratherton, still standing, staring after her.

* * *

In the days ahead, Rebecca worked a decided change in the previously even tenor of life at Cedars. The formerly still halls of the house rang with the squeals of laughter and children playing. Two new puppies, a litter of kittens, and a frog were introduced into the household, which added to the constant flurry of excitement. The staff was kept busy preparing picnic lunches, and there were frequent raids on the attic trunks for costumes for impromptu dramas or for bizarre items for treasure hunts. Perhaps most remarkable of all to at least one noble member of the household was Alexandra's renewed interest in music — not the pianoforte, at first, it was true, but Rebecca's Portuguese guitar.

One afternoon, close to a month after their cousin's arrival, the girls, released from their lessons, went eagerly in search of Rebecca. They found her in the summer garden, strumming softly on her guitar while baby Anthony slept on a blanket in the shade of an oak tree.

"Cousin Rebecca," exclaimed Zenobia, plopping down on the blanket beside her brother. "We've been looking everywhere for you."

"Hush, Nobie. You'll wake up Anthony," her sister scolded, but her eyes were on Rebecca's fingers, moving nimbly over the guitar strings. "What is that you're playing, Cousin Rebecca? Is it a Portuguese song?"

"Mm-hmm," Rebecca murmured. "A ballad about a young girl mourning for her lost love." For a few moments longer, she continued to play, while Alexandra looked on, her expressive eyes dark with silent yearning.

As the final notes quivered and faded, Rebecca laid the flat of her hand over the strings.

"That was beautiful," Alexandra breathed. "Where did you learn to play?"

"In Elvas, when the colonel was overseeing the evacuation of the men wounded at Talaveras." Rebecca's sudden smile banished the faraway look from her eyes. "A young soldier taught me during the long days of his convalescence." She did not mention that the soldier had been her dearest friend since childhood or that in the end he had died, not of his wounds, which had been well on the way to healing, but of the fever that had taken ten thousand of his comrades. "Come, would you like to try it?"

Without waiting for an answer, she drew the child down on the blanket beside her and, putting her arms around her, showed her how to hold the guitar and place her fingers on the strings. A rapt light lit Alexandra's face as a chord vibrated on the breeze. Eagerly she asked to be shown another and yet another.

In a very short time, Alexandra, who had a true gift for music, was strumming the chords in accompaniment to a simple melody sung by Rebecca and Nobie. Rebecca, glancing up, was the only one to see the duke's brooding figure framed in the bay window overlooking the garden. For a moment she watched him, feeling his eyes on her. Then Anthony awakened, voicing his displeasure of a soaked nappie. When she looked again, Ratherton was gone.

Until that afternoon, she had seen little of the duke, who made it a practice to absent himself from the house till all hours of the night. Having lived nearly all her life among men, she would hardly have been shocked to learn that the duke kept a mistress. Nevertheless, the suspicion that he spent his time with Mrs. Wendover or someone like her somehow did not set well with her. She told herself that her feelings sprang only from concern for the children and her growing affection for them. Indeed, she could not see how she could reconcile the differences between father and offspring if he were never around to see them.

She was, consequently, more than a little surprised when she came downstairs to dinner that evening to find Ratherton waiting for her in the company of Miss Twickum. His grace, she noted in amusement, wore a glazed expression.

"You are just in time, Miss Marsh," beamed the spinster, a plump woman past middle age who was dressed in lavender silk with a frivolous white lace cap over improbably blond curls. "I was just telling his grace you would very likely be along shortly, and here you are. How very fortunate we are that his grace has decided to enliven our little company with his presence. Oh, not that it has not been perfectly congenial this past month with just the two of us at dinner," she hastened to assure Ratherton, who gave every indication of one contemplating the merits of a swift murder by strangulation. "For it has. Miss

37

Marsh and I are fast on the way of becoming boon companions. It is only that there is nothing like having a new face at the table to introduce an added spice to the conversation. Would you not agree, Miss Marsh?"

"Oh, indeed, Miss Twickum," Rebecca replied with a gravity belied by the unmistakable twinkle in the look she gave Ratherton. "Your Grace," she murmured, and dropped into a curtsy. "How good of you to join us."

"The pleasure, Miss Marsh," drawled the duke, bending his dark head over her hand, "is all mine." Glancing up at her, he added softly between his teeth, "You took your blasted sweet time getting down here. Another moment alone with Miss Twickum would very possibly have been her last."

The dimple leaped irrepressibly to Rebecca's cheek.

"Oh, no, Your Grace," she exclaimed sweetly, careful to keep her voice lowered. "How can you say so, when she has taken such pains to assure you of the honor you bestow upon us by your presence?" Smiling limpidly in the face of his sardonically arched eyebrow, she gently pulled her hand free. "Miss Twickum, how very well you are looking tonight. I trust you have overcome your indisposition of yesterday and are quite ready to enjoy a hearty meal?"

"Could I interest you in a breath of fresh air, Miss Marsh?" queried the duke after dinner, breaking the silence that had lain for some few moments over the three occupants of the withdrawing room. "I venture to suggest," he added dryly, "that far from objecting, Miss Twickum will not even know we have gone."

"No, I daresay she would not," agreed Rebecca, smiling in gentle amusement at the picture of Miss Twickum, snoring peacefully in the overstuffed wing chair nearest the fireplace. "Poor dear, she is a very kind-natured, gentle soul. She seems quite at peace here at Cedars, and who can blame her? I believe the dowager duchess quite terrifies her."

"The dowager duchess delights in terrifying kind-natured souls," observed Ratherton cynically, having just been forced to suffer through an entire hour of the spinster's uninterrupted chatter. "Especially when they are as hen-witted as your Miss Annabel Twickum. Oh, don't say it. In fact, don't say anything. You might awaken her."

Taking Rebecca's hand, the duke drew her to her feet and led her through the French doors out on to the second-story terrace flanked by columns.

It was a lovely evening. The air was redolent with the perfume of lilacs and roses, and a three-quarters moon shone brightly overhead, shedding a soft, silvery light over the garden below. Rebecca inhaled deeply, savoring the fresh scent of rain on the breeze.

"I no longer wonder," she exclaimed softly, "that Eleanore loved this place. It is everything that she claimed it to be, and more. I regret deeply that I did not come sooner. I should have liked to see her one last time, here, in the surrounds that she loved so dearly."

Ratherton's lean frame stiffened ever so slightly.

"You say that as if you know it to be true," he said, his face hidden in shadows.

"But I do," replied Rebecca, frowning slightly with puzzlement at the oddity of his comment. "Perhaps she never expressed it in so many words, but it was nevertheless implicit in all of her correspondence to me. Surely you, of all people, never doubted it."

"No, how could I?" he drawled, maddeningly unreadable. "What—else did she reveal to you in her correspondence?"

"Nothing, really. She used to write of small matters pertaining to the household and the children." Rebecca hesitated, wondering how far she dared test Ratherton's mood. "In her last letter she spoke of nothing but the great joy she felt at the discovery that she was increasing—her hopes that at last she would provide you with the heir which had hitherto been denied her. Perhaps you can find some small comfort, Your Grace, in the knowledge that she wanted that more than anything."

"Good God," he uttered savagely, "what an innocent you are. So she told you that, did she. And did she also tell you that she had been warned after her second lying-in that another pregnancy might kill her?" At the harshness of his short bark of laughter, Rebecca nearly winced. "No," he said, "I can see that she did not."

He turned away from her, and for a moment Rebecca thought that he meant to leave her standing there. Then he struck the side of his fist against a marble column and, leaving it there, leaned his weight against it.

"It seems I must beg your pardon, Miss Marsh," he said in accents, heavy with irony. "You must forgive me. I do not usually forget myself. Certainly I did not lure you from the house to discuss matters that were better left alone."

. Rebecca drew in a long, steadying breath. "Indeed, Your Grace. Then why did you 'lure' me out?"

He laughed and turned to look at her out of eyes that glittered in the moonlight. "Anyone but you, Miss Marsh, would not ask such a question. One would almost believe that no man has ever paid you marked attention before."

"Then you would be mistaken, Your Grace," Rebecca replied, outwardly composed. "Is that what you are doing? If so, I should prefer that you did not. It could only complicate matters and make my continued presence here impossible."

"Should it?" he murmured, observing the shimmer of moonlight in her hair. "Then of course that was never my intention. Far be it from me to do anything that would induce you to leave Cedars, just when you have begun to work miracles here." His lips twisted in a wry smile as he saw the frown start in her eyes. "No, don't deny it. You saw what it was like when you arrived. I am not so far removed from what is going on here that I have not seen what you have done."

Rebecca gave a dismissive gesture of the hand. "I have done nothing that you cannot do, Your Grace," she said.

"What utter nonsense. You have brought life back into this house. Good God, I never thought to hear laughter or music in these cursed halls again. When I saw Alexandra today in the garden, I began to think that perhaps there was hope, at least, for her. And for Zenobia. They have been made to suffer enough for events that had nothing to do with them. If something is to be salvaged of their innocence, it will not be their father to whom they must look."

"Now you are being absurd, Your Grace," Rebecca insisted. "Perhaps if you were not gone so much from the house, you would see that the girls want only to love you. As for Anthony, he is too young to know anything of past events. He will never know his mother. I pray you do not intend to let him grow up without learning to know his father."

A cynical gleam flickered in Ratherton's eyes. Until that afternoon, he had not laid eyes on his youngest offspring since

40

the memorable day of the child's birth. The truth was he had purposely distanced himself from matters of the household long before Eleanore's death, and, afterward — well, afterward, it had seemed much simpler to continue as he had before.

But naturally Miss Marsh was not to know that. He had few illusions as to how she would judge him when she gained possession of all the sordid details of his last years with Eleanore. And gain them, she would. If not from one of the staff, then from someone else.

The thought was not one to give him comfort. Had anyone told him little more than a month ago that a meddlesome, persistently managing female with flaming red hair and impudent, laughing eyes could wreak such havoc on his well-guarded existence, he would have called them mad. But that would have been before Miss Marsh had come like a breath of life into the dreary confines of Cedars and granted him a glimpse of what it might have been like had things been different.

And why should he not have it now the way it had been meant to be? he thought bitterly. He had not asked for the circumstances that had driven a wedge between Eleanore and himself. He had done what necessity demanded, had adhered to the boundaries that Eleanore herself had laid down for him, even going so far as to allow into his household the governess Eleanore had insisted upon — Miss Blydesdale, the paragon, sent to them by Caroline Wendover. It had been the final straw, having meant, that henceforth even access to his own children was to be denied him. Not that it had happened over night. Oh, no, it had been a gradual freezing out. First the fishing trips had been deemed improper activities for females, and then the evening romps in the nursery before bedtime, until his only part in his daughters' lives was limited to an occasional buss on the cheek.

But he had agreed to allow Eleanore the complete running of the house. And clearly, matters pertaining to the nursery and schoolroom fell under that category. Even so, he was well aware that he should have exercised his rights as a father to object to the manner in which he was being cut out of their lives, even as he had been already cut out of Eleanore's. And now, thanks to Rebecca, he was being offered a second chance.

41

In a single, wild moment, it came to him that he had every right to grasp at the opportunity fate had cast in his way. He doubted not that he could make Rebecca love him. The children and Cedars had already won a place in her heart, and she would not gladly leave them. He had only to bide his time, he told himself.

"You make it all sound so very simple, Miss Marsh," he said, resisting the urge to crush her to his chest and taste those cursed alluring lips. "Tell me what you would have me do."

"Make yourself available to the children, Your Grace. Learn to know them. You have already won Zenobia's trust. Her affection is yours for the asking. Alexandra, however, may prove more difficult. She holds things inside and does not readily give vent to her feelings. In that, she is very like you, I think."

"Hornet," he said feelingly.

"You asked, my lord duke," she retorted, laughing. But almost immediately she sobered. "There is something else. Alexandra blames herself for the loss of her pony, which is perhaps understandable considering the nature of the accident. But somehow I feel there is something more to it than that. I believe it is somehow all mixed up with her refusal to indulge her natural love for music. Oh, I know it makes little sense. Perhaps if I knew more about what happened, I . . ."

"It happened on the day her mother died." Rebecca stared at Ratherton, rendered speechless as much by the content of his statement as by the chilling harshness with which he had uttered it.

In the sudden stillness, the rustle of leaves on the breeze sounded unnaturally loud. Rebecca nearly started as Ratherton's dispassionate voice broke the silence.

"Naturally I was the one who had to tell them," he said with a cynical twist of the lips. "Alexandra was supposed to be practicing her music lesson. Miss Blydesdale thought it better that the children be kept ignorant of what was going on behind those accursed closed doors." A harsh bark of laughter seemed torn from him. "As if you could keep something like that from them. When I went in search of her, Alexandra was nowhere to be found. One of the stable lads reported that her pony was missing. When we found her, hours later, she was half frozen and barely conscious. I did what was necessary for the animal and carried Alexandra home." His face a mask in which his eyes

42

glittered, hard as diamonds, he seemed almost to have forgotten Rebecca's presence. "She never said a word, then or later, about what had happened, and nor did I, though perhaps I should have done. I can only suppose that she overheard the staff talking and in her grief, turned to her only friend in need."

"Castor," Rebecca murmured, seeing it all as it must have happened — Alexandra blinded by tears, the stone wall, the pony's tormented screams. She shuddered. "How dreadful for you both. But now it is over, and it is time the wounds were healed. I wonder, Your Grace," she said, lifting her eyes to his.

A single black eyebrow rose toward the duke's hairline as he read the look in her eyes. "Why is it that I have the distinct impression I am about to be made a party to one of your colorful exploits? I am not, I trust, going to be induced to lead an expedition against river pirates."

"Oh, nothing so colorful as that," she answered, smiling. "It is only that I have just remembered hearing that it is nearly time for the pony races to be held at Balmer Lawn. Is it not the usual practice to round up a number of the wild ponies to be sold at auction before and after the races?"

"It is, Miss Marsh," drawled Ratherton, "every August. But it won't work. Do you think I have not already tried to persuade Alexandra to accept a replacement for Castor? She would have none of it."

"No, of course she would not," Rebecca readily agreed. "However, it was not Alexandra whom I had in mind."

Chapter Three

"But I don't want to go to Balmer Lawn," Alexandra insisted stubbornly, as she watched her cousin add the finishing touches to her toilette — a straw hat with a rounded crown and up-turned bill, which perched saucily atop Rebecca's red curls, a Spanish vest of pale green sarcenet, which admirably set off her gown of sprigged muslin underneath, and, finally, elbow-length white kid gloves. "Why can we not stay here? A picnic in the park would be ever so much more fun."

"I am sorry that you feel that way, Alexandra," said Rebecca, stuffing a lace handkerchief in her reticule. "Truly I am. Especially since any day now I shall be summoned to join the colonel in London. This might be the last time for a very long while that we shall all be able to go out together. And you know how excited Zenobia is about going to pick out her very first pony. Naturally you must do as you wish, but I think it would be a shame if you were not there with us, don't you?"

Alexandra, leaning with her back against one of the tall posts of Rebecca's bed, stared glumly at the toe of her patent leather shoe. "Yes. I suppose so." Suddenly the child lifted troubled eyes to Rebecca. "Do you really have to go, Cousin Rebecca?" she blurted. "To London, I mean. You seemed happy here. I-I thought you liked us."

"Oh, but I do like you, Alexandra," Rebecca exclaimed softly, crossing the room to take the girl's hands in her own. "Never think that I don't. But that does not mean that I can stay here with you forever. Even people who care for one another cannot always be together. And simply because we are parted

44

does not mean that our friendship must come to an end. We shall write to each other, and I shall come again to visit whenever I can. Now that I've found you and Nobie and Anthony, I do not intend to lose you."

"I don't believe you," Alexandra cried, twisting her hands free. "It will be just like Mama all over again." Fighting the tears that threatened, Alexandra ran to the door. "I hate you, Cousin Rebecca. I wish you had never come."

"You have a perfect right to feel that way if you like, Alexandra," Rebecca said quite calmly before the child could bolt from the room. Alexandra stopped, her back to Rebecca. "Very often we cannot help the way we feel. But nothing you say or do can change the way I feel about you. You will always have a special place in my heart, Alexandra." Taking up her reticule, Rebecca crossed to the door. "We shall be waiting in the carriage," she said, pausing before Alexandra's rigid figure, "if you should decide to change your mind and come with us."

Calmly, she walked past Alexandra and made her way to the nursery where Nurse waited with Anthony. Rebecca took her time, going over the last-minute instructions with Nurse for the baby's care and gathering up the things that he would need on the day's outing. Nevertheless, when she at last came downstairs with Anthony in her arms, she was conscious of a sharp pang of disappointment to find that Alexandra had yet to join the others in the carriage.

"I'm afraid she isn't coming," Rebecca said in answer to Ratherton's pointed query. "No, please," she added softly, as she saw his lips thin with grim resolve. "She must be allowed to make up her own mind."

Grimly, he gave into her, though he must have seen through her pretense of composed acceptance, and handed her up into the carriage. It was not until he lifted a booted foot to the carriage step that a clear voice rang out behind him.

"Cousin Rebecca—Papa, wait." Panting a little, Alexandra came up beside the duke. "I'm sorry I'm late," she said, stoically meeting her father's eyes. "Please, sir, I should like to go with you, i-if you still want me, that is."

"I cannot imagine why we should," reflected the duke, with a sternness belied by the faint twitch at the corners of the handsome lips. "It seems, however, gudgeon that you are, that the entire day will be spoiled if we do not." Suddenly picking her up

45

beneath her arms, he swung her up, causing her to squeal in startled delight. "Now in, brat, before you make us late for the races."

Balmer Lawn basked in the sun, a low, rolling heathland bounded on the west by the slow, curving arm of a river near the banks of which snuggled a cluster of cottages, an inn, and yards and paddocks teeming with ponies. A festive air was generated by the mill of carriages, horses, and people in the narrow, winding lanes and over the down, made colorful by a red and white-striped pavilion. The girls exclaimed at the sight of stalls in which vendors offered everything from marchpane and dainty pastries to steaming beef, mutton, or kidney pies and pickled pigs' trotters.

Even as the carriage came to a stop and the duke helped Rebecca and the girls to descend, the loud report of a shot rang out, signaling the start of a pony race.

Anthony squirmed in Rebecca's arms, excited by the noise and confusion. "Oh, no you don't, little man," she scolded, laughing. "You are far too young to head off on your own. And so are your sisters. Stay close, Alexandra and Nobie. It would never do to become separated."

Leaving the carriage in the care of the groom who had ridden behind on a hack in order to lead home any new additions to the stable, Ratherton and his excited entourage leisurely made the rounds of stalls, stopping occasionally to sample the wares, until Rebecca was moved at last to scold that they would all have bellyaches if they did not soon desist. Inevitably, they were drawn to the pavilion and the wooden benches filled with spectators. Another round of races had just come to a finish, and as the track was cleared, half a dozen wild ponies were herded, darting and plunging, on to the down.

"Oh, look," breathed Alexandra, her eyes fixed with longing on a sleek bay mare with a foal at heel. "Is she not beautiful, Cousin Rebecca?"

"A fine lady," murmured Rebecca, exchanging glances with Ratherton. "Good legs, tall for a New Forest pony, and her head daintier than the others I've seen. I should say she has some Arabian in her."

"I like the foal," Zenobia piped up. "And look. There, at the

46

white one. Oh, I like him. I don't think I should be afraid of falling off if I had him, Papa, he's so small. May I have him, Papa? May I?"

"Perhaps," Ratherton tempered, "if he proves on closer inspection to be sound and of an amiable disposition. However, you should take into consideration that there might be another later on that you like better."

"Oh, but there won't be, Papa," Zenobia insisted. "I'm sure of it. As soon as I saw him, I knew that I should never be afraid of him."

Laughing, Rebecca was at last moved to say, "I am afraid, Your Grace, that Zenobia is one of those rarities—a female who will not change her mind. And what of you, Alexandra?" she asked gently. "Is your heart quite won by your dainty little mare?"

Instantly, Alexandra's face clouded over, and with a determination that wrenched at Rebecca's heart, she tore her eyes away from the bay. "No. I could never love anything so stupid as a pony. I wish that I might never have to see another one as long as I live. May we go now, Papa?" she asked, turning her back on the ponies. "Please, I want to go."

"Yes, perhaps we should," Rebecca said quickly, the desperation in Alexandra's voice unmistakable. "It is time I changed Anthony, after all. If it please, Your Grace, Alexandra can come and help while you and Nobie see about the pony."

Alexandra stubbornly kept her silence as she and Rebecca made their way back to the place where they had left the carriage, and Rebecca, biding her time, made no attempt to woo her out of it. Neither one was prepared to be accosted by a fashionably dressed woman in the company of a Town beau.

"Why, it is little Alexandra," lilted the lady, blocking their way in the lane between two stalls. "Though I daresay I hardly recognize you. You have become all arms and legs since I saw you last. It was after the unfortunate incident with your pony, was it not?"

"Yes, ma'am." Alexandra squirmed, a hot blush staining her cheeks.

"My, what a fright she gave her father," confided the woman to her companion, a slender gentleman of indeterminate years, whose dissolute features, while handsome, showed the ravages of drinking and vice. "I have never seen Trevor so unnerved as when he thought he had lost his older daughter as well as his wife."

"Ratherton unnerved?" queried the gentleman. "You exaggerate, surely, m'dear. I have seen the duke risk a fortune on the draw of a card without turning a hair. And if you had ever faced him across either pistols or swords, you would not have questioned the state of his nerves, but only his lack of them."

His companion laughed, a sort of tinkling sound which was no doubt thought to be charming to gentlemen. "Yes, well, I daresay on that particular day you would not have recognized in him our impervious Duke of Ratherton." The woman's eyes, an opaque ceramic blue, turned back to Alexandra. "I do hope you have devoted some thought to the little talk we had afterward, Alexandra. While painful, it was meant to be instructive. The last thing we should ever wish, after all, is to add to your father's burden of grief."

"Alexandra," said Rebecca, her arm going around the child's shoulders. "I see your father's groom. Perhaps you would be so good as to go and ask him to fetch down the little bag we brought for Anthony." She took her gaze off the dark-haired beauty to smile bracingly into Alexandra's dark, questioning eyes. "Go," she said, giving the child a gentle nudge. "I shall be along presently."

"Yes, Cousin Rebecca." Alexandra flashed her a grateful look before dipping a curtsy to the lady. "I beg you will excuse me, Mrs. Wendover," she murmured and fled.

" 'Cousin Rebecca,' is it," queried Caroline Wendover, deigning at last to acknowledge Rebecca's presence with the faintest arch of an eyebrow. "I beg you will pardon me for what must have seemed a rudeness. I fear I mistook you for the children's nursemaid. After all, the care of an infant is the sort of thing that is better left to servants. Naturally if I had observed more closely, I should have seen my error instantly. You are, of course, Miss Rebecca Marsh of whom Eleanore used to speak."

"I am, and you are Mrs. Caroline Wendover, of whom I have heard a great deal," Rebecca replied coolly, well aware that she could never have been mistaken for a nursemaid.

"No, have you?" Mrs. Wendover gave vent to her tinkling laugh. "I'm sure my ears must be burning. But then, of course the duke and I are very old friends."

"Are you? Odd, I cannot recall that his grace has ever mentioned you. Are you here for the races, Mrs. Wendover? Or were you more in mind of purchasing a pony?"

Caroline Wendover's smile grew noticeably stiff and her gaze more coldly calculating. Obviously Miss Marsh was neither a fool nor a simpering miss.

"Oh, merely for the diversion," she answered, in accents of boredom. "It is so tedious in the country, you will agree, that even anything so rustic as this is a welcome distraction. And you, I must assume, have come here with Ratherton."

"Ratherton and the children, of course," said Rebecca, unconsciously rocking Anthony, who had fallen asleep with his head on her shoulder. "We came in the hopes of finding a pony for Zenobia."

"Quite the little family gathering. My congratulations, Miss Marsh," Mrs. Wendover purred. "I did wonder why I had not seen his grace lately. I must say you have achieved in a short time something that not even Eleanore could do in thirteen years of marriage. I should never have believed Ratherton would fall to anything so mundane as a family outing had I not been here to see it for myself."

"I daresay, Mrs. Wendover," Rebecca replied pointedly. "As for my cousin, I am quite certain she would be only happy and relieved to see her loved ones together, as a family should be. If I have had any small part in achieving that, then I shall leave Cedars with a lighter heart."

"Oh ho! Best beware, Caroline," warned the gentleman, apparently greatly entertained by the exchange. "We've a rare one here. A lady of wit *and* quality."

"I wish you will not be absurd, Westbrook," Mrs. Wendover snapped, then smiled acidly at Rebecca. "I believe you are not acquainted with my escort, Miss Marsh. Allow me to present to you the Earl of Westbrook."

"Charmed, Miss Marsh."

"My lord," murmured Rebecca. "And now perhaps you will both excuse me. I should not wish to keep Alexandra waiting too long without me."

The ride home was a deal less boisterous than the ride over to Balmer Lawn. With the duke once more at the reins, they went at a goodly clip. Rebecca, seated beside Ratherton, cradled

Anthony in her arms while the girls slept in the back.

They had gone for some time without talking, though, had Rebecca not been so deeply preoccupied, she might have observed that the duke's gaze strayed speculatively more than a few times to the clear-cut profile of her face. When at last he chose to break the silence, Rebecca was jarred out of her thoughts.

"I beg your pardon, Your Grace. What did you say?"

Ratherton's lips twisted in a wry grimace. "I have not spent the last month going on fishing expeditions, reading bedtime stories, and making myself accessible in general to my children — at your request, I might add — without coming to know that it was not I who was the object of your meditations. I asked if it was Alexandra who was troubling you."

"Only partly, my lord duke," Rebecca confessed, smiling a little at his description of the past four weeks. True to his word, he had been more often than not in their company, so much so that Rebecca had found herself watching for his tall figure to appear, striding across the lawn toward her or appearing unexpectedly to share in afternoon tea in the schoolroom. She had learned to look forward to the quick exchange of wits, the quiet conversation about books and politics and any number of a wide range of subjects while they watched the girls fish or pick berries or simply romp with their growing menagerie of puppies and kittens, baby ducks and whatever else had taken their fancy. They had been long, carefree days, untroubled by anything more eventful than the occasional afternoon shower, and yet they had passed so swiftly that already they seemed unreal to her, as if she had only dreamt them. She had been thinking how greatly she would miss them, would miss the sun-dappled forest, the narrow, twisty roads and quaint villages, the elusive wild ponies, Cedars and the children — and Ratherton.

Silently she chided herself for a fool. She should have seen it coming, should have realized that no woman could long remain inured to the duke's devastating presence. Indeed, it had been inevitable from the first moment she had laid eyes on him, dark, brooding, strong-willed, and virile. And yet it had been the softer side of his complex character that had eventually beaten down her resistance — the gentleness in the strong slender hands, which could with equal ease master a spirited animal or smooth a tumbled lock from a sleeping child's forehead; the ready sense of humor, which displayed itself in a wry twist of the lips or the dark head thrown back in laughter; his keen wit and compelling grasp of matters of the intellect. He was everything she had ever looked for in a man, and so much more, and yet instinctively she had fought the silent promptings of her own unruly heart.

He was Ratherton, and he had been married to Eleanore, who had loved and been won by him. Somehow it did not seem right that she, Rebecca, should enjoy the happiness that fate had denied her cousin.

Strangely enough, it was not until her encounter with Caroline Wendover that afternoon that the scales had been stripped from her eyes, and she had realized with sudden blinding clarity that she had fallen hopelessly, irrevocably in love with the duke. Mrs. Wendover had made it quite clear she believed Rebecca had used the children to win Ratherton's regard and that, furthermore, she had succeeded so well that he was behaving wholly unlike the Ratherton everyone, including Eleanore, had previously known. She had made it sound as if Rebecca had deliberately set out to win the duke for herself, Good God, as if she had stolen the duke from Eleanore, or at least her memory. It had not mattered that it was patently absurd, that she was hardly the sort of female to whom the duke would ever have been seriously attracted. *She,* through no fault of her own, had become terribly attracted to *him.* Suddenly she could not be sure that she had not had some unconscious personal motives in persuading him to spend more time with the children. She was only human after all.

Oh, what a bumblebroth she had made for herself. When one came right down to it, it hardly signified whether she was guilty or not of having tried to send out lures to the duke. Obviously it was what everyone else would think, and that she found galling in the extreme.

Even more galling, however, had been finding it necessary to steel herself even to face Ratherton again with at least a semblance of her usual composure. Indeed, it had been all she could do to sit in such close proximity to him, when she was suddenly and so acutely aware of the warmth of his lean body next to her, of the familiar scent of his shaving soap mingled with the subtle aroma of tobacco and clean linen assailing her nostrils.

For a time Anthony, weary of the close confines of the carriage, had afforded some diversion from the unsettling sensations Ratherton's nearness and her own newfound awareness were arousing in her. But even that had been denied her once the baby had received his bottle and fallen contentedly to sleep in her arms. Then the impossibility of her situation had struck her, along with the realization that she could not remain even another day at Cedars without giving herself away.

"If not Alexandra," persisted the duke, his gaze probing on her face, "then what, Miss Marsh?"

Rebecca drew a long, steadying breath. "I have been trying to decide, Your Grace," she said evenly, "how best to inform you that I must be leaving in the morning."

She had expected him to display a measure of surprise, perhaps even to voice an objection. She had not expected him to show no reaction at all other than a brief tightening of his hands upon the reins.

"I was not aware that you had received word from the colonel," he commented after a moment.

"That is because I haven't," Rebecca answered, refusing to resort to a lie, which in the end could only complicate matters further. "It has nothing to do with the colonel. I simply feel that everyone would be better served if I removed myself from Cedars with the least possible delay."

"I, on the other hand, can conceive of nothing which could be farther from the reality," rejoined the duke in steely accents. "Nor do I find that an acceptable explanation. I must assume that something has happened to drive you away. Is it something *I* have said or done?"

"No, how could it, when you have been everything that is agreeable. Nothing has happened, Your Grace," Rebecca insisted with all the firmness at her command. "I shall always remember Cedars with the greatest possible fondness."

"Then, for God's sake, why, Rebecca?" thundered Ratherton, abandoning all pretense at polite civility. "If the children and I are to lose you, surely we have a right to know why."

"There is nothing *to* know," Rebecca replied. "Nor are you losing me, not in the strictest sense. It was never intended that I should stay longer than a few weeks. I'm afraid you will simply have to accept that I have my reasons for going a day or two earlier than planned. Now lower your voice, I beg you. You will achieve nothing by upsetting the children."

As he could hardly argue with her final admonition, the rest of the drive was accomplished in silence, a silence that stretched endlessly and did little to ease the tension that lay like a physical thing between them.

Rebecca could not have been more relieved when the welcome lights of Cedars at last reared up before them, a relief that was to be short-lived in the extreme. No sooner had they gotten the children down and into the house, than a booming voice and the appearance of an imposing figure of a man striding toward them with outstretched hand announced the arrival of a new complication in her already complicated existence.

"About time you got back, Ratherton. Couldn't get this butler of yours to tell me where you keep your cigars. Demmed fool's bloody deaf or something. Ran out of my own on the ride over with the duchess. Demmed fine woman, that. Don't mind telling you straight out what she thinks. Reminds me of you, Rebecca. Well, you might as well tell me. When's the wedding going to be? I've demmed little time before I have to report back to Wellington."

"Wedding?" exclaimed Rebecca, staring at the man's strong, still-handsome features, which bore a marked resemblance to her own, as if she had never seen them before. Instantly, Anthony started violently and, screwing up his pudgy little face, began to cry vociferously.

"What wedding, Papa?" yawned Zenobia, stirring sleepily in her father's arms.

"Papa's and Cousin Rebecca's," Alexandra exclaimed, her face lighting up with understanding. "Papa's going to marry Cousin Rebecca!"

"No, Alexandra, it's all some sort of misunderstanding." Bouncing the squalling infant in her arms, Rebecca turned back to the instigator of mayhem with a martial light in her eyes. "There isn't going to be any wedding," she stated unequivocally. "Nor can I conceive where you could have come up with such an outlandish notion."

"Got it from your future mama-in-law. Makes sense, don't it? Was the reason she brought you all the way back to England."

"No, did she?" murmured Ratherton, apparently much struck by the notion.

"Well, of course she did," affirmed the gentleman. "Said so, didn't I? Now maybe you'd like to explain what you meant about there not being any wedding. You know I've never interfered with you, Rebecca. Don't intend to start at this late date. But if there's something I should know, I'd like to hear it now."

"If you mean, sir," interjected Ratherton with a noticeable lack of humor, "have I been playing fast and loose with your daughter—"

"Really, Your Grace, I must object," exclaimed Miss Blydesdale, plainly scandalized as she arrived on the scene. "Must I remind you of the children?"

"Oh, button up," commanded the dowager duchess, who, aroused from her bed by the sounds of pandemonium, had become an interested observer from the gallery overhead. "If you must do something, I suggest you take the children upstairs."

"—For I must presume that she *is* your daughter," continued Ratherton, grimly ignoring the interruption and Miss Blydesdale, who was attempting to free Zenobia's clasped arms from about her papa's neck, "and that you, by process of deduction, are Colonel Marsh, her father, then you very greatly mistake the situation. While I cannot answer for what my mother may or may not have told you, I can assure you that I have never made your daughter an offer, nor have I by word or deed led her to believe that that was ever my intention."

"Indeed, Colonel, he hasn't," Rebecca confirmed, her eyes stinging and her straw hat knocked to a precarious angle as Baby Anthony got a death grip on a red lock of hair.

"Well, that seems plain enough," observed the colonel, apparently oblivious to events going on around him. "Though if you never wanted to marry her, I hardly see why you couldn't have let me know what the devil you were about. It would have saved me the trouble of coming all the way to Hampshire. Devilish far out of the way place, Hampshire."

"No doubt I should apologize for the inconvenience," drawled Ratherton in exceedingly dry tones. "I did not say, however, that I did not *want* to marry Miss Marsh." Then turning his attention to the struggle being enacted between his daughter and the governess, he quite effectively put an end to it. "Enough, Zenobia," he ordered sternly. "You will go quietly upstairs with Miss Blydesdale. You, too, Alexandra. I shall be up later to explain things to you both."

"No, by gad, you didn't!" the colonel ejaculated after a moment's apparent reflection. "Demmed if I know what you *are* trying to say, Your Grace."

"He's trying to say," offered Alexandra helpfully, as she evaded Miss Blydesdale's grasp, "that he *does* want to marry her. And *she* would, too, if Mrs. Wendover hadn't done something to hurt her. Oh, please, Cousin Rebecca, don't heed whatever it was that she told you. She was always telling Mama things that hurt her. I used to see Mama crying after Mrs. Wendover's visits and then there would be a dreadful scene. Papa would go away in an awful fit of anger. And now you are going to go away, too."

"Alexandra!" Miss Blydesdale uttered in accents of horror. "You are too young to judge the actions of your elders. You misunderstood—"

"No, it's true, and you know it." Alexandra stood at bay, her gaze coming to rest accusingly on the governess's flushed face. "Why don't you tell them, Miss Blydesdale? Cousin Rebecca is always nice to you. She'd never treat you the way Mrs. Wendover does."

In the sudden silence occasioned by Baby Anthony's having been dislodged from Rebecca by the dowager duchess herself and handed over to a housemaid to be hurriedly carried upstairs, Miss Blydesdale could be heard drawing a ragged breath.

"Well, Miss Blydesdale?" interjected Lady Zenoria. "Is what Alexandra says true?"

"You don't understand," said the spinster, looking suddenly old indeed. "Mrs. Wendover was my patroness. My last family was going to pension me off with hardly a shilling to my name. She promised me a small stipend if I—"

"Miss Blydesdale, don't," murmured Rebecca, filled with pity as she saw all too clearly how it must have been. The elderly governess, with nothing to look forward to after all her years of service but a life of penury, had been all too vulnerable to anyone unscrupulous enough to take advantage of her. "You don't have to say anything."

As if suddenly freed from an overwhelming burden, Miss Blydesdale deliberately straightened her shoulders. "No, I know you mean to be kind, Miss Marsh, but it's time the truth was told. You should know, Your Grace, that Mrs. Wendover did everything she could to break up your marriage, even going so far as to enlist my services as a spy. My heart fairly ached for what she did to Lady Eleanore. That poor, trusting child. She believed everything Mrs. Wendover told her, all those stories about — well, you know, Your Grace. The least said, the better. I always doubted there was a word of truth in them. Naturally I shall pack and be out of here by tomorrow, Your Grace."

"We shall discuss your future in the morning, Miss Blydesdale. In the meantime, take the children upstairs," said the duke ominously, his eyes on Rebecca. "Miss Marsh, if you would be so kind, I should like a word with you — in private."

"I should rather not, Your Grace," Rebecca demurred, little trusting that look or the sudden unevenness of her own pulse. "I believe enough has been said for one night."

"Oh, come now, Miss Marsh," Lady Zenoria insisted. "The last thing I should ever have taken you for is a coward. Go with him, child. Surely, Colonel, you can exert some influence over her."

"Wouldn't dream of it, dear lady," said the colonel. "Doubt if it would do any good anyhow. Rebecca's devilish independent. Best thing is to leave it to the two of them to work it out. Now, m'boy, just where did you say those cigars were?"

"I suggest you look in the desk in my study, Colonel. And while you are at it, you might sample some of the brandy in the decanter. You, too, Mother, if you are so inclined. And, now, Miss Marsh," said his grace, "I believe a stroll in the moonlight is in order."

Without waiting for an answer, Ratherton took Rebecca by the arm and led her, resisting, to French doors which opened up on to the garden, the very garden in which Alexandra only a few weeks before had first given in to the allure of the Portuguese guitar.

"I think, Your Grace, that this has gone quite far enough," Rebecca pronounced in chilling tones. "We have nothing to say to each other which has not already been said. I shall be leaving tomorrow with the colonel, and there is nothing you can do to change that."

Ratherton advanced purposefully toward her.

"What did Caroline Wendover say to you, Miss Marsh?" he demanded. "Did she tell you that for the last six years of our

56

marriage, I slept away from my wife? Perhaps she even intimated that I spent that time with her, is that it? God knows it was on everyone's lips that Caroline and I were lovers. Is that why you have formed this sudden disgust for me?"

"Mrs. Wendover said nothing of the kind, and if she had, it would have little signified. I am not so green that I do not know the ways of the world. I should hardly have been shocked to learn you had taken a mistress under the circumstances. I should only have felt pity for you and for Eleanore."

"How very generous of you, Miss Marsh," said the duke. "However, it is not your pity that I want. Nor was there ever a mistress. Not then, and certainly not now. Only the nameless faces of Cyprians. When it was made clear to me the dangers of sleeping with my wife, I stayed away from her, even going so far the last year or two of taking up residence in the dowager house, when, that is, I was not frequenting the gambling hells in London." He laughed, a cynical laugh that tore at Rebecca's heart. "Do I paint you a grim enough picture, Miss Marsh? If you had not formed a disgust of me before, the sordid details of my pleasurable pursuits in London should be enough to send you fleeing from me. Is that it? Is that what she told you?"

"No," answered Rebecca, turning away from him to hide the pity in her eyes. "I wish you would not pursue this any further. Mrs. Wendover said nothing of any consequence."

Rebecca's heart nearly stopped as she felt him come up behind her.

"It is not like you to varnish the truth," he said. His hands, closing about her arms, rendered her peculiarly weak. "Look at me, Miss Marsh, and tell me you are not lying. Or, at the very least, that you do not hold me responsible for Eleanore's death."

At that, she did come around, her face registering her horror at such a notion. "No, never! Nor will I listen to you accuse yourself."

"And yet it's true. I took her to my bed. How ironic that after five years, I should weaken at the crucial moment. No doubt I could blame the brandy in my veins or the darkness that made me mistake her in my drunken stupor for someone else. After all, I should hardly have expected Eleanore in my bachelor quarters in London. Oh, it was not a rape, if that is what you think," he added bitterly, misreading the emotion in her eyes.

57

"Better that than what it really was—a sacrificial offering."

"No, you are wrong, Your Grace, it was never that," murmured Rebecca, so many things at last made clear to her, not the least of which was why he persisted in holding himself aloof from his infant son and heir, while accepting the ready affections of his daughters. "Don't you see? Eleanore never stopped loving you. It was the one thing I most remarked in all of her letters to me. Her love for you and the children and for Cedars. She did not go to you in London in the hopes of begetting an heir. I doubt not that was the farthest thing from her mind. She went because she could no longer bear a life without you. She was willing to gamble everything to have it again the way it had once been for the two of you, for however long chance or fate might allot her. Can you not see that you gave her what she most wanted? You came home to her, my dearest lord duke, and you made her last days the happiest ones of her life."

"You have made me see a great deal, Miss Marsh," he said, his eyes glittery in the moonlight, "not the least of which is something I have known almost from the moment I laid eyes on you."

"I-indeed, Your Grace?" faltered Rebecca, little trusting the sudden leap of her heart. "And what is that?"

"That whatever happiness the future might hold in store for me depends wholly on you, Miss Marsh. I love you, Rebecca, and I want you for my wife. And that is why I must insist," he added, moving to imprison her in his arms before she could make even the feeblest attempt to escape him, "that you tell me what Caroline said to poison your mind against me. I warn you, I shall not let you go until you do."

"And I warn *you*, my lord duke, that I am not so easily coerced." Hardly had the words left her mouth, than Ratherton crushed her lips beneath his in a kiss that battered at the walls of her already tenuous defenses.

When at last he released her, a dizzying eternity later, her head was spinning and her knees threatened to buckle beneath her.

"Tell me, Rebecca," he demanded huskily, lifting his head to study her face.

"I-I told you, Your Grace," Rebecca somehow found the wit to answer. "She told me nothing of consequence. We only exchanged pleasantries."

"Liar," he growled. Ruthlessly he bent her once more to his will.

Never had Rebecca thought that torture at the hands of the duke could be such blessed sweet torment. And yet it must have been, for when he lifted his head the second time, she discovered her traitorous arms clung about the back of his neck and she had actively been aiding him in her punishment.

This time Ratherton's breath came, swift and shallow, and his eyes smoldered with barely restrained passion. "Tell me, Rebecca, or by God I cannot answer for the consequences."

"Tell you what, my lord duke?" Rebecca queried, her eyes dreamy, but the dimple, irrepressible, in her cheek. "That Mrs. Wendover was so careless as to make me realize a terrible truth about myself?"

"The devil she did," muttered Ratherton, frowning with a fierceness that must have gratified even the most hardened of hearts. "What truth?"

Rebecca, taking instant pity on him, cradled his dear, beloved face between her hands and gazed into his eyes with undisguised fondness. "That no matter how hard I tried not to, I had fallen hopelessly in love with my cousin's husband. And that, my dear lord duke, I could not countenance. Not if it meant I had, no matter how innocently, used the children as an excuse to be near you. And not if it meant I had somehow stolen what should have been Eleanore's."

"And what if you had?" he demanded, tightening his grip on her as if he thought she might even yet try to escape him. "Were those reasons enough to run away?"

"It seemed so at the time," she replied. "But that was before you told me about you and Eleanore."

"And now?" he murmured, a dangerous light in his eye. "Damnit, Rebecca. Are you going to marry me or not?"

"Now, my dearest, I know that Eleanore had her happiness and I have every right to grasp mine. Yes, of course I am going to marry you. After all, I could hardly leave now, when Anthony is on the point of taking his first step and Zenobia to begin her first riding lessons. And if you think I should ever dream of missing Alexandra's face tomorrow when she sees her bay lady in the stable, you are very much mistaken."

"Witch," growled Ratherton in such a way as to make

Rebecca's heart beat with happiness. "How the devil did you know I had purchased the bay and her foal?"

"Because I have come to know *you,* my lord duke," Rebecca answered, drawing his head irresistibly down to hers, "just as your mother intended I should."

Her Special Day

by Teresa DesJardien

Clarice, Lady Cawley, esteemed wife of Sir Horace Cawley, and mother of the six younger Cawleys, swayed gently in the pew. Her vision dulled and narrowed down to twin tunnels, and she bumped against her husband, whose hand shot out to grab her elbow even as he twisted to inquire in a whisper what she was about. She could not give an answer, instead slumping in the other direction, against her eldest son's shoulder. It was as the young man turned and instinctively reached for her other elbow that her eyes rolled back in her head, and the lady's consciousness faded away under the astonished stares of her shocked family members.

Five minutes later, Clarice roused to find herself laid out upon a pew, her son vigorously fanning her face, her daughters whispering back and forth in high agitation, and the face of her husband, Horace, hovering over her with a terrible frown as he patted her hand rather briskly.

"My dear!" he cried. "Are you quite well?"

"I fainted," she said, astonished to find it was true. "I've never fainted before in my life," she heard her own voice, weak and quite unlike her, go on to say. It was then, as she struggled to sit up, a multitude of hands reaching to assist her, that she realized the entire populace of the church was staring at the spectacle she had unwittingly created. "Take me home!" she whispered at once to Horace, her pale cheeks suddenly flooding with color.

He promptly responded by offering her his arm; her son, Sutton, offering his as well. She hated hobbling out like an old woman—she was, after all, only thirty-seven years old—but she was grateful for their assistance nonetheless.

63

"Oh, Mama," cried her eldest, Muribelle, once they had exited from the church, "this does not mean you are increasing again, does it?"

"Indeed not!" "Heavens, no!" Clarice and her husband cried at once.

"Such a question!" Horace continued in a scolding tone.

"But you must admit it is a logical question," Sutton, their second eldest, put in.

"I am *not*, and that is an end to the matter," Clarice said with finality.

"Muribelle, see to the younger ones, please," Horace said, seeing from the corner of his eye that Peter was trailing the family by a significant eight yards or better, and would slip away if not attended to promptly.

Muribelle gave an impatient sigh that reflected the long suffering she had endured as the eldest child, but moved at once to do as she had been bid.

As Horace handed Clarice into their coach, he announced, "My dear, I must say that this is all for the day. You have been working too hard on this betrothal party of Muribelle's. You must cease, must take a day of rest. I insist; you must put up your feet and relax today."

"Don't be ridiculous, Horace! The party is tomorrow. There are a hundred things to be done between now and then," Clarice protested, even as she leaned back into the squabs in an unsteady posture quite unlike her usual self.

Horace replied crisply and to the point, "That is why one has servants, my dear."

"Now you know I must see to every detail—"

"You 'needn't'; it is simply your habit to do so. No, truly, Clarice, you are not to overtax yourself any more than you already have. Just give me your lists and I'll see everything is arranged just so."

Sir Horace's wife looked on that fellow with a supremely doubtful eye, but then a wave of nausea seized her, and she realized she really was wanting for a lay-down. "If you think . . . ?" she murmured, tentatively surrendering to his dictates.

"I insist!"

He turned to his children, the last of whom was climbing atop the overlarge and overstuffed coach, to say, "Mama is to have a special day. No fuss, no interruptions, just a quiet lay-down. Do you hear what I say?" His usually gay blue eyes turned serious behind his gold-wire spectacles. "No running to her to solve a dispute. No asking her if you 'may go here or may go there'. No requests, no intrusions on her rest at all! Mrs. Pattick or Miss Harrod will have to be your sources today," he said, referring to the nanny and the governess. "Or the housekeeper, Mrs. Davis. I will be available should you have questions as well, naturally. This is an absolute pronouncement — am I understood?"

Five of the six heads bobbed, until Peter — the sixth and youngest — also belatedly joined them, realizing that Papa really was soliciting their agreement and not just lecturing.

"Fine then," Horace pronounced, climbing in and managing to find a place next to his wife. He turned to her and inquired, "Do you feel I ought to send for the doctor?"

"Gracious, no!" she said with feeling. "I am only a little tired, with perhaps just a touch of the grippe."

"Fine then. Your lists?" He put out his hand.

She delved into her reticule, producing the three separate sheets of paper that represented the hours of work and forethought she had put into her daughter's betrothal party. She hesitated a moment before handing them over. "It is all recorded there, and neatly so, I trust. It should not be a *great* deal of bother . . ." she said uncertainly.

"Of course not, my dear! You shall awaken to the party tomorrow, refreshed and gay, content in the knowledge that all will be ready for your guests," Horace assured her as he tucked the sheets into his coat pocket.

"Yes, well . . ."

"Mama, I am not so very sure —" Muribelle began to protest, even as the three other siblings who rode within all erupted into sudden and clamorous speech, to agree or disagree as was their wont. Peter repeatedly said, "Mama!" over and over, trying to catch his parent's eye as he tugged on her sleeve, wishing to impart his own six-year-old opinion, even while his sisters loomed over him, nearly drowning out his voice with their own multiple exclamations.

"Now, quiet everyone!" Horace boomed, making the windows of the carriage rattle, and causing his wife to startle. Sutton leaned down from his seat atop the unfashionably large — yet for such a crew, essential — stagecoach, only the curls at his brow and his blue eyes visible, upside down. Sir Horace rapped on the window glass, motioning for his off-spring to sit upright again. Once he was obeyed, he let down the window, that the two boys might hopefully hear his dictates as well, and loudly exclaimed, "Your mother requires silence and peace, and I'll have it this very moment, thank you!"

Fortunately, at just this moment the carriage came to a halt before their town house, so although quiet was never given a true chance to reign, at least the children were released from their confinement. They tumbled onto the pavement, in-stantly scattering in six different directions. "Muribelle," cried their father, "you will gather your siblings at once! In the li-brary in five minutes, if you please!" He then offered his arm to Clarice, who took it with a large sigh as she moved to step down from the carriage.

"I'll be quite ready, come my wedding, to be rid of the lot of you," Muribelle grumpily told her two sisters, Anna and Lissy, as she caught each of them by one arm.

Clarice clucked her tongue disapprovingly, but had no time for a lecture on pretty manners. For, as soon as her slippered feet touched the ground, Horace scooped her up into his arms.

"Horace!" she gave a little shriek. "Don't be a goose. Re-member your back!"

"I'd rather put out my back than have my wife prostrate on the walk before our door. Do cease your wiggling, Clarice, or I really shall have a difficulty and drop you most unceremoni-ously!" he warned, as their startled butler pulled open the front door to admit them.

As soon as he had seen his wife settled on her bed, safely nestled in her devoted housekeeper's care, Sir Horace as-cended to the second floor (three flights of stairs up if one started in the basement, as his back told him with each upward pull of his legs), his steps accompanied by the hum of voices which grew as he approached where his six offspring awaited him in the library.

Muribelle, Sutton, Wyatt, Anna, Lisette, and little Peter, everyone of them speaking, and half of them involved in some sort of physical battle. Horace cleared his throat loudly, abruptly disrupting the turmoil as he had hoped he might, as

66

six pairs of eyes swung around to stare at him.

"My children," he intoned in his very firmest father voice. "You have all seen for yourselves that Mama is overtired. It is entirely up to us to see that she is rested for tomorrow's activities. I want you to tell me how this may be accomplished? You there, Peter, you must speak first."

Peter looked startled, putting both hands to his face shyly and glancing warily at his siblings. "Um," he said, shifting his weight from one foot to the other. "Be quiet about the house?" he suggested finally.

"Exactly. Very good, Peter. And you, Lisette? What way may you avoid disturbing your mother?"

"No arguments?" she piped in her eight-year-old voice, full of the hope that she had guessed correctly.

"Quite, quite!" He turned to Anna.

"Ah . . ." she said, grinning, then turning sober again when she saw Papa did not smile back. "Uh, perhaps we could keep from making messes?"

"Yes! That is an absolute requirement! All outside play today, though I doubt there will be a great deal of time for play, eh? And what of you, Wyatt, what have you to say to the matter?"

Wyatt stood in all his fourteen years of dignity, ignoring Peter who absently hung on his older brother's coat now that his attention was no longer so keenly required. "I should think we will be required to help with the arrangements."

"Yes, you shall. That brings me to Sutton and Muribelle, for whom I have planned specific tasks." Horace reached into his pocket, ignoring the sudden frown on his eldest daughter's face, and sixteen-year-old Sutton's parted lips that had not quite managed to completely smother the protest that had risen there. "Muribelle," Horace said as he glanced over the three lists briefly. "Ah, yes, as I had thought . . . You will see to all the party clothes."

"I still do not see why the younger ones are to be allowed at *my* betrothal par—"

"That subject has already been discussed and dismissed, as I recall, Muribelle! We are all one family, and this is a special occasion, and—by gum!—we are all going to enjoy it *together*. End of subject. Now, your mother has here that we are all to wear blue, or you young ladies may wear white, if you so

67

choose. Make sure the laundrymaid has everything we might need all washed and ready, plus see to it that any garments you feel require it be mangled. We must be neat and shiny as new pins tomorrow."

"But the servants detest mangling, especially when the weather has turned warm," Muribelle protested, her face reflecting that she would detest giving the instruction almost as much as the servants detested having to give a sheen to the garments by way of the awkward two-person pressing machine.

"Which is why you will see that it gets done, hmm?" her father replied, his blue eyes taking on a steely edge.

If Sutton had meant to say anything, now he firmly bit it back in light of his father's obvious determination to be intolerant of protests.

"Sutton, you and Wyatt are to see to the arranging of the furniture. Make sure the servants understand that Mama means to use the silver services, and also make quite certain that none of the chairs end up against the stucco. You know how easy it is to damage the chairs' lacquer or the walls!" He gave them just as steady a look as he had given his eldest, under which both boys blushed, having ruined a good chair or two in their day, to say nothing of the chunks of stucco that had been knocked from more than one wall. "We are seating two-and-seventy guests, plus our own household, so obviously you will need to use the ballroom at the top of the house." Under his breath he added, "Never thought to see a purpose for such a room, but I suppose I should be glad I need not acquire a hall now. I only hope our meal may arrive there at least half warm."

Sutton and Wyatt exchanged glances, at once quite unconvinced that it would be so. Horace handed Clarice's neatly penned instructional sheet to Sutton, then turned to his remaining offspring, stooping down a little to be more on their level, one hand propped against his thigh.

"You three are to see to the food." He held up the one remaining list. "It is all written down. All you need do is take it to Monsieur Cook and see that he understands. You must stay with him for a while, to be sure that he comprehends, his English being so uncertain as it is. Anna, you are quite capable of reading everything on this list, and explaining what it is if he does not know. Yes?" He handed her the sheet.

She read the list with studious care, then nodded with a

smile, finally winning a smile in return from her Papa.

He straightened, clapping his hands together and rubbing them with satisfaction. "Not so very difficult, is it? Of course not. A job for everyone, and everyone has a job. Well then, off with you! This party is to be for nuncheon tomorrow, so we must be all but ready by this evening, that we have time to dress tomorrow morning, and see to all the little details that must come at the last moment. Go, go, I say!" He waved his hands in the air, the children scattering at once as though they were leaves before a wind.

Sir Horace tucked his thumbs into his waistcoat, well satisfied with himself. After a moment, he crossed to the service table, poured himself a splash of port, gathered a newspaper under his arm, and descended to the floor that held his bedchamber.

His wife was already asleep under the covers of their bed, her light brown hair uncovered — no doubt because it was the middle of the day and pleasantly warm — and unbraided, perhaps to avoid a headache. After securing the bolt on the door — he fully intended his wife should not be intruded upon — he slipped off his pumps, and gingerly settled beside her, doing his best not to rustle the newspaper too much, nor rattle his glass against the bedside table.

He once gave a hearty sigh, filled with the joy of simple pleasures as he read beside his slumbering wife, until he, too, took advantage of the peace and quiet to indulge in a little nap.

"How many did Papa say we were seating?" Wyatt asked, rubbing his jaw as he stared at the list Sutton was holding before them. They alternately stared at the list and then at the bare ballroom before them, conspicuously empty of furniture.

"Two-and-seventy. Plus the eight of us."

"Do we have eighty chairs?"

"Nodcock! Of course not. But, see here, it says on Mama's list that rented chairs and tables ought to be delivered to the house. I wonder when, though? It seems it should be quite soon, or else how will we have time to have them arranged? Do you suppose something has gone wrong with the order?" Sutton allowed a flicker of doubt to pass over his features.

"Does it say who is to deliver them?"

"No," Sutton said, chewing on his lower lip.

"What are we to do?" Wyatt cried, throwing up his arms in exasperation until an idea struck him. "Oh, we must ask Papa, of course!"

"No!" Sutton cried, horrified. "You know he'd ring a peal over our heads. I'd feel a perfect fool for not being able to arrange a few chairs and tables." He folded the paper and slipped it into his jacket pocket. He straightened his shoulders and announced firmly, "I know what we must do. Fetch your riding boots, little brother."

Within minutes the two oldest boys were quit of the house, passing out the front door toward the mews where their horses were boarded.

Below stairs, in the rear basement, their eldest sister heard the sound of a door, but since doors opening and closing were a constant in her family's home, paid no attention. She sat glumly trying to decide between the two dresses the laundry-maid held up before her, her eyes swaying between the two with no real interest. "Oh, I don't know." She sighed.

The maid, Lilly, closed her eyes for a brief moment, but in no other wise indicated that she was more than ready for the young miss to decide which gown she would wear the next day. "How about yer pretty sarcenet with t'gold netting, Miss Muribelle? It's already hangin' in yer wardrobe, an' I'd be 'appy to press it fer yer in t'morning, so's it'd be fresh and crisp as could be . . . ?" she suggested hopefully.

"I was wearing that dress when Fenton proposed," Muribelle said, smiling slightly.

"Ooh, perfect then. Loverly," Lilly encouraged.

"But, the thing of it is, it is to be my betrothal party. I cannot wear the same old dress! Fent . . . Mister Penville has not seen either of these two. Yes, it must be one of these," Muribelle said, sighing again. Mama had said the girls were to wear white, but surely Mama had not meant to include *her* in that dictate? Of course, it *was* a nice dress with a pretty flounce, but still. . . .

"Should I cover my eyes then?" a male voice said, causing Muribelle to spin with sudden animation.

"Fenton!" she cried, her hands coming together as she danced across the cool flagstone floor to his side. "I never heard you come in. Whyever were you not announced?"

70

"Hassup tried, but there seems to be no one about. We split up, vowing to search the house until we found bodies, dead or alive." He smiled down at her. "How pleased I am not only to find that everyone is apparently still quite well, but also fortunate enough to be the one to specifically find *you.*"

She smiled back at him, her glum mood utterly erased. "But to answer your question: no, you must not cover your eyes. Well, perhaps you should, and then only take a quick peek, so quick you cannot remember what you see. Of these gowns: which should I wear tomorrow? I know you say I look splendid in white, but that seems to me to be too predictable for a betrothal party, don't you think?" She nodded toward where Lilly stood, the maid not quite able to erase the look of gratitude Mr. Penville's appearance — and his part in at last a decision — had brought her.

Fenton glanced toward the indicated gowns.

"Just a quick glance!" Muribelle laughed, lifting her hands to cover his eyes for him.

He slid them to one side, made a play of glancing at the gowns, then pulled her hands back over his face. "The yellow. Definitely the yellow. With your dark hair, you will look like a wildflower, bold and beautiful, yet delicate and serene." He then pressed his lips to her nearest wrist.

She gave a soft sound that was no real protest, and made no move to lift her hands away. "You speak as a poet," she said, her voice grown velvety.

He kissed her other wrist, and then she moved her hands, that she might gaze into his eyes.

A discreet cough from the laundrymaid interrupted the moment, and made Muribelle laugh even as she blushed. She seized her betrothed's hand and, pulling him along behind her, moving out of the basement and up the stairs. "Take me for a drive, will you please, Fenton? It is such a lovely day, and I have not seen you for two whole days. Lilly," she cried over her shoulder as her fiancé nodded his ready agreement, "do see that all that gets done."

"All . . . ? What, this?" the maid called after her, then looked down at the small pile of laundry at her feet when she received no answer, her mistress having quickly and laughingly disappeared up the stairs. Shrugging, she moved in Miss Muribelle's wake, wondering where she might find a footman to help her fill the large washtub with heated water.

As the maid mounted the stairs, she was greeted by the three youngest Cawleys, who were peering at a piece of paper. As she passed, she made little note of the fact that the oldest of the three, Miss Anna, was wielding a lead pencil.

The three waited until the maid was gone, then resumed their discussion. "I do not care for lobster patties," Lisette said.

Anna dutifully crossed it from the list.

"What else does it say?" Peter chimed in.

"You can read it," Anna scolded.

"But I like it better when you read it."

"All right then, but just one more time. I'll leave out all the terrible things we do not like, and read only the ones we do. 'Roast beef with beef stock gravy'. 'Yorkshire pudding'," she read, pausing to glance down the list. She double-checked, then announced, "That's it. That's all that is remaining."

"No vegegibles?" Peter lisped.

"No vegetables," Anna assured him.

"No oyster sauces!" Lisette grinned.

"No oyster sauces. But, I believe we ought to have a dessert with this," Anna said, nodding knowledgeably.

"No syllabub!" Peter cried, making a face.

"No syllabub," his siblings echoed, and Anna emphasized the point by crossing it off the list with a second, darker line.

"Tarts," Lisette suggested helpfully. "And strawberries with cream."

"And marzipan." Peter rolled his eyes and licked his lips. "And sugar plums."

"Sugar plums are for Christmastime," Anna said, writing with care, making her best script letters.

"Or special occasions," Peter argued.

"I suppose a betrothal party *is* a special occasion," she conceded, adding it to the list.

"Oh, cake! I think you must have cake at a betrothal party, don't you think?" Lisette asked.

"Quite right, Lissy," Anna agreed, writing "fancy cake" on the list.

"What are we to drink? Mama wanted that Champagne punch," Lisette said, her lip curling.

"It is not terrible, but I think . . ." Anna pressed the pencil to

72

her lip and rolled her eyes heavenward as though for inspiration.

"Lemonade!" cried Peter.

"Yes, lemonade," his sisters agreed, their heads bobbing in chorus.

"But no wine at all," Peter went on, proud of his success. "Uncle Acton always gets so silly from wine. Mama was quite scanda . . . scanda . . ."

"Scandalized," Lisette helped.

"Scandalized last time he was here. So, I say, no wine."

"Papa *is* always going on about the expense of keeping a wine cellar, so I think that is a good suggestion, Peter. No wine." She made sure the word was neatly scratched through on her list. She stood up, her face beaming. "I think we have done very well. Come on then, let us take this list to Cook. He will need time to have everything just right." She took up one of Peter's hands.

Lisette gathered the other, and the three marched triumphantly down the stairs, toward the kitchens.

"Madame," said the cook, a puzzled frown on his face. "I wish for you to make ze question for me," he told the housekeeper before him in his accented English.

"Question? What do you mean, Monsieur?" Mrs. Davis asked.

He handed her the paper he held before himself. "Zis list — I say to myself, is zis so? Is zis as Lady Cawley wishes it?"

The housekeeper read through the list, noting the markouts and the childish scrawl. "Well, of course not, Monsieur!" she cried, trying to hand it back to him, but he refused to accept it.

"The children, zey say 'Papa give us this list'. Zey say he say 'go and tell Cook to make ze wonderful foods.' I zink 'no, it is not so', but zen I zink 'perhaps it is so?' Madame, I do not know, now. I ask you, you go to ze Lady Cawley, and you ask if is so, *non?*"

The housekeeper, Mrs. Davis, took a deep, aggravated breath. "As if I do not already have enough to do, Monsieur! I am overseeing the cleaning and the polishing — !" At his stubborn look, one very familiar to her, she ceased to list her own problems, with resignation saying, "Very well then! I will go

73

and ask her. She is resting, and it is true Sir Horace has said she is to have a quiet day, so perhaps she *did* dictate these changes instead of making them herself, though that seems most unlikely. I will inquire for you, Monsieur."

"I will wait," the cook said with a firm nod of his head.

Mrs. Davis climbed the stairs to where the bedchambers resided, knocking at her mistress's door quietly. When there was no answer, she knocked a little more firmly, and when there still was no answer, tried the doorknob, only to find the door was bolted. That startled her for a moment, for only external doors were ever locked and that only at night, but then she thought twice, and pressed her ear to the door. As she had half expected to find, she heard a familiar snoring, loud enough to permeate into the passageway if one but listened for it. It was clear that Sir Horace was asleep within, which meant his wife must be also decidedly exhausted, if she could sleep through such a ruckus. That being the case, it behooved her not to wake either of them. She moved away from the door, grateful that none of the lower servants had caught her at her wrongful — however useful — eavesdropping, and proceeded to explain to Cook why she could not inquire as to the list's actuality.

"What must I to do?" the Frenchman cried.

"I will inquire as soon as I may, but for now—" Mrs. Davis tapped the sheet against her chin, deciding quickly. "Dessert dishes *do* require a deal of preparation time. If Lady Cawley does indeed desire them all, then we had best have them ready for tomorrow. There will be time enough for changes should this not be so."

"Everything takes ze time for the preparation!" Cook cried, his cheeks stained red with frustration. "I cannot do some of zese, zen some of zem, zen some more of somezing else! I must very soon know, madame. Very soon!"

"Of course you must. Begin with the cake, Monsieur. I will speak with Lady Cawley as soon as I may," she soothed.

Somewhat mollified, the cook retreated, muttering under his breath.

Muribelle walked in the front door, her cheeks tinged pink from the carriage's spirited clip through the park, but mostly from the brief kiss she had just exchanged with Fenton, daringly, on the front steps. His hand was caught in hers as he followed her over the threshold, and for a moment she thought he might try to steal yet another kiss. She danced away, knowing any one of her siblings would be more than happy to report such an event to Mama or Papa, and thereby bring a lecture on propriety down about her ears. Still, if she could find a place where no one might think to wander, it would be no terrible thing to have perhaps just one more kiss . . . ah! She knew the very place.

Pulling on his hand and smiling invitingly at him, Muribelle led him quickly through the house and on to the back patio. She closed the patio doors, and, speaking softly, urged him to a bench that was somewhat sheltered by a rose bower. To her pleasure, she saw that the books of fashion plates remained on the bench where she had left them this morning before church. Perfect! Not only would she have Fenton to herself, but she could also take the opportunity to solicit his opinion on a matter or two regarding the wedding.

Fenton settled beside her as she placed the books on the ground before them, and sat up to part one open in her lap. His arm slid along the back of the bench as he looked over her shoulder, until his hand had slowly crept around to encircle her waist. Twice she leaned into him, a silent and relatively irreproachable caress of sorts, even should Mama see it, but then she would lean forward again to fetch another set of tinted drawings.

He smiled at her three "best choices" for a wedding gown design, nodded at the colors she thought would best suit him and his best man, murmured approval of the wedding feast menu, shrugged when she asked if the Champagne ought to be iced or not, and only scratched his ear and rolled his eyes when she solicited his knowledge regarding how many groom's guests were to be invited.

She smiled at him, just faintly exasperated with his obviously growing lack of interest, and said, "But, Fenton, dear, I am assured I have requested that information at least twice from you."

He stifled a sigh, almost smiling back, but not quite. "I haven't made the list yet. Besides, it will just be my fellows from school and my club and all. That's all I can think of." At her steady gaze, he added, "Father is giving me some names, and my Aunt Felicity has offered to arrange a list, but I'll confess I have not gone past her home to see what she has accomplished."

"Please see her today, will you?" Muribelle said, the corners of her mouth unsure whether to turn up and win a smile from him, or turn down to show him he had been remiss. Finally the smile won, for after all the poor fellow had no mother to help him at such a time.

"I wi—Oh, I quite forgot! She has probably gone to Bath by now. Her rheumatism."

Muribelle closed the book in her hands, a frown flickering over her face. "Then you must write her at once. And specify that you require the list at the very earliest possibility. It is only six weeks until the wedding, Fenton! People must have their invitations very soon!"

Fenton's mouth slanted to one side, but he bit back the comment he was going to make. Muribelle did not miss the motion, and cried, "What were you going to say?"

"Nothing."

"It was something. I saw it in your eyes."

"It is just that," he cried suddenly, "who does not know we are being married? It's been in the papers. The banns have been posted. It's no surprise. Everyone has already made their plans, bought their gifts, and so on! What difference does it make whether they get their invitation six weeks ahead, or two?"

"What difference?" Muribelle echoed, her eyes rounding. She sat away from him, causing his arm to fall from her waist. "What difference? Why, Fenton Penville! I cannot believe you would say that. You know what difference, or at least you should! It is only good manners to give one's guests timely notice! If I did not send out my invitations until a mere two weeks before the wedding, I should be considered the most shocking, ill-bred creature in London! It just isn't done."

"Neither is kissing on the front step," he grumbled, his face flushed red with annoyance.

Muribelle gasped, and suddenly her ire turned into a terrible melting disquiet in her stomach. She could not believe it: not only had Fenton Penville voiced a perfectly silly argument, *while* raising his voice at her, he had also thrown a tender moment in her face, presenting it as something common and quite possibly vulgar.

76

Now she stood, her hands trembling at her sides, a sudden blurring mist clinging to her lashes. "I bid you good afternoon, Mister Penville," she managed to say stiffly, just before she turned her back and fled, just able to keep her sobs held within, if not her tears.

Sutton approached the house, his steps slowing as a look of puzzlement settled on his features. There was a large cart before the house, filled with what he all at once recognized as table and chair legs. The look of confusion turned to one of astonishment, and suddenly his feet were flying forward. Belatedly, Wyatt came behind him, though the look on his face testified to the fact that he had not yet solved the puzzle as to this rather peculiar delivery. He only understood when he heard his brother cry, "I say! You aren't from Swallow and Sons, are you by chance?"

"No, sir!" was the crisp, slightly indignant reply from a tall, lean man who stopped instructing the workers who were just beginning to unload the cart and stepped toward Sutton. He gave a quick bow. "We are from Young, Bittner, and Canney."

"Mama already arranged — !" Wyatt said in understanding, only to receive an admonitory glance from his older brother which stopped him in midsentence.

Sutton turned back to the man, his thumbs seeking his pockets in a manner very like Father's. "I thought it was quite queer that you should be here already, given that I have just hired you. Only you are not *you* . . . er, that is to say, you are not of Swallow and Sons."

The man blinked several times, but his face remained schooled to a polite indifference. "Where do you wish for us to arrange the tables, sir?"

Sutton turned to Wyatt briefly, his eyes rolling once in his head in a manner that suggested he had a thought as to how to handle the situation. He leaned toward his younger brother to whisper quickly, "We must cancel."

When he turned back to the deliveryman, he encountered a slightly suspicious stare.

"Are you the responsible party, sir?" the tall man inquired.

"Responsible?" Sutton echoed.

"For payment, sir."

77

"Good gad! Mama did not pay?" Wyatt cried.

"It was arranged that Lady Cawley would pay upon arrival, master . . . ?" the man replied, asking for a name even as he glanced about as though he were looking for someone who might be of more help.

"Sutton. Lady Cawley's son, you may be assured. Will you pardon us for one moment?" Sutton asked with a polite smile that ceased to exist the moment he turned and seized his brother's arm to drag him aside. "What to do, Wyatt?" he whispered furiously. "I've reserved the other agency, and they made me give them half the fee, nonrefundable! Out of my quarterly funds! I can't afford this fellow as well!"

"We'll have to ask Papa for the funds."

"Then he'll know we made a muddle of things! No," Sutton straightened, tugging at his waistcoat as though to firm his sudden resolve. "No. We must have the other company service the affair, that's all. I'll simply send this fellow packing."

Wyatt watched with admiring eyes as his brother strode straight-backed across to the man from Young, Bittner and Canney. He watched his brother's chin come up, watched the masterful way he spoke, his hand making a small shooing motion. He saw his brother neither flinch nor step back when a deep redness filled the man's face; he regarded with a flicker of pride how Sutton absorbed the man's obviously heated words. He saw the exchange of comments — increasingly shorter and louder — and admired Sutton's unwavering stance. Then, he felt admiration shift into a wave of relief at the thought it was not himself that had to deliver — loud enough to be heard by all and sundry — Sutton's final words of, "I wish you to leave the premises, now, sirrah!"

The man stiffened, and his voice dropped considerably. He said something very briefly, etched the barest of bows — more an insult than an honor — and turned his back to Sutton with a military precision that any soldier would admire. He shouted out a single command of, "We leave, at once," and promptly proceeded to do just that.

Wyatt watched as his brother tugged down his waistcoat again, as one might after a round of fisticuffs, his shoulders slanting back and his chin rising in a sure sign that he was not only affronted, but perhaps also a bit uncertain.

"What did he say to give you such a high color?" Wyatt demanded, his eyes glittering, once his brother had crossed to his side.

"When this is all over," Sutton said, with a lift of his chin indicating the direction of the ballroom high over their heads, "remind me to inform Mama that Young, Bittner and Canney are no longer available for services pertaining to this household."

"Oh," said Wyatt, making a mental note to be quit of the house that day.

A clattering from down the street caused the brothers to turn as one, and they saw another large cart arriving, loaded with the likes of what they had just sent away.

"Maybe it's just as well," Wyatt said, though his tone implied he would not wager a monkey on it. "At least these fellows from Swallow and Sons are very quick and prompt."

"Which is why I no longer have any of my quarterly available to me any longer, my dear brother. Haste costs dearly," Sutton said sourly, walking forward to wave the cart toward the rear entrance of the house.

The boys surveyed the room.

"It doesn't look right, does it?" Wyatt said, scratching his cheek. "Though I'm not sure why that is."

Sutton nodded slowly, equally at a loss to explain why.

"Maybe they should be further apart?"

"No." Sutton shook his head now, his cupped hand to his chin, his elbow supported by the arm crossed over his chest.

The butler turned from where the last table was being set up, crossing over to the young masters. "And are the linens being delivered by another place of business, Master Sutton?"

"Linens?" Sutton echoed, flushing scarlet.

Wyatt nodded and said, "Yes, that's what's missing. Of course, linens!"

Sutton cleared his throat and mumbled, "No delivery, no, Hassup. We'll just make use of what Mama has about the house."

"But, Master Sutton, we do not have twenty table linens, not to mention those needed for the service tables," Hassup cried.

"We don't?"

"Where would they be stored? As it is, Lady Cawley had to

install another wardrobe for nothing but bed linens, and we had to place that in her chambers, as there is no more space for so little as a box below stairs. Monsieur, the cook, was threatening to quit if he had to surrender any more room over to storage, if you recall. No, Master Sutton, we perhaps have a half-dozen, or maybe as many as eight . . . but, more than twenty, no, of course we do not have such a number on hand."

"Then we'll leave them bare," Wyatt offered.

Hassup looked at both boys as only a long-time servant could. He spoke slowly, enunciating the words to make clear his point, "We *must* have table linens until the dessert is served."

Sutton's shoulders slumped. "I cannot hire them. I haven't a farthing to call my own. What of you, Wyatt, have you any of the ready?"

"None at all. I went to Hatchard's and bought a supply of books to take back to Eton with me."

"Books! Good gad, I didn't even know you could read," Sutton grumbled.

"Just because I like to play at a sport or two does not mean I cannot read," Wyatt began, warming up to the old argument. "In fact, if you ever bothered to lift your eyes from those risqué novels you think I don't know about—"

"Mind your tongue!" Sutton ground out, his face coloring before the servant's silent observation. "This gets us nowhere. Think, man, think! What are we to do?"

"I say we assault the linen closet and see what's there. Wouldn't a sheet be near as good as a table linen, I ask you?"

"Wyatt! I declare I have maligned you most unfairly! It seems you *do* have a modicum of intelligence. That's the very thing," he cried, ignoring Hassup's attempts to add his own undoubtedly disapproving opinion, at least to judge by the censure in his features. "Come on then, brother. Hassup. Let us see what we can find to put to use!"

"And flowers," Wyatt said as they exited the room. "Seems to me there ought to be flowers."

"It's on Mama's list. She wrote that she meant to make use of the flowers from the orangery. We'll do that next, after we see what may be done about the linens."

"By jove, we are clever fellows, aren't we?" Wyatt smiled at his slightly taller brother.

"By jove, we are. Papa knew it, even if Mama was less sure," Sutton agreed, as Hassup followed in their wake, wisely keeping his opinion on the matter to himself.

Horace had been awake for over an hour by the time his wife stirred beside him. "Good evening, sleepyhead," he said, smiling down at her as he set aside the paper he had resumed reading.

"Evening? Have I slept so long then?" she asked, pushing against the feather mattress to sit up against the headboard next to her husband. Her hands wrapped around his arm and she laid her head on his shoulder, her dark hair spilling across his chest as she yawned. "What time is it?"

"Nearly six."

"I feel better," she announced.

"I'm glad. Feel up to some supper?"

"Supper. Yes, I'll have to see to that —"

"Not at all. No need for you to disturb yourself. I'll ring for it, and we'll eat together up here in the room. Mrs. Pattick can see that the children are given a meal in the nursery."

"Muribelle will simply adore that," Clarice said with a wry smile. "But I confess, I *am* hungry, and I *am* willing to allow you to spoil me this way."

"Then so it shall be. As my lady requests."

She turned up her face to smile at him and their eyes met.

"You should wear your hair down more often," Horace said in a low voice, reaching a hand to gather up the silky length, letting it slide through his fingers.

"We should nap together more often," she replied.

A spark leaped in his eyes. "I quite agree. Just how well are you feeling now, my dear?"

"Quite well," she replied, blushing even as she gave a throaty laugh.

"That's a very good thing, as I intend to put off dinner for a while now. I seem to have developed an entirely different appetite all of a sudden," he said, as one hand reached for his glasses, which he placed atop the table near the bed, then lifted the other to caress her face even as he leaned down toward her. She raised her lips to his, surrendering to his suggestion without the slightest protest; in fact, with quite some participation. Horace pulled her onto his lap, continuing the kiss, and she wrapped her arms around his neck.

It wasn't very long before buttons were being undone, and hands were exploring, when a sudden sharp rap at the door startled them both.

"Blast it!" Horace growled. "Ignore it!" he added. Clarice gave him a shocked look, but then she giggled conspiratorially and settled back down on his lap. He began to undo yet another button when another knock resounded.

"Sir Horace!" called the housekeeper, Mrs. Davis, through the door. "Sir Horace, it is nearly the supper hour." There was a pause, and then the voice continued, "Might I have a moment of your time? Sir Horace?"

"Excuse me," he ground out to Clarice, shifting her to her side of the bed. He crawled off, shrugging his shirt back over his shoulders. He crossed to the door, slid back the bolt, and pulled it open. The housekeeper's lips parted, even as her eyes rounded at the sight of his open shirt, but before she could speak, he said firmly, "We would like a tray sent up, please. Knock once and leave it outside the door. We are not to be disturbed for the rest of the evening."

"But, Sir Horace—"

"I believe I made myself quite clear, Mrs. Davis," he said, shutting the door and sliding the bolt back in place.

Mrs. Davis stared at the closed door, then drew herself up. "Well, I never," she said to herself, unused as she was to such ways from Sir and Lady Cawley. She flushed scarlet at the memory of Sir Horace's bared chest, and—turning to flee the scene of such unusual immoderation—decided at once that she most certainly would *not* disturb them anymore this day.

Horace made sure the bolt was secure, then turned back to face the room.

"Oh, Horace, she will be quite scandalized," Clarice said, half prepared to laugh.

"It's good for her. Far too stuffy by half," he assured his wife, crossing to her slowly as he removed his shirt and tossed it on the floor, his blue eyes flashing.

"Oh, Horace," she said again, but then it was quite some time until she spoke in anything other than a throaty whisper.

"Wyatt!" Sutton squeaked at the window.

The lad left off tying his cravat to join his brother at the window. He paid no attention to the beauty of the bright morning, seeing only the cart in the street below their town house as it turned around the corner, obviously heading toward the back door. "What's that?" he said, though he had a strong suspicion he knew exactly what it was.

"Flowers!" Sutton spoke, the word sounding like a curse. "Why didn't Mama note that she had already ordered all these things? What are we to do with another mass of flowers? I thought the ballroom was just fine the way it is, but now, with these, it will be crowded and overdone. There'll hardly be room for the guests!"

"Go turn him away, as you did with that other fellow."

"And how am I to pay?" Sutton wailed. He reached for his jacket, dragging it on without consideration for its fine workmanship. He tugged at the lapels and the sleeves, straightening his spine. "But, perhaps you are right. It is worth an attempt. Perhaps he will allow us to be billed — many of the finer places do." He paused, giving his younger brother a stern look. He snapped, "Well, come on then! Can't see why I should have to do it alone a second time."

Wyatt grabbed for his jacket, trepidation replacing the anticipation that had formed on his features.

They marched, shoulder to shoulder, down the hall, and then in unison down the stairs. They heard the stir of arrival below them as they advanced down to the laundry room, the hum of voices exchanging information, and hurried forward to intercept the proceedings. Three steps above the bottom, Sutton's head shot forward as he half crouched on the stairs, peering into the half-lighted room before them. "Devil take it!" he hissed, earning Wyatt's admiration for the well-phrased curse, only to have his blood freeze a moment later when Sutton added in horror, "Mama!"

Indeed, Mama had come before them. She was directing that the flowers proceed at once to the ballroom above.

"What now, brother?" Wyatt gulped, his voice a whisper. "Do we confess all, ere she discovers it for herself?"

Sutton's eyes bounced around in his sockets as he searched his brain for an answer, and finally discovered one as he began to back up the stairs. He intoned quietly and solemnly, "Every soldier understands that sometimes there is a need for a retreat to be sounded."

He promptly turned on his heel and fled, Wyatt immediately behind him.

Clarice followed the men up the stairs, the scent of flowers bringing a smile to her lips, suggesting the gaiety that was ahead of them this day. Really, she felt much, much better. Horace had been quite correct in insisting she rest yesterday. Now she quite felt up to the obvious demands the day would bring, she thought as she tied the strings of a kitchen apron at her waist as she walked, anticipating the need to help arrange the flowers just as she thought they ought to be.

The men stopped at the doorway, not moving into the room. She stepped forward, assuming they were awaiting her instructions. The lead man turned to her and said, "M'lady, where would you be wishing these 'ere?"

"Well, I particularly wanted white roses for the service tables—" she began to explain as she stepped into the room, but then the words died in her mouth and she gasped. The room was already filled with flowers—quite a profusion of them, in fact. Her eyes flew around, taking in the variety of colors, the way they were slapped and slumped into a collection of bowls and pitchers, and she knew in an instant that each and every one had been harvested from her orangery. *Cut,* not carried in their pots, but *cut,* and a very great many of them. There were clusters of her prize hydrangeas, a distinctive shade of pinkish-blue she had achieved from careful monitoring of the minerals they received in their feedings. There was her particular favorite red rose, the one with the streaks of yellow, and handfuls of pink and purple pansies were strewn everywhere in bowls, stripped from their plants. She nearly moaned aloud, wondering if there was a single flower left to bloom in the orangery, and had to wonder how many of her plants would suffer from being so denuded?

As the shock began to wear off just a little, she saw more. She saw the nearest handful of tables had proper linens upon them, but beyond the row of six stretched a sea of varying cloths. Here was a white bed linen, stained on one edge where one of the children had wiped a bloody nose late one night; there was a thick, grayish sheet, the variety used in the colder climes of the servants' quarters; another table hosted a coarse dark brown woven blanket. The differences went on through the room, with only six of the twenty tables properly dressed. Clarice raised a hand to her forehead, turning to stare blindly at the deliveryman. "Oh my," she breathed.

He stared back, obviously wondering if he ought to be disapproving.

"Oh my," she said again, her hand moving to her breast. "I . . . I . . ." she tried to think what to say next, but for a moment her mind was blank. Finally she said, "You must simply place the flowers here, in the hall, on the floor. If you would, please. My servants . . . ?" she glanced back at the room, her eyes assessing as she mumbled, "No. My children . . . !"

Then her usual bearing of composure returned, and she made a motion with her hands that indicated they should set down their burdens. "Yes. Yes, indeed. Please bring all the plants here and leave them in the hallway. And leave a path, that we might move through them into the room. My servants will arrange them shortly."

"As you wish, m'lady," the deliveryman bowed.

Clarice turned and fled down the stairs, calling, "Horace! Horace!" unmindful of the stares of the staff. She was intercepted by Mrs. Davis, who supplied the information, "He's just gone out to the tobacconists', my lady."

Clarice flew to the door of the nearest room that overlooked the square below the house, which happened to be the sitting room that Muribelle had taken over as a bedchamber. Muribelle looked up from the table upon which her arms and head had been bent, tears marking her cheeks and puffy eyes testifying that the weeping was not new. She jumped at her mother's unannounced entrance. She was equally startled when she saw her mother press against the windowpane, then heard her swear, "Drat! He's gone already."

"Lady Cawley!" Mrs. Davis gasped from the open door, casting a warning eye toward the impressionable young lady in the room.

"Whatever is happening?" Muribelle asked, reaching to wipe her face with her hands.

Her mother whirled to face her, and for a moment Muribelle was astounded to see that Mama had quite lost her composure. "Mama, are you well?" she cried.

Clarice gathered herself with a visible effort, taking three deep breaths until she quite resembled her usual self. When she spoke, she spoke softly, as she nearly always did. "Muribelle, whom did your father appoint to see to the ballroom?"

"Sutton. And Wyatt."

"I see. Thank you, Muribelle." She paused then, and added ominously, "Have we any notion of where Sutton and Wyatt might be at this moment?"

The housekeeper and the daughter shook their heads.

"Not in this house, I am willing to wager," Clarice muttered to herself.

Muribelle sniffed, and Clarice's eyes finally focused on the occupants of the room, noticing at last that her daughter's face was awash with tears. Her expression softened with perplexion as she moved at once to put her arm around her daughter's shoulders. "My dear, whyever are you crying? And all night, too, by the look of you. You mustn't have puffy eyes for the party—"

"There won't be any party!" Muribelle wailed, leaping up to fling herself into her startled mother's arms. "Or at least," she blubbered, "I shan't be there!"

"Whatever can you mean?" Clarice cried, but got no answer for several minutes as Muribelle soaked her shoulder with tears. Finally the girl managed to gasp out, "We had a-a disagreement. He-he was so horrid, Mama. Horribly horrid, I tell y-you."

"Oh my dear. Well, you must tell me all about it," soothed Clarice, leading her over to the settee before the vanity, looking up to catch the housekeeper's eye. "Mrs. Davis, if you would be so kind as to await me in my sitting room?"

As the housekeeper departed, she made Muribelle sit down and began to brush her hair, knowing that the motion would calm her even as it freed her tongue to explain.

Ten minutes later Muribelle had sobbed out her explanation. "A-and then I said 'I b-bid you good day, Mister Penville!', and he stormed out of the house. And h-he doesn't love me, or he w-wouldn't throw my kisses back in my face that way. And he's shallow, and mean-spirited, and horrid-horrid-horrid!" she cried with vehemence.

"Oh dear," Clarice said under her breath as she finished securing her daughter's hair with a colorful ribbon. She caught

Muribelle's eye in the mirror, set aside the brush, and laid her hands firmly on the girl's shoulders. "Then of course you must not marry him, Muribelle. Not if you feel that way about him."

"Yes," Muribelle said, but she did not nod in agreement and her voice was less than firm.

"It's too bad, really." Clarice gave an exaggerated sigh. "At first I thought this was just the Betrothal Argument, but when you explained, I could see at once that it was more than that."

"The Betrothal Argument?" Muribelle echoed, turning her doubting features to face her mother.

"The traditional one. The one every couple has before the wedding. It's meant to clear the air, of course, as one must. Weddings can be such tediously emotional affairs! I'm sure you've heard the matrons speak of it . . . but then perhaps you haven't, being so popular as you are at parties. No time to sit with the older women and hear us repeat our tales to one another."

"I'm sure no woman has had such a terrible row as this," Muribelle interjected.

Clarice opened her mouth as if to speak, only to close it and stop a nod in midmotion. "No, no, of course not," she said soothingly. "No, they are usually just little things, such as how 'his Mama insists she will only wear green'; or — well, I guess you are old enough to hear this now — I recall one bride whose husband's mistress was at her wedding feast! Oh my, I'm afraid *that* row began at the feast and we were all a party to it! And I remember one family where it came about that a twin had died unexpectedly and his family had merely substituted his twin brother in his place. Poor girl didn't realize it until her wedding night! And she could not abide the twin, as they all knew, of course. Terrible, shocking business!"

"Mama," said Muribelle, doubt creeping into her voice, "are you roasting me?"

"Not at all!" Clarice cried as though offended. "Every word is true. But, of course, what has that to say to the matter? You have had a terrible row, and fences may not be mended, not at this late date."

"You are making me feel a fool," Muribelle sniffed.

Clarice smiled briefly to herself, glad to find her daughter wasn't one at all. She folded her hands before her skirt. "Then what do you suggest, Muribelle? Shall we cancel the party and the wedding, or shall we send for Mister Penville and see if perhaps he is feeling just a little bit foolish as well?"

"I'm not saying I forgive him," Muribelle replied stubbornly, but her chin sank meekly to her chest as she murmured, "but you have my permission to send him 'round a note to call upon me, if you wish."

"I think that would be wise," Clarice said, reaching to pat her daughter's face. "Now wash that pretty little face, Muribelle, and I'll have some cucumber slices sent up for you to put over your eyes while you have a little lie-down. I'll send that note right away."

Clarice turned down the hall to her room, finding the housekeeper awaiting her as requested.

"My lady," Mrs. Davis greeted her anxiously.

"One moment, please," Clarice replied as she crossed to her secretary. It was the work of two minutes to pen the note, at the bottom of which was added in underlined letters: "It would be most advantageous if you could please bring your list of invitees with you, even if it is only a partial list." She sealed the folded letter with a wafer, and then handed it to the housekeeper. "Please see that this is carried by a footman at once to Mister Penville's home. He need not await a reply unless the gentleman indicates he wishes to send one."

"Very good, my lady. Now, as to a very important matter—"

"Yes, yes, I know. The flowers." Clarice sighed.

"Flowers, my lady?" Mrs. Davis frowned. "I know nothing of flowers . . . except all the vases are missing, and not to mention Monsieur assures me his kitchens are missing quite a number of bowls . . . ?"

"Then if not the flowers, what?" Clarice asked, her face paling.

"It is the menu, my lady."

"The menu?" Clarice echoed faintly.

The housekeeper held up the modified sheet of paper that the children had presented the chef. Clarice looked it over, and very nearly groaned aloud. "Do not tell me this is all Monsieur has prepared? One main entrée? No vegetables, no soups, no salads, no breads?"

"Yes, it is all. Are you saying these were not your instructions?" She drew herself up defensively. "You must know I tried to verify this list, but my lady was not to be disturbed! Sir

Horace made that very clear to me," Mrs. Davis cried. "What was I to do, my lady? I had to think the children would be in their governess's care. That they would not be so presumptuous. . . . I had to think this was what you wished."

Clarice gave her housekeeper a level look that made the other woman flush and nearly take half a step back. Then the lady of the house sighed, remembering Horace had chased the woman away last night, and how she had allowed it to happen. This, then, was her just reward for lying abed when she was no longer ill.

"You and I both know that my children are entirely capable of avoiding Mrs. Pattick's attentions, and that they are also entirely capable of being presumptuous. Ah, well." She sighed again, glancing at the ormolu clock on her mantelpiece. "It is nearly ten o'clock. There is no time to start new preparations, I suppose?"

"Very little time, my lady! We could perhaps hasten to the bakers, and I'm sure a vegetable dish of some kind could be put together, perhaps . . ." her voice trailed off doubtfully.

Clarice folded the paper deliberately, thinking rapidly. She slipped the paper into the pocket of the apron, and decided all at once, "No. No, let us not begin new preparations. Monsieur will already be at wit's end, if I know him at all. To add more demands to the kitchen now would result in even more disasters than I have already uncovered this morning. Mrs. Davis, go to him at once, tell him to put back the beef and pudding until supper, and ready only the desserts. As elaborate as he may make them. We are going to have 'a profusion of sweets to celebrate the sweethearts' . . . that is, presuming my daughter agrees to remain one of those sweethearts."

"My lady?"

"Never mind. Just please see that the note is delivered as soon as possible, and see that Monsieur has his new instructions," Clarice declared, gathering up her skirts. "And have Lilly bring my gown here to my room. The blue gown with the silver netting; it is not in my wardrobe. And tell her to be ready to help me dress at a moment's notice. I'll have little time left for dressing when I am through putting the ballroom to rights."

"At once, my lady." Mrs. Davis made a curtsy and departed, shaking her head at the folderol that went on in this household.

89

Clarice stepped back, and nodded slowly, growing more and more satisfied with what she saw. The ballroom was filled with a profusion of color. She had scrounged every kind of colored fabric she had in the house, and cut or folded them into equal squares. Two chambermaids had been set to sewing with a rapidity that had little to do with accuracy, but which ended in a multicolored pile of equal-size spreads. These Clarice placed at a crosswise angle over the various fabrics already on the tables, so that only four corners of the various linens and blankets underneath showed. She was careful to coordinate the top and bottom colors, so that now the brown blanket was cross-covered with a cloth of gold, and now the bloodstain on the white bed linen was hidden by a lovely plaid she had brought back from her honeymoon in Scotland. And each table had a bouquet at its center, with flowers and a bowl or vase also chosen to complement the colors of the cloth upon which it resided. On the particularly unspectacular and unflattering dark green blankets that covered the service tables, she had not only arranged flowers in her grandmother's silver epergnes, but had also hand-sewn flowers and greens along every edge, including the fabric folds that stretched down to the floor. Behind the two seats where Muribelle and Fenton presumably would sit together, she had arranged a large urn — so large she had to stand on tiptoe to place the flowers as she wished them to be — and filled it with some of the larger flowers, arranged in a kind of rainbow effect, going from palest pink to deepest violet.

The room had become a riot of color. If she had not known better, she might have thought the whole eclectic effect was quite deliberate.

"Will it do?" she asked the two maids who still were placing last-minute stitches.

"It looks right beautiful." "Loverly," they gushed, sighing as one.

"I think you may be right," she said and nodded again. "At any rate, it matters not, for there is no time to change it. Now, if you will see that all these clippings are swept up and the floor polished anew — "

"My lady?" she was interrupted by the maid, Lilly, who had just come from mounting the stairs.

"Lilly, there you are. Just the one I needed to see. You must help me dress," Clarice said, wiping her green-stained hands on her apron as she moved toward the maid and the stairs.

"O'course, my lady. Which dress would you be wantin'?"

"Why, the blue with silver net, of course. Did Mrs. Davis not tell you?"

"Aye, she did that. Only . . ." the maid's voice dwindled away. Her usually boisterous manner was nowhere in evidence, causing Clarice to come to a halt before she ever put her foot down the first stair, and she felt her mouth twitch. Really, this was becoming just too absurd. "Only what?" she asked, her voice wavering.

"Only it ain't ready, m'lady. I never knew you wished it!" the maid cried, alarmed by the unsteady quiver in her mistress's voice. "Oh, I'm that sorry, I am, m'lady, only no one ever said special-like, and I thought to meself that you had what you'd be wantin' an' all. I mean, Miss Muribelle never said nothing 'bout the clothes, 'cepting what was already in the washroom, an' that weren't much!"

Clarice looked on, her chagrin rising in her throat, becoming an unexpected bubble of laughter that threatened to burst past the twitch at her lips. "I don't suppose any of the shirts have been mangled?" she managed to say calmly, though she was unable to suppress the smile that spread across her lips.

"No'm," peeped the maid uncertainly, almost smiling along, but obviously afraid she was misinterpreting the mistress's mood. She opened her mouth to offer an explanation, but Clarice held up a restraining hand, grinning openly now.

"No. No, do not explain to me. There is nothing to be gained by it. We may do well enough without the shirts mangled. That is, presuming there are some clean and ready to be worn, I pray." Then she could no longer keep from laughing aloud, from exasperation and from a growing acknowledgment of the absolute chaos of the day. Her laughter filled the ballroom, and she remained smiling as she added, "Though I find it difficult to hope it could be true. Oh, Lilly, do go at once and ask each and every member of this family if they have something presentable to wear. Anything! I had once thought we might be dressed in similar colors, but now I only care that we are dressed in something, anything, at all fashionable. I presume I am not mistaken to think my pomona green gown is pressed and ready?" She laughed again, and the maid dared to smile as she nodded enthusiastically. Clarice went on, "In point of fact, we may as well be as the flowers in this room: see that everyone wears a different shade, if you will. And I want a list. Don't worry about your spelling — I just want to know what to expect next!" she cried, lifting her hands in a gesture of surrender, even as she turned to hurry down the stairs, her laughter trailing behind her.

"My lady," intoned Hassup.

His words stopped her before she could descend to the kitchens to assure herself the chef was not unduly upset by the latest change to the menu.

She turned to him, her eyes wide as she said, "I cannot imagine what this will be!"

"My lady?"

She waved her hand in the air, and urged, "Do go on; you had something of which you wished to inform me?"

"Indeed, my lady. Was my lady aware that naught had been ordered for beverages other than lemonade? In point of fact, a rather large tub of lemonade?"

"No wine? No Champagne?" Clarice asked, knowing the answer before the butler could indicate this was true. She pressed a hand to either side of her face, firmly suppressed the last vestiges of her laughter, allowed her shoulders to come up around her ears, then relaxed with a hearty sigh. "This at least is more simple. See that all the usual wines are brought up from the cellars at once, and the reds allowed to breathe."

"Very good, my lady. I believe our stock is adequate. I must say I am not too surprised to learn this is what you wish, despite Monsieur Chef's claims to the contrary."

"Yes, well, Monsieur was misled. Is there anything else?"

"Yes, my lady. I thought perhaps my lady might wish to know that the Masters Sutton and Wyatt were quite recently seen playing cards in the stables at the mews."

Clarice nodded, for she and the butler had long ago come to the understanding that the young masters required monitoring. She did not utter the words "so that is where they are hiding!" that sprang to the tip of her tongue. "Please send a footman at once to gather them, and be sure they understand the message means they are to come at once. Is that all?"

"No, my lady. Mister Penville has called."

The sudden pinched look that came to her face lasted only a moment before relaxing somewhat, and she nodded, making a dismissive gesture. "Then please ask Miss Harrod to join Muribelle in the calling room, and then show him in."

The butler cleared his throat. "I have already attempted to do just that, but Miss Muribelle refuses to come down, and Miss Harrod is in a near-faint at having to entertain the gentleman by herself, my lady."

Clarice could not stop herself from rolling her eyes in front of the servant. However she managed, by pressing her lips together, to keep from uttering an oath aloud. "Very well," she said in a measured tone, "I will go and speak with Muribelle. You will join Miss Harrod."

"Toward what purpose, my lady?"

"I don't *care*," she said between clenched teeth, though her expression remained calm. "Offer them tea, or port, or see if you can get them to play dominoes. Anything you can think of, only do not allow Mister Penville to leave!"

She did not wait for the butler's assurances, turning with a swish of her skirts to mount the stairs once more.

She knocked on Muribelle's door, just managing to refrain from tapping her foot.

"Who is it?" came a faint, muffled voice.

"Mama," Clarice answered, not waiting for an invitation. She entered the room to find Muribelle prone on the bed, her face buried in the pillows. The girl looked up at the sound of her mother's entrance, and Clarice knew a moment's relief to see that she had not been weeping again. If anything, her face was mulishly set.

"I won't go down," Muribelle declared, burying her face anew.

Clarice crossed to the bed and grasped her daughter's shoulders. She pulled firmly up, and Muribelle surrendered to the demand, swinging her legs around to sit up. The girl then promptly melted into her mother's shoulder as that lady sat on the bed, cradling her oldest child as a storm of tears ensued.

"Oh dear, I had thought perhaps we might avoid new tears," Clarice murmured.

"I can't help it!" Muribelle wept, her shoulders shaking.

"I know, I know. And this time I won't even make you explain, because I believe I know why you refuse, all of a sudden, to see Fenton."

Muribelle's lower lip came out, but she was listening closely despite her tears.

"I know it is because you are embarrassed. You realize that perhaps you were a little harsh with Fenton, for he is, after all, Muribelle, only a husband-to-be. And it is difficult enough for husbands to understand the intricacies and delicacies of household planning, even after a score of years, let alone a mere bridegroom. I am sure Fenton thought something like 'oh, a list of guests. Yes, yes, I'll get around to it,' and I am equally sure it never occurred to him that you might need it in a far more timely manner than he thought to supply it. Not because he meant to upset you, but merely because he did not realize how important it was to you. Oh, give men a war to be won, and they can make the most intricate battle plans, and careful evaluations of the enemy, and all that goes with such a campaign, but ask them to name who should sit next to whom at dinner and they know nothing. It is as though they have special blinders that don't allow them to see the particulars of their everyday lives. So that is left up to the wife."

She patted Muribelle's shoulder, then brought up her other hand to pull a small lacy kerchief from the wrist of her long sleeve. She passed this to the girl, and said, "Time to dry your face, darling." As Muribelle complied, Clarice went on, "What I am telling you, my dear, is that in major matters you *should* consult with your husband, and when he happens to care enough to disagree with your proposals, you should listen to what he has to say — which will undoubtedly complicate your life and plans — and certainly you should comply . . . if his thoughts are at all sensible. However, if his judgments are entirely untenable, then you must promptly find another way to go about getting done the things which must be done. He may resent, for a short while, that you went about it differently, but in all he will be satisfied as long as the plans flow smoothly. *This* then is the secret to a joyous marriage."

"But I *had* to have that list from him — !"

"Indeed you did. But could you not have called upon his father and written his aunt, and gotten it yourself that way?"

"Oh," Muribelle said, her shoulders slumping. "I never thought of that."

"You will, next time," Clarice assured her.

"Next time?" Muribelle echoed, her eyes wistful though her mouth did form a small smile.

"Yes, next time! Another row is inevitable, and I'll not tell you otherwise. A friend once told me that marriage is a very convenient way to have love and hate all under one roof, where the battles thereof can be privately conducted, over and over again. I am not sure I quite agree with such an assessment, but there's a grain of truth in it. You must expect to be both angered and inconvenienced by Fenton, as he must with you. That is, very simply, a facet of residing together." She hugged Muribelle about the shoulders, and added kindly but firmly, "Now that you understand that, you realize you must go down and apologize."

"Why must *I*? I daresay I was not nearly so rude as Fenton!"

"But you admit you *were* rude, and it is only right that you should express you are sorry for it, even if it was the lesser sin. You know as well as I this is what is *really* bothering you now, and that is why you do not wish to join him below stairs. It is never easy to say 'sorry', but it is a skill all spouses must develop.

"Well, my dear," Clarice said, standing and pulling Muribelle to her feet as well, "there is nothing for it. It must be done. And I will tell you a secret: you will feel ever so much better once it is done and over with. And I suspect you will not be the only one to utter an apology."

Muribelle sniffed, not quite convinced. "So this is my first taste of real marriage?"

"I'm afraid so." Clarice pulled her toward the vanity, turning her to face the mirror where their reflections looked back at them. "But remember, daily life is seldom so traumatic. And if you and Fenton truly love one another, then for every tear you shed, a corresponding smile awaits you."

"I don't know—I've shed an excess of tears in the last two days." Muribelle hiccupped. "There is a great deal of ground to be made up."

"Count the smiles in the church on the day of your wedding," Clarice advised with a soft smile as she pressed on her daughter's shoulders, signaling her to be seated before the vanity.

"Oh, Mama, you are a romantic peagoose!" Muribelle smiled at last through her tears.

"Now, look in the mirror, note that we are both smiling—that's two!—and allow me to help you put yourself to rights. Mister Fenton Penville awaits you."

"Oh, Mama, do help me hurry! He won't leave, will he? I have left him waiting below for over half an hour already," Muribelle cried in new agitation.

"He won't leave."

"But how can you know that?" Muribelle cried, frantically pulling pins from her hair, which scattered about onto the floor.

Clarice bent to retrieve some of them, then reached for the hairbrush. "Because I simply do not have time to deal with the fact should he do so," she mumbled around the pins she had stuck between her lips.

Clarice took the last stair up from the kitchens, at last smiling in relief, even as she ran her wrist across her forehead and sighed in something very like exhaustion. Everything seemed to be back in order. Monsieur was happy once more, well pleased to find he had, in however roundabout a fashion, done nothing wrong. He was content enough that he was putting extra effort into the elaborate cake that would serve as the "sweets for the sweethearts" centerpiece, adding floral flourishes in colors to match the pink-to-violet flower display that would form a backdrop for the betrothed couple. She had seen the flurry of footmen carrying the wines to the ballroom above, and she knew the tables and flowers were in as good an order as she could make them. Now she need only peep in on Muribelle and Fenton to be sure their situation had not managed to go awry again, see that everyone was dressing for the occasion, and be dressed herself.

Just as she crossed by the vestibule, the door was opened by Hassup to admit her husband. "Horace!" she called to him, relieved to see he was returned in a timely manner.

"Darling," he called back, brandishing a wrapped package. "I thought we were a bit short on cigarillos. Went and picked up three dozen."

If he had come home an hour earlier, he might have gotten

the lecture of his life. Now Clarice had no time — nor energy — for it. She shook her head abstractedly and replied, "How very nice, dear. I am so glad that you are home, as you may be a great help to me —"

"I say," he interrupted, having divested himself of his coat and beaver, to cross to her side, "you are looking a trifle peaked. Are you not feeling well again today?"

"No, I feel quite well. It has just been a rather hectic morning —"

"Wouldn't know it! Everything's in order at first glance." He circled the hall and stairwell with his eyes, then turned again to look down at his wife, who had grown suddenly quite still and silent. "Oh, I say!" he cried, alarmed by the growing scowl on her face. A scowl he had not seen often, but recognized at once as a danger sign. He cleared his throat and attempted to land on the side of her good graces by asking, "A bit hectic, you say?"

"*Very* hectic."

"Things did not progress quite as planned?"

"To the best of my knowledge, absolutely nothing progressed quite as planned."

Her eyes, usually so soft and filled with amusement, had now gone quite steely, holding him in place.

"I see, I see," he murmured, lifting his chin and glancing anywhere but at her. There was no point in exasperating her — as he invariably did on just such occasions, although he was always at a loss to say exactly why it should be — so he rushed on, saying, "But I interrupted you, my dear. You had a task you wished me to fulfill?"

She could see that he was well aware he had somehow put all her party plans awry, though it was equally obvious she would have to explain, later tonight, exactly why that was. Indeed, he had no way of knowing that each and every one of his children had altered the careful plans she had made. She decided he had suffered enough, for now; she released him with a sigh. "Indeed." She then glanced at the wall clock and gave a little cry. "Oh, Horace, it is nearly eleven-thirty! I don't know how I'll be able to be dressed in only half an hour! And I've yet to look in on Muribelle — Great heavens! Muribelle must begin dressing now, too. So you see, yes, yes, there is something you must do for me! Do please go and see that all the other children are dressing, will you? I am quite sure Mrs. Pattick

97

has her hands full. And make sure their faces and hands are clean, especially Peter's."

"At once, my dear," he assured her, slipping away before her agitation could turn to ire with him once more.

She fairly flew to the sitting room, relieved to see the door was left open. It was a minute's work to slip next to the open doorway and peep inside. Muribelle and Fenton were standing facing one another, smiling, speaking in low voices. The governess, Miss Harrod, was also smiling slightly, a reliable indication that all was going well. Hassup was gone, no doubt to his personal relief, on to other duties. Clarice stepped back quietly, then made a play of swishing her skirts and stomping her feet a bit, then proceeded, thus announced, into the room. All heads swiveled to note her arrival.

"Ah, Muribelle!" she called. She nodded at Mr. Penville in his party finery of fashionably tight buff pantaloons, blue superfine jacket, and a powder blue waistcoat shot with gold thread. "You are looking most fine today," she told him.

"Thank you, Lady Cawley," he replied. He opened his mouth to respond in kind, but was stopped.

"Don't you dare compliment me!" Clarice said in a pleasant scold. "I have not yet dressed, my hair is at sixes and sevens, and I know I look a fright."

"Mama, only see! Fenton has brought the list for the wedding invitations," Muribelle said, brandishing the list, her eyes fluttering shyly between her fiancé and her mother, apparently abashed and pleased at once.

"How thoughtful, Fenton," Clarice approved.

He flushed a little, but his eyes held hers as he silently thanked her for the advice in her note to him.

Clarice smiled, but there was no time to reflect on either their happy reunion or her part in it. "I am afraid I must disrupt this charming scene, and steal my daughter away for the next half hour."

"Half hour?" Muribelle cried, glancing down at the small watch pinned on her dress. She gasped. "Oh, Mama, we must hurry!"

"Indeed we must. Fenton, please make yourself comfortable. I see at least one morning newspaper on the table there, and if that is not sufficient just ring for Hassup, and he will find the others and bring them to you. Muribelle. Miss Harrod, if

98

you please?"

She led the way upstairs, leaving Muribelle in Miss Harrod's hands while she turned toward her own dressing room. To her enormous relief she found Lilly waiting within for her.

" 'Ere's the list yer wanted, m'lady," Lilly said at once, handing her the paper with the labored writing on it.

"Why, Lilly, only look. You have spelled 'clothes' quite correctly — I do believe that is a first. My congratulations."

"Oh, thank yer, m'lady!" Lilly glowed, giving a little bob of a curtsy as a thank you. "I really am gettin' better at me letters, ain't I?"

"Yes, you are." Clarice smiled and nodded, running her eyes down the list. She liked her servants to have a little knowledge of the printed word; how was one to give any devotional time to the Holy Bible if one could not read it? Horace laughed at his wife but tolerated her opinion, although he sometimes murmured that the practice had led to his servants being a bit high in the instep — as he had judged Mrs. Davis to be last night. Clarice nearly blushed now to think of how he refused to bow to the housekeeper's notion of propriety, and she allowed herself a brief smile that acknowledged he had most deliberately startled the dear woman away from their bedchamber door to remind the woman of her place.

She read the list over again, seeing that Muribelle had decided on her jonquil gown, here noted as "the yeller dress." Sutton and Wyatt had obviously — and wisely — returned with the footman who had been sent to bring them home, for the one had agreed to bottle green, and the other to bishop's blue. Anna had no doubt delighted that she was not to wear the ubiquitous white of a young lady, for here it was noted she had chosen "flowers," a gown Clarice recognized by the one-word description as a Sunday best, and which was colorful and pretty. Lisette was to be in her fawn with mulberry ribbons — quite delightful with the child's long dark curls cascading down her back — and Peter was to wear the Devonshire brown that had just recently been purchased for him; its rich reddish-brown color brought out the highlights in his soft brown hair. Yellow, green, blue, mulberry, brown, and a flowered print — what did that leave for the masters of the house? Horace could either sport his dark blue, or else his evening blacks if he was inclined to be as sober as all that, but what for her? The pomona green now seemed a tame choice, one that would fail to make it seem the entire day had been planned just as it was presented. Equally, no pastel would do, ruling out half her dresses. The blue was too tame, the gold too much like the bride-to-be's choice, and even the rose was too docile.

Then she saw just the gown hanging to one side in the wardrobe and smiled, for she had dared to wear the gown only once before, to see the incomparable Edmund Kean at the theater. She had so wished to make a splash that night, for Horace and she had rather gained a reputation as homebodies. Well, this gown could never be accused of being a boring old matron's dress, as had been proved that night if one judged by the number of compliments it had garnered. It was the fashionable color known as morone, or as she thought of it herself, a red very like that of a peony. It was an unapologetic color, the cut was cleanly styled, and the bodice cleverly set with matching lace arranged to accentuate without actually revealing. Yes, it was exactly the gown for this occasion. She may be merely the mother of the bride, but she would be a very dashing one in this dress.

She turned to Lilly, whose eyes went around with something somewhere between reservation and awe at the daring color and cut, and cried, "Come along, Lilly. I've hardly any time to get my gown on, let alone my hair up in anything near the mode. Praise heaven that this dress is pressed!"

They set to with the energy of troops preparing for imminent battle. A quick disrobing was followed by an even quicker sponge bath, a powdering, a brushing out of hair, a resumption of fresh linens and stockings, shoes, and finally the dress. Clarice was pleased to see that it suited her as well as she had remembered, and she did up her last few buttons as Lilly was sent to fetch her mistress's garnets from the connected sleeping chamber she shared with her husband. The gems were not the shade of her dress, but their yellow undertones allowed them to be a most effective foil, perhaps even to the point of making it appear that one had been prepared just to suit the other. She was grateful she had to spend no additional time trying to select some other bit of jewelry that would be just right for the party—not too extravagant, but also fine enough to show they had more than just a ballroom as a token of their financial well-being. Once the sparkling gems were set about her neck, wrist, and ears, she had to sit still while Lilly brushed and tugged her hair up into a braided crown, making use of the curling iron — into which was dropped, by use of small tongs, glowing embers from the small fire in the dressing room grate — to make tiny pincurls around her face and along her nape. They added a special softness that Horace had more than once told her was most fetching. If it were evening she might have reached for the rouge pot or the kohl — just the tiniest, cleverest bit to add a mere hint of accent — but certainly not during the day, when such artifice was readily apparent.

Having the maid work with her hair had relaxed her, so that when she rose to her feet, she was not so distracted that she could not see in her mirror that her ensemble was just the thing. A quick glance then at the clock above the mantel showed that there was ten minutes to spare before the guests should start arriving. She sighed, relieved to find that somehow she had managed to bring not only the party but also herself back into a state of order.

There was a knock on the dividing door, but Horace did not wait for a summons before he cracked open the door. His head and torso came through the opening, and he did not step in, causing his wife to wonder instantly if maybe he wasn't deliberately using it as a shield?

"Clarice," he said, his face looking pinched, "I find I really must be changing my clothes now. . . ."

"Yesss?" she said, making it a long, questioning sound as a suspicious misgiving rose in her eyes.

"I cannot do so if I must spend the next ten minutes looking for your children."

Her eyebrows shot up. *"My* children?"

"Our children then, of course. But the thing of it is, Peter and the girls can't be found." Seeing the horror that rose at once in her eyes, he added quickly, "Not to panic! They're already dressed. Mrs. Pattick saw to that, but while she was seeing to Muribelle —"

"Muribelle?"

"Well, yes, she had a small rip in her gown —"

Clarice put a hand to her cheek and murmured some unintelligible word.

" — Which Miss Harrod was making quite a mess of, as I understood the problem to be. So, anyway, Mrs. Pattick was seeing to the rip, and the younger ones slipped away. Hassup is out in the lane looking for them, and I have set several footmen and the two older boys to searching the house, so you see I have quite taken care of the problem, except that, of course, I must be dressed myself—"

"Get dressed," Clarice echoed, coming to the door. She put her hand on his chest and pushed him back through the opening. "But you are under the strictest instructions not to attempt the Mathematical with your cravat — you will never be ready in time. Something simple will suit the occasion well enough. Are we agreed on that?"

"Agreed," he said hastily, following the word with the quick, sunny smile he always used when he wanted to turn around one of her moods. "You look splendid," he told her sincerely, then leaned forward quickly, pecked her on the cheek, and leaped back, pulling the door closed behind him.

She struggled, trying to retain the scowl that had been growing over her features, but Horace had done his usual magic. Instead she merely cast a quick, amused and exasperated glance toward heaven, then exited the room.

A footman went flying by her. "Any sign?" she called.

"No, m'lady," he called back just as he mounted the stairs by twos.

She hesitated a moment, wondering which of the children's multiple hiding places she ought to try first. The roof—which was of course forbidden—or the large kitchen cupboards? No, it would be far too busy down there for even three rather little children to slip in unnoted . . . or the storage wardrobe in the nursery? Yes, that was a possibility. The girls might not wish to become too filthy, not in their party clothes, although of course Peter wouldn't have a thought for such. She followed up the stairs.

They were not in the wardrobe, much to her chagrin. She almost left the room, when she heard a small muffled sound. She turned slowly, listening, but no further sound came. "Anna? Lissy, Peter?" she called loudly.

This was followed by a stifled giggle, coming most definitely from the direction of the beds. Clarice moved at once, lifting up a corner of the comforter that topped one of the wooden frame beds. This was met with a scurrying sound and a little peep of surprise.

"Children, you are to come out from under there at once!"

This pronouncement was met with absolute silence.

"Although I am entirely unwilling to get down on this floor and look, I am perfectly aware that you are under these beds," Clarice said firmly. She lowered her voice to add solemnly, "And if you are not out by the time I count to five, not a one of you will be allowed to attend the party."

This announcement caused a brief, whispered conference.

"One," said Clarice. "And you will have to spend the entire afternoon at your lessons. Two."

This caused another brief conference, and Peter wormed out, rolling over to look sheepishly up at his mother.

"Traitor," came a scold from under the bed.

"Three. Did I mention there will be no ices after our afternoon strolls for a month?"

Lisette squirmed out, making a great deal of pretended sneezing so as to avoid meeting her mother's eye.

"Four. Dear me, do you know I am looking for someone to take care of every last garment that needs to be restitched?" Clarice said ominously.

Anna squirmed out at last, casting Peter a dark look. "You gave us away!"

Clarice stepped among them, silencing the argument before it could begin. "Only look at your clothing! All of you rumpled, your bow out of place," she said to Lissy, then to all of them, ". . . you are all very fortunate that the chambermaids must sweep out under the beds every week or else you would all be irreparable messes. Lissy, go dampen your hair with a wet brush — it is flying all about. Oh, and Peter! You have quite lost a button!" she cried. "Anna, you are to take Peter to the laundry room and sew his button on again. Make sure you use only white thread now!" she said as Anna made a face and acted as though she would protest. "And if you, and Peter, are not ready in the ballroom in exactly five minutes, you will make me severely regret persuading Muribelle that you all ought to be included on her special day."

Anna frowned — she was coming of an age that wished to be included in the doings of adults — and caught up Peter's hand, grumbling, "Come on then, Petey."

Clarice turned to her third daughter, reaching for and

quickly putting the maroon hair ribbon to rights. She then gave Lisette a kiss on the cheek and said, "Up to the ballroom with you, little miss. Stay there and be ready for the party to begin, and no sampling any of the treats Monsieur has set out. You do know that we are to have a great number of desserts today, don't you?"

Lissy ducked her head, but Mama was smiling, so she shyly smiled, too, when she glanced up from the corner of her eye. "Peter was the one who wanted marzipan and sugar plums."

Clarice nodded seriously, though her eyes still glittered. "And I suppose they overruled your desire to include any vegetables on the menu?"

Lissy giggled, then shook her head.

Clarice gave her another kiss, and with a pat on the back sent her toward the stairs. "Go along now. Tell Anna and Peter that because of this little escapade of yours, you will all be required to have a second vegetable choice on your plate each night for a week."

Lisette's shoulders slumped, but she did not protest, recognizing the fairness of her mother's proclamation.

"For now, do keep an eye on Peter. I'll be up promptly. . . ." Clarice watched Lissy go up, then added under her breath, "I hope."

Just at that moment, Wyatt flew into the room. At the sight of his mother, he slid to a stop and made a thick swallowing sound. "I . . . I was sent to look for the younger ones—"

"I have located them," she said, crossing her arms and allowing a stern expression to cross her face. "We must talk. Myself, you, and Sutton."

Wyatt nodded, scratching behind one ear and staring at the floor as he shuffled his feet. "Now?" he said to the tiling.

"Not now. Now you need to find Sutton, and both of you need to ascend to the ballroom. I expect you to keep the children in order and see that nothing is touched or upset until I can join you up there. Am I clear on that?"

"Yes'm," Wyatt mumbled, starting to back up.

"And Wyatt?"

"Yes'm?" He did not cease to move, though he did slow down a little.

"I also want to be clear that I expect you and Sutton to help me nurse or replant my orangery until I am satisfied it matches

104

its former state."

"Yes'm," he said, unable to quite keep from making a face that reflected his abhorrence of gardening. He added in a low voice, "Sorry about the problem with that delivery fellow." At his mother's blank stare, he went on, "You know, that establishment . . . 'Young' and something . . . ? Ah, I have it, yes, Young, Bittner, and . . . Canney . . ." He looked up, his words fading away at the disapproving look on Mama's face.

"There was a problem with the delivery of the tables and chairs?" she said, her voice tight. "And now that we are speaking of the matter, why is it that no proper linens were delivered?"

Now Wyatt backed up hurriedly again. Just as he disappeared through the doorway, he cried, "This really is not a good time, is it? No, I think not. We'll discuss it later, shall we? I've got to find Sutton now, Mama . . . !"

She closed her eyes, but then opened them. "That has to be the end of the bad news, doesn't it?" she murmured aloud. She threw up her hands for a moment, and cried, "I no longer care if there is even one thing left to go wrong! I am going to my party, and refuse to deal with even one more thing," she announced to the silent walls. She then gathered up her skirts and moved with determined steps down the stairs.

She actually gave a sigh of relief to see Horace, Muribelle, and Fenton all waiting, in fancy dress, by the front door, ready to greet their guests. Muribelle had her hand on Fenton's arm, and his hand was covering hers possessively. A good sign, a happy sign. It seemed her protest may have been heard by the fates.

She smiled a slightly crooked smile at the couple, who happily smiled back, and stepped next to her husband. Just as she opened her mouth to begin to explain in a low voice what kind of day it had been, there was a knock at the door. Hassup moved, opening the door to their first party guests. The moment was gone; perhaps that was just as well, she thought with a silent sigh, for she would have no doubt ended the tale either in a fit of tears or hysterical laughter, and neither would do just now.

"Why, it's so very charming!" Lady McEvie cried. "And so

105

like you, Lady Cawley, to come up with a fresh and clever theme. I declare, I do so look forward to attending your gatherings, and today you have outdone yourself. Everything so fresh and colorful! I vow, I wish I were half so clever as you."

"Thank you," Clarice murmured sincerely. It was not the first compliment that she had received, and so she knew that she had succeeded. The festivities were unfolding very well, for although the guests had at first been startled to learn that they were only having desserts for their nuncheon, fortunately Monsieur's creations had proved to be most delicious. Once their stuffiest guest, the commanding Lady Brackwell, had declared herself delighted with the frosted peach tarts, others had joined in the spirit and helped themselves with hearty appetites. Muribelle and Fenton were glowing as a young couple ought, and the sewn flowers were not drooping too sadly yet. The five younger Cawleys were behaving themselves well — all of them, no doubt, anxious to prove to their parents that they were not entirely wayward creatures — and she did not regret her decision to include them in the festivities. Anna was in fact entertaining a group of matrons with her chatter, and Peter was giving flattering and rapt attention to the hunting tales of Lord Rackley, Fenton's father. Lissy was floating about, offering her opinion on which were the finest tidbits to be had from the trays the servants offered to the guests, and Sutton and Wyatt were part of an animated conversation at a table filled with a handful of young bucks who were Fenton's friends.

Lady McEvie moved away, replaced by a larger form. Horace looked down at his wife, his blue eyes pleased behind his spectacles, two glasses of Champagne in his hands. She accepted one of them, as a quick glance showed her that the footmen were now circling among the guests with trays of the bubbly liquid.

"It is nearly time to lead everyone in a toast to the betrothed couple," Horace said. He added, just for her ears, "My very dear wife, it seems you have arranged a grand success today."

She smiled, to soften her scold as she said, "With little thanks to you."

He smiled, too, his eyes dancing as he accepted his justified reprimand. "How can you say that? Bishop Abel is, even as we speak, enjoying one of the cigarillos out in the corridor."

She laughed softly and teased, "Ah! Well, thank goodness

you made sure we had enough."

"I *am* sorry, you know. Foolish of me, I see now, not to make sure things were progressing as I had thought they would. I *know* the children are capable of carrying out such tasks, but I rather suppose a little guidance might have helped things to go along . . . ?"

"A little." She smiled again, shaking her head at him in amused exasperation.

"Still, I *was* otherwise occupied most of yesterday afternoon and evening." He grinned at her, his eyebrows dancing suggestively.

"It is difficult to regret that," she said with obvious sincerity, leaning into him.

His free arm slipped around her and he held her close to his side. "I rather fancied it myself. Perhaps we ought to declare more often that Mama needs a special day of rest. Once a month or so, don't you think?" he asked.

She laughed then, and replied with feeling, "No, please! I think I will need at least a year to recover from my first special day of rest."

He pouted down at her for a moment, but then they laughed together, and were still laughing when they raised their glasses to offer a heartfelt toast to the betrothed couple's future happiness.

The Butterfly Net

by Melissa Lynn Jones

The ticking sounds coming from the little clock on the night table seemed inconsiderately loud. From his chair at the foot of the bed, Avril Heneley, Baron Ranstow, silently debated about whether he should order the annoying mechanism removed or simply throw the blasted thing out of the window. Although anxious for some positive action, he managed to restrain himself from doing either.

A brief, unintelligible mumbling recalled his attention to his purpose in being here. Before he could rise from his seat, however, the nurserymaid was already leaning over the bed with a damp cloth for her charge's flushed cheeks. Her motions seemed to soothe the child, and, after wetting the cloth and applying it a second time, the servant dropped the towel back into the washbowl. She returned to her place in the corner.

"Thank you, Nurse," he thought to say quietly. Then, for the dozenth time, "And you're sure the doctor said it wasn't serious? He gave instructions for the tea but said nothing else to the point?"

The maidservant, very young and new at her post, helplessly shook her head.

The hour dragged slowly past. Once, the child whimpered in her sleep, but she merely pulled the covers up over her face and rolled to her other side without waking. The baron resettled himself as well. Unaware of it, he crossed his long legs and began swinging one snugly booted foot in time with the clock's ticking.

After another hour, the thin film of travel dust coating his smart Hessians, toe to elegant tassel, attracted his attention. He crossed his calf over his knee and idly traced the tip of one

111

finger down the fine leather. Flexing his ankle and observing the long dark streak he had made, he wished he had at least taken a moment to change into more comfortable clothing before setting up this vigil. The night promised to be a long one.

Upon his homecoming earlier in the evening, the baron's initial concern had been only for a refreshing bath followed by a good country supper. Normally, he would have come down to Wilts for his summer sojourn two weeks sooner than this, but the press of business had kept him in town. But when his mother had sent him a hurried note, explaining that she must leave Ranstow-on-Avon for a few days, he had come at once. Especially since she had advised him that the nursemaid was but recently employed — Nanny Rice having lately retired — so the baron had delayed only the length of time needed to pack a small bag. He had instructed his valet to follow him after closing up his lodgings in town.

Of course, it was unthinkable to leave a six-year-old child alone in the care of servants, although, certainly, no one had suspected that his daughter was about to take ill. Apollonia had complained of a headache that very morning, just an hour or so after his mother's departure. Baron Ranstow was glad to have arrived when he had.

But he felt so damnably *useless*. All he had been able to do thus far was to sit here, hour upon hour, watching and waiting.

The nurserymaid gave in to sleep somewhere nearing two of the clock. Gentle snores issued from her corner of the room. When fever made the child moan and restlessly turn over a second time, the baron stood and started over to wake the servant, but the little girl quieted before he could do so.

Avril Heneley stretched the tired muscles distributed about his large frame and thought to loosen his cravat. The folds of starched linen immediately came undone, almost as if by themselves, so he removed the dratted thing and dropped it onto a stool. He then decided he might as well take off his coat. This last provoked something more of a tussle, though, since his shoulders were wide, and his waist strongly indented the coat had a fashionably form-following fit. Finally releasing himself from the garment, he draped it atop his neckcloth. His square, handsome features looked haggard. For two days he'd been on the road and he was exhausted. He sat back down to listen to the hours tick past.

112

A small bird outside the window at last announced the approaching dawn. Another bird ventured an answering chirrup; soon the air filled with the sounds of their morning greetings. The sky gradually lightened to a soft gray, while high, sun-warmed wisps of cloud turned rosy in celebration of the day's beginning. The clock didn't seem quite as noisy as before, although the nurserymaid's snores gained that much and more in volume.

The village doctor came up about ten. While Lord Ranstow wrestled with the problem of getting back into his coat, the physician examined the sleeping child and directed low-voiced questions to his lordship about how his patient had passed the night.

Nurse roused herself, and Lord Ranstow readied a few questions of his own. As the doctor put away his instruments, he entreated, "Please, Doctor, what's wrong with my daughter? She scarcely took a bite of supper last night, and since then, she's had nothing but a few swallows of weak tea. I must know what illness she has contracted. How could this have come about and so suddenly, too?" He looked at the small shape nestled under the rumpled covers, running nervous fingers through his already tousled dark hair.

Otherwise occupied, the physician didn't reply at first. He was busy at rummaging in his pocket for several paper-wrapped parcels of James's Powders. He said, "She's to have a quarter of a packet, fully dissolved, mind you, every three hours. Don't give her any more than that, for the dosage is prescribed by weight and could prove harmful if too much is allowed. Stir it in with the tea, if you like."

"But, Doctor," Lord Ranstow pressed, "the way she sleeps; it cannot be normal after so many hours!"

Gathering up the round-topped, gold-headed cane that was a badge of his calling, the physician replied, "Nor is it, my lord, not in the ordinary way. But Miss Apollonia is ill, remember, and rest is Nature's way of healing a febrile condition. It's a shame Lady Ranstow had to be gone at just this particular time, but I do assure you that we'll have your daughter back to skinned knees and torn smocks in a bang."

"But how much longer—"

"However long it takes," came the brief answer. Then, apparently, realizing the insufficiency of his response, the physician

113

said more kindly, "Lord Ranstow, it's only a juvenile bout of fever and a moderate case, at that. I wish we knew more about these things, but you mustn't fret, such illnesses come and go quite easily in children. All we can do is to try and make her as comfortable as possible over the next few days, while we wait for her health to return." With a conscious eye to the anxious father, he added, "There is absolutely no danger, my lord. And there's no reason why you should be here beside her every moment. You look as though you could do with a bit of sleep yourself."

Relieved in some degree, the baron nodded and, glancing over to be sure Nurse was now awake and aware of her duties, made to accompany the doctor downstairs. After seeing the man out, he decided that possibly the physician was right, and a few hours of rest were in order. First, however, the idea of food was an attractive thought. The tray brought up to the nursery last night was inadequate to this morning's needs.

Buttered eggs, black coffee, and a thick slice of smoked ham soon had him, if not precisely at high romps, at least not so wholly done in. He was further cheered when he returned upstairs to find that his valet had finally arrived and was even now unpacking fresh clothing. Lord Ranstow filled his man in on the situation, then requested the valet to prepare him a bath, while he stepped down the hall to give Apollonia one more quick look in.

The little girl lay burrowed deep beneath the covers — far too many covers for this warm day, the baron feared. With the windows shut tight, the room seemed overwarm. Nurse didn't seem to mind it, though, as she sat with a pile of linens before her, patiently stitching lace onto a pair of pillow slips.

On an impulse Lord Ranstow stepped nearer to the bed and gingerly sat down at its edge. He fished under the covers until he discovered his daughter's small hand and gave it a reassuring squeeze.

Unfortunately, this disruption to her rest had an unexpected effect.

The little girl shoved out from under the assorted sheets, blankets, and coverlets with a surprising burst of energy. Her head popped free and she mewled a soft "Papa?" before regurgitating copiously onto the floor.

"Oh, my God," he groaned, loosening her hand and grab-

114

bing a blanket to try and contain the mess. Manfully, he resisted an embarrassing plea from his own stomach to respond with a more overt display of sympathy.

Clamping his teeth against his escalating nausea, his lordship grimly ceased to breathe. He also gave up his hold on the blanket, seeing an immediate need for lending a hand to his daughter's support. Nurse, at once understanding his predicament, hurried over to his assistance, grabbing up the earthenware washbowl to employ as a catch basin.

She misjudged the violence of the child's convulsions, however. Before she could get the bowl into any useful position, the small body lurched forward in a final heave, knocking the bowl against the nightstand which, along with the half-filled water pitcher and the table clock, toppled to the carpeted floor. With a heartrending moan, the little girl spewed the remainder of both her supper and her tea onto the embroidered front of her father's primrose silk waistcoat.

"Lawks a' mercy!" the nurserymaid screeched, turning this way and that, unsure what next to do.

Raising his daughter and hugging her to him, Lord Ranstow shut his eyes and shook his head against the awful sight. Awkwardly, he stroked the nape of the child's small neck, alternating with little pats to her back as he helped her to rinse out her mouth. Using the balance of the oxygen from his strained lungs, he said through gritted teeth, "I am so sorry, sweetheart. Are you feeling better now?"

He eased her back down to the pillows, quite unable to await her reply. He leaped over the broken crockery to rush to the window and throw it wide, there to lean his head out, taking great gulps of fresh, unsullied air. When he felt he had himself back under control, he shut the window and turned round to assess the damage.

Damage indeed. One look sent him flying out the door in desperate search of assistance.

Miss Selina Springer strolled up the smoothly raked gravel drive at a leisurely rate. Tall elms lined both sides of the approach, their midmorning shade exceedingly pleasant on a day already turned warm. In the spaces between each tree, dark-leaved masses of rhododendrons bloomed with colorful aban-

115

don: some in bright pink and others in the gayest of reds.

Mrs. Goodge, the vicar's wife, was to have accompanied Miss Springer on this, her first call upon the dowager Lady Ranstow, but the Goodges' son and daughter-in-law had unexpectedly arrived at the vicarage for one of their rare visits, necessitating a last-minute change in plans. It didn't really signify, of course, since her ladyship's invitation had been an informal one. To be sure, at the advanced age of seven-and-twenty years, Miss Springer felt herself capable of undertaking the business alone.

A terraced series of stone balustraded steps led the way to the manor's double-wide front door. Like most country houses, there was no bellpull; instead, centered on the door's outer surface hung a rather hideously fashioned gargoyle mask with a heavy metal loop passed through the flared nostrils of its bronzed nose.

"Where *could* they have had such a thing from?" Miss Springer murmured in disgust.

Reluctantly, avoiding the monster's upturned snout, she grasped the hand-sized ring and applied the knocker. She then gave her skirts a quick little shake to release whatever dust might have collected about the hem, for this was her best black bombazine, worn especially for the occasion. She also adjusted the tasseled ends of her pelerine. The left one had a habit of becoming snarled unless closely attended, and Miss Springer felt it was important for her to appear the genteel spinster lady — which by all accounts, she was.

She was startled when a man on horseback, a groom by the look of him, came charging from around the rear of the house to gain the drive. He set off down the raked gravel, attaining a full gallop before disappearing from sight. The neatly built little spinster wondered at it. Frowning slightly, she turned back to the knocker.

With only a small grimace of distaste, she took a firmer hold upon the ring. She rapped on the door with a short progression of determined taps. Still, it was not until her third try that the door began to swing inward . . . giving the lady reason to wish she had waited for Mrs. Goodge.

The widening aperture disclosed a presence every bit as frightful as that deplorable gargoyle knocker.

Sans cravat and wearing a filthy yellow waistcoat and dark-colored coat — this last unbuttoned — the man before her made an undeniably shocking sight. His hair was uncombed, his boots begrimed, and, unless she was badly mistaken, he was not even properly shaven! Of a certainty, his was the most disreputable visage Miss Springer had ever in her life encountered. Had she come to the right address?

But she knew very well that she had. The Ranstows were the only family of note in the neighborhood, and this great house could belong to no other. As for how the dowager Lady Ranstow regarded *this* base-looking character, Miss Springer could not so much as begin to guess.

She struggled to disguise her disquietude to say uncertainly, "I am Miss Springer, and I believe Lady Ranstow expects me?"

The repulsive man simply stood there. He stared out at her as if not comprehending a word. Was he, then, one of those unfortunates who were naturally slow of understanding?

Very much at a loss, she fixed his eyes and tried again, taking care to speak precisely. "Miss Springer. Miss Selina Springer. Her ladyship is expecting my call today. From the Springer Home for Children? I am patroness there."

Suddenly, his face came alive with eager interest. He beamed upon her — literally beamed — for the broad whiteness of his smile effectively eclipsed the evil-looking growth on his jaw. "Oh, that *is* the dandy," he proclaimed with astonishing enthusiasm. "From the Home for Children, you say? Yes, yes, that should certainly do us. You shall come with me this instant, Miss Springer, and very welcome, too!"

Distracted by his attractive smile, Miss Springer obligingly stepped inside. She felt confident that the man was a gentleman, at least, since his accents and his courtesy marked him as clearly as any guild stamp on fine gold. Somewhat bemused by the comparison between his handsome smile and his conspicuously disheveled appearance, before even she knew it, she had responded to his gesture that she should precede him up the elegant width of the inside staircase.

Not halfway up the steps, however, other considerations imposed themselves on her mind. She caught herself midstride and turned about. "But, where is it that we are bound, sir? I don't wish to be rude, but you've also neglected to tell me who you are. And where is Lady Ranstow?"

He met her look of polite inquiry with an oddly distrait ex-

117

pression. Yet he answered her readily enough. "Please, Miss Springer, there is no time for explanations. We must hurry before anything else happens to her, you see."

Miss Springer swiftly assessed his apparent distress and could only assume that Lady Ranstow had some urgent need of her assistance. Remembering the groom's pelting descent down the drive, she lifted her skirts exactly one inch the higher to speed her climb to the next floor. Perhaps there had been some terrible accident!

Reaching the top of the staircase, she paused, this time in perplexity over which direction to take. Should she proceed to the next flight of stairs, just ahead and down a short hallway, or, perhaps, take one of the long corridors, branching off to either side?

Her escort resolved the dilemma by taking up her arm to tuck within his own. He promptly started them off to the right, down an inner hall which seemed to go on forever. They passed door after closed door at an alarming rate before he stopped and turned the handle at one entry. He stepped inside ahead of her.

"Miss Springer!" he declared to the room at large. He sounded quite as proud as if admitting Queen Charlotte herself.

No matter the sober maturity of her dress, Miss Springer found herself choking back a giggle of sheer nervousness. She collected herself and took one step forward, only to realize that she had been brought into someone's bedchamber — someone's very *untidy* bedchamber.

To her right was a clothes press with the doors standing wide, and beyond that, a young maidservant leaned over an unmade bed, carrying a tiny sleeping gown trapped under one arm. The maid crooned softly to whomever it was that lay there; although, betwixt the mishmash of coverlets and the servant's intervening form, Miss Springer's observation was limited to the discovery that the person abed was too small to be Lady Ranstow. Two other servants, one a butler and the other apparently a footman, were standing nearby as if unsure of their part in all this, and on the far side of the bed, an older woman in a checked-and-white apron held a large bundle of cloths. These she seemed to be deliberately dropping, one by one, onto the floor. Oddly, a little clock protruded from her apron pocket.

Miss Springer extended her inventory to include a jumble of what appeared to be pillowslips on the floor by the window, along with a spool of white thread, while a length of cloth which looked suspiciously like a man's crumpled cravat was flung across a footstool on the near side of the room. Above everything else, she detected a most appalling odor.

Before she could comment or even think to form a question, her escort turned back to face her. "Well?" he encouraged, motioning for her to come further into the room.

Miss Springer took an immediate step *back*. She loosed her hold on his arm and gripped the strings of her reticule with both hands, wondering what sort of slapdash mummery these people would have her involved in.

The man's next words were even more confusing, as, pointing toward the bed, he announced, "She's there. So you are needed, can't you see?"

Barmy-brained. Yes, completely off his hooks, the trim little spinster decided, with an eye to the erstwhile gentleman's singular state of undress. For in all the years of living with her father — a learned, if adorably absentminded man, may the saints give him welcome — never had anyone seen Father in such slubberdegullion disarray. Nor had her dear departed parent ever so lost touch with reality as to speak with such incomprehensibility as this man did, either.

Almost at once, though, the sensible spinster had to discard the idea of her current companion's being an addlepate. The village gossips would have warned her long since if the neighborhood housed any sort of zany; moreover, the dignified lady whom she had been introduced to last Sunday was not the type to knowingly tolerate this degree of chaos — a dowager baroness, after all.

So what went on here? And where was Lady Ranstow?

Brought to the end of her tether, Miss Springer primmed her lips and allowed a modicum of resentment to surface. "And what, precisely, am I supposed to see, sir? A bedchamber at sixes and sevens? No, instead, I think it is time I see her ladyship. Perhaps she can explain the meaning of this . . . this rare *mess* you've hauled me into."

He dropped his jaw — his darkly shadowed and unkempt jaw — looking no end confused himself. She gave him a look right back and, for the very first time, really looked at him.

Inches above her own, Miss Springer perused long hazel-colored eyes with tired-looking creases about them. They were intelligent eyes, too, she had to conclude. Widely spaced above broad cheekbones, they were parted by an assertively out-thrust nose, while his unruly dark hair was gloriously thick, but clipped short, in what must be the new Bedford crop which she'd heard was all the rage. The man was tall, but because of its being the same height as her father's had been, Miss Springer found the familiar size reassuring.

His jaw was another matter. Square of shape, it bristled with that decidedly evil-looking black stubble she had noted before. She skipped over the dismaying detail as best she could, returning to the needed inspection. His lips? Ah. Now those she had to approve. They were full, nicely curved, and were bracketed to either side by deep, friendly creases.

In seconds, though, she was back to examining his eyes. She was startled to discern that his was a highly expectant expression — apparently, there was something he wanted from her, something vastly important. But she had no idea what he expected, no idea what to do!

Qualmish, Miss Springer continued to stare. Somewhere in the back of her mind, it registered that the servants had all stopped moving about and were openly gawking, but it hardly concerned her under the circumstances.

A muffled sound from within the bed restored the scene to animation.

"Papa?" came a thin cry. "I don't feel so good again."

With the same decisive energy with which he'd brought her up here, the man now drew her over to the bedside. The serving maid carrying the tiny nightdress instantly whipped that item behind her, jumping back a pace and giving Miss Springer room to see.

Horrified, she realized that it was a child who lay there, a very dirty and obviously ill little girl. The tot's cheeks were flushed with the dry, parched tightness connotive of fever, and her eyes, of a peculiar shade of hazel Miss Springer had already come to recognize, were slightly glazed and unfocused.

"Dear God in heaven," the diminutive woman gasped in dismay. "This is really too bad!" Shocked right down to her summer-weight, knitted cotton drawers, she swung round to demand an explanation.

120

"She's sick," her escort said, looking unhappy. "Mother's gone, and Apollonia is taken sick."

Miss Springer felt a little sick herself. And just whose mother could he mean? His or this poor child's? She put him this very question.

The fellow scowled and dared to look as if he thought *she* was the hoddypoll here. "My own, of course," he said succinctly. "She's gone down to Dorset and left me to take care of Apollonia. But I can't, you know. She's ill. You can see for yourself."

Miss Springer thought she might burst with frustration. Any fool could see the child ailed, so he didn't need to keep on repeating the fact. Oh, how *could* she have mistaken the light in those beautiful, woodsy eyes for being mentally apt rather than acutely insane? And hadn't she read somewhere that there was a close correlation between intelligence and mental derangement? She forgot about his lovely eyes and handsome smile. With a barely suppressed shiver through her small frame, she decided to humor him until she could make her escape from this hubble-bubble house with all of its strange inhabitants.

"Yes, well, I must be very sorry your mother is gone," she managed on placating notes. "But exactly how you expect me to get her back for you, I'm sure I don't know. Oh!" she exclaimed, as though on a sudden thought. "Perhaps I could go and seek her out. Yes, I do think that would be best." She gave him a winning look, wondering if now was the time to try and slip away.

A second whimper from the bed stayed her. Was it safe to leave this pathetic babe in what was, quite possibly, a madman's care? She reconsidered, lightning fast, then reminded herself that she was Miss Selina Springer, granddaughter of the late Admiral Sir Christopher Springer who had never in his entire career fled from certain disaster. If only she could find Lady Ranstow!

While she dithered, the child's father, if that's who he was — Miss Springer wasn't sure of anything just now — chose the moment to put in further arguments.

"But I've already told you," he said in bleak tones, "Mother's gone down to Dorset and won't be back for two or three more days. It's an imposition, I know, but I need you to help me tend Apollonia. Nurse does her best, I'm sure" — he turned and scanned the several servants, who, goggle-eyed were standing fast and observing this farce in progress — "but neither she nor Mrs. Wooten has ever had children of their own. And the doctor? He cannot even name the malady which has stricken my daughter. Miss Springer, you must, please, *help* me."

It was the slight crack in his voice which tipped the balance of Miss Springer's wildly fluctuating opinions. Whatever else this man was, short or tall, deranged or no, and handsome or ugly as bedamned, he *did* care for this little girl. "So then, good sir, do I at last understand you? You want me to administer to the child's care, is that it?"

She didn't know whether to feel glad or sorry when he nodded and broke into a wide, relieved-looking smile.

Lord Ranstow held serious doubts about having enlisted the neatly made, black-clad little patroness's assistance. *What did she mean by saying she should go in search of his mother?* Was the woman daft?

He leaned his broad back against the copper-lined tub, absently dipping and squeezing the water from the bathing sponge in his palm.

He had realized during the previous night that Nurse could not be left in sole charge. The young maid was devoted to Apollonia, he believed, but she was too inexperienced to be of real use in a sickroom. And, neither was Miss Springer any sort of shuttle-head, he consoled himself, for, once decided, she had begun ordering everyone about with gratifying proficiency. True feminine competence had flowed through her every instruction as she had taken command.

"Bring clean bed linens and let the floor wait. Hand me that gown. Oh. You men are not needed, so please take yourselves elsewhere. The doctor has already been sent for? Good. And for pity's sake, someone open a window so that we can breathe in here!" Yes indeed, she had taken hold in fine style.

His lordship continued toying with the sea-sponge while he sorted through other, less comforting impressions.

When he had heard someone at the door after sending out the groom and recruiting the house servants to go up and help in the sickroom, he had thought at first that his luck was in and that it was the doctor returned. Instead, he had been confronted by a disturbingly pretty female, albeit somberly attired, who had said she was come on a visit to his mother. He had allowed himself to be reassured by her no-nonsense manner, though, and by her mention of the Springer Home for Children.

Certain misgivings had followed.

To begin with, Miss Springer was too young for the role she claimed. In his experience, a lady patroness was a middle-aged woman of unshakable aplomb. While the trim, short-statured little spinster had a deal of poise—he laughed softly when he remembered what a picture he must have made when he had answered her knock—it was obvious, nonetheless, that she was some five years younger than himself. Besides which, she had a disconcerting habit of swinging her great blue eyes up at him when he least expected it.

Her dress, at least, was unexceptionable. His mother frequently appeared in a similar model and owned a pelerine of the same type Miss Springer seemed to favor. Nothing alarming in that. Yet his mother had never stepped so lightly, nor with such delightful, hip-swaying rhythm as he had observed when Miss Springer mounted the stairs ahead of him.

No. Something was not right about all this. Something about Miss Selina Springer was most unsettling.

When he had finished his bath and a shave, he accepted his valet's help in fitting a lightly starched neckcloth into place. He castigated himself for never being able to get the cursed thing wrapped and tied properly without assistance; he also suffered his man to help him into another well-tailored coat. Passing up the opportunity for the nap he so needed, he then headed back to his daughter's room.

He hesitated at the door and tilted an ear to listen but received only silence for his trouble. Twisting the handle, his lordship pushed open the door.

The sight which greeted his eyes was reassuring. His daughter seemed to be asleep in a clean bed, a sheet and one light blanket spread smoothly over her. The room had been repaired to its customary standards, and, with the window left open a few inches, the air inside felt cooler. He was especially glad to perceive that the awful smell had been vanquished.

Miss Springer sat in the stuffed chair at the foot of the bed, her skirts draped just so. He didn't see Nurse but felt no unease on that account, for it was plain that the black-begowned woman had everything under control.

"We should see Doctor Coleson here shortly," he whispered as she looked up. "Is there anything you need for now?"

It required effort for him to get this last question out due to the difficulties in relating anything of sense when looking down into large, limpid blue eyes. If that wasn't enough, Miss Springer had sometime discarded her bonnet to reveal a perfect, heart-shaped face, the satiny sheen of fine, light-brown hair just visible around the margins of her tiny frilled cap. It made him aware of her as an attractive, mayhaps even desirable, female.

Nearly as distracted by his . . . his staggeringly handsome appearance, Miss Springer could only shake her head "no."

Who would have thought he'd clean up so nicely? she mused in strong amazement. For, without those scareful whiskers and dressed to advantage as he was, she was put to some trouble remembering the one thing she simply must ask him. She could have got the needed information from the housekeeper or one of the other servants, but she preferred they not realize the extent of her absurd ignorance. Focusing her thoughts away from his dizzyingly handsome countenance, she reminded, "You do realize, sir, that you have never told me your name. Nor," she added, keeping her voice low so as not to disturb the child, "has anyone, saving myself, mentioned Lady Ranstow today."

He looked much struck by this. "Never say so!" He, too, held his voice to a whisper. "I don't know what I could have been thinking of, Miss Springer, but I really thought you knew. I am Avril Heneley, Lady Ranstow's misguided son." He essayed a slight bow. "And my lady mother left in a rush yesterday upon receipt of the news that one of her cousins in Dorset—I forget the exact number of removes—had, er, passed on to his reward. She must have forgotten her invitation to you in the exigencies of the moment." Darting a quick glance toward the bed, he then said on still-softer notes, "And Apollonia is my only daughter, as you might already have supposed."

She arose to make the obligatory curtsy. "I believe I comprehend how it was, my Lord Ranstow."

"Oh, no need for that, Miss Springer." He looked uncomfortable at the acknowledgment of his rank.

Dutifully rising, she sought to further clarify matters. "So

124

then, Lady Ranstow, the *dowager* Lady Ranstow, has the up-bringing of your daughter? I recall hearing something about your lordship's being a widower who spent most of his time in London, but I hadn't realized the whole."

At his puzzled look, she explained, "Up until recently, I lived in Warminster and was first introduced to her ladyship following church services this past Sunday. And now that I think of it, I do seem to remember a little girl going on to Lady Ranstow's carriage while we chatted; it must have been your daughter I saw. I should have realized before." She began to feel very foolish.

How he might have responded was lost when the particular child under discussion made a restless movement, evidenced by a rustling sound from the crisp, newly made sheets. Holding her skirts against the possibility of their making a similar noise, Miss Springer moved to the bedside.

The little girl's eyelids fluttered open. She rolled her head to look about the room, then said in querulous tones, "Where is Nanny? I want her."

"There, there. No need to bestir yourself," Miss Springer shushed her gently. "Your nurse is resting but will soon be restored to you. Would you like some tea in the meantime? I understand the doctor wants you to have it as often as you will."

At this, Apollonia sat up. "I don't *like* that stuff," she pronounced crossly. "I won't have any more of it, ever. And I don't want Nurse, I want *Nanny.*" She wriggled back under the covers, saying faintly, "I feel awful."

"Poor dear, I don't doubt it." With a dampened cloth, laced with a sprinkling of lavender water, Miss Springer dabbed at Apollonia's forehead. "Do try to relax now. Doctor Coleson is on his way."

The child exerted herself sufficiently to swat at the cloth before pulling the pillow over her face. She twitched beneath the covers a few times, then seemed to fall into sleep.

When she had quieted, Baron Ranstow explained about Nanny Rice's retirement. But since Nanny's present abode was a full day's journey away, there didn't seem any hope of securing her services in a timely manner. In conclusion, he asked, "Do you not think I should send for Nurse, then? It might be better if she was here when Apollonia next awakens."

Lifting her eyes to meet his, Miss Springer answered with

some firmness, "No, I don't think so. The poor maid needs her sleep, for I understand that you and she were in here all night. You should be following Nurse's example this very minute. But of course I won't presume to order you to it, as I did her."

No sooner said than Miss Springer was put to wondering at the admitted temerity. She had issued commands to the young nursemaid, the housekeeper, the butler *and* the footman, very much as she would have done had they been in her own employ. She had acted like someone with every knowledge of what she was about — when she was actually anything but! Her experience with sickrooms was limited to those few short weeks last fall, during which her father had fought an inflammation of the lungs. Unsuccessfully.

She blinked back a burning sensation behind her eyes, feeling both bereft and terribly inadequate.

The baron must have realized something was amiss, for he drew her away toward the window to ask, "Won't you at least permit me to stay till the doctor arrives? I'm hoping he'll advise us how best to get Apollonia's medicine to her, if she continues to refuse the tea."

Apprehending that she had allowed her own upset to interfere with a proper regard for a parent's natural fears, Miss Springer made haste in answering. "Oh, but you will want to see him when he comes; I didn't intend you to think I meant otherwise. This concerns your daughter, after all!" Feeling guilty at her lapse, she added, "And I can remain for the entire afternoon, needs be, so there's no problem in both you and Nurse having plenty of time for respite." His grateful smile told her that she had done well in offering these assurances.

Now then. She had only to make do until the nurserymaid returned, and so might yet acquit herself honorably.

Some little time later, Miss Springer felt less certain of fulfilling her aims. The doctor came up and seemed as pleased as the baron with her presence. No doubt the two men assumed that, coming from the orphanage as she did, it qualified her particularly to oversee Apollonia's care. But when a sleepy-looking nurse peeped in about five of the clock, and she, too, seemed prepared to rely upon Miss Springer's continued attendance, it left the young patroness with little choice. Sensible of the nurserymaid's drooping eyelids, she sent the young servant off to get more sleep.

Since the days were growing longer, Miss Springer knew there would be adequate light for making her return to the Home as late as eight of the clock, or even half past that hour. Time was not what worried her, though. Rather, it was her own competence, or lack thereof, which was frightening. She wondered if she might better confess her ignorance and let the house get along as best it may. Still, it hardly seemed appropriate at this late hour. These people were depending on her to sustain them; for the nonce, she would just have to administer to the child as the doctor instructed.

Twice Miss Springer prepared senna tea with the powders Dr. Coleson specified. Each time, the little girl spurned her efforts, fretfully demanding her "real" nanny. Driven nearly to distraction, Miss Springer persisted in her efforts until Apollonia took a few disgruntled swallows.

She was just straightening the sheets after one of their more active bouts — wherein she had all she could do to keep the child from tossing the unwanted liquid to the floor — when the baron requested entry.

Opening the door to him, she noted that he was not so stylishly dressed as he had been the last time she had seen him. He wore a loosely tied scarf rather than a proper neckcloth, and, instead of a well-fitted coat, he had on a relaxed style of jacket, buttoned, and made from some subtly patterned material. Despite the comparative casualness of his dress, however, to Miss Springer's eyes, he looked marvelously up to snuff.

A slight heaviness around his eyes indicated he had but recently arisen from his slumbers. He refused her advice when she suggested more rest, though. "No, I've had quite enough, thank you," he said in quiet reply. He flexed his shoulders as if easing a cramp, then fetched the room's other chair from its place by the window. He brought it nearer to hers at foot of the bed. "So how does my daughter fare?" he asked while seating himself.

"Well enough, I suppose," she returned doubtfully. "I cannot say that the fever has abated to any degree, but neither does it seem any worse. Doctor Coleson did warn us that her temperature might rise, though it appears he may be mistaken. And there have been no other signs of biliousness, thank goodness."

"A large blessing, to be sure. Miss Springer —" he said next, then appeared to hesitate over his words. "Miss Springer," he started again, but stopped.

"Yes, my lord? What is it?"

"Well—" He looked a trifle embarrassed. "I just wanted to thank you for staying. You cannot know how fortuitous your arrival seemed, for I was at my wit's end, I don't mind telling you." He thrust strong fingers through his hair, leaving a few strands to stand straight up.

Diverted rather than critical of his newly mussed hair, Miss Springer did not respond right away. She saw nothing of the gargoyle about him now; instead, his appearance was endearingly careworn, making her wonder how she had ever thought him terrifying. More importantly, he had nothing of the off-putting *tone* so usual to a man of his high position in the world.

And he was a father. A man devoted to his daughter's well-being. Miss Springer suddenly felt out of place.

Shortly thereafter, the housekeeper brought up a large tray for them. It was loaded with thick sandwiches, various condiments, cheeses and sliced fruits, together with an assortment of pastries. Mrs. Wooten set the tray on a small table at the far side of the room, close by the window. Just as Miss Springer began to fear they would be required to take the dreaded senna tea with this repast, the footman came in, bearing a smaller tray. This one held a decanter of sherry and a welcome pitcher of lemonade.

The baron stood and helped the petite woman to her feet so that the footman could rearrange the chairs. When the servants left them seated before the table by the window, the baron returned to the subject of his indebtedness.

"What I've been trying to convey to you, Miss Springer, is my deep appreciation for your being here. Oh, I know you'll think me foolishly concerned, for indeed, Doctor Coleson assures me I've no real cause to be worried, but I cannot feel easy in my responsibilities. As you know, I spend most of the year in London, while Mother insists that she and Apollonia do better to remain here. So you see, Miss Springer—" he looked earnestly into her eyes—"I've never even *seen* a sick child before." He looked sorrowed by his lack.

Miss Springer bit back the urge to make a like admission. Her own experience with children, sick or well, had begun a scant two months ago when she'd taken up residence in the

Home. Since then, not a single child had suffered so much as a sniffle! But she dared not reveal her deficiencies in the given situation. To do so might pacify her conscience but could only add to his lordship's unease. No, she must bide her time and withhold pointless confessions. And wouldn't Twinny just stare if she could see her now?

But the matron presiding over the Springer Home for Children, that good woman more fondly known as "Twinny" to her charges, was not to see Miss Springer anytime soon. Miss Apollonia's fever began to rise, even as the doctor had predicted. The distraught baron prevailed on a reluctant spinster to send word to the orphanage that their patroness-in-residence would remain at the manor at least until the morrow.

With the baron's and nurserymaid's assistance, Miss Springer labored for hours to keep the child content. Bowl after bowl of lavender water was applied, and Miss Springer had the happy thought of replacing the senna tea with lemonade. The little girl seemed to accept the change and made no more demur about taking her medicine.

Somewhere nearing two of the clock, the exhausted nursemaid again succumbed to sleep in her usual chair by the window. Baron Ranstow had caused a second stuffed chair to be brought for himself, and he and the little spinster spoke quietly together, smiling conspiratorially from time to time when Nurse emitted an especially loud snore.

Believing it inappropriate to discuss their separate worries, particularly with the child drifting in and out of wakefulness, Miss Springer led the conversation into divergent channels. ". . . So while I cannot say I'm an authority, I perhaps may claim some expertise on the subject," she said just after the clock on the nightstand struck three.

"I should think you could, at that," the baron acknowledged, "for I well recall your father's work. His *Entomology Defined* was a encyclopedic exposition, yet written in layman's terms — why, I have a copy myself! And *you* did those wonderful colored plates? You must be very proud, Miss Springer." He looked rather impressed.

"As to that" — she smiled, allowing him to appreciate a tiny crinkling effect above the tip of her straight little nose — "I didn't color every copy, never think so. Rather, I did the original manuscript, leaving the work of reproduction to the water-

129

color artists at Mister Clowes' print shop. Mister Clowes put out two hundred copies with hand-colored plates, and three hundred more were offered with only the line drawings. Since you purchased one from the first group, you are aware of the added expense. But they were rather nice," she said modestly. Then, on a thought, "And, please, if you don't think it too forward, my name is Selina."

With a huge smile, the baron agreed. "And I am Avril. For it cannot be pushery when a famously accredited lady like yourself offers friendship. Having participated in cataloguing your father's collection is no mean accomplishment."

Feeling better about having introduced the intimacy — it was the first time she'd requested anyone to use her christening name in a decade — Selina smiled. She rolled her own name about in her mind for a moment; it had become unfamiliar to her ears since her father's death. *And his name is Avril.* She smiled yet wider.

Pulling her thoughts back into order she inquired, "And your business in London? Is it something to do with the government?"

He seemed pleased to discuss it. "Yes, indeed. You see, I'm a partisan in the effort to reform and, hopefully, mitigate the penal code regarding the prohibition against any soldier or mariner who presumes to beg in public. As it stands now, the law prescribes the death penalty for such behavior, unless the poor beggars first obtain written permission from their commanding officer or a magistrate. Lord Ellenborough opposes me in the House of Lords, but with the unwearying efforts of men like Samuel Romilly, I hope to see the statute struck by the end of the year. That's why I didn't come down earlier in the summer, as I am used to do." With this, his countenance took on a guilt-ridden look. Selina longed to comfort him.

"But, my lord . . . Avril —" She found the sound of his name on her tongue even more pleasant than his release of her own. "Surely, you cannot blame yourself for what's happened to your daughter. What you're doing in Parliament is important for all England."

His response came on dejected notes. "But what matters England, if my own house suffers. One tear from my daughter means more to me than anything else possibly could."

"But that's so much fiddle-faddle!" she expostulated, surpris-

130

ing herself as much as him. She next made herself gentle her tones, if not her sentiments. "I've no children of my own, so perhaps I shouldn't speak out, but I do think it unlikely that a six-year old is irrevocably harmed by a single incident of parental omission. Whereas, if what you say about the current law is true, there are men in imminent danger of dying because of an unjust law. If you have the opportunity to remedy their situation, to have this dastardly statute repealed, then go *to* it, I say!" She glared at him quite fiercely.

He frowned and seemed to consider. "Well, I'm not sure but that you may be right to some extent. Enough about me, however. I'd like you to tell me more of your father. Have you always helped him in his work?"

"From the time I was old enough to carry my own catch-net," she answered proudly. She had to laugh. "But I don't suppose the scores of beetles and borers I brought home as a child were truly of much interest to him. Can you believe it, though? — he never once let on. Father accepted my every offering, helping me to inscribe the correct names for my finds on little cards for each one."

"I'm envious," he remarked. At her quick, concerned look, he explained, "My own father died when I was but a lad, so I missed that sort of guidance. Tell me, what else did you do together?"

"Well, it's rather ironical, but I know just what you mean about losing a parent. My mother died when I was very young, so I've often wondered about what I might have missed. Nevertheless," she went on thoughtfully, "I don't remember, as a child, feeling myself shortchanged. Father always took me with him on his expeditions; we went from Scotland to the wilds of Cornwall in a near-constant search for new specimens. He was a great fisherman, too. I think my fondest memories are of the two of us wielding our rods in search of the wily, brown-speckled trout."

Restless thrashings from their patient's bed interrupted. The little girl broke into a violent sweat, keeping her two caretakers busy at dabbing her limbs with cooling cloths, exchanging her night dress for a dry one, and switching damp sheets for fresh. Finally, the child settled into a profound sleep, her color receding to more normal tints as her cheeks and forehead cooled.

131

"She'll do! By God, she'll jolly well do!" his lordship exulted. His daughter had passed the crisis.

Just as relieved as anyone could be, Selina smiled so widely she thought her face might split. She turned her head to look beyond his lordship's shoulder to the still-sleeping nurse, wanting to share her joy with the world. Instead, she received a tremendous jolt as his lordship abruptly leaned over and centered a kiss — right on the bridge of her nose!

Nonplussed, Selina lost her bright smile and gaped stupidly up at him.

"Selina?" he questioned softly. He stepped closer, a tiny furrow collecting between his brows.

She felt the heat from his broad chest leap the small distance between them. He leaned still closer, the soft material of his jacket brushing lightly against the tassels of her pelerine, while his gaze fixed upon hers. Assailed by a ridiculous and unaccustomed timorousness, she pulled her eyes away.

His gruff throat-clearing brought her back to her senses. "Miss Springer, pray forgive me for —"

"My Lord Ranstow, I don't know what —"

The simultaneous rush of words brought them both to embarrassed silence.

Then, God help her, her lips quirked. Precisely at that moment, one corner of his mouth lifted. Seeing each other's reactions soon had Selina struggling mightily, trying to contain her mirth sufficiently not to disturb either Nurse or the sleeping child. The baron was soon working nearly as hard while great, irregular bouts of silent laughter shook him.

Like two naughty children, they held their sides even as every shared glance sent them into further paroxysms. Finally, when she thought she could manage a decent whisper again, Selina said, "Really, if we aren't the most foolish pair?"

"Just so!" he responded on a grin.

The next day, Selina was returned to the Springer Home for Children in fine style. His lordship had sent her out in his own emblazoned carriage, drawn by a pair of high-bred bays. He didn't accompany her, of course, not yet fully confident about leaving his daughter, however rapidly she seemed to be recovering.

"Oh, my very dear Miss Springer!" Selina was greeted by

132

Mrs. Twenbury, the orphanage's matron, when she stepped down from the carriage. "Never tell me your mission was successful?"

Not misunderstanding the question, Selina dismissed the carriage with her thanks to both driver and footman before answering, "Well, if you're asking me if I accomplished what I'd set out to do, Twinny, regrettably, I did not. Her ladyship has gone from the county for a few days, while, as you might have understood from my note, other concerns at the manor took precedence."

She smothered a wry chuckle at Matron's not unexpected response to this. "I still can't believe it, Miss Springer. You? Nursing a sick child? Why, we both know you cannot tell a paregoric draught from a peppermint. Oh, that poor child! However did you manage? But I suppose it must have gone well with the little one, or you wouldn't be here and looking so pleased with yourself."

Having no wish to disclose other possible reasons for her cheerful state, Selina merely said, "Indeed, I'm happy to report that Miss Apollonia is much better. The fever broke late last night and, after the doctor was in this morning, he agreed that she might progress to coddled eggs and toast for her lunch."

"I don't suppose there was any opportunity for mentioning the needs we have here, then," Matron said on a disappointed note. "But what we are going to do about Denis and his shoes, I cannot imagine. Running barefoot during summer is all very well, but come winter . . . ?"

"Yes, I know," Selina soothed. "But as I've told you, it shall be taken care of in one way or another. I still have five copies of Father's book remaining, all with colored plates, so you needn't fear that young Denis will go without new footwear for much longer." She didn't mention how she had done the coloring in all five volumes herself, knowing that if it ever became necessary to sell them, the additional money they would bring must be sorely needed.

"Oh, but miss, I'd hate for you to give up your father's books!"

"No matter, Twinny, no matter. Whoever needs more than one copy of any book? Still, it is a shame that when Grandfather endowed the orphanage, he hadn't the foresight to realize what wartime prices could do. We mustn't blame the admiral too severely, though, since until I came here in May, neither did I realize what shifts you were put to in trying to provide for the children." She picked at the left tassel on her pelerine while they walked inside the building.

"How, miss, don't take on so. No one could have known. I didn't realize myself what trouble we were in for the longest time. When the solicitors didn't come for the usual accounting last year—" She looked suddenly horrified by her inadvertent reference.

Selina took no offense. "No, I quite understand, Twinny. That was when my father died. But long before that, *he* should have warned you that the budget was slim, though I fear Father was never much for considering financial affairs. And then, stupid me, I assumed, as you apparently did, that the Springer family still had the wherewithal to support the orphanage. In fact, right up until the day I arrived, I had thought my coming would be of some benefit. I hadn't realized that I would be merely adding another mouth for you to feed."

"My dear Miss Springer, never say so!"

"Oh, but I *will* say so. After months of wrangling with the lawyers over my father's estate, or, rather, what I discovered was left of it, I never even thought to request an accounting for the Home. What a complete nigit I was!"

"Not that it would have made any difference," the matron commented sadly.

"No. Not that it would," Selina agreed.

In truth, Selina had barely recovered from a severe depression caused by the unexpectedness of her father's death, when next she had discovered that her once-comfortable circumstances were also at an end. She learned that her father had been living off his principal for many years, and that, by the time he succumbed to the bout of pneumonia contracted during an ill-advised fishing trip last November, even their house in Warminster was mortgaged to the fullest amount.

Her notion to move to the orphanage had solved no problems, however. Twinny had welcomed her with opened arms—but with dauntingly empty pockets. They had money enough for food, thus far, as Twinny's cookery could make the cheapest cuts of meat seem a feast, but funds were insufficient for the children to have new clothes, new toys, nor even a pencil.

* * *

Exactly four days later, Miss Selina Springer was again attired in her best black bombazine. Along with the baron's daily messages to keep her *au courant* with the details of Apollonia's improvement, yesterday's note had also included an embossed card of invitation from the dowager. Apparently, her ladyship had returned to Wiltshire. Today's luncheon, according to the dowager's inscription, was planned in celebration of her granddaughter's restored health.

Selina dearly wished she had some other gown to wear. Nothing else in her wardrobe could be deemed suitable for the occasion, though. These last few years she had tended toward mostly plain, practical gowns of twill stuff, whereas the black dress — made up in the days after her father had died, and before she had realized her pecuniary difficulties — was of good material. It was also the only thing she owned which was less than two years old.

As it was, she and Twinny worked for two full hours yesterday: brushing, cleaning, and pressing the bombazine, making sure the dress was again presentable. Her muslin pelerine had been carefully washed and ironed, her cap freshly laundered, and even her reticule had been refurbished with the addition of a new string-cord Twinny had unearthed. Selina would have felt quite up to the nines, were it not for the fact that she had long since come to loathe black. Worse, his lordship — *Avril* — would recognize the bombazine for having spent the better part of twenty-four hours in its company.

With a small sigh, Selina wished things otherwise.

Once again the Ranstow carriage was sent round for her. On the ride up to the manor, Selina dismissed all thoughts of her gown to appreciate the dissimilarity between this visit and her last. *Avril kissed me,* her heart sang. And he had sent her at least one brief note every day since. She had not written him back, of course, since for a maiden lady to do any such thing, even at her advancing age, could only be considered *fast.* But his notes to her had each one been signed, "Most affectionately, your very own — Avril."

Oh, she had no intention of placing too much significance on a kiss, and certainly not when that kiss had been applied to her nose! But what had led her to feel a certain interest, was,

135

instead, the baron's open and friendly manner.

Her only previous beau, and that several years ago, had been a young man of a far less consequence, yet one whose every word had seemed a great deal more *consequential*. Indeed, after months of courtship, his ponderous air had led her to end the relationship.

Unluckily, other than her father, not once had Selina met a man who seemed to understand that life was rightly balanced between matters both weighty and light. She had thus depressed interest from men who were too serious-minded or those too frivolously inclined. When every gentlemen of her acquaintance was found to fall too readily into one category or the other, she had given up hope of finding a suitable partner-for-life.

Until now.

For the first time in years, Miss Selina Springer was brought to contemplate the possibilities implied by the married state.

And when she was announced to the gathering in Lady Ranstow's drawing room, her eyes went immediately to the tall gentleman standing behind the dowager's chair. Selina was warmed by the baron's welcoming smile as he stepped forward to bring her up to his mother, who kindly presented two fingers for her to shake.

Lady Ranstow also wore black, but unlike the dull, cloth-covered buttons of deep mourning which finished Selina's gown, hers were of fine black jet. "So pleased, Miss Springer," her ladyship drawled in the unhurried manner Selina recalled from their initial meeting at the church. "Regrettable that Cousin Charles *passed on* at such an unfortunate time, but I understand you responded to *our need* like a true Good Samaritan." Selina noted a sharpened look to the lady's eyes with this last.

"I did what I could, ma'am," she answered. "But between the baron's exertions and your staff's commendable efforts, I confess that there was not much for me to contribute."

"Oh, no, Miss Springer, you do yourself an injustice. Too, too modest. Really. For the way my son has explained it" — again, Selina caught that same, sharpened look — "you were a veritable Boadicea in defense of her territory."

Selina was surprised into a chuckle. "Oh, hardly that, my lady. Perhaps it would be more apt to compare my efforts to a reluctant Miss Lucy Selby as exposed by Mister Richardson's pen. But speaking of young misses—" She turned to where a lovely child with green-brown eyes sat upon a nearby sofa. "The Honorable Miss Apollonia Heneley, I believe?" She grinned over at the fairy sprite and offered the child her hand.

The daughter of the house, dressed in some dreary shade of lavender, promptly slid to her feet and made a very nice curtsy in her direction. "So pleased, Miss Springer," she piped in an odd imitation of her grandmother. "I am only sorry our first meeting was not on more convivial terms. I ask you to accept my sincerest apologies."

She sank into another pretty curtsy, which, together with her stilted little oration, left Selina wholly speechless. The words "convivial" and "sincerest apologies" sounded strange coming from the lips of a six-year old.

No one else, however, seemed to see anything amiss. Mrs. Goodge and her husband merely looked to Selina as if waiting their turn to be noticed, while the baron and his mother smiled and nodded at the child with obvious approval. The only other luncheon guest was Mr. Patrick McKeone, the parish curate, and he didn't seem to be interested in anything beyond making his polite "how-do's." Selina shook hands with each in turn, then sat down to join in the general chitchat.

She took a place on the sofa with Apollonia. At a break in the talk, she smiled over at her and said, "I am delighted to see you so well recovered, for you must know that your father was terribly worried about you."

"One might even say," the baron came up to them in time to add, "that I was brought to a state of the most severe disorder. No sight for the squeamish, to be sure." He gave a mock shudder of horror.

"Oh, I quite agree," Selina quipped, put in mind of the gargoyle knocker. "A terrible, beastly spectacle, sir!" She rounded blue eyes at him.

Blue eyes and hazel twinkled brightly at each other until Apollonia intervened. "I'm sorry, Papa—Miss Springer," she said in a small voice. This time, her words seemed entirely genuine, and there was no denying her discomfort.

"Oh, good heavens, no need to be in a pother over it," Selina rushed to console her. "A sad look-out it would be if a person couldn't take ill without reproaches falling on

137

her head for what could not be helped. Why, you were a perfect lady, all things considered."

"Of course, she was," confirmed Lady Ranstow, overhearing. "Apollonia is never anything less than a lady, are you, my dear," she said indulgently.

Apollonia instantly straightened her features. "No, Grandmama," she replied.

"So then, shall we just put this little incident behind us?" Lady Ranstow said smoothly. "Ah, and here is Mrs. Wooten, come to tell us our luncheon is prepared. Shall we go in?"

Courteously, the baron held out one arm to his mother and the other to Apollonia. Her ladyship directed that the vicar and his wife follow next, leaving Selina and Mr. McKeone to complete the party as they repaired to the dining room. There, a delightful lunch lay spread out before them.

Their little gathering made a cozy one as most of the leaves to the cloth-draped oval dining table had been withdrawn, making the table almost circular in shape. They were favored with fish and a soup, turkey stuffed with truffles, pork in a pomona green sorrel sauce, Welsh mutton, and Swiss cabbage mixed into an attractive salad with several other cold vegetables.

To Selina's amazement, ices were brought at the end of the meal. She discovered that this was Avril's contribution; he had arranged for the treat to be shipped specially for the occasion.

But nothing could have been more astounding to Selina than the dowager's preferred subject of converse. The entire meal was taken up with detailed descriptions of funerals! Her ladyship proceeded with a point-by-point report on her cousin's last rites, with references to an assortment of other such events as she'd attended. The vicar was led to relate particulars from the memorials and internments over which he had presided throughout the years; Mr. McKeone willingly offered similar depictions.

Rather distressed by it all, Selina learned that it was the dowager's habit to participate in every mourning service possible; it seems she made it her business to provide the black crêpe falls for the bereaved's hatbands, which she would often prepare in advance with the embroidered initials of those persons expected soon to number amongst the deceased. Evidently, Lady Ranstow missed no opportunity to take a part in mourning ceremonies, whether she was well acquainted with the *dearly departed* or not. In the case of the cousin from Dorset, Selina learned that her ladyship had not even previously met that gentleman!

By the time Lady Ranstow got round to encouraging Selina to describe the events surrounding her own father's funeral, Selina had had enough. If the topic bothered *her*, she feared its morbid influence on a child. Not that Apollonia had seemed overly affected, for she had attended her meal all the while, paying no obvious attention to the adults' discourse.

Still, Selina refused to participate and instead remarked brightly, "Oh, but I'd far rather you tell me, Lady Ranstow, whether it was you who are responsible for those wonderful rhododendrons lining the drive. I've never seen their like before; are they some special variety?"

The dowager looked startled by the abrupt change in topics. Before she could say anything, however, Selina found herself with an ally. "Yes, I've often wondered about them myself," Mrs. Goodge ventured with enthusiasm. "It has been some eight or nine years now since the bushes were planted, or so I recall, but the only ones I've seen elsewhere have all been white. And aren't they sometimes called 'oleanders'?"

Until now, the baron had not seemed overly interested in the lunch conversation. He now advanced, "Yes, Mother, do tell us. Are they all of the same species?" He seemed to consider a moment. "And I also remember that it was some friend of yours who brought the plants—from Cuba, wasn't it?"

"Jamaica," her ladyship corrected, accepting the change in topic with grace. "And they are called by both names, oleander and rhododendron, but they are, for all that, the same plant. They grow into reds, at least three shades of pinks, and the more common whites. Lady Kiley, an old school friend of mine, brought an assortment of them with her when she returned to England to put her boys in school a few years ago. She insisted I have a portion in the colors of my choice, before she sent the rest on to Kew Gardens as a manifestation of her affection for the queen." The dowager looked rather pleased at everyone's sudden interest.

"So you have manifestations to match royalty?" Apollonia quickly asked, ignoring her dessert. "Grandmama, you never told me!"

Selina hid a smile at the little girl's flourishing of what was, very likely, a new word. Apollonia was wonderfully keen-witted. It reminded Selina of herself as a child, when she had hung on her father's every utterance.

"I do not suppose," the elder woman responded, a small frown marking her brow, "I particularly thought to mention it before. But why do you ask, dear? Is it important?" The dowager didn't seem to notice the child's unusual perspicacity.

"Oh, yes, I should think it is, Grandmama!" the little girl crowed. "Just think, our gardens compare to the best!"

Everyone laughed at the child's ingenuous comment. Soon after, her grandmother dismissed her with a smile, declaring that a nap for a so-recent invalid was in order. The rest of their group yielded to the baron's suggestion that a brief stroll through the gardens might prove pleasant. Adroitly maneuvering Mr. McKeone into his lady mother's company, he and Selina took a position behind the others.

"The strawberry cream was to your liking, Selina?" He bent his head to hers with a knowing grin. "I saw you accept seconds, and you looked very much as though you wanted to beg thirds. You could have, you know. For you were the real guest of honor today, though Mother suggested that naming you such would only have brought you discomfort. She reminded me that you are a newcomer to our circle and so might not like our singling you out."

"How very, um, thoughtful of her," Selina said wryly, having already taken that lady's measure and, therefore, having an idea about the real motivation behind the dowager's alleged concerns. "But the reason I abstained from accepting that last serving was probably the same as your own: Apollonia. Oh, yes, I saw your eager gaze upon the confection. But when the footman offered, you said, 'No, I haven't room for another bite.' And when anyone could see you were just aching to have it, too!" She laughed when he responded with a contrived and deeply lugubrious expression.

"Ah, the things we do for our children," he remarked on a sigh, not sounding in the least unhappy. "Speaking of which" — he checked their progress on the path — "I want to come and visit the orphanage, if I may. I understand that you've a round dozen youngsters there, so I thought, well, I thought that perhaps I could repay you for your care of my daughter by making

140

some small gift which your own charges might like."

His hopeful look made her heart turn completely over. "How kind. How truly kind of you to think of them! Yes, there are a few items which the children might enjoy."

Selina secretly crossed her fingers behind her back at this outrageous understatement. More than just a few things were needed. But a review of the dowager's reception today made her reluctant to approach her ladyship for a contribution just yet.

Of a surety, she understood that there was no *absolute* certainty that her friendship with the baron would continue to develop as she had begun to wish it might, but she regarded that what she felt for *Avril* was something quite, quite extraordinary! She was also as sure as she could be that he returned her feelings — twenty-seven years had earned her a feeling of confidence in her own good judgment — but experience also warned her that Lady Ranstow might view things in a different light.

Budding dreams of the future notwithstanding, though, the orphans' needs must be seen to. It was Selina's duty to inspire interest in their plight wherever she could.

"Have you never been out to the Home, then?" she inquired accordingly. "It's in a lovely old house to the south of the village, with two large rooms for the girls, and two more for the boys. We have a playroom covering most of the top floor, a parlor which Matron uses to teach the children their manners, and a larger room set aside for academic instruction. I'm helping with those particular studies now myself," she added with some diffidence. "I remember my grandfather's insistence that 'None can make a sailor who can't count out the bells.' "

"A worthy goal," her companion agreed. "But in answer to your question, I'm afraid I've not seen the orphanage except from the road, having left the care of local charitable causes in my mother's hands."

Selina bobbed her head at the truth of this, for Mrs. Goodge had already told her as much. On a impulse, she then extended the invitation. "And would not Lady Ranstow and Apollonia care to come with you? You needn't fear that our lot is too rough and tumble for genteel society. Twinny's lessons have seen to that."

"Twinny?"

"Mrs. Twenbury. She's been matron at the Home for years

past counting, and while I wasn't given the opportunity of meeting her till recently, she is a perfect pattern for the children. Industrious, patient, and unfailingly cheerful. Believe me, she can kiss a bruise and heal it quite as quick as quick may be, repair a torn dress in a trice, or whip up a syllabub that would send you into transports of delight."

"Better than a strawberry ice?" he quizzed, flashing her a dazzling smile.

"Oh, well, at least as good, I think."

"You admire her a great deal, don't you." It was a statement, not a question. A statement which felt like a hug.

"I do," she answered consciously. "More, perhaps, than any other woman I've ever met. But there's another thing about Matron you should know, or rather, about how unlike her I am." She hurried into her next words. "You see, sir, when you told me how you had never seen a sick child before this past week, I should have told you that neither had I."

He looked uncertain, as if he thought she jested. "But surely, Selina—"

"No," she interrupted, hating the necessity, "my only encounters with the younger set have been those of the last eight weeks."

"But you permitted me to think—"

"I did, yes," she said, feeling properly ashamed, "and I must ask your pardon for it. But I would like to have it on the square between us."

"Well, if that isn't just the *dandy!*" he exclaimed suddenly, at the same time grasping her hand. "I caught you up in our troubles without giving you a moment for thought, and you never once let on! So it is I who must beg your pardon, Selina, for I am so accustomed to my mother taking charge of these matters, that I never considered what a burden I might be laying on your shoulders. Why, the credit for my daughter's recovery belongs to you. Double and double again!"

"But you didn't really need me. You did very well with Apollonia!" She was incensed that he would so underrate himself.

"I most certainly did need you. But still, I had my own contribution to make, didn't I?" He spoke as though the notion surprised him. His voice lowered and he looked deep into her eyes. "Selina—" She thrilled anew at the sound of her name on his sweet lips.

There was no time for whatever delights might have followed, though, for Lady Ranstow had realized how they had dropped back from her group.

"So what are you two discussing and so seriously?" she drawled, leaving the party from the vicarage behind as she glided up to the truants. "You must not monopolize Miss Springer's time, my son, when she and I are only barely acquainted."

Selina heard the unmistakable rasp of steel in the dowager's voice. She hastened to loose her hand from his lordship's hold and said, "I was explaining to Lord Ranstow that my position as patroness of the Children's Home is new to me. I am hopeful that you will soon come and see how we go on there, for I will appreciate any suggestions on its management."

"Yes, do join us, Mother," the baron entered lightly, folding his now-freed arms across his wide chest. "For I intend going, and I'm sure Apollonia will enjoy the outing as well."

"Never say you mean to take your daughter *there?*" her ladyship burst out, losing her languid air. "What can you be thinking of, Avril? Apollonia is much too young to be exposed to such shab-bag sorts, whatever Miss Springer thinks!"

Before Selina could defend either herself or the Home, the baron stepped into the breach. Within an instant, Selina was set to wondering why she had ever supposed his lordship lacking in *tone*.

"Mother, I will have you to understand that the thought of visiting the orphanage was mine," he said at a languid speed of his own. "If you don't care to come with us, you need not do so, but Apollonia *will* come with me. Vicar? Mrs. Goodge? Mister McKeone? You will join us?" he added as they reached her ladyship's side.

With a look as sharp as any, Mrs. Goodge quickly answered, "Oh, but so many people at once! No, no, Lord Ranstow, that won't do. We'd have those dear little ones all in a taking, what with so many visitors to please at the same time. Besides, Vicar and I go often to the Home, so you are better off without us causing added distractions. Right, John? Patrick?" More than a hint of her mettle was heard and understood.

Strangely, Selina thought she saw Mrs. Goodge then send a little wink in her direction.

"Am not."

"Are too."

"Not!"

"Oh, yes, you are, for my grandmother *says* so."

Bustling up to this scene, Matron demanded, "Denis Trogmorton! What are you about, arguing like that with our guest? Apologize this instant, young man."

"Hold a moment, Twinny," Selina advised. Her bombazine skirts rustled as she came up from behind, for, once again, she had felt it appropriate to appear in her best gown. She and the baron had been inside viewing the latest drawings done by Selina's students, when the sound of raised voices had brought them out to the porch on the run. With Matron's silent permission, Selina leaned down and held the little boy steady with her eyes. "Denis, since you are the host, I want your explanation first, if you please."

Not unwilling, the little fellow promptly pointed at Apollonia. *"She* says"—he scowled menacingly at the prim young miss—"that I am a 'mere blot on Sosity's kitchen.' I'm not, though, am I?" He began to fidget and look worried.

Apollonia sniffed in disdain. "That's nonsense. I said 'blot on Society's escutcheon.' "

"Yes, dear, we'll get to you in a moment," Selina said calmly, trying hard to suppress a quick sputter of amusement.

"Mother," she thought she heard Avril mutter from somewhere behind her.

At that, Selina barely averted a chuckle. Indeed, although Lady Ranstow had not accompanied her son and granddaughter today, like the baron, Selina suspected that the dowager could rightly be credited for Apollonia's little comment. The minx parroted her grandmother's every word. "A-*hem.* Now then," she said sternly, keeping her attention on the matter at hand. "Denis, what else?"

"Well, I collect she's just mad 'cause I named her 'Apple.' But I didn't mean it for anything bad, Miss Springer. Honest."

"Apple, is it? But that's a very nice name you've given her, Denis. Very nice, indeed." She turned to Avril's daughter. "You see, dear, Denis sometimes finds names for his friends. Mrs. Twenbury is Twinny, Margaret Pritcher—you remember seeing her, the older girl with long black hair—is now known to us as Magpie and—"

"She chatters *all* the time," Denis entered helpfully.

"Just so. But please, Denis, take care not to interrupt again unless it's urgent," Selina admonished him gently. She returned her attention to Apollonia. "Also, we have Queen Mary, that's Mary Gumps who has such nice posture; Bow-Peep, whom you may have noticed as the littlest girl; and then, of course, there's Tools the gardener, and so forth." She was glad to note that Apollonia began to look interested.

"Then, what about you, Miss Springer? Do you have a name, too?" the little girl finally asked.

"Yes, do tell us," Avril said with a smile in his voice.

Without looking back at him, Selina responded to the little girl's question with all due seriousness. "Oh, well, Denis tells me that I haven't been here long enough to acquire a proper name just yet. Sometimes these things take time — isn't that right, Denis?"

The boy grinned and bobbed his head.

"Apple!" the tidy little miss pronounced on a sudden giggle.

A silent look then passed between the tiny hazel-eyed girl and young Denis. Without warning, they both suddenly took off, racing for the rope swing that hung from the stout old oak tree at the end of the walk.

Selina stood up and looked on in approval. She thought it was marvelous how the two youngsters communicated a mutual desire without another word needing to be spoken between them.

And the next day, the Springer Home for Children saw still more marvels.

Packages and parcels from the village shops began to arrive. There was a selection of novels for the older girls, pictorial alphabets and tales of Mother Bunch for the younger children, cock-horses in number, an assortment of whistles, pens and watercolor sets, and even new half boots for young Denis — of leather!

"Oh, Twinny, how could he have known?" Selina cried happily. "I never said anything to him, considering it best if he decided on his own gift. It's beyond belief that he should mark our needs and so accurately!"

"So, miss, what made you think I'd be closemouthed about it?" the matron said in scolding tones. "No reason why I shouldn't give out a suggestion or two, now is there?"

145

The marvels continued. Accompanying this display of the baron's largesse was a note which begged Miss Springer to prepare herself for a fishing expedition two hours hence. After reading it, Selina grasped Twinny's shoulders for a hug, then danced away up the stairs. "And this time, *this* time, I won't be in *black!*" she trilled back down.

In strictest concentration, past the pale dappled shadows of the yellow-green willow trees overhead, Selina narrowed her eyes—eyes as blue as the color of her otherwise serviceable gown. Her cork, floating some yards away on quiet waters, bobbled ever so slightly. It was the second week of August, and her third fishing expedition with Lord Ranstow.

"Easy. Easy there," she murmured to herself, cautiously relaxing her wrists.

"Got something?" the baron asked on hushed notes.

"Maybe and—Yes!" she cried out, bringing her rod up with a sharp snap before deftly starting to play out her line.

Backing out of her way, Avril grinned with triumph as he observed her display of skill.

She let out her line by careful increments, following the increasingly forceful tugs against her rod as she moved on down the bank. From time to time she halted, then played out more line.

Apollonia's attention was caught by the ongoing activity, and she scurried over, Nurse trotting right along behind her. The baron gestured for them to be quiet; obedient, they stilled to watch the drama unfolding before them. It took all of fifteen minutes, but by the end of which time, Selina popped a shimmering trout into her creel, her audience looking on in awe.

"Must go all of two pounds," Avril declared admiringly.

"Two and a half," Selina straightly insisted.

"Three!" Apollonia cheered, which started everyone to laughing. The little girl blushed and implored, "Well, it could be, couldn't it, Miss Springer? It's much bigger than the one you caught last week."

"Possibly, possibly. But then again, your father may be right. Fishermen do have a tendency to boast, you know."

"And entomologists?" Apollonia asked, enunciating with her usual precision. "Do they always boast?"

146

"Yes, entomologists, too, I'm afraid," she had to agree. "You see, dear, it is the hunter's lot to come home empty-handed rather often, and so to balance out these failures, a brag or two sometimes seems useful."

" 'Odds so!" The baron looked wise. "Does that mean if you've caught a perch, you may claim it for a whale?" Everyone laughed once more.

"Show me again, Miss Springer," Apollonia broke in next. "I want to catch something, at least *one* something today."

"Very well, Apollonia—"

"Apple!" the young miss piped up.

"Yes, of course. Come with me, Apple, and we'll see what we can do about improving your technique."

But it was not a fishing rod which interested the child, for three weeks ago, Selina had brought Apollonia a small gift of her own. She'd dug out an old catch net and had Tools shorten the pole to make it of a size the little girl could handle. It was a very good net, too, made from a loop of wire with fine white mesh that was just heavy enough to swing well. Tools had sawed and sanded the wooden shaft to make it look like new.

The country surrounding the lower Avon supported a variety of wildlife, or, at any rate, a goodly selection of that type of wildlife which most interested Miss Apple today. There were dragonflies and fire flies and today's special quarry: butterflies. So while Selina set off with the child in earnest search of this last, Lord Ranstow remained behind, comfortably sprawled across their picnic blanket, while Nurse munched contentedly from a cluster of red grapes which the baron had offered from the basket of food they had brought with them.

His lordship disguised a smile at the servant's enjoyment of the treat. Leaning back, he allowed the sun to dazzle his eyes between half-closed lids. He gave thought to Miss Selina Springer's chance advent into his life.

From the moment when he had opened the door and seen her blue eyes staring up at him, he had been drawn to the pretty spinster lady. He was aware that the attraction between them had grown apace, producing a powerful bond. They discussed his Parliamentary efforts and her interests in insects and the Children's Home with equal ease. Her cares were his cares, giving him to feel a growing richness in their friendship which surpassed all previous experience.

147

Certainly, Avril had loved his first wife but had to appreciate that what drew him to Selina went beyond the giddy attachments of youth. Joanne Heneley had been precious to him, yet so young when they had married that he had never had the opportunity to know her as a woman. If Joanne had lived, perhaps real closeness would have come with their union in time — he very much liked to think so — but he had met, married, and lost his young wife in the scant space of a year. He had mourned her loss sincerely, too, but gradually his sorrow had lessened, leaving him merely a lonely man.

His involvement in the business of government had helped to keep him busy during his time of grief; however, Selina was the first woman of his acquaintance who had shown any real concern for his work. His mother rarely displayed any interest; London's political hostesses wanted only to sway him to this cause or that. But Selina? She was his own, personal partisan. In one month's acquaintance, he felt closer to her than he would have ever thought possible.

He leaned back further and shaded his eyes with his hand while he watched his daughter with her new mentor. He saw the little girl creep through the tall grasses at Selina's called instructions, and for some reason he was brought to recall the abysmal sense of emptiness he so often suffered during the long months in town while the House was in session. But the constant come-and-go of London was no fit place for a child. Or was it?

The baron began to wonder.

To be sure, he had realized long since that the dowager was much given to manipulating him to her own desires, and it was at her request that Apollonia stayed at Ranstow-on-Avon while he went up to town. Usually, his mother's advice was sound — but was it always? And, wasn't Apollonia Joanne's very special legacy to him? Of course, his work in the House was important, but was there really any reason why he couldn't have his work *and* Apollonia's company?

And he now wanted more than that. He wanted Miss Selina Springer.

He hadn't the least doubt that she wanted him, too. Those clear blue eyes could disconcert him but would never lie to him. Well, almost never. Sunlight glanced off white teeth when he remembered her delightful confession about her not having cared for a sick child before. But the important thing was, after long discussions about his political beliefs and hours spent assessing the needs at the Springer Home for Children, he had seen how she cared for *him*.

He must not delay in putting the question to her, either. His concerns in London could not go untended much longer; Mr. Romilly's work was so close to success that he must return to London as soon as possible. Parliament would reconvene in September this year, but he was resolved not to leave just yet. Not before he had matters at home in satisfactory train.

Consequently, when Selina and little Apple returned — the latter chattering in excitement while she thrust the contents of her net in his face — he said solemnly, *"Libellula gigantis,* I presume?"

The little girl chortled in glee. "Oh, Papa, you *do* know about them!"

"Surely I do. In fact, when we get home, I'll show you some pictures that our Miss Springer did for a book on the subject."

"But I so wanted to catch a butterfly this time. I have five dragonflies already. This is my first really big one, though." The little girl peered intently through the folds of her net, not, apparently, too disappointed.

"A fine catch, indeed." He winked at Selina. "But come —" He swung the little girl onto his hip, grabbing up the blanket with his other hand. "It's time you had a rest, child." He carried her over to Nurse, who settled the blanket in a shady spot, suitable for a nap.

Selina watched this pleasing domestic scene for a moment, then went about securing the captured dragonfly in a container she had brought for just such an eventuality. When Avril returned and extended his hand, she tapped the lid to be sure it would hold, then reached up for his support as she came to her feet.

He led the way back to the water's edge, taking them down the tree-lined bank and away out of sight. He slowed, then stopped. And just like Denis and his "Apple" had once before, neither spoke before they moved in unison. Instead of running for a tree swing, however, they moved, inexorably, into each other's arms.

Sun-warmed lips, slowly, gently came together, the kiss deepening in degrees to attain a stunning intensity. Selina felt a profound sense of awe for how this man knew, and without need for words, when to laugh and when to be serious. The intimate contact ended as softly as it had begun. "Oh, Avril," she sighed, drifting on waves of euphoric pleasure, "I do love you so." She then drew back to look up at him, startled at having voiced her sentiments aloud!

He merely pulled her back within his embrace, snuggling her head, just *so*, beneath his chin. "Did you think I didn't know, sweetling?" A smile colored his voice. "After so many fishing trips"—he pulled back a tiny space and grinned—"surely, you didn't think a fine trout was all I was after? Why, we've shared three kisses—um, four now"—he said, nuzzling her lips—"and, of course, I knew you loved me. My dearest Selina, you love me, and I am your own. We love each other now . . . we will love forever . . . and for always."

"Oh, Avril," she whispered again, if more than four kisses later. "I both knew how you felt and didn't know. I mean, I knew what I was feeling, and what I thought I saw in your eyes each time we met, but—"

"But until we heard the words, we neither could be perfectly sure. Yes, I understand." He lifted her chin for another kiss. When both were sated, at least temporarily, he bent one knee to the ground.

Selina, not wholly unprepared, had expected to find the conventions prescribed for a proposal to leave the swain looking silly. She quickly discovered it did nothing of the sort! His hair gleamed in the shifting sunlight, his strong shoulders spread below her as if able to take on the world, and his smile? His smile was only for her.

"Will you have me to wed, Selina? Will you accept my hand and my love? For both are yours, freely given. Love me, Selina. Love me," he said in soft command.

What was there for her to say, but "yes"? And "Yes!" she cried out gladly.

While Apple dozed in her nursemaid's lap on their way back to the Children's Home, Avril quietly took up Selina's hand. He pressed it within his own. "Before we part for the day," he said, low-voiced, so the servant couldn't hear him above the sound of the rotating carriage wheels, "there is something else I will mention. I want you to understand that there will be no more traipsing off to London alone for me. I would have you and Apollonia nearby from now on. Are we agreed?"

"Oh yes, Avril, we are." She returned the pressure of his fingers.

But things were not to proceed so smoothly as that. Imparting the news to his lady mother that evening made it plain to the baron that the dowager was not best pleased. That was no deterrent to him, however. It was, instead, Selina's response to the dowager's reaction which had the baron thrown top over tail. He was, in fact, put into the cursedest dilemma of his life!

"She'll come around, Selina," he said the next day, and not for the first time during that dreadful hour. "Even if she doesn't, it's nothing for you to blame yourself about; neither should it change our plans. I have already told the vicar to begin reading the banns; in three weeks more we will be married, and in four, we will be on our way to London."

"I don't blame myself," Selina replied, adamant. "But I cannot in good conscience cause a separation between Apple and her grandmother. Six *years* they've been together, and I shall not be left feeling responsible for isolating Lady Ranstow from her granddaughter."

"They won't really *be* separated," he said, echoing an earlier statement. "If Mother won't come to London with us, I'll leave her here at the manor, and we can visit her in the summer."

"No!" Selina all but wailed. "She must share in her granddaughter's life, just as she always has done. I tell you, it must not be this way!"

"Then, if I left my daughter here—"

"You are not to consider such a thing. I would see you and Apple together, no matter what!"

"But, love, be reasonable. You want me to go to London for the sake of my work there. You want Apple with me. You want my mother with Apple. And you want me with you, admit it."

"Yes, yes, I want it all." Visibly seeking to calm herself, she leaned against the ancient oak at the end of the path leading to the orphanage. She reached over to rub the back of her hand against his freshly shaved jaw. "Avril?" she said a minute later. "I am not about to give up one particle of our happiness. You are right, though, for I want you, I want your efforts in the House of Lords, and I want your entire family. I won't say your

151

mother has to love me, but she must accept your desires for a wife and daughter by your side. Anyway," she added prosaically, "I believe your mother is bluffing."

"What!" his lordship practically howled. "If you know that—"

"Yes, well, she may not know it yet herself. I think that neither does she know how to manage her way out of this coil she's caught herself up in, so . . ."

"So?" He found himself intrigued.

"So we will just have to render her a little assistance, won't we?" And with that fine intention, the sensible Miss Selina Springer began sorting through various plans to reverse her ladyship's declared position.

Neither were the baron and his intended alone in their aims. For no sooner had Lord Ranstow left the house that morning, on his way to see Selina at the Children's Home, when another interested party set to work.

Knowing her grandmother, and in some ways, better than either her son or soon-to-be daughter-in-law, Miss Apple Heneley entered her ladyship's bedchamber that very same morning. She had seen and heard enough during weeks of visits to the Home and during their fishing trips for a sharp young miss, who wasn't *always* sound asleep, to see which way the wind blew. Bracing her elbows on the edge of the mattress, she cupped her tiny chin in her hands.

"Grandmama," she began artlessly, "why do you suppose Miss Springer doesn't have a nickname like the rest of us?"

The doting grandmother, ensconced in her bed as was customary at this early hour, looked up from her breakfast tray in surprise. "Why, what diddle-daddle nonsense is this, Apollonia? *I* certainly have no nickname. That would be vulgar." She took a small sip of her chocolate, then grimaced as the familiar sweet drink seemed unwontedly bitter this morning.

"Oh, but you do," the little girl reminded, looking innocent. "Else I would call you 'Grand*mother*' all the time. And, you know, I shouldn't like that. It would be—I don't know, so faraway sounding. Besides, I like calling you 'Grandmama,' Grandmama." She giggled at the duality of words.

"Perhaps you are right, dear." Her ladyship gave up on the

152

chocolate and reached for a square of toast.

"And I wish you to call me 'Apple' from now on. Please say you will, pleeeease, Grandmama?"

Unable to resist this appeal, Lady Ranstow said grudgingly, "Very well then, I shall begin calling you 'Apple.' But only at home, mind you."

"Yes, Grandmama. Grandmama?"

"What is it now?"

"Miss Springer gave me a very nice catch-net. Have you seen it?"

"Yes, dear," Lady Ranstow said vaguely. She had just bitten into her nicely browned toast, and for some reason, it felt like sand in her mouth.

"So I was thinking," the little girl went on. "Instead of putting initials on all those nasty black things you make for when some-one dies, you could put *my* initials on my new catch-net for me. Couldn't you, Grandmama?"

That returned ladyship's attention. "But what's this, Apol . . . er, Apple? Just what is wrong with my contribution of mourning attire? And," she said, more warily, "what is so 'nasty' about black? I have worn black every day since your grandfather *passed on.*"

Rolling her big green-brown eyes, Apple heaved a remark-ably capacious sigh. She said glumly, "I didn't know *him* either, just like all those other people you go to see dead." Then, her eyes widened on a thought. "Oh, they aren't *specimens* now are they? I mean, when somebody dies, you don't pin them up on cardboard for everyone to come and admire, do you?"

Her ladyship looked prodigiously shocked. "The very idea! Of course not! You know we respect the dead far more than that."

Apple settled her chin deeper into her hands. "But black makes you look *old,* and you aren't really, are you, Grand-mama?"

"Well—" The much-beset grandmother began to look un-certain.

"I mean, you *could* wear butterfly colors if you wanted to, and then you'd be pretty, too, don't you think?"

"And just what would you consider 'butterfly colors'?" Lady Ranstow questioned in an ominous tone.

Without a sign of conscious intent, the little girl dropped her

153

hands and lifted her face to answer in some exuberance, "Yellow, green, red—lots of colors! Miss Springer wore a blue dress when we went fishing yesterday, and she looked *much* prettier than she ever did in black. And she hasn't even got a nickname like you, Grandmama!"

Unconsciously, Lady Ranstow preened for a moment. "Yes, well, you must know your grandfather had several rather endearing names he used to call me by, and he also was used to say that I did very well in apricot." Losing herself in memories, she added, "And I wore a delicate ivory on the night of my come-out and sea-foam green when your grandfather proposed, as I recall it."

"Oh, do the shops in London have all those colors, Grandmama?" the little girl asked in admiring tones. "When I went with Papa to the village shops to search out toys for the orphans, I didn't see anything like that. They had mostly ugly browns and mauves and grays. Probably because they don't show grime, isn't that so, Grandmama?"

"Grime?" the dowager questioned in horror. "I hadn't realized before . . . and our house livery is mauve. I have always preferred subtle colors, but perhaps it *is* time for a change. Yes, I'm sure it is. I'll send off for samples as soon as may be; it wouldn't do for us to be thought shabby—not at all!"

"But, Grandmama," the tireless little miss advanced, "wouldn't it be easier if you went up to London instead of sending for samples. There must be so many lovely new colors to see there."

"I assure you, we can discover them from samples in the comfort of our own home, Apollonia."

The child seemed to take no umbrage at the reversion to use of her full name, for she heaved a long sigh and said, "It's just that I am so very anxious about it, Grandmama."

Putting her breakfast tray aside, for the first time this morning, the elder Ranstow spoke rather crossly to her granddaughter. "Anxious? And what is there to be anxious about, I'd like to know?"

Mild hazel eyes drifted over to the breakfast tray and Apple took up a piece of toast. Between bites, she got out, "It's just that I was thinking: If I was a merchant and knew that a client lived off in the shires somewhere, I would be sure and send out samples for the colors which wouldn't sell in town. We're likely

154

to see only the most awful things, I'm afraid." She shrugged philosophically and picked up her grandmother's teacup, apparently not finding the brew at all bitter while she finished it off. "But, then," she opined, returning the cup to the tray, "I suppose we are hardly butterflies are we, Grandmama?"

It was as easily done as that. Whatever plan the former Miss Selina Springer might have devised to reconcile the dowager Lady Ranstow to her new daughter-in-law would never be known, for, just one month later, a procession of loaded carriages left Ranstow-on-Avon on their way to London Town. The leading vehicle contained three proud generations of Heneleys; it also sported, oddly, a white pennant which was embroidered with yellow and bright red thread. If one were to look closely, the embroidery formed an emblem: a fat round apple with a delicate yellow butterfly perched atop.

More oddly still, if one looked very, *very* closely, the gaily flying pennant was not actually a pennant at all.

It was someone's butterfly net.

Blissful Betrothal

by Valerie King

Love is a circle that doth restless move
In the same sweet eternity of love.

— Robert Herrick

Chapter One

Olivia Charing stood at some distance watching the dairy maids in Green Park milk their cows. A fresh morning breeze swept her dark blue silk pelisse tightly about her legs and the sun, shining in grave contrast to the drenching of the night before, warmed her straw bonnet. She shook her head thinking how odd it was to see cows in London since all surrounding the park were gray buildings grown black with coal dust, a dust which belched day and night from even blacker chimneys. But what seemed worse to her was that a constant din of noise rose from the streets like a cacophony of geese driven to a perpetual state of excited honking and complaining.

In May, London was an exceedingly noisy place and as foreign to a country lady as these cows were to cobbled streets, to the rumble of a constant flow of carriages, and to the hawking of wares from salt boxes to candles to chamber pots.

Olivia and her daughter had arrived in London only the day before. She had slept so poorly that she had wanted only to take a walk in a quiet place in order to restore her sensibilities. Green Park had been recommended to her by the concerned butler, a bent, considerate man who was himself a permanent fixture of the town house she had hired for the remainder of the season.

Olivia had not been to London in over seventeen years when of the same tender years she herself had enjoyed her first season. She had forgotten how London seemed to have a life of its own, sweeping its visitors up in a clamor of movement and soot, so much so that upon first arriving in Brook Street she had known a strong inclination to order her portmanteau strapped back on to the boot of her carriage, to command her

159

beautiful daughter, Jocelyn, to remain within the muddied coach and to fly back to the small village of Old Turvey — seven miles from the large township of Bedford — from whence mother and daughter had just arrived.

She would have, too, had the marriage settlements for Jocelyn and the Earl of Braunston not already been agreed upon and signed.

In three weeks, Jocelyn would become the Countess of Braunston, her future secured. Olivia reflected upon the remarkable good fortune which had brought the dowager Lady Mary Braunston — the earl's grandmother — to one of the Bedford assemblies which she and Jocelyn had attended. Jocelyn had been recommended to her ladyship by a mutual friend as a potential wife for Lord Braunston. Olivia had found the old woman provoking, disagreeable, and impertinent. But she had raised her daughter well and had watched with considerable pride as Jocelyn, in her serene, well-bred manner, turned aside every reproach designed to reveal an unformed character.

In the end, Jocelyn had been approved. She was, according to Lady Mary, just the sort of refined young woman required to complete the earl's happiness. His lordship had been married and widowed, his darling wife of ten years having left behind a small daughter in need of an affectionate, youthful mother. Apparently, Lady Mary had seen Jocelyn with the village children and had been convinced that here was the mother her beloved great granddaughter, Daphne, could love.

Before the documents had been signed, however, Lady Mary had paused and regarded Olivia quite strangely for a moment, then asked rather cryptically, "But can she make him a good wife? I have been so concerned about Daphne, I — oh, but never mind, of course she will. Jocelyn's character has been proven to me times out of mind. She is quite dedicated in her principles — he will have no need for worry."

Olivia had frowned slightly. "To own the truth," she admitted, "I have experienced some anxiety that she might, well, that is, Lord Braunston is a Man about Town. I only hope she will be sufficiently *amusing* company for him."

"She is a trifle *staid* for so young a lady," Lady Mary had added with a nod of her head. "But then I had much rather she were of a more serious turn. Braunston may be used to moving

MORE PASSION AND ADVENTURE AWAIT... YOUR TRIP TO A BIG ADVENTUROUS WORLD BEGINS WHEN YOU ACCEPT YOUR FIRST 4 NOVELS ABSOLUTELY *FREE* (AN $18.00 VALUE)

Accept your Free gift and start to experience more of the passion and adventure you like in a historical romance novel. Each Zebra novel is filled with proud men, spirited women and tempestuous love that you'll remember long after you turn the last page.

Zebra Historical Romances are the finest novels of their kind. They are written by authors who really know how to weave tales of romance and adventure in the historical settings you love. You'll feel like you've actually gone back in time with the thrilling stories that each Zebra novel offers.

GET YOUR FREE GIFT WITH THE START OF YOUR HOME SUBSCRIPTION

Our readers tell us that these books sell out very fast in book stores and often they miss the newest titles. So Zebra has made arrangements for you to receive the four newest novels published each month.

You'll be guaranteed that you'll never miss a title, and home delivery is so convenient. And to show you just how easy it is to get Zebra Historical Romances, we'll send you your first 4 books absolutely FREE! Our gift to you just for trying our home subscription service.

BIG SAVINGS AND FREE HOME DELIVERY

Each month, you'll receive the four newest titles as soon as they are published. You'll probably receive them even before the bookstores do. What's more, you may preview these exciting novels free for 10 days. If you like them as much as we think you will, just pay the low preferred subscriber's price of just $3.75 each. *You'll save $3.00 each month off the publisher's price.* AND, your savings are even greater because there are never any shipping, handling or other hidden charges—FREE Home Delivery. Of course you can return any shipment within 10 days for full credit, no questions asked. There is no minimum number of books you must buy.

GET
FOUR
FREE
BOOKS
(AN $18.00 VALUE)

ZEBRA HOME SUBSCRIPTION
SERVICE, INC.
120 BRIGHTON ROAD
P.O. Box 5214
CLIFTON, NEW JERSEY 07015-5214

AFFIX
STAMP
HERE

in the highest circles where ladies and gentlemen of considerable wit make up the numbers, but it would never do to have his new wife simper and behave the hoyden."

"No, no, of course not!" Olivia had agreed readily and the subject was let drop.

Though Olivia's fear that Jocelyn's somewhat narrow interests — like reading Hannah More's improving works and taking extracts from the same every Sunday night — might not be the scope of entertainment Lord Braunston desired for himself, this was not her current distress.

Of the moment, she had begun to wonder whether or not, in her profoundly earnest desire to see her daughter well established in the world, she had erred. Not that her daughter had been complaining of late, only that she had reverted to a truly wretched childhood habit which indicated her spirits were overset. Whenever she grew nervous, she sucked on the tip of her first finger.

Reviewing the process of presenting her daughter with the prospects of marriage to Braunston, she could not be entirely content with her own conduct. Was it possible, in her zeal to make certain her daughter did not suffer as she had suffered in her own marriage to Jocelyn's father, she had persuaded her against every proper inclination? As Olivia traversed the brilliant, green sward steadily advancing toward the milkmaids her conscience smote her. She felt ill with worry. Jocelyn was a biddable young lady, an excellent daughter and after several weeks of long and sometimes unhappy discussions, Olivia had finally convinced her to accept Braunston's proposals.

Good lord, she thought. Her daughter did not even know the earl, since he had at the time been in Vienna and had requested his grandmother, Lady Mary Braunston, to find a mother for Daphne and a proper countess for himself. What had she been thinking? Surely she had pressured Jocelyn too forcefully on the points of greatest interest to herself as a mother — that her daughter not experience the exigencies of poverty which her own marriage had forced upon her. She had loved her dear Edward quite madly but year after year of practicing the most horrendous economies upon the meagerest of vicarage incomes, had taken a toll on the beauty of their love. When Edward perished after having been caught in a snowstorm in only a threadbare, one-caped greatcoat and afterward died of an inflammation of the lungs, she determined that no such hideous fate would ever befall her beloved Jocelyn. Olivia had lost her husband and the freshness of her love for him because of their relative poverty and she simply would not permit her daughter to endure the same. Her last speech to Jocelyn had been delivered through a mist of tears, a display which she was now persuaded had brought Jocelyn's resolve to an end, at least in part. When her daughter's particular friend from childhood, Alfred, had also added his opinion that she would do well to accept of so handsome an offer, Jocelyn had finally acquiesced.

Olivia had tried to reassure herself that Jocelyn would be happy in her marriage to the earl and there was a time when it seemed Jocelyn was so reconciled to her forthcoming marriage that she seemed quite content. But whenever the actual wedding plans were discussed, her daughter became oddly nervous in her movements, and inevitably, her finger found its way past her lips.

Though Jocelyn's skittishness could be attributed to the normal sentiments of a young lady — just turned eighteen — about to embark on the unknown course of an arranged marriage, still some instinct warned Olivia all was not well. The path had been set, however, and no amount of regretful or fearful ruminations on her part would change what was now the unchangeable future.

When she was but a few feet from the rosy-cheeked dairy maids, she heard the ecstatic squeals of a very young girl coming from somewhere behind her. She was about to turn around to see where such a joyous sound originated, when the child collided with the back of her legs.

Olivia gave a cry of delight herself, having always taken pleasure in young children. She had initially thought the child had merely run into her while playing, but when Olivia was kept off balance, nearly toppling over several times, she realized something was wrong. For some reason the girl was either having difficulty herself in gaining her own balance or perhaps had become trapped in the skirts of her pelisse.

A man's voice called to the child from a distance.

Finally, Olivia was able to turn awkwardly around in order to discern what was wrong and saw at once that the child was hugging the back of her knees very affectionately, as though

162

she knew her, thus keeping her tottering on her feet.

The young girl, a pretty little thing with enormous blue eyes and long red curls trailing from behind her dark green velvet bonnet, smiled seraphically up into her face. "Mama! Mama!" she cried happily, over and over. "I have found you! I have found you!"

Her euphoric words startled Olivia. "No, no, my little darling," she responded gently, as she bent down to detach the child from about her. The young girl looked up at Olivia and with eyes wide with innocence tilted her head. In quick stages, her joyous expression disappeared. In its stead, as she recognized that Olivia was not her mother, a dullness blotted out the initial brightness of her eyes.

Olivia had seen the look often enough. Death was a familiar visitor to her own village and in her own life. Her heart went out to the unfortunate child who had mistaken her for someone she had clearly lost. She immediately took her by both hands and dropping to her knees on the damp grass, exclaimed, "Oh, but I wish I were your mother, for I have not seen such a pretty girl as you in all my life, save my own daughter of course. And where did these lovely red curls come from?"

"Papa says they belonged to Mama."

Olivia touched one of the curls and opening her eyes very wide said, "Then she must have been a beautiful lady to have had hair this color."

"She was. There is a picture of her in the long gallery. There are other pictures, too, but some of them frighten me."

Olivia nodded in wise agreement. "I know precisely what you mean. In my mother's home was a picture of her grandfather. He wore a patch over one eye and sported the longest hair one has ever seen, it was gray and hung about his shoulders in waves of curls. When I was about your age, I was convinced he was a Barbary pirate and meant one day to steal me from my bed and carry me across the oceans."

"And did he?" the young girl asked, the dullness to her eyes disappearing entirely.

"I'm afraid not," she answered with mock disappointment. "As you can see, I'm still here. The truth is, he wasn't a pirate at all. Only a judge and sat behind a very tall wooden desk hours upon end and listened to people talk. Quite unexceptionable and I think, quite dull! May I tell you a secret?"

The little girl nodded vigorously.

In a whisper, Olivia responded, "I wish he had been a pirate!"

A man's amused voice intruded, "Indeed, ma'am? How singular!" His voice trailed off, however, in a strange manner as he caught her eye.

When Olivia glanced up from the child's face, she found herself looking into the bluest eyes she had ever seen. She had been told the Earl of Braunston had quite remarkable blue eyes but none could have been lighter, clearer or more piercing than those of the stranger who stared back at her. He was quite handsome, too, and was probably very near her in age. When the ignoble thought flitted across her mind, *I wonder if he is married,* she found a blush rising to her cheeks. She wanted to say something to him, particularly something very clever, but it seemed that by gazing into his extraordinary eyes, she had lost all ability to converse.

Not that he was faring much better, she realized. No words passed his lips and something in his expression told her the same mute spell which now afflicted her had been cast over him as well.

Somewhere in the mists of her mind, she wondered what was happening to her. She saw him extend his hand to her and she even watched in a curiously detached manner as her own hand met his. Dreamlike, she placed her palm within what proved to be a strong, comfortable clasp. He then gently lifted her from her knees and at last spoke, "You were speaking of pirates, ma'am, to my daughter?"

Was it her hearing or was his speech unaccountably slow. "Yes," she responded. Why did it seem her own voice echoed through her mind as though traveling down a long, mysterious tunnel. "I trust you have no objection, sir. She seemed distressed, you see. I believe she thought I was—"

"—yes, I know. I am grateful. Her mother wore this color quite frequently—a beautiful blue. It becomes you as it did her."

Lord in heaven, how handsome he was, she thought, her heart beating with butterfly quickness in her breast. His black hair was silvered at the temples ever so lightly, his black brows arched over his incredible eyes, his cheekbones high and arresting, the lines of his face strong and patrician leading to a

164

firm chin. He was dressed elegantly in a coat of blue superfine which fitted his broad shoulders to perfection. His neckcloth was arranged in a mode she had never seen before but gave every indication it had been the work of meticulous hands. Moderate shirt points touched his cheeks and accentuated the fine lines of his face. He wore a red waistcoat and buff knee breeches. Tasseled Wellington boots gleamed brightly against the green of the grass. The soft morning sunshine and a gentle breeze enhanced the sense of magic which seemed to have surrounded Olivia the moment the gentleman spoke to her.

"Papa, I thought she was my mother. Who is she?"

"I am Mrs. Charing, my dear," Olivia said, watching with great approval as the man lifted his daughter easily into his arms.

"Mrs. Charing?" he cried in disbelief. "You are not perchance, Jocelyn's mother, are you?"

Olivia frowned. How could he know of her daughter and why was his expression one of horror? She did not understand. "Yes. Jocelyn Charing. But we are only just arrived in London and have few acquaintance here. How is it poss —"

She felt her heart constrict within her at the sudden realization of who he was. It couldn't be! She pressed her hand to her breast and looked everywhere but at him. She knew her cheeks had deepened in color and she was afraid she might cry for reasons she was loth to admit.

"I am Braunston," he stated.

"I know," she whispered, finally permitting her gaze to be drawn back to his. Did she see an expression of acute anguish in his eyes, or was she seeing only the reflection of her own sudden unhappiness? She finally quieted her heart and gathered her thoughts together sufficiently to add, "I mean, of course you are Braunston and this must be Daphne. By your grandmother's description of you both, I should have known you in a trice. Only it seems so impossible that I should meet you here in the park." With her throat closing up with tears, she addressed the child. "Daphne, you may find this very odd, but in only three weeks I shall be your new grandmama. Would you like that?"

"Papa, is it so?" Daphne asked, slipping her thin arms about his neck and staring at him in wonder.

"Yes, it is," he responded, kissing her cheek.

Daphne's eyes again brightened and in a sweet manner as she lay her head on her father's shoulder she said, "I think it would be better if she became my mama instead. Couldn't she, Papa?"

"No, my dear. I'm afraid that would be quite impossible at this eleventh hour."

Chapter Two

Olivia pushed open the door of the library on the first floor of the town house. Her legs seemed laden with weariness as she slowly entered the chamber, her thoughts unhappily fixed on the memory of a pair of blue eyes. The entire distance from Green Park to Brook Street she had attempted to right her sensibilities, to order her mind and thoughts, and more than once had chided herself for behaving like a silly chit just out of the schoolroom. But it seemed the cruelest twist of Fate for her to have waited so many years and to have refused so many highly eligible offers because her heart was not engaged only to meet her ideal in her daughter's betrothed.

She still could not credit it had happened. She had tumbled in love in a manner she had only dreamed about and to some degree believed could never happen to her. But there it was, a fire burning brightly in her heart which even the slightest memory of Braunston kindled anew.

Heaven help her! Her daughter's betrothed!

She had tried to remind herself that she knew very little of Braunston, but her sentiments seemed to have fixed themselves the moment he lifted Daphne in his arms and the child affectionately put her arms about his neck.

The despairing train of her thoughts was disrupted suddenly when her daughter called to her from across the cozy chamber.

"Mama!" Jocelyn cried, apparently surprised by her entrance.

Olivia had not known her daughter was present in the chamber when she entered it. "Jocelyn! I am sorry! I didn't see you. How very odd!"

"Nor I you — that is, whatever is the matter, Mama?"

Jocelyn was sitting in a chair by a cold hearth with a rug thrown over her knees. Olivia had a momentary glimpse of her daughter shoving something hastily into her lap desk as a faint blush suffused her cheeks. She wondered vaguely if she ought to be concerned, but her own chaotic thoughts soon dismissed her concern as absurd. Jocelyn's principles, just as Lady Mary had suggested, were well established and she would no more engage in improper conduct than the sun would set in the east. Trying desperately to ignore the flames burning steadily in her heart, she crossed the room to her daughter and placed a loving kiss on her cheek.

"Nothing of significance," she said, hoping that Jocelyn would not notice how her hands trembled. "Only the smallest annoyance. You see, here I am in my shabbiest gown and pelisse and a bonnet with frayed ribbons and who must I meet in Green Park? Really, it is quite amazing when I consider it!"

Jocelyn shook her head. "We've only been here little more than a night and a day and we are acquainted with scarcely no one. Who, then did you chance upon?"

"None other than Braunston — and his daughter, Daphne."

"No!" Jocelyn breathed, clearly stunned. Her smooth complexion lost its glow and a veil of anxiety clearly lowered over her large, enchanting green eyes. She was so pretty, Olivia thought, even with her expression fraught with distress. Her hair was a lovely light blond in color and her face was decidedly heart-shaped. Her mouth gave her the appearance of one Cupid had kissed more than once. Her features were delicate, her hands and feet quite small, her stature, though dignified, still childlike. An air of fragility hung about Jocelyn like a fine silk shawl over a ball gown of satin and tulle. When Jocelyn began sucking absently on the tip of her finger, she appeared little more than a schoolgirl. Braunston and his strong shoulders were certainly fit to keep guardianship over such a wife.

"Jocelyn, please," Olivia reproved gently, touching her daughter's hand and drawing it away from her lips.

"I am sorry!" she cried, aghast. "Such a dreadful habit! I cannot conceive how I came about to be snared by it all over again, like a baby. Forgive me, Mother, only tell me of Braunston. Was he very gentlemanly or was he, as *some* suggest, rather harsh."

168

Olivia was surprised. "Harsh?" she cried. "Who has been saying such things to you? I saw nothing of harshness in him. Truly, he was all that was gentlemanly, particularly given the circumstances."

"Then why do you look so sad? Tell me the truth, Mama," Jocelyn demanded, folding her hands tightly upon her lap. "You do not like him, do you? I can see it in your eyes."

Olivia was so surprised, so taken aback, that she could only stare at her daughter for a long moment before answering. When she spoke, she could not restrain giving full voice to her opinion. "Not like him? Jocelyn, he is a wonderful man and will make you the very best of husbands. He held Daphne in his arms most tenderly and spoke to me with respect and good humor. You must trust me in this. Only, tell me who has spoken ill of him."

Jocelyn's lip trembled. She lifted her hand as though to begin sucking the tip of her finger, then again hastily clasped her hands together. "No one, that is—not precisely no one. It is just that Alfred—"

"—not Alfred," Olivia interjected impatiently. "Jocelyn, you must not let him—"

"—but Mama, he said Lord Braunston once fought in a duel!"

Olivia regarded her daughter for a time, then turned away, moving to stand near the fireplace. She was caught in a most awkward position, one she was certain rarely afflicted a mother in that it seemed to her that her own standards were considerably less exacting than her daughter's. Not that she approved of dueling, not by half. But given the nature of the offense—that of another gentleman having called the earl a liar—there had been nothing left but for Braunston to have called the man out. To her knowledge the affair had ended when his offender had missed his shot completely and Braunston had deloped. In her opinion, he had acquitted himself in the most gentlemanly, honorably manner possible, but to her daughter, well, he might as well have killed the man.

"Jocelyn," she began, staring into the cold grate. "I am acquainted with the particulars of this duel, and I am persuaded he could have done nothing less than to have behaved as he did."

"But Alfred says a true gentleman would have merely turned

169

aside the insult, turning his cheek as it were. As for myself, I had rather not be married to a man who duels. I only wish I had known this before agreeing to marry him. What if I should wake up some morning a widow?"

"I doubt it would ever come to that."

"But how do you know it wouldn't? Besides, it isn't just that he duels, Alfred says he is known to frequent Watiers where the play is quite *deep*."

Olivia straightened her shoulders and felt defensive suddenly. "Alfred told you that? And what else did he tell you? That he drinks four bottles of Madeira each night with dinner, that he keeps raucous company and frequents the opera! Good heavens, Jocelyn. If you are to be Braunston's wife, you must come to know him for himself and not to listen to mere gossip!"

"Alfred does not *gossip*, Mama!" Jocelyn returned, deeply offended.

"Well perhaps he ought to then," she retorted cryptically. "I don't like to mention it, but your dear Alfred seems like a terrible bore besides having filled your head with a great deal of nonsense!"

"Nonsense? You consider dueling and gaming to be matters of nonsense?"

"Certainly not," Olivia responded, flustered. "I only meant that when partaken of to excess these pastimes can be quite dangerous—"

"—you think dueling is a mere pastime. Oh, Mama! I never understood you before. Hannah More says—"

Olivia lifted her hand and silenced her child. "—I don't give a fig for what Hannah More says. Yes, yes, I know she is a paragon, but we are speaking of Braunston, not a monster. I know of only one duel, I did not mean for it to sound as though I approved of dueling. As for gaming, I suggest you reconcile yourself to a gentleman and his love for the company of other gentlemen which is of course the primary reason a man will *frequent* the club to which he belongs. Lady Mary assures me he does not play *deep* as Alfred might have you believe." When she saw that Jocelyn was prepared to argue further, she again lifted her hand and exclaimed, "Oh, pray do not let us brangle on this score. I am still suffering a trifle from the headache. Rest easy, Jocelyn. Braunston is an excellent man. Truly, he is."

With that, she turned on her heel and with tears burning her eyes, quit the chamber.

Jocelyn watched her mother leave and only after the door had been shut upon her for a full minute did she realize she was sucking her finger again. She had not done so in ages, certainly not since Alfred had befriended her three years ago. His presence in her life had been as an anchor to a ship in a storm, holding her steady in any adversity. She dearly wished for him now to help her through this final trial of meeting the man she was to marry. That was impossible, of course, for many reasons, not least of which was because she was in love with Alfred.

The moment he entered her mind, a wonderfully warm sensation spread throughout her heart. Lifting the lid of her cherrywood lap desk, she fondled a stack of letters, bound by a green velvet ribbon — all from Alfred, of course. Most were part of a correspondence they had enjoyed when he reentered Old Turvey society upon completion of his final term at Oxford. He loved to write and she, to read. He would call upon her every Tuesday and Friday and leave her with a sonnet or an essay he had composed. Her heart twisted up very tightly as she let her fingertips touch the edges of the top two letters. These had been waiting for her upon her arrival in Brook Street.

First one tear, then another, plopped onto the bodice of her embroidered muslin gown. She missed Alfred dreadfully and felt in her heart she always would. She had in a distant manner, since she was five years his junior, grown up with him. He was the squire's son, a neighboring family of diminishing fortune — the crop failures of recent years having ruined many of his tenant farmers. The passing of the Corn Laws, so devastating to the farmers with small acreage, had sealed the Lovell's fate, at least for the time being. Alfred had been instructed to wed an heiress or the family was sure to suffer for decades to come.

Alfred was a good son, a proper son, and had made it clear to Jocelyn that he must at least attempt to oblige his beloved parents. That was why he had encouraged Jocelyn to accept Braunston's generous offer since he simply could not in good conscience offer for her himself. In the second of the two letters

171

he had indicated he would be coming to London for the strict purpose of getting himself a wealthy wife, if he possibly could.

More tears fell. Jocelyn quickly withdrew her lace kerchief — never far from her — from the depths of her beaded reticule and dabbed at her cheeks. She did not want to continue in so hopeless an avenue of thought, but her mind quickly ran to their last parting — so painful, so sad! They had actually met secretly, in a thicket in the beech woods near his home. Words of undying love had been exchanged, and a final kiss shared, a joining that had almost been Jocelyn's undoing. But Alfred had been gentlemanly to the last, and had been the one to insist that in a few years, she would have forgotten him completely and that she was bound by every dictum of their society which they both loved, to marry Lord Braunston.

He was so strong and the firmness in his voice as he bid her farewell had given her the courage to travel in silent mourning without one spark of regret.

But now, as she closed the lid gently on Alfred's letters, her finger again found its way into her mouth. Her mother could not deceive her. Something had occurred in her encounter with Braunston to have overset her mightily. She was very close to her dear mama and however many words of protest her mother might speak, the sadness in her eyes had convinced Jocelyn she was marrying a monster.

Withdrawing a sheet of writing paper, she began penning a missive to Alfred explaining her mother's odd behavior after her accidental meeting with Braunston. Would he still advise her to marry a man who caused her mama to look as though the earth had caved in on her?

Chapter Three

Five days later, Olivia sat in Lady Mary Braunston's drawing room, to the right of the dowager who was dozing gently in a chair by the fire. Across from her Jocelyn giggled behind her fan, for the poor old woman's mouth had fallen slightly agape and a faint whistle sounded through her nose every time she drew in a breath.

Olivia shook her head reprovingly at her daughter, but since she was finding it difficult not to smile in return, every once in a while a giggle continued to rise from Jocelyn's throat.

Her daughter was dressed in a fine, sprig muslin gown — one of several Olivia had had made up for Jocelyn before coming to London. It was pale pink and embroidered with little bluebells all about the bodice. She wore a cameo tied on a silk black ribbon about her neck. And though at home Olivia had been pleased with the results, here, against the quite fashionable world of the *beau monde* — not least of which was the elegance and sophistication of Lady Mary's silk gown draped with jewels — she feared her daughter looked little more than a country dowd.

Not that her own appearance was much better. Her gown, which had served her well at the local assemblies in Bedford, was nearly five years old and its simple print and lack of ruffles about the hem bespoke a rustic. She had never been one to repine overly much about such matters, but now, with her daughter betrothed to a man who she had come to understand in the past several days was considered a Leader of Fashion, she found herself decidedly uncomfortable in her surroundings.

As she glanced at her daughter, she saw that Jocelyn appeared awestruck. She was looking all about the elegant chamber decorated in blue silk-damask, entirely *en suite,* the draperies, walls, and furniture covered in the same costly fabric. Poor Jocelyn, she thought, as she watched her dear daughter's expression. The several days which had transpired since their arrival in London — the presentation of her daughter at a ball given by Lady Mary, the crushing embarrassment Jocelyn experienced at the extreme notoriety which abounded about her as the earl's betrothed, the halting conversations she had endured with his lordship — had amounted to at least three serious bouts of tears and one hysterical moment when Jocelyn had proclaimed she couldn't marry Braunston, she simply couldn't!

For her part, Olivia had been able only with the strongest of efforts to keep the initial *tendre* she had felt for the earl in check. It seemed whenever Jocelyn was not present, she and Braunston fell into an easy discourse made more agreeable and more wondrous with each new meeting. The truth was, she simply did not understand why Jocelyn did not enjoy and value his company as she did.

The door opened and a rush of cool air flowed into the drawing room from the hallway. Olivia turned and saw that Lord Braunston had at last finished his port and was ready to join the ladies. He stood in the doorway, elegant as always in his evening dress. He wore a black coat — which Olivia had learned had been created by no less a master than Weston — black pantaloons, black silk slippers, a white waistcoat, starched shirt points which never seemed to wilt even in the stuffiest of ballrooms and a neckcloth tied in his usual fashion, a mode she had come to understand the *ton* referred to as, *a la Braunston.*

She was proud of him, very much so, and had her daughter shown even the smallest sign that she was tumbling in love with him, she would have been inordinately content.

He smiled at her as he entered the chamber. She rose to greet him, crossing the room with her finger to her lips. In deference to Lady Mary's dreamy state, she spoke in a hushed whisper. "If you should not object to retiring to her ladyship's music room, Jocelyn has expressed a hope she might perform for you. She is an exceedingly accomplished musician, though I beg you will forgive me for praising my own child to the skies. Quite a fault, I know, but I promise you, you

174

will not regret acquiescing."

"Your pride does you honor," he responded kindly, smiling down on her. "And of the moment I confess I have no other desire than to hear your daughter play."

Braunston looked into Olivia's face and knew a tug on his heart so strong he was certain her own fingers must have reached into his breast and accomplished the deed. Ever since he met her in Green Park, he had been experiencing all the wonderful sensations of love he had hoped to share with Jocelyn. How cruel Fate had been in arranging this marriage, he thought. For however much he valued the daughter, her air of breeding, her sensible conversation — when he could coax her to speak — her long list of accomplishments, it was the mother who lit up his heart with the brightness of a thousand candles. She had but to appear anywhere within his range of vision, and it was as though everyone else ceased to exist.

Did anyone suspect the truth? he wondered. He made every effort to conceal the state of his feelings. How successful he was, he couldn't know, particularly since his senses became so disordered when he was near her.

He was older than Olivia and had already teased her several times about calling her his mother.

How could he ever call her anything so stupid, he thought, as he gazed into her soft hazel eyes and marveled again at the golden flecks blended with grays and browns. Over her shiny blond hair, she wore a delicate cap of tulle, trimmed with lace — an indication of her *advanced years* — a cap he longed to tear away from her curls that he might let his fingers ramble freely through her tresses. She was as pretty as a spring morning to him, full of the promise of new life. Why hadn't his grandmama thought to arrange for him to marry the mother instead of the daughter? The devil take it!

Still, did anyone suspect the truth?

Whenever he saw her, conversed with her, danced with her, he knew an intense desire to hold her close and to kiss her. She had told him about Edward and her difficult life of relative poverty, a life which, since her husband's death, had been devoted exclusively to the securing of her daughter's future. Though he found himself pleased he had been able to relieve her of the burden of Jocelyn's care, how much he wished instead he could lavish upon Olivia her every heart's desire.

"Is something amiss, my lord?" he heard her query. He wanted to tell her that *everything* was wrong. Instead, he shook his head and turned away from her. Begging Jocelyn to take his arm, he recommended they leave his grandmother to the obvious sweetness of her dreams.

Olivia followed behind her daughter and future son-in-law. Her hands were trembling again, as they frequently did when in his company. This time, they shook because of the warm manner in which he had ceased speaking and merely looked at her, in silence, for an unconscionably long time. What had he been thinking, she wondered, her cheeks glowing with a warmth that brought her cold, trembling hands up to cover them. Jocelyn should not see her with her complexion high. Did her daughter suspect the truth? Her thoughts tumbled over one another. Did Braunston feel as she did? Or was she merely seeing what she wished to see? Yet if he was experiencing sentiments toward her as powerful as her own for him, how terrible for Jocelyn? Oh, lord what a coil!

Lord Braunston led the ladies through an antechamber adjoining the drawing room, and into another though smaller receiving room, dressed elegantly in a gold damask. The chamber contained a silky horsehair sofa, several empire chairs covered in striped, gold and white silk, a burnished rosewood pianoforte and a gleaming harp.

She sat down on the sofa and once Braunston had settled Jocelyn before the pianoforte, he joined her, causing her heart to leap. Truly, he should have sat in a chair, yet the best vantage point for appreciating had set Jocelyn's talents was the sofa.

But to be so near him!

She began fanning her face gently, which caused him to ask solicitously if the chamber was too warm for her. She snapped her fan shut and responded that she was quite comfortable. Did he know that it was his nearness and the way he looked at her which caused her to feel that an enormous blaze, instead of a moderate fire, had been lit in the hearth?

Several branches of candles bathed the chamber in a cozy glow lending an intimate ambience which further set her heart to beating strongly.

Jocelyn, with her back perfectly straight and her hands arched beautifully over the keys, began her exceptional progress through the precise, powerful movements of a Haydn sonata.

The music helped Olivia to calm herself and after a few minutes she was able to set aside her disturbing thoughts. She watched Jocelyn play, feeling her mother's heart swell with pride. She had scrimped every day of every year in order to give Jocelyn the best music master the town of Bedford could provide. Braunston would have no cause to regret his marriage to Jocelyn on this score.

After a time, the earl leaned close to her and whispered, "She plays remarkably well, you are to be congratulated. And don't think I am unaware of the sacrifices you have made. You've been a good mother to her, Olivia. If I have only one regret, it is that Jocelyn does not yet seem comfortable with me."

Olivia looked into the clear blueness of the earl's eyes and felt lost. He was too close to her and she found it difficult, yet again, to think. Something to the rise and fall of the music, particularly beneath her daughter's inspired fingers, seemed to increase her sensitivity to Braunston's presence and she found her breathing had grown quite shallow. "You must give her time, my lord," she responded in a whisper.

As he regarded her, his expression grew quite intense, his gaze shifting from her eyes to drift over her face, from her forehead, to the line of her cheek to her lips. A rush of sentiment poured through her, alarming her terribly, the original *tendre* she had felt for him breathing life anew, only this time stronger and more vital than before. It was a long time before he drew his gaze from her lips, back to Jocelyn who was fully involved in performing the sonata. Only when he no longer held her attention captive did Olivia realize she had been holding her breath. She released it in a long, slow sigh.

"I'll give her all the time she needs," he whispered. "I only wish — " His words trailed away to nothing.

"Papa," a small voice called from the doorway.

Lord Braunston, his attention riveted to his daughter, first scowled mildly at her, then bid her with a smile to join them on the sofa.

"I heard music," Daphne said, her nightdress of fine woolen stuff dragging behind her as she lifted the oversized skirt away from her feet and ran to her father.

He took her on his lap and bid her be very quiet while

Jocelyn played. Daphne listened attentively for a few minutes, then turned to Olivia. "Grandmama," she whispered, extending her arms to her. Olivia pulled her from Braunston's lap and took her into her arms, holding her close. Whenever the two families were together, she and Daphne enjoyed a special comraderie, perhaps because of their unusual meeting. She began speaking to her in low tones, explaining what Jocelyn was playing and how long she had studied before she could move her fingers across the keys so rapidly.

Daphne listened to her, asked whispered questions, and demanded to know if she would be living in the same house as Jocelyn and her papa.

"No, I'm afraid not. But I will come to visit very often and if your father does not dislike the idea you may spend the summer with me in Bedfordshire. We have a peach orchard in which you may climb as many of the trees as you like, a garden where you may help me pick the vegetables and cut the flowers, and a clear stream and a pond where I will teach you to swim—"

"—to swim! Papa, Papa. Grandmama will teach me to swim."

"So you swim?" he asked, turning astonished eyes upon Olivia.

"I hope I don't offend you, or your notions of propriety, but with so many rivers about—not to mention ditches which fill dangerously full of water at given times of the year, my parents insisted their children learn to swim—even their daughters."

"I think it an excellent idea."

"Oh, Papa. What fun we shall have, only why doesn't Grandmama live with us? We have a pond—the one you swim in—she could teach me there."

Olivia met his gaze over the child's head. He looked at her evenly, and the unspoken anguish in his eyes caused her heart to again beat painfully fast in her breast.

Chapter Four

Lord Braunston held the reins of his evenly matched bays lightly in hand. Glancing down at the silent figure beside him, he repressed a sigh. It had been a full fortnight since he had made his betrothed's acquaintance, and in that time, he had still been unable to warm toward her, nonetheless ignore what proved to be his growing sentiments toward her mother. He was not certain if his intuition was correct, but he suspected that Jocelyn harbored some mistrust of him, yet he could not imagine what he might have done to have caused her to think ill of him.

Again he suppressed a sigh, a sensation of hopelessness dragging at his heart.

Perhaps if he and Jocelyn were nearer in age, he might have been able to make greater inroads with her affections. After all, she had a great deal to recommend her. She was very beautiful in her petite, youthful way, her manners were precise, her good breeding evident in the choice of her words, in all matters of etiquette and in her many accomplishments. She was fluent in both Italian and French, she displayed remarkable ability with the use of the watercolors, she would please even the most fastidious of hostesses — and had done so already — with her performance on the pianoforte. Her singing voice was less attractive, but her general deportment when she entered a room and greeted her new acquaintances was friendly and polite. If she lacked Olivia's buoyancy and liveliness, he truly could have no complaint of her as the next Countess of Braunston.

He called gently to his horses and encouraged them into a trot. They were heading to Hyde Park at the correct hour of four at which time the *beau monde,* in all its brilliance, would be assembling. Most to display their latest costumes, whether a fashionable new gown from a modish shop in New Bond Street, or the absurd apparel of the extreme dandy. "What do you think of Petersham?" he had queried one afternoon of Jocelyn. Lord Petersham had created his own style of trousers, worn exceedingly full at the hips with pleats extending from the waistband. For himself, he thought them ridiculous and amusing. But Jocelyn's response had disturbed him.

"Disgraceful!" she had pronounced.

He had looked at her with surprise, thinking perhaps she was saying what she felt might please him. But when he realized she was being perfectly serious and expressing her true opinion, he recalled feeling slightly horrified. In a kind tone, he had said, "I don't think they are disgraceful, precisely. Absurd, perhaps."

Jocelyn had merely stared at him for a long moment, her complexion paling at his reproof. He watched her start to lift that most dreaded finger to her lips, then return it hastily to her swansdown muff. Afterward she had compressed her lips tightly together and responded, "You are right, of course."

The impatience which coursed through him in that moment had so alarmed him, that for the first time since Jocelyn's arrival in London, he had seriously doubted his ability to ultimately find contentment with her. Once the door had opened for admitting these doubts, he wondered why the devil he had permitted his grandmama to persuade him to enter into an arranged marriage in the first place — except that he had desperately wanted a mother for Daphne. Was it anyone's fault that he had been disenchanted with the grasping females of his acquaintance who had sought him in the most unprincipled manner following his wife's early demise? He had forgotten what it was like to be a sought-after Matrimonial Prize and he had detested every false smile and practiced flirtation more than life itself. He still shuddered at the memory of it, of coy missives, of broken boot laces, of limbs pretended to be injured that he might be forced to carry one of his pursuers to a nearby carriage.

That Lady Mary had chosen the granddaughter of one of her school friends ought to have warned him he was in serious jeopardy though he had been comforted, if only for a moment, upon having met Jocelyn's mother before meeting Jocelyn herself.

His initial reaction to Olivia, a quite inexplicable desire to take her forcibly in his arms and kiss her, had given him hope that the daughter would be like the mother.

But how different they were! When he had gently broached this difference with his grandmama, she had beamed proudly and responded that Jocelyn was just like her mother — so honorable and accomplished, a perfect woman to become the next Countess of Braunston.

He had trusted his grandmama. They had had many long discussions over the sort of wife he needed for himself and the manner of mother Daphne would most benefit by. Why had he believed she could choose wisely for him? How could he have been such a sapskull, such a completely romantic fool, to have embarked on such a course particularly since he now realized he had believed love would follow easily if an excellent woman were chosen for him?

And Jocelyn was excellent. But perhaps too much so, he thought, as he again regarded the bonnet covering half her face. Her sobriety of perception caused him again to sigh. Jocelyn just didn't laugh enough to suit him.

The entire betrothal, from first meeting Olivia in Green Park, to watching his intended suckling the tip of her finger, to listening to her quite stuffy opinions on matters of decorum, had begun taking on the proportions of a nightmare.

For these reasons, he had decided he must make an effort to spend time alone with Jocelyn and had begun by making daily excursions with her to Hyde Park — without Olivia. Perhaps if he could encourage her to speak and they could come to some measure of understanding with one another, the marriage, which by every unspoken law of his peers must take place, might be a happy one.

But even now, as she compressed her lips in obvious disapproval of the lively Winsford twins who were flirting harmlessly with two young officers, his heart sank.

The park was full to overflowing on the fine spring afternoon. The sun shone warm upon the gaily decorated bonnets of hundreds of ladies. Several Cyprians displaying their wares quite generously, drove by in a light blue phaeton and pair, nodding and smiling to him. He knew of them, of course, as did any male among the *ton*. But he kept a discreet distance having come to understand that greed was the only motivation of these ladybirds. And he wanted love, a lasting love such as he had enjoyed with his darling wife of ten years. How much he missed her, her bright conversation and charming manners. She was all he had ever wanted and had looked forward to a long life with her. When she had died of a fever two years ago, he had thought his life had come to an end.

The unhappy rambling of his thoughts was disrupted when he realized Jocelyn was speaking. By the nature of the morsel he caught, he comprehended she must have been speaking for some time.

Her words were halting. She was clearly embarrassed. "So I hope you will agree, for the sake of our children, that you will reconsider your practices of dueling and gaming."

She turned to look up at him, her large green eyes hopeful.

"My what?" he queried, confused. "Dueling and gaming?"

Jocelyn nodded, appearing very childlike as she regarded him, a fluff of perfectly formed blond curls gracing her brow.

He was stunned. *Dueling and gaming* "I don't take your meaning, Jocelyn. I don't *duel.*"

"You did once because a man called you a liar. I — I know of it from an unexceptionable source."

"Well, yes, that much is true, but that was in my *salad days.*" He felt very strange defending himself to a young lady half his age. He supposed any bride must have a right to know that her children would not be lost to her husband's instability of character, but the fact that Jocelyn made mention of a duel which had occurred eleven years earlier, was nothing short of a considerable shock.

When she clasped her hands tightly together on her lap, however, he found his growing irritation and impatience with her beginning to rise within him. He knew she meant to say more on a subject which he wished she would let drop and braced himself.

In a low voice, she added, "I hope you don't mean to make light of one of the king's laws"

She is very young, he reminded himself, trying to control his temper. He gave the horses a slap of the reins and increased their pace.

He knew now he was in the devil of a fix. How was he to

182

marry a young lady who behaved more like his mother toward him than a wife? He was about to tell her that he did not appreciate her *motherly* reproofs when he happened to glance at her. He saw that her gaze was fixed in some horror upon a young man mounted on horseback.

Braunston scrutinized the boy, for he couldn't have been much older than Jocelyn, and his first impression was of a provincial with an ill temper. The beaver hat gracing a head of red hair, was a style worn ten years ago. He was dressed in an unfashionable brown velvet coat fitting poorly across his shoulders, his knee breeches had seen finer days and his top boots, though gleaming, were considerably worn. It was obvious the young man knew Jocelyn for he watched her with an intense expression, his lips compressed firmly together in a manner which seemed identical to the disapproving expression Jocelyn frequently sported. He looked back at his betrothed and saw that her color was high as she stared straight ahead, her attention turned purposely away from the young man, her hands now knotted tightly together.

What the devil, he thought. Who was this young country pup? A beau? Was Jocelyn in love with him?

What a pretty fix they were in if she did. One thing was certain, he must find occasion to speak with Olivia, alone — and the sooner the better!

Chapter Five

The next day, Olivia paced the wooden library floor, marching to and fro in front of the fireplace. Her heart was in her throat as she awaited the arrival of Lord Braunston. Her nerves were raw and her fingers like ice. This latter condition had already caused her to cast all caution to the wind — she had actually had a large fire built in the grate, against the habit of years of practicing the strictest of economies — in hopes of warming her hands and relieving the terrible anxiety, or was it excitement, which beset her.

It would seem Braunston had a matter of great import to discuss with her.

She suspected he wished to speak with her yet again of Jocelyn and her reserved demeanor toward him. This much did not distress her, for she would merely represent to him, yet again, his need for patience with so inexperienced a young woman.

On the other hand, when he had made clear he needed to speak with her *in private,* all thoughts of Jocelyn had immediately fled her mind. Visions of actually being alone with the earl invaded her brain like Wellington's troops on the field at Waterloo. She was overcome with swirlings of ignoble sentiments made worse by the fact that when he had made his request last night at Lady Aldworth's ball they had been waltzing together. At the time, thoughts of enjoying his company *tête-à-tête* somehow became confused with how wondrous it was to be whirled about a ballroom held snugly in his arms. The euphoria she had felt still afflicted her. All morning, she could think of nothing else than seeing him, *alone.*

"Oh, dear!" she cried into the library air. "I am in the basket! Indeed, I am!"

Fortunately, Jocelyn would know nothing of the visit. She had promised to take Daphne on an excursion — just the two of them — to Richmond Park and it would be some time before she returned.

Stopping abruptly in her pacing, Olivia crossed to the rose-colored wing chair near the fireplace. She plunked down into the chair, despair pulling at her heart.

She had reason to believe Gregory — he had insisted she call him by his Christian name — was as sorely afflicted as she was. Earlier in the evening, he had requested the waltz they had later shared. With several curious tattlemongers standing nearby, she had stumbled over her words trying to refuse him. The truth was, she feared dancing with him. He would have none of her refusal, however, and pressed her, drawing close and with a terrible glint in his blue eyes, begged to know why she would not dance with him. She could see they were being eyed curiously by several known gossips not the least of which was Lady Jersey whose nickname *Silence* bespoke her propensity to waggle her tongue.

Their whispers seemed to fuel Braunston's intentions. The more Olivia became disconcerted by his behavior — the more she wrung her hands and attempted to excuse herself — the more he insisted. His blue eyes fairly blazed as he demanded in a teasing whisper to know if she thought so poorly of him she would not even dance with him. She had somehow, in the absurdity of his words, forgotten her surroundings entirely — including the gossiping Tabbies standing too near for comfort. "Think poorly of you!" she had cried in a return whisper. "My lord, I am persuaded the sun rises with you!"

How could she have said anything so horridly daring to him. She had immediately flung her fan up between them, her cheeks burning hot with embarrassment. "That is not what I meant to say," she amended, averting her gaze from his. But the harm was done.

"I think you meant every word of it, Livvy," he had countered. "And you will dance with me."

"Yes," she had said at last, but not before she caught the eyes of the ladies near her and saw that they stared at her in the most horrified astonishment. How much had they heard, how close had he been standing to her? Did anyone suspect the truth, that she was suffering from the most dreadful of *tendres* and could not seem to escape it?

But worse, what manner of mother was she to have said such a thing to her daughter's betrothed?

The set that followed beneath the glow of three brightly lit chandeliers had been nearly as bad. She had become utterly lost in the enchantment of being held in Gregory's arms and she had moved with him, in the breathless, rhythmical swirls of the dance, as though her feet had wings. Never had she enjoyed dancing the waltz as much, never had a partner seemed to fit her to perfection, never had each turn of the dance felt so smooth and so effortless. His gaze had been only for her and she had given herself fully to the moment, knowing that once he was married, she would take care never to dance with him again.

Afterward, he had expressed forcefully his need to speak with her in private, about Jocelyn. From that moment on, her thoughts were fixed on the hour, eleven o'clock, when he would arrive.

She was not aware that the intensity of her thoughts had moved her to sit on the very edge of her seat, leaning forward and staring at nothing as one transfixed by an alarming vision. When a knock sounded on the door she literally fell off the edge and tumbled to her knees. She began laughing a little hysterically, and was about to rise to her feet and bid the butler enter, when the door opened.

That was how Braunston found Olivia, her gown curled about her knees and feet, her face lit with amusement, one hand clapped over her mouth. Until this moment, the earl had been denying the scope of his feelings for his betrothed's mother. But seeing her in so ridiculous a position and laughing about it, somehow forced every sentiment rushing wildly to the surface of his heart. He loved her and had been in love with her the moment Daphne had nearly toppled her over by holding the back of her knees. How sweetly and lovingly she had spoken to his daughter with complete awareness of the trial the child had suffered. There was more brightness, joy, and love in this woman than he had ever known before and he wanted her so much it was as though a vise had trapped his heart in a deathlike grip.

"What are you doing?" he cried, closing the door behind him. He crossed the chamber quickly to hold her elbow gently as she rose to her feet.

She laughed outright and said, "I fell off the chair when I heard your knock. How could I have done so? I feel like a perfect Bedlamite."

She was now standing and had no further need of his assistance, but he couldn't seem to release her arm from his grasp. Instead, he looked into her smiling face, glowing from her escapade, and every rational thought deserted him — in particular the reason for begging an audience with her in the first place. Without consideration to the truly reprehensible nature of his actions, he caught her up in his arms and kissed her.

Olivia knew she should protest. Her mind told her to push him away. But the feel of his lips upon hers in what she could only deem was the most forceful kiss she had ever received in her entire existence, quelled all resolve. Instead, she leaned into him, slipping her arms about his neck and abandoning herself completely to an embrace which had haunted her in her dreams for three nights in a row. She felt as though she had come home as one who might after having been forced to trudge through the countryside for days on end. Odd feelings of thirst and hunger were instantly allayed by his embrace, as was the desperate sensations of loneliness and anxiety. Her mind ceased to move in its usual way, time slowing, even the feel of the floor beneath her feet disappearing entirely. Her heart alone beat steadily and surely against the impropriety of being kissed by the man her daughter was to marry.

After a moment, he drew back from her slightly, his gaze marred by terrible pain. She knew the total of his thoughts in this moment — that there was no future for them and never would be. To her surprise, he did not release her as she expected him to. Instead, he pulled her close and held her in a tight, desperate embrace. Tears welled up in her eyes then trickled down her cheek to stain the fine bottle green fabric of his coat. She felt him sigh deeply, his shoulders rising and falling, his breath warm on her neck. She wanted to ask, "What are we to do?" But the words were so hopeless in nature that they did not even dare rise to her lips.

When at long last he released her, she returned slowly to her chair. She could not look at him, but instead let her gaze rest on the glow of coals burning hot in the grate. Her fingers became icy again, and even the warmth from the fire could not seem to restore them.

When he finally spoke, it seemed that his words traveled a distance of miles instead of a few meager feet. "I came to speak to you of Jocelyn, or at least I thought I had. But now I wonder if I just wanted to hold you in my arms once before my wedding. I shall go now. Remember that I shall always love you."

Chapter Six

Jocelyn saw Alfred and her conscience smote her deeply. For the first time in her life — save for the truly unconscionable assignation she had arranged with him before leaving Old Turvey — she had committed a terrible trespass against her mother's trust. She had agreed, by secret correspondence through her maid, Nancy, to meet with Alfred at Richmond Park. When he saw her and his face lit up with a joyous smile, the despicable nature of her crime dimmed perceptibly. All she felt now was an overwhelming sensation of happiness at the mere sight of the man she loved.

"Who is that smiling man?" Daphne asked, tugging on Jocelyn's arm. Over the past fortnight, Jocelyn had become attached to the little girl who would soon be her new daughter. She looked down at the long red curls trailing behind a diminutive bonnet trimmed with artificial red cherries. "His name is Mister Lovell and he is a particular friend of mine from Old Turvey."

Alfred seemed nervous once he drew close. His initial enchanting smile became compressed and a worried frown marred his freckled brow. He made Daphne's acquaintance with a polite bow, then begged the ladies to walk with him beside the lake where several pleasure seekers were rowing boats. A light breeze kept the surface of the lake in a ripple of movement as the trio began their progress along the pathway.

Alfred immediately addressed Jocelyn's former concern. "I cannot like meeting in this reprehensible manner, Jocelyn. It is not seemly. And the park is terribly crowded today. What if we meet up with some of your new acquaintance?"

"But I simply had to speak with you alone and Regent's Park is much worse, which was my first thought, though not frequented as much by the *beau monde* as is Hyde."

"Very well! I suppose there was nothing for it, but only this once! You are to be married in less than a sennight and I want you to know I came only to assure myself of your contentment and of Braunston's character. I don't mean to make light of your distress regarding his reputation, Jocelyn, but I believe you have made too much of the gossip you have heard. Though I do not approve of dueling or of gaming in any form, I don't think Lord Braunston is the hardened gamester you portrayed him to be in your letters. I have made numerous queries since my arrival and I am satisfied that he will make you an excellent husband. He is not as sober a man as I would wish for you, in part because I don't believe he has the proper ability to curb your penchant for melodrama, but taken as a whole, he will do quite well."

Jocelyn sniffed trying to hold back her tears. "He is not you, Alfred, and I suppose that is all that matters to me."

"I forbid you to cry. Think of Daphne. What will she be thinking of her new mama?"

"Is Miss Charing crying?" Daphne asked, curious. She released Jocelyn's hand and stared up into her face. "I can see she is, but only a little bit. I wish we had gone to *Gretna Green*. That was where I met Grandmama. Papa and I went there to see the cows and then I saw Grandmama. She was wearing a blue pelisse. Miss Charing, you would like the cows. They wouldn't make you cry at all! Shall I ask Papa if I may go with you to Gretna Green?"

"Gretna Green?" Alfred cried, startled. "My dear child, who has put such a notion into your head? I wouldn't consider— that is—Gretna Green?"

Jocelyn smiled and whispered to Alfred, "She means Green Park, silly! Not Gretna Green, though I should like to see Lord Braunston's face if Daphne asked to accompany us to Gretna Green."

Alfred responded gravely, "It is not proper to even speak lightly of so horrendous a course."

Jocelyn was too content at having Alfred by her side to engage in a quarrel. Besides, he was right. She ought not to make light of *elopement*. If a small part of her wished that Alfred would sweep her away in a post-chaise and four, journey along the Great North Road to Gretna Green and marry her out-of-hand, she ignored such heinous desires. As much as she loved

190

Alfred, she would rather marry Braunston than subject any of her family to the scandal always attached to Scottish border marriages. Instead, she sighed. "So you believe I have no cause to worry about my forthcoming nuptials."

Alfred's voice sounded pinched as he responded, "No, Jocelyn. No concern whatsoever."

"Have you—have you perchance found your heiress since your arrival?"

Alfred shook his head. "I have discarded that notion entirely. Papa and I argued at length over the prospect but I am become steadfast. I have no wish for a wife at the present and I came to London only to assure myself regarding your happiness. From here I intend to travel north and meet with Coke of Norfolk who has made considerable improvements in methods of farming. I mean to concentrate all my efforts on rebuilding the estate, in particular the rent rolls by improving the land—perhaps then I will marry."

"I wish I had known as much before accepting of Braunston's hand, Alfred. I should have removed to Bedford and taken up a position in a dressmaker's shop and waited for you."

Alfred looked down at her and smiled faintly, sadness ruling his eyes. "I would never have permitted you to do so. No, I am persuaded you ought to marry Braunston. I am convinced it is the right course for you."

"The expression in your eyes insists otherwise. No, don't argue. Speculation is useless anyway. I will marry Braunston on Saturday, only would you meet with me *alone,* one last time before you leave London? If I brought my maid, would you meet me in Green Park? Mama says the dairymaids are quite charming as they tend their cows. You can even purchase a glass of fresh milk from them if you so desire."

A long, heavy silence followed her request. She looked up at the profile of her beloved and sighed. He was not handsome as many young gentlemen of her acquaintance were, but every freckle on his round, stolid face had become precious to her. She could see by the manner in which his gaze was fixed upon the path just ahead of his feet that he was considering her scheme. She knew it went sorely against the grain with him, but after all, in only five days she would probably never see him again. When he still did not answer her, she took hold of his arm and squeezing it gently, pressed him, "Please, Alfred. One more time only, and without *little ears* along to disturb our discourse?"

When she reminded him that he would undoubtedly never have another occasion upon which to be alone with her again, he turned to look at her, his light blue eyes full of anguish. "As you wish," he whispered. "Tomorrow at one o'clock. But never again."

"One o'clock, then," she responded resolutely.

The next day, Lord Braunston held Daphne in his arms and encouraged her to speak. He stood near the gold sofa in Olivia's drawing room where she was seated and commanded his daughter with a gentle smile, "Tell Grandmama what you heard Mister Alfred say to Miss Charing."

He then looked at Olivia, his eyes full of meaning, and waited.

Daphne stated, "Miss Charing wanted Mister Alfred to take her to Gretna Green."

When his daughter said nothing more, the earl prompted her further. "Did he say when he wished to do so?"

"This afternoon at one o'clock."

Olivia glanced at the small white clock on the mantel and saw that it was half-past one already. Jocelyn was indeed gone from the town house but had said she meant to go to Hookham's and would return in an hour or so. She had even taken her maid with her. Rising from the sofa, she placed a hand against her breast, trying to still the sudden erratic beating of her heart. "Are you sure?" she whispered breathlessly, looking up at Braunston. Her knees had begun to quiver and she wondered how it was she could stand at all.

Still holding Daphne in his arms, Braunston quickly took Olivia's arm and begged her to reseat herself. "I have given you a severe shock, Olivia, and I am sorry. But the landlord at Mister Lovell's hotel said your daughter's friend had already paid his shot, packed his portmanteau and quit the premises. When asked if he knew where Mister Lovell was going, the man said he had posed the very same question to the fiery-haired gentleman. Mister Lovell's response was quite firm, *I am taking the Great North Road and heading to my future.*"

Olivia's hands began to tremble. "And Old Turvey is *not* along the Great North Road. It can't be possible! It simply can't be. But it seems odd to me now that when Jocelyn said she saw Alfred in Hyde Park, I had expected he would pay us a morning visit, and he did not!"

"I don't know what is transpiring, or whether or not to give full credence to Daphne's story, but she said Mister Lovell was with them in Richmond Park yesterday — about the same time I, I called upon you here."

"Oh, dear," Olivia murmured. "But are you certain?"

"Yes. It would seem Lady Aldworth saw them together as well. And you may imagine how readily she conveyed this disastrous information to Lady Mary. She wasted precious little time in turning her horses the direction of Grosvenor Square."

"I still can't credit that it could be true. Not Jocelyn! On the other hand, she has been so blue-deviled of late. I don't wonder if she has been —" She could not finish the thought.

"— if she has been what?"

"I believe she might have been corresponding with Alfred. You see, he has been her most particular friend for ages!"

"Good God!" he cried, still holding Daphne close and running his free hand through his thick, black hair. "A love match! It can be nothing else. Olivia, why didn't you tell me? Why did you permit her to enter into an engagement with me?"

Olivia felt a blush burn her cheeks. She could not look him squarely in the eye. "Mister Lovell, Alfred's father, would never have permitted the match. He has no objection to Jocelyn's birth and breeding, of course, but as to her lack of fortune, his own estates are in such shambles because of the disastrous crop failures of his tenant farmers in recent years, that he simply couldn't, in good conscience, encourage the children. Poor Alfred has been instructed to get himself an heiress." A certain bitterness rose from her heart and invaded her words. "Why is it, Gregory, that love and a fortune rarely combine to make life a pleasant prospect? Oh, but never mind! I wander from the point and from the concern of your visit. A match between Jocelyn and Alfred was not to be thought of, wholly ineligible on every score —"

"— except that they love one another. I take it you would not have permitted the marriage either."

Olivia swallowed hard, giving her head a quick shake. Lifting her gaze to meet his, her eyes brimming with tears, she felt his disapproval of her attitude and retorted, "You forget that I loved Edward with all my heart. Ours was a love match. But everyday that should have been a joy was dimmed by the oppression of our joint lack of fortune and prospects."

Lord Braunston relented, the intensity of his harried expression softening. "I am being unkind," he said quietly. He glanced down at his daughter whose head was nestled in his shoulder and realized the nature of their discussion was hardly suitable to her tender years. He encouraged her to go in search of Cook, who he was persuaded by the aroma redolent in the town house, had been baking macaroons all morning. Daphne had no resistance to her father's suggestion and with a flip of her muslin skirts, a miniature of the grown-up lady she would one day become, skipped from the drawing room.

When her footsteps had disappeared down the hall, he continued, "The truth is, I am as much to blame. I should never have trusted my grandmama to find me a suitable wife. Had the London seasons not become intolerable to me, and had I not wanted a mother for Daphne so very much, I would have waited until I found the woman my heart longed for."

Braunston drew close to her and sitting down beside her, took her hand. Giving it a gentle squeeze, he said, "I only wish I had met you first. Yet it seems utterly ironic to me that I would never have met you at all save for having sent Grandmama to find me a wife. Good lord, it is all too hopeless to consider. My duty now is to climb aboard my curricle and pursue Mister Lovell and Jocelyn. When I return—"

Olivia pulled her hand away from the earl's tender clasp and covered her face in shame. "She can't have gone to Gretna Green! Not Jocelyn! There must have been some mistake! She would never have dishonored you so completely! Nor me! Never! Daphne must have been mistaken."

At that moment, one of the upper maids appeared in the doorway, a perplexed look in her eye as she extended a letter toward Olivia. "I beg your pardon, ma'am, but I found this on Miss Charing's pillow. I thought it might be of importance and brought it to you directly."

Olivia clasped a hand to her breast and gasped. Braunston was on his feet immediately, crossing the room in several long strides. He took the missive from the maid's now trembling fingers and bid her tell no one of its existence. She bobbed a frightened curtsy and was gone.

When Olivia took the letter from Braunston she quickly broke the wax seal and unfurled the single sheet of paper. The message was wretchedly brief and to the point.

> *Mama, I have gone with Alfred. I shall return as quickly as possible. I am writing this as a precursor to the full confession I mean to make regarding my conduct when next I walk through the doors of our town house. I was not honest with you yesterday — Alfred joined Daphne and me at Richmond Park. Today's excursion is unforgivable, I know, but I cannot help myself especially in light of my wedding on Saturday. Pray do not be angry.*
> *Your wretched but loving daughter, Jocelyn.*

"Pray do not be angry?" Olivia queried. "I am not so much angry as stunned. Oh, Gregory, have I failed so miserably as a mother that my only child should disgrace me so completely."

Braunston slipped an arm about her shoulders and drew her close, comforting her. "Of course you have not failed her, she is simply misguided of the moment. I will find her and we shall resolve this difficulty in a sensible manner. I only wish she had come to me before acting so hastily." He placed a kiss in her hair and began, "I ought to leave at once, particularly with the sky looking so dark and unfriendly, although — "

But he got no further, for at that moment, Lady Mary Braunston, who had entered the town house unbeknownst to Olivia, now stood mute on the threshold. "Merciful heavens!" she exclaimed "So this is how it is! Lady Aldworth and a dozen others told me how it was, and though I had my suspicions — madame, I don't hesitate to inform you that I find your conduct outrageous! And as for you, Braunston, how could you sit there *flirting* with your future mama-in-law when your betrothed was seen not a half-hour past in the company of a red-haired youth. What dreadful bumblebroth has been brewing this past fortnight that I must arrive only to find Mrs. Charing snugly in your arms and Jocelyn apparently engaged in conducting clandestine *tête-à-têtes* with a mere country rustic?

Chapter Seven

Olivia hurriedly retrieved a kerchief from the deep pocket of her gown and soundly blew her nose. She rose quickly to her feet as did the earl. He crossed the chamber and slipping his arm beneath his grandmother's elbow drew her to a chair where he said, "Do not condemn Olivia and as for what you saw, don't be absurd. I was merely comforting her. It would seem Jocelyn has eloped to Gretna Green with Mister Lovell."

Lady Mary sat down and appeared to be in a state of shock. "Gretna Green?" she cried, pressing a hand to her wrinkled cheek. "I don't hesitate to tell you I have never been more astonished in all my life. But are you certain? Of all the females I have ever known, she would be the least likely to behave so very badly. Jocelyn eloping — incredible, nay, impossible! Why, I have never known a young woman to be so high in the instep as she. Do you know last night at Almack's she cleared her throat and nodded to a crumb of cake which had fallen upon my lap. I confess I was dumbfounded and would have been amused had I not found the incident to be quite so irritating. Good heavens, she behaves more like a matron of seventy than a young woman. I cannot credit, therefore, that she has gone to Gretna Green. Are you positively certain?"

"It would seem Jocelyn has been in love with a gentleman by the name of Alfred Lovell for some time — unbeknownst to me."

Lord Braunston handed his grandmama the cryptic missive Jocelyn had left for her mother and agreed that though the specifics of her adventure were left unstated, a misdeed of no small proportions was in the offing. Combining the letter with Daphne's report served to convince her ladyship that an elopement had indeed taken place.

"What do you intend to do?" she queried with a despairing

shake of her head.

"I must go after them. There can be no two opinions on that head. Perhaps you can stay with Olivia and support her while I'm gone."

"Oh, no!" Olivia cried, crossing the room to stand next to him. Placing her hand upon the sleeve of his coat, she gave it a gentle twist of her fingers and said, "I mean no offense to your grandmother, but I intend to go with you. Who will be Jocelyn's chaperone and protect her reputation once you have found her? She will be traveling alone with two men and I cannot conceive of a worse scandal than that!"

Both Lady Mary and Lord Braunston protested vehemently, but Olivia remained steadfast. When five minutes had passed, she straightened her shoulders and cried, "She is my daughter, and I will go with you!"

Lord Braunston finally capitulated, saying, "If we leave immediately, we shall be able to overtake them before we reach the fourth posting house. A sluggish pair of post-horses will be no match for my bays!"

Olivia needed no further encouragement and literally ran from the room to her bedchamber where she gathered up a warm traveling cloak, a bonnet, a pair of gloves and serviceable half boots of orange kid. Without taking the time to change into her boots, she flew down the stairs. With Lady Mary left to take charge of Daphne, a few minutes more and they were gone.

"One more macaroon, please, Grandma-great!" Daphne cried beseechingly, wiping away crumbs from the front of her muslin gown.

"No," Lady Mary said, shaking her head when she saw that Cook held up no fewer than four fingers behind Daphne's back in reference to the number of biscuits the child had already consumed. "You've had your fill. And now we must go."

"But where is Papa?"

"He left with Mrs. Charing. They had an errand to attend to and you are to come home with me."

"Are they going to the park to get some fresh milk like Mister Alfred and Miss Charing?"

Lady Mary's thoughts were drifting far from the child as she walked up the stairs from the kitchen to the first floor of the town house. "No, they are not. Besides, Mister Alfred and Jocelyn did not go to get some milk. They decided to take a journey into the country and your papa and Mrs. Charing have gone to join them. I expect they will return by evening."

"Could we go to the park, then? I should like to see the cows though I don't think I want to drink the milk again. It was warm!"

Lady Mary turned to glance down at her great granddaughter. "See the cows?" she queried, her attention now riveted to Daphne. "Whatever are you rattling on about? And what do you mean Mister Alfred and Jocelyn went to get some milk?"

"Yes, to Gretna Park to see the cows and get some milk, like Papa and I did the day we first met my new grandmama."

"Gretna Park?" Lady Mary queried. "You mean Green Park, don't you?"

"Yes, Gretna Green Park, the one Mister Alfred and Miss Charing went to."

Lady Mary felt a severe palpitation disturb the ordinarily stead rhythm of her heart. "Oh, dear!" she cried. "Daphne, did you tell your papa, *Gretna Green Park?*"

"I don't know. I suppose I did. At least I know I said Gretna Green. Isn't that right, Grandma-great?"

"No, dear. In fact, in this particular instance, I believe it is very, very wrong."

"Will Papa be angry with me then?"

"I'm afraid so," she responded quietly. She considered what next she ought to do. Her first instinct was to send one of the footmen racing after her grandson, but just as she reached the entrance hall and was preparing to issue the command to Olivia's butler, the words did not find their way to her lips.

They will discover their error soon enough, she thought, when they find no trace of either Alfred or Jocelyn along the road.

As she quit the town house and walked onto the flagway, she knew a curious sensation, very much like guilt. She knew she was conspiring with Fate. Looking up into the rain-laden clouds, she bid them drench her grandson and Olivia, trusting that they might become bogged down somewhere for an hour or two, or if Braunston was very fortunate, the entire night!

Merciful heavens, what a scandalous thought! But when she

had first stood upon the threshold of Olivia's drawing room and had seen the gentle, quite affectionate manner in which her grandson *comforted* Mrs. Charing, her eyes had been opened to a truth she had been denying from the first. There had been just such an ease between Braunston and Olivia, such as she herself had known with her own dear Everard so many years ago, which could only be construed as love. Only why hadn't she seen it before!

Lady Mary remembered the gossip which had been related to her by Lady Jersey that Braunston had practically forced a reluctant Mrs. Charing to waltz with him. He had become quite insistent, as it happened. Furthermore, Olivia had spoken scandalous words to the earl before finally agreeing to dance with him, something about the sun rising with him.

"Oh, dear—"

Daphne pulled at her great grandmother's hand and when Lady Mary turned to look at her she saw that the young girl was deeply distressed, large tears brimming in her eyes. "Have I been very bad?" Daphne asked. "I didn't mean to be."

Lady Mary smiled at her and gave her hand a squeeze. "No, my child. In fact, somehow I wonder if your little mistake has not been a very good thing. Now tell me of Mister Alfred. Was he kind to Jocelyn?"

"I suppose so, though he did seem to correct her all the time but she never once put her finger in her mouth like she does when Papa is around."

"I see. Was he happy to meet Jocelyn in the park?"

"First he looked happy, then I think he was rather angry that she had asked him to meet him at Richmond Park, then he looked happy again, until she begged him to meet her at Green Park. He told her it would be the very last time he would ever see her."

"Well, never mind. Oh, look, it is raining! How—how unfortunate!"

"Papa will get very wet, and Grandmama, too."

"I know, poor things! Well, never mind that. Your father is old enough to take care of himself and Mrs. Charing, too. Now, into the coach with you.

Chapter Eight

Before Braunston and Olivia reached the outskirts of London, it became necessary to exchange the earl's curricle for a post-chaise and four. Olivia ran into the taproom of the coaching inn, escaping the steady spring rain, while Gregory made arrangements with the hostler for a more comfortable coach.

Shaking off the drops which had collected on her cherry red cape, Olivia pressed a concerned landlord for information regarding Alfred and Jocelyn. The rotund, frowning man—a father himself of several hopeful children—relayed unhappy news, for not an hour earlier just such a young gentleman and lady as she described had hired a post-chaise and pair.

"Do you recall their destination?" Olivia queried, as the landlord hung her cape on a peg by the door. "Did it seem they would be traveling a considerable distance."

"Aye, that they did. Spoke of going north. She were quite lovely, innocent and shy gazing up at him with youthful admiration gleaming in her blue eyes as she did."

"Did you say her eyes were blue?" she asked hopefully.

"Aye."

"But Jocelyn's eyes are a striking green. Tell me, are you certain they were blue?"

He shook his head. "Nay. 'Twas possible they were green, I suppose. The lighting in this inn isn't at all as revealing as the sun outside. I could be mistaken."

For the barest moment Olivia had permitted herself to hope that perhaps the landlord had erred. But as she glanced about her, she realized that the rather cloudy diamond-paned windows, shaded by half-drawn shutters, were not at all conducive to discerning the color of anyone's eyes, nonetheless those of a shy young lady eloping to Gretna Green.

When Braunston heard all that she had learned from the landlord, he shook his head. "At least they're only an hour beyond our reach. With a little good fortune we shall overtake them well before nightfall since the hostler has agreed to part with his best rider who he recommended to me as a man quite eager to *spring 'em!*"

The postilion did just that but after a mere twenty minutes on the road, the post-chaise struck a rut and lost a wheel two miles past a small village.

With the rain still afflicting their journey, Olivia sat within the awkward confines of the tilting carriage while Braunston and the post-boy wrestled with the errant wheel. She sat half reclining on the seat and was jostled by every rough movement of the men as they struggled to make a temporary repair. All the while the rain beat in a monotonous pattern on the roof of the vehicle until she thought she would go mad.

An hour later with the damaged wheel partly restored to the post-chaise, the entire equipage limped to the next village where a replacement was sought along with dry clothes for the earl and the postilion. Olivia's spirits were revived by two strong cups of hot tea, but her nerves became chafed sorely by the necessity of waiting.

Time had become her enemy.

Every minute spent motionless, whether repairing the wheel, drinking tea, or exchanging one's wet clothes for dry raiment, took Jocelyn further out of reach. And if Olivia did not find her daughter tonight, and bring her safely back to the shelter of her motherly protection, her reputation would be damaged forever. A scandal of horrendous proportions would ensue, afflicting Jocelyn and her progeny for the remainder of her days, nonetheless plunging poor Lady Mary into social exile as well.

If once or twice the considerably ignoble thought crossed her mind that given her sentiments for Braunston and his for her, they ought to simply permit the lovers to make their journey to Gretna Green, she quickly chided herself for even giving shape to so selfish a notion. Besides, Jocelyn simply couldn't marry Alfred, she couldn't! She would permit no daughter of hers to suffer as she had.

Two complete hours passed before the post-chaise resumed its trek north. The postilion rode the lead horse hard, water dripping from the brim of his hat as mile after mile passed beneath the pounding of the horses's hooves. At every stop along the Great North Road, Olivia was able to find news of Jocelyn and Alfred. But it proved to be small consolation as night fell, the dark road becoming impossible to travel in the rain.

When they sought shelter in a small hamlet, Olivia found herself nearly beyond exhaustion. She had never been one to travel well and the exigencies of following a couple apparently intent upon reaching the Scottish border in excellent time, left her feeling that every muscle in her body had been bruised and every joint torn asunder.

Lord Braunston bespoke rooms for the night and a private parlor for dinner. The appearance of a repast of pigeon tarts, boiled beef, and cold breast of chicken did little more than cause Olivia to push her fork about her plate in an absent manner.

"You appear fagged to death, my dear," he said gently. "I knew you should have remained at home."

Olivia looked up from her plate and blinked twice at the earl. He had spoken sympathetically, but his words served as a welcome reproof. She sat straighter in her chair and after telling him she was only mildly fatigued from the journey, set about eating everything before her.

He laughed at her once or twice, telling her she needn't prove herself to him, but the entire incident served to restore her strength. When the rain stopped, she suggested the possibility of continuing on but he insisted it was impossible.

"The clouds are low about the countryside and there is no light for the road. We lost a wheel once already, I daren't risk more. It was bad enough breaking down during daylight, but what would we do at night? No, it will not serve!"

Olivia felt her throat constrict. She was completely sick at heart at the very thought that her darling daughter, without benefit of matrimony, would actually spend the night with a man at some nameless inn on the road to Gretna Green. Before she knew what was happening, two tears rolled down her cheeks. She wiped them away quickly, apologizing for becoming a watering pot.

Lord Braunston, seeing Olivia's unhappiness, begged her to impart her thoughts to him. She did not hesitate to tell him the whole, at which time he drew her to a settle near the fire and begging her to sit beside him, held her close, comforting her as he had earlier.

"You are very kind," she said at last, drying the tears which had continued to seep silently from her eyes.

"I'm not kind at all," he said quietly, squeezing her gently as she laid her head upon his shoulder.

"What nonsense is this?" she queried with a watery laugh. She drew back from him slightly, just far enough away to look into his eyes.

"Is it kindness," he asked, "to be listening to the concerns of the woman I love, when I ought to be traveling all night in order to discover the whereabouts of the miscreants? No, it is pure selfishness. I have lost my heart for pursuit. I want only to be close to you and for the past two hours have thought of nothing more than kissing you again. I am not kind, I am utterly wicked."

"Then I am just as wicked," Olivia whispered.

"My darling," he returned. "What a hopeless pair we are." His lips were quickly upon hers as he slipped his arms firmly around her waist and pulled her close. "I love you," he said between kisses, his lips wandering over her every feature, hungrily. "I love you to the point of madness."

Olivia submitted to his tender assault until guilt rose hotly in her mind. Suddenly she pushed him away and gained her feet. "I cannot!" she cried. "Oh, my poor, unhappy Jocelyn. Whatever are we to do?"

With that she ran from the parlor.

Lord Braunston remained for only a numb moment by the settle. His thoughts and therefore his actions became swift and sure. He knew precisely what he needed to do. Feeling it useless to discuss the matter with Olivia since an argument would undoubtedly ensue, he scribbled a hasty missive and bid the astonished landlord see that she received it in the morning.

He eyed him warily as he took the folded sheet of paper and with his cheeks beginning to flame with indignation, exclaimed, "I won't 'ave a lady without even a proper maid with her spending the night with you takin' off without so much as a by your leave. I seen the lady run up the stairs and she weren't none too 'appy."

Lord Braunston comprehended the man's concerns instantly and allayed the landlord's fears by producing three sovereigns and pressing them firmly into his palm.

"A bit havey-cavey, if you ask me. And when was you thinking to be back?" the landlord asked, his expression impudent.

Lord Braunston restrained his mounting temper with only the greatest of efforts. "I'll have none of your impertinence, my good man," he returned coldly. "And if Mrs. Charing has been treated with even the smallest mite of contempt while I am gone, I'll see that your establishment is burnt to the ground. Do you understand me?"

The landlord seemed considerably taken aback. "Yes, sir," he responded, his broad cheeks paling. "I only meant —"

"I know what you meant. I shall return sometime tomorrow, so take care that the lady's every needs are attended to."

"Yes, sir. Of course, sir. Very good, sir."

With that Braunston moved into the cool night air and making his way to the stables, roused the inn's hostler from his slumbers and hired a gig with two extra carriage lamps, a pair of sturdy horses and was gone.

A half-hour past midnight, Lord Braunston pounded upon Mr. Lovell's door. When the landlord had told him that the young man fitting his description was posing as a mere Mr. Smythe, a fury as none he had ever known filled him. How could Jocelyn and this *Alfred Lovell* fellow have been so inconsiderate of Olivia's feelings to have eloped. He wanted only to grasp Mr. Lovell's shirt firmly in one hand and with the other, to draw his cork, to satisfy the rage which now flowed in every vein!

When Mr. Lovell opened the door, blinking his eyes at the sight of the candle held high to his face, Lord Braunston withheld his temper only with the severest of efforts. He immediately pushed past him and scanned the bed, but there was no one else to be found beneath the bed covers nor even the appearance that the young man had been sharing his bed at all.

"Where is Miss Charing?" he cried, wheeling on *Mr. Smythe*.

But when *Alfred* pulled his cap from his head, revealing the accusing shock of red hair, only then did Braunston examine the young man's face. He could remember very well the man on horseback at Hyde Park who Jocelyn had later referred to as Alfred Lovell.

And this was not that man!

"Good God!" the earl cried. "Who the devil are you?"

The young man responded unequally, "I — I don't know, sir, I mean that is to say, I know who I am but who is it you suppose I am and what is worse, who did you expect to find in my bed? The er, unfortunate Miss Charing, I presume?"

Lord Braunston did not answer his question, but took a step forward holding the candle higher and letting a little more of the dim yellow light flood the boy's face. "You are not Alfred Lovell, are you?"

"No. George Smythe of Lincolnshire, more lately of London where I had recently gone to fetch my sister from Miss Plimpton's Select Seminary for Young Ladies. She is in the adjoining chamber." He gestured to the doorway to his right.

"Is she rather diminutive in stature and does she have blond hair in stark contrast to your red hair?"

"Yes."

"And is she very pretty?"

Mr. Smythe smiled crookedly, pride beaming in his eyes. "Every buck within a ten-mile radius of our home is anxiously awaiting her return."

"Oh, good lord in heaven," the earl breathed, lowering his candle, at last realizing he and Olivia had been chasing a phantom. "I beg your pardon," he said, bowing formally. "I have erred greatly and you've been most patient. You may return to your bed, I promise I shan't disturb you further."

"Good night, then, Lord Braunston."

The earl was surprised that Mr. Smythe knew who he was, but the young man smiled broadly and said, "I had you pointed out to me once at Hyde Park. My good friend, Captain Silsoe of the Horse Guards, directed me to examine the exquisite folds of your neckcloth."

On impulse, Braunston withdrew his card form the pocket of his waistcoat and presented it to young Mr. Smythe. "When you are next in London, pray call upon me and if there is any service which I can render you, I vow upon my word as a gentleman it shall be done."

"Sir!" Mr. Smythe exclaimed, but handed the card back to him. "I intended not to solicit your benevolence by telling you I know of you. It is too much."

"It is hardly enough. I can think of few less wretched occurrences in the course of traveling, particularly when escorting one's sister home, than to have one's sleep disturbed. Pray, keep my card and make use of it at your least whim."

Mr. Smythe hesitated, but only for a moment as he looked down at the card. A conscious expression overtook his face as a slight frown formed between thick, red brows. "There is one matter, if it would not be too inconvenient—"

"—you have but to name it."

The young gentleman laughed, his cheeks suddenly rosy with embarrassment. "Well," he began enthusiastically, "had I a fortune I would give it all to go just one round with Jackson." He lifted a glowing face to the earl.

Braunston let out a crack of laughter, "Done, you silly cub. Present this card to Mister Jackson with my compliments. He will honor your request." He then clapped Mr. Smythe on the shoulder and bid him good night.

As he passed through the doorway the young gentleman laughingly said, "You may disturb my slumbers any night, my lord."

The earl smiled in return. "Go back to bed, jackanapes!"

Chapter Nine

"So it is all settled, then?" Olivia asked, stunned, her heart feeling strangely battered. She was standing near the fireplace in Lady Mary's drawing room, her cloak still draped about her shoulders, the cherry red of the fabric in marked contrast to the blue silk damask of the walls and furniture. She and Braunston had literally raced across Mayfair having learned from her butler in Brook Street that both Jocelyn and Alfred were currently paying a morning visit upon the dowager. Lady Mary had sent word to Olivia's butler that she was expected to call upon her immediately after her arrival in London.

"Yes, Olivia," Lady Mary responded. "There apparently will be no repercussions to your, er, *adventure*. No one is the wiser and the story I have circulated that you were called from town to visit your very ill relation—an infirmed aunt—just outside of London, seems to have satisfied those few who dared broach the subject in the first place. To my knowledge, no one saw you on the road together, so there we are—Jocelyn admits to having erred in meeting clandestinely with Alfred, for his part, Alfred has agreed to stay in London in order to present a proper appearance, and the wedding will take place as scheduled."

Olivia glanced at Jocelyn and saw the deep anguish wrinkling her young, pretty features. She watched the silly, wretched finger rising from off her daughter's morning gown of pink cambric to slip absently just past her lips.

She is little more than a child, Olivia thought. She looked back at Braunston and saw that he was watching her with a stubborn glint in his eye. She was not surprised by his expression, she knew precisely what he meant by it.

"Then I am content," Olivia returned dully, feeling numb with shock. She had never expected this. She had fully expected that after having passed a scandalous day and a night in the company of a man who was not her husband, not only would her reputation have been ruined, but the wedding would not have been allowed to take place. When she first heard Lady Mary state in her strangely flat manner that she had arranged everything to a nicety and that no real harm had been done by the misunderstanding Daphne's words had created, she had felt the strongest desire to scream. Somewhere in the hopeful recesses of her womanly mind — so completely at odds in this moment with her every motherly instinct — she had believed Fate had so disturbed the wretched course of Jocelyn's betrothal to Braunston that Lady Mary would find it necessary to bear the brunt of society's disapproval and abort the unhappy nuptials.

But no such happy Fate, if so it could be termed, had presented itself. Instead, Lady Mary had used all her abilities to maintain a discreet appearance before the world until her grandson and Olivia could discover their mistake and return to London. There was nothing for it then — Jocelyn would marry Braunston on Saturday, three days hence.

"Come, Jocelyn," Olivia said quietly. "We should return to Brook Street." She avoided looking at the earl as she thanked Lady Mary for all her efforts in averting a scandal.

"Should I accompany you, Mrs. Charing?" Alfred queried, rising to his feet and appearing nonplussed.

Lady Mary had suggested that Alfred remain in London at present that he might attend the wedding. It would seem several members of the interested *haut ton* had seen the interesting couple — albeit with Jocelyn's maid in tow — at Green Park and the usual drift of gossip had resulted. His continued presence as an accepted friend of the Charings was a requisite to forestalling further unflattering rumors.

"Yes, if you please," Olivia responded. "You may escort us home and then return to your hotel." Alfred acquiesced with a polite bow.

When Olivia had made her curtsy to Lady Mary, along with Jocelyn, she moved toward the door where the earl had remained during the course of the entire interview. He did not look at her, but stood very straight, his jaw working strongly.

She could see he was angry with her.

Earlier, when he had returned to the inn after his night's escapade, he had presented two possibilities to her — either that circumstances might forbid his marrying Jocelyn once it became known he had been with Olivia overnight or that should it happen no scandal resulted from their absurd flight north, then Olivia must end the engagement between himself and Jocelyn as quickly as possible. Only she had the power to take such a step since he was bound as a man of honor to the documents he had already signed. He would ruin himself and his family by jilting her daughter, a course not to be thought of.

But Olivia had winced at the suggestion for reasons Braunston had been unable to comprehend. She knew he had fully expected her to joyfully agree to his suggestion but when she tried to explain the depths of her maternal feelings where Jocelyn's future was concerned, that she simply could not disrupt the advantageous betrothal, he had been dumbfounded.

She had withdrawn her hands from his intense clasp, refusing to discuss the matter further. Turning away from him with a pained apology on her lips, she had seen the expression of shock strike his face almost as surely as if she had used her hand. As long as she lived she would never be able to forget the hurt she had caused him.

Still, she remained steadfast.

The truth was, if she ended her daughter's engagement, Jocelyn was likely to insist upon becoming betrothed to Alfred — and that she could never permit. Why couldn't Braunston understand she could never allow her daughter to marry Alfred Lovell? She hadn't told him as much but she thought it likely he discerned her thoughts since they had scarcely spoken the entire return trip to London.

Now, as she passed into the hallway, she was surprised that Braunston followed after her. When he took her forcibly by the arm she looked up at him, wondering what he meant by it. He asked Jocelyn to permit him a moment's private speech with her mother, gesturing for her — and Alfred — to descend the stairs, if she wouldn't mind terribly much. "I will keep her only a few minutes, I promise you," he assured them.

Jocelyn stumbled over her words, begging him to speak with her mama as long as he wished. She then turned to hurry down the stairs where she said she and Alfred would await her mother.

Olivia wanted to ask Braunston what he meant by forcing her in this manner, but he was before her, turning her bodily to look at him and staring down at her with his blue eyes sharp with reproof. "Was I so mistaken in you?" he queried, in a harsh whisper, unwilling for either Jocelyn or Alfred to hear him.

Olivia was completely taken aback. "Whatever do you mean?" she whispered in return. "And why do you look at me as though I have done some great evil?"

"Because you have!" he cried. "You and you alone have it in your power to end this absurd charade. Instead, I fear you mean to see it through? Do you really want Jocelyn to become my wife?"

Olivia tried to avert her gaze, but he forbade her by taking her chin in his hand and forcing her to look at him. "Don't turn away," he commanded. "Answer me from your heart."

Swallowing hard, Olivia breathed, "Of course I don't."

"Then what is it? Why don't you spare us all? Why are you being so deucedly stubborn? Are you as all the other Match-making Mamas I have known, wanting desperately for a handle to your daughter's name? But that won't fadge. Any of those ladies would have been happier to have had the title for themselves — which I would gladly bestow upon you if you would but gather your wits about you — yet you have not wanted the title for yourself. What is it, Livvy? Why is your chin so set against ending this?"

She couldn't speak the words. Even though she felt them in her heart, somehow she knew that saying them aloud would diminish her in his eyes. She remained mute, merely staring back into his startling, blue eyes, begging him to understand. He searched her gaze and queried softly, "Does Jocelyn know that you love me?"

Olivia shook her head, tears starting to form in her eyes.

"It would make no difference if she did, would it?" he asked. Again she shook her head.

"She will be obedient to the end, you know she will, to both you and Alfred. Alfred wants her to marry me also, doesn't he?"

Olivia nodded as tears began to run freely down her cheeks.

210

"For God's sake, what is it then? What could be better than your wedding me, and Jocelyn marrying the man she loves? Why must she marry me when she obviously doesn't want to! My word, Olivia, even now she is sucking her finger! Why do you hold her to this!"

The earl seemed harried beyond measure, his temper rising, a flush of pure frustration covering his cheeks. He looked down at Alfred and Jocelyn. Alfred stood apart from the woman he loved, his stoic gaze fixed steadfastly ahead as though he were preparing himself to face the future inexorably alone. He was a highly responsible young man, and the earl had learned from his grandmother that the reason he had told the landlord at his hotel that he was heading north was because he meant to pay a visit upon Coke of Norfolk. His respect for the boy had risen sharply upon learning of his desire to restore to prosperity the land he would one day inherit. As a man he knew that Alfred's future was secure because Alfred would make it so.

He looked back at Olivia who was now dabbing at her cheeks with her kerchief and blowing her nose. With startling clarity he came to understand her resolve to see the wedding through to the end, that Olivia's primary and sole concern in this circumstance was, and had always been, her daughter's comfort and security.

He drew in a sharp breath and at last released her arm. "I understand now," he said more kindly than before. "But you are wrong. You are wrong about Alfred and you are equally wrong about Jocelyn and what she needs. She is not you, Olivia. And if I am not mistaken, she would not suffer quite so badly as you have given the same circumstances. But beyond that, Alfred will care well for her, better, I fear, than Edward was able to care for you. Besides, didn't you once tell me Edward was content with his lot?"

"Yes," she responded, still drying her eyes. "And it wasn't just that he was being brave, I believe he was truly happy and used to laugh at me when I would save every tuppence from my housekeeping funds to purchase fine fabrics for Jocelyn's gowns."

"Did Jocelyn value these *furbelows* as you did? Truthfully, now."

"Probably not nearly as much as I did."

"She is her father's daughter," he said. "And you are being

211

inordinately selfish in forcing her down this path."

"Selfish?" Olivia cried, greatly shocked.

"Why does that surprise you? Whose feelings are being considered in this situation — yours or Jocelyn's?"

Olivia opened her mouth in surprise, words failing her. Finally, she said, "I — I had never thought of it in that manner before. It would seem that I am quite flawed."

"I could more easily forgive you this one flaw if it had not been so unrelentingly combined with another more insidious defect."

Olivia blinked at the earl and in a cool voice queried, "And what is that, pray tell."

Lord Braunston smiled, "Only that you are one of the most stubborn females I have ever known."

"I? Stubborn?" she cried, again shocked. "How do you mean?"

"I'll admit you have the appearance of gentleness and meekness, but I have come to believe there can be as much stubbornness in a female who persistently, but *gently,* presses those about her to behave as they ought as one who screams and cries and succumbs to fits of hysterics."

Olivia could not help but smile sheepishly. He had the right of it and she knew it. All along, she had doubted her wisdom in having *pressed* Jocelyn so tirelessly as she had. She looked down at her daughter and felt her heart twist within her breast.

"Jocelyn," she called to her, placing her hand on the smooth oak banister.

"Yes, Mama?" Jocelyn said, taking a hopeful step forward.

Olivia began descending the stairs. "How would you feel if you were forced to endure the next ten years as you had the last eighteen? Think for a moment before you speak — I want an honest response."

Jocelyn cocked her head and queried, "I don't take your meaning precisely."

"We have not had an easy existence all these years, you and I. Would it distress you to continue to live as you and I have lived?"

"You speak in relative terms, don't you? I mean, there were so many less fortunate than we that I never gave it a moment's thought. I realize the Misses Hargraves and other young ladies wore new ball dresses at every assembly, but I didn't give a fig for that. I have been very content in our little cottage. I have needed little more than the friendships I treasure"—here she glanced shyly up at Alfred and smiled—"and was happiest when I could ease the sufferings of the poor in our neighborhood."

"You weren't *unhappy* then?"

"Of course not! You loved me so well! And though I know you made sacrifices, I did try to tell you how silly they were, like the time you had that amethyst-colored gown made up for me when you still wore your ball dress from five years earlier. To own the truth, I think it was you who suffered. You have such a lively disposition, Mama, and a real love for finery and a manner of frippery which I do not. Alfred says I am very much like my father. It was you who always seemed to kick up a dust about things which never seemed very important to me."

Tears again brimmed in Olivia's eyes as she reached the bottom of the stairs and gathered her daughter into her arms. "You don't wish to marry Lord Braunston, do you?"

Jocelyn didn't answer her for a moment. When she did, Olivia could feel that a sob had caught in her throat. "I will marry him, if you wish me to, mama."

"You darling girl," Olivia whispered. Setting her gently away from her, she looked her straight in the eye and said, "Will you forgive me for loving you too much?"

Jocelyn's lips quivered. "Does this mean I don't have to marry Braunston?"

Olivia smiled through a haze of tears. "That's right. You do not have to marry Braunston." She watched her daughter sigh heavily with what she could determine was nothing less than profound relief.

Extending one hand to Alfred and the other to Jocelyn, Olivia directed her question to Alfred, whose cheeks had become quite flushed. "Do you wish to marry my daughter?"

"Mrs. Charing!" Alfred cried, hope burning brightly in his blue eyes. "It is not to be thought of."

"It is very much to be thought of, Alfred. Only tell me this, do you wish to marry my daughter?"

"Of course I do."

"Then that is all I need to know. When we return to Old Turvey, I shall speak with your father and we shall see what can be arranged. For now, please accept my apologies for having been such a ninnyhammer. If I hadn't been thinking only of my own wishes for Jocelyn, just as your father has had primarily his own particular concerns at heart all these years, none of us would be standing here right now."

Jocelyn drew close to Alfred. Appearing very grown-up, she said, "But, Mama, had I not accepted Lord Braunston's offer, you might never have made his acquaintance and that I think would have been almost as great a tragedy as my having wed him."

Jocelyn looked at Braunston, who had by now joined Olivia at the bottom of the stairs, and with a smile of embarrassment on her lips, said sweetly, "I regret to inform you, my lord, that our betrothal is now at an end. Also, it has been brought to my notice, during these past few minutes—and by several hints your grandmama let drop not an hour past—that you are very much in love with my mother. I look forward very soon, then, to being able to call you *Papa*."

Lord Braunston moved past Olivia and for the first time in his acquaintance with Jocelyn, embraced her. She hugged him soundly in return, the restraint which characterized their relationship of the past three weeks, disappearing entirely.

"Hallo, Grandmama," a small voice called out.

The next moment, Olivia felt her knees buckle as Daphne bounded into her and grasped her knees from behind just as she had that first day in the park.

"Daphne, my little darling," Olivia cried, whirling around and dropping to her knees to gather the child up in her arms. Daphne giggled, her sweet embrace a promise of the future.

Lord Braunston stooped down beside Olivia and petting his daughter's red curls, said, "Would you mind terribly if Mrs. Charing were to become your mama instead of your grandmama?"

"Miss Charing is not to be my mother?" Daphne asked, her eyes wide with wonder.

"I'm afraid not," Jocelyn interjected quickly. "But if my mother marries your father, then you and I shall be sisters!"

"We would?" Daphne cried. "Would we all live in the same house and swim in the same pond?"

"For a time," Jocelyn said, glancing back at Alfred and taking his arm gently in hers.

Lady Mary's voice boomed down the stairwell. "Olivia!" she

cried. "Have you finally settled this absurd business?"

Olivia rose to her feet and slipped her arm through Braunston's. "Yes, ma'am," she called up to her. "I believe I have if you don't mind a slight alteration in the wedding plans."

"Grandma-great!" Daphne cried. "Everything is changed. Mrs. Charing is to be my new mama."

"At last." Lady Mary sighed, descending the stairs slowly, her knotted fingers grasping the banister with the necessary care of age. "I don't like to mention it, but for a moment there I feared you actually meant to permit Jocelyn to marry my grandson."

Olivia was surprised. "But you said nothing to me and when I saw that all had been as before, I supposed you meant—"

"—I only wanted you to come to the decision yourself."

"You were right to do so."

Reaching the last step of the stairs, Lady Mary held out her arms to Olivia and embraced her gently, placing a kiss on her cheek. "I know now that Gregory will be very happy. You are exceedingly well suited, you know, almost as much as Alfred and Jocelyn. Now, let me think. We have three days in which to set everything to rights and to inform the guests that you will be the bride instead of your daughter."

"Ma'am!" Olivia cried, greatly astonished, "you cannot be serious! You cannot imagine that I would even consider walking down the aisle in place of Jocelyn?"

"Whyever not?" Lady Mary responded, "especially since, to my knowledge, the entire *beau monde* has been considering it a likelihood this past sennight and more. You have hardly been discreet—the pair of you, what with Braunston kissing you whenever he is able and you, Olivia, speaking of *the sun rising* in front of Sally Jersey, no less. Goodness gracious, have you no sense at all?"

"No, ma'am, I am convinced I do not, so I will most gratefully leave all to you."

"Now that is the first reasonable thing you have said since I first made your acquaintance. Will you then stay for dinner? Or perhaps we should all simply clamber aboard my barouche and travel to Green Park, where, I understand we can each partake of a glass of milk."

The dryness of her tone was lost on no one.

When a general round of laughter ensued, she then bid the

215

company return to her drawing room where they might at their leisure work out the more delicate aspects of what had not precisely been a blissful betrothal.

Daphne took her great grandmother's hand, falling into step beside her. As they began mounting the stairs, she said, "I don't like drinking milk from cows—it's too warm. I like it from Cook's pitcher with two or three macaroons . . ."

Olivia encouraged Jocelyn and Alfred to follow behind Lady Mary. She had intended to trail after them, but Lord Braunston held her back. "All's well that ends well?" he queried.

"Very much so," she breathed. When he took the opportunity, while everyone had their backs turned to them, of taking her yet again in his arms and kissing her, she was unable to say more. Somewhere in the back of her mind, she knew she ought not to permit Braunston to kiss her, but it seemed as always the moment his lips touched hers, all proper intent deserted her.

"I have never seen anything so shocking," Jocelyn exclaimed in a disapproving whisper as she gained the landing and discovered her mother in the earl's arms.

"Hardly a proper example for Daphne," Alfred returned with a severe shake of his head. "You ought to speak to your mother, Jocelyn. This will not do."

"You're quite right, and I shall do so as soon as we return to Brook Street."

Lady Mary however also glanced back at the scandalous sight of her grandson holding Olivia in his arms and murmured, "I can only say I am grateful the wedding is to take place in three days. Indeed, I am."

"Grandma-great," Daphne whispered. "Why is Papa biting Mrs. Charing?"

"I'll tell you when you're older, child, when you're about seventeen."

Daphne moaned in disappointment. "But you already said that the time I saw Jack biting one of the upstairs maids. If Jack was biting her, why didn't she cry? Besides, I don't think he was biting her at all. I think you made that up. My friend Mary said he was kissing her. And what about the time . . ."

Olivia finally drew away from Braunston and with a teasing smile and a laugh catching in her throat, said, "I wish you would stop *biting* me, Gregory! Really, it is too much."

"It is hardly enough," Lord Braunston returned. And as the rest of the family disappeared into the drawing room, he again assaulted his bride-to-be.

Again, Olivia failed to protest. She was far too happy, and too greatly relieved to do little more than murmur sounds of encouragement as Braunston tenderly kissed her again.

Gifts of The Heart

by Mary Kingsley

Chapter One

Robert Evans, the Marquess of Stowe, glanced out the window of the traveling carriage and then reached up to grasp the strap, bracing himself for the sharp downhill turn into the drive. Stowcroft, at last. It had been a long, weary trip from London to Devon, though the roads were in good shape and the weather was fine. His own impatience was what had made the trip so long. Never had Robert wished so much to be home. Never had he needed it quite so much.

The carriage swept past the lodge, where the gatekeeper rushed out, tugging at his forelock. Beside him his wife, still wiping her hands on her apron, dropped into a hasty curtsy. News of Robert's homecoming hadn't reached here, then, though he hadn't really expected it to. He had made his decision to return too quickly to send a letter ahead. Eliza would be surprised to see him. Surprised, and glad? Lord, he hoped so. He found himself leaning forward, as if to hurry the carriage along. He needed to see Eliza again. He needed to confirm, despite the hint in his sister's last letter, that she was well. Eliza was, quite simply, all he had.

He knew it didn't seem that way to the outside world. His pedigree was long and his estates, if not vast, healthy. He took his seat in Parliament every year and enjoyed a position of influence in the Whig party. He would have been a supremely happy man, had Eliza ever bothered to come to London with him. Instead, she chose to stay behind at Stowcroft with their children, whom she claimed needed her more than he. It was an old argument, one he no longer fought, though now that Laura, their youngest, was nine, he hoped things would change. He was tired of living away from his wife.

The carriage dipped into a sun-dappled glade, the wheels rumbling briefly over the planks of a bridge, and then emerged again into sunlight. Before him was the house, a comfortable Elizabe-

221

than manor of gray stone, set on a plateau of emerald green turf that led to a cliff. Beyond was the shining sea, sparkling in the sun. He was home.

As the carriage drew up under the portico, a footman raced to open the door for him. Robert descended and strode into the house, past a startled-looking Shannon, the butler, and the curtsying maids. "Welcome home, me lord." Shannon followed after him, grinning. Hiring him had been Eliza's notion, a butler who performed his duties impeccably, but with the Irish tendency toward song and irreverence. Robert still wasn't quite accustomed to him, after ten years. "And fine it is to have ye here, me lord. Will ye be wanting refreshment? Or will ye be going to your rooms to bathe?"

"Neither," Robert said crisply, thrusting both hat and stick at him. "Where is Lady Stowe?"

"Why, in the garden, me lord. Where else would she be?" Surprise showed for a moment in the bright blue eyes, and then something else, an expression Robert couldn't identify. "Sure, and glad she'll be to see ye. She's—"

"Thank you, Shannon," Robert said, cutting him off, and turned away. He was never certain whether to upbraid the man for his impudence, or to return his cheerful smile. This house was certainly run differently than it had been in his parents' day, a fact which his mother, on her infrequent visits, lamented. Robert liked the informality, even if it did sometimes make him uncomfortable.

From hall to antechamber to drawing room Robert strode, again looking neither to right nor left and so ignoring the rare Grinling Gibbons carvings in the hall and the exquisite Adam mantelpiece in the drawing room. The quickest way out to the garden was by the French windows that opened off the drawing room. So intent was he on his destination that he didn't notice the figures gathered on the terrace, until he heard voices. "Father!" someone gasped, and he turned, startled, to see his daughters with their governess.

Good lord, they had grown. Though he had just seen them at Christmastime, both girls seemed to have added inches to their heights. In addition Delia, the oldest of his children at fourteen, no longer had the shape of a little girl. The thought gave him a pang. "Delia. Laura." Smiling, he walked toward them. They continued to stare at him, their eyes wide and startled, and then dropped into curtsies. Something twisted inside Robert. In the past Laura had always run to him, to be hugged and to tell him all her news. Now she, like her sister, was holding back. "Have you been behaving yourselves?"

Delia's eyes were downcast. "Yes, Father."

Damn, he hadn't meant to say such a thing. "You've grown."

"Yes, Father."

"Papa." Laura, no longer able to contain herself, danced about in front of him. "My garden is ever so much bigger this year, and the carrot tops are showing already!" She threw herself at him, and he gathered the small body close, some of his tension dissipating. "Everything's growing! Want to come and see?"

"Not just now, muffin." He smiled down at her, to take the sting out of his refusal, and was rewarded with a blazing smile of her own. "Perhaps later. I need to see your mother. Where is she, do you know?"

"In the rose garden, Father." Delia hung back and his impulse to embrace her as well faded. She always had been more reserved, and more difficult, than her sister. "Will you be staying long?"

"For a time. I will see you at dinner."

"Yes, Father."

"Yes, Papa."

He bowed, and turned away. Lord, he'd made a mull of that with Delia. When had his children grown up? It seemed just yesterday they'd been babies, yet Delia was practically a young lady. Time was passing uncomfortably fast. Yet, what could he have said to them? Faced with their startled, wary looks, he had realized he was a stranger to them. An unwelcome stranger. Just so had he once looked at his own father. Until now he would have said he'd had nothing in common with that august personage. Now he wondered.

He heard Eliza before he saw her; she was humming a country air, apparently unaware of his presence and just as apparently at peace with the world. Something inside Robert relaxed. She wasn't ill, then. Thank God. Only now did he admit to himself how worried he had been about her, and how scared. Life without Eliza, even if he did live apart from her, was too frightening a prospect to contemplate.

He turned past the yew hedge that sheltered the garden, and there she was, her back to him as she checked the leaves of the rose bushes for insects. Over her arm hung a flat basket filled with a riot of color, yellow daffodils and orange jonquils, purple iris and blue narcissus. As always she was dressed with little regard to fashion or convention, in a sack dress of some subdued color, with a battered straw hat upon her head. That last made him smile. She wasn't a beauty, his Eliza, at least not in the conventional way. Her light brown hair was too fine and soft to style neatly, her mouth a bit too wide for beauty, her chin a bit too square and determined. Her eyes, though, mirrored the depths of the sea, sometimes a serene aqua and other times a stormy gray, depths that had drawn him in long ago, as had the petal softness of her fair skin. Unfortunately she tended to freckle; hence, the hat. He could remember one night, when they were first married, when he had kissed every one of her freckles . . .

"Ahem." He cleared his throat, uncomfortable with that line of thought.

Eliza turned, her eyes inquiring, the basket held across her body. "Robert!" she exclaimed, joy lighting her eyes to a clear blue. "You're home!"

Robert inclined his head. "As you see, madam."

"Oh, how wonderful — isn't it?" She took a step forward and stopped, reminding him too clearly of Laura's reluctance to greet him. "Is all well?"

"Yes. Why wouldn't it be?"

"Because you rarely return home before Parliament finishes session."

"We were accomplishing little. It's been a difficult year."

"Oh." Eliza bent her head, examining a rose leaf. "No sign of aphids yet, thank goodness."

"Good," he said meaninglessly. "Eliza, you are well?"

She glanced up, surprise crossing her features at the concern in his voice. "Of course I am. Why do you ask?"

"I had heard — never mind, it hardly matters now."

"Have you seen the girls?"

"Yes, just now." He held out his hand. "Come, talk with me and tell me what's been happening."

Eliza hesitated for a moment, an odd look on her face, and then nodded. "Very well," she said, lowering the basket. For the first time he saw what the basket had concealed, the fullness of her breasts, her softly rounded stomach. There was no mistaking the signs. Eliza was pregnant.

Chapter Two

They stared at each other across a tangle of glossy dark green leaves, as effective a barrier as a thorn hedge. "Well," Robert said, not moving. "Were you planning on telling me?"

"Yes, of course I was." Eliza walked sedately toward him, the impulse she'd felt to dash into his arms like a giddy girl quelled by the look on his face. "When you came home."

He inclined his head. "As I have, madam."

Unexpectedly Eliza felt the old familiar prickle of annoyance. Must he be so cool, so imperturbable? Once she'd been attracted to him precisely because of such coolness, his ability to handle everything thrown at him. More than once she had needed his calm steadiness to counterbalance her own flights of emotion. But must he never show any feelings? Here he had just learned he was to be a father again, and they might have been discussing the weather for all he cared. If he cared. "It's your child," she said aggressively.

Robert's eyebrows went up in mild surprise. "I never thought otherwise, Eliza. I know you wouldn't play me false."

"No matter my other faults?"

"Why are you cutting up at me so?" he asked. "Have I done aught to upset you?"

No. You only stayed away for four months. And that, she should be accustomed to. "No, of course not. Forgive me, Robert. You know when I am increasing I am subject to megrims."

"Mm-hm." The look he cast her seemed to say she was subject to megrims most of the time, which, she admitted, was true. At least where he was concerned. "Are you feeling well?"

"Yes, quite well. Oh, Robert, I am glad you're home." At last she went to him, putting her hand on his arm and smiling up at him.

For a moment Robert stood still under her touch and then pulled back, though he was smiling. Eliza felt again the familiar pang of disappointment and hurt. She should have expected it, should be used to it by now, but Robert's coolness always surprised her and always hurt. She should know better than to make the first move, yet she always did, despite the risk of rejection. Someone had to bridge the gap between them. From long experience, she knew it wouldn't be him.

"It's warm," he said abruptly, and held out his arm. "You should be resting. As I recall, you're usually tired by this time of day."

Suddenly Eliza had to stifle a yawn. It was true, when she was increasing she did rest in the afternoon. Imagine him remembering that. "I'd like to rest," she admitted, and laid her hand on his arm, grateful for its strength. Whatever else she said about Robert, he'd always been there for her to lean on. "Will you be home for a while?"

"I don't know. I don't seem to be needed in Parliament just now."

Eliza's eyes opened wide. "Why? What happened?"

"Nothing in particular. I don't happen to agree with the government's policies. Or, for that matter, my own party's."

"And they're not listening to you? Oh, Robert, when they know how often you've been right in the past—"

"It matters not." He looked down at her, his gaze suddenly sharp and keen. "It was Twelfth Night, wasn't it?"

She didn't pretend to misunderstand. Twelfth Night, the last time she and Robert had lain together, after the ball they had given. The night her child was conceived. "Yes."

"Damn." It was a measure of his agitation that he swore in her presence. "My apologies, Eliza," he said formally, as they reached the terrace. "It will not happen again."

Eliza opened her mouth to speak, but at that moment a childish voice from the other side of the terrace distracted her. "Mama! Did you see my garden?" Laura cried, running up to her.

"Yes, Laura, I did." She smiled, but inside she was annoyed, which startled her. She loved her children and loved being a mother to them. There was more to her than that, though. Before the children had come along she had been Robert's wife. She always would be.

"I'll leave you now, madam," Robert said with a slight smile, and gently pulled away.

Eliza turned. There was still so much to discuss. "But, Robert—"

"As you see, I need to wash the dirt of the road from me. You will excuse me?"

"Yes, of course." Eliza watched him as he left, a slight frown puckering her brow. It was going to be difficult this time. Very difficult.

"Mama?" Laura said, breaking into her thoughts. "Is Papa going to stay this time?"

Eliza forced herself to smile. "I hope so, Laura. Now, let's go see how your garden is doing," she said, and turned away.

Laura bounced into the schoolroom, where Delia sat, half-heartedly working on her sampler. "I'm so glad Papa's home!" she announced, throwing herself down onto the window seat. "Do you think he'll want to see my garden?"

Delia looked over the top of her sampler. "I'm tired of hearing about your garden. And your dress is dirty."

Laura glanced down at the hem of her blue muslin dress, which was indeed smudged with dirt, and shrugged. "Mama says that happens when you work in a garden. I think Papa might stay this time," she said, kicking her heels back against the window seat.

"You're such a baby," Delia replied scornfully. "He won't stay. He doesn't like it here."

"I am not a baby! And he does so like it here."

"Girls," Miss Stevenson, their governess, said from her seat at the table, where she was going over their lessons. "Quietly, now."

Delia and Laura cast her furtive glances and then ignored her. "I'm not a baby!" Laura hissed. "Papa likes me."

"Why isn't he ever here, then?" Delia hissed back.

"Because he's busy in London. Mama says he's—"

"Too busy to be with us."

That stopped Laura for a moment. In the darkest moments of the night, she sometimes wondered why Papa stayed away.

Was it something she'd done? She tried to behave, really, she did, but when he was home she always did something that made him mad. He didn't yell, not the way Mama did, but instead lowered his voice, which somehow seemed worse. And he had a way of looking at one, so steady and direct, that one just had to squirm. She'd be a good girl, Laura vowed once again. "You just don't want him to know you like Michael Slocum."

Delia's head jerked up. "Don't you tell him, you brat! Or I'll—"

"Heavens, what is going on in here?" Eliza said from the doorway. Both girls froze, and then relaxed, at the mildness of her tone. "Are you squabbling again?"

"No."

"No."

Eliza exchanged a wry smile with Miss Stevenson and sank down next to Laura, stretching out her legs. " 'Tis a hot one today. What are you fighting about?"

"Nothing," Laura muttered.

Eliza glanced down at her and then looked over her head at Delia. Delia worried her sometimes. She always had kept herself to herself, but lately she did so more tenaciously. She was growing up, Eliza acknowledged with an inward sigh, and yet now, with her eyes seeking Eliza's for reassurance, she looked very young. "Delia?" she said quietly.

Delia shook her head and looked down at her sampler. "Nothing, Mama," she said, and then went on to give the lie to her words. "Does he know about Michael?"

"Your father? No, I don't imagine so." Eliza bit back a smile, relieved at the mildness of this problem. Delia was in the midst of her first romance, with Sir Peter Slocum's son, and was taking it very seriously, more seriously than Eliza thought it warranted. Michael was, after all, not much older than Delia. She couldn't imagine Robert playing the heavy-handed father over this. "Shall I tell him?"

"No! I mean, yes, well—"

"Trust me, Delia." Eliza leaned past Laura to lay her hand on Delia's. "He'll find out anyway, and better it comes from us. He wants you to be happy."

"Then why is he never here?" Delia burst out.

"He's very busy in London," Eliza said, the words sounding

228

hollow even to herself. "I'm going to take a rest. Laura, do change your dress."

"Yes, Mama," Laura said, sounding so subdued that Eliza looked at her quickly. Both girls were sitting still, their heads bent. Eliza could only guess at their confusion. If it were like hers they were unhappy, indeed.

"It will be all right." She bent and put her arms about them, drawing them close. "I promise it will be all right."

Both girls held on for a moment, and then Delia drew away. "Yes, Mama."

"Good." Eliza patted Laura's shoulder and pulled back smiling at both girls. "Mind Miss Stevenson now," she said, and went out.

By evening matters hadn't improved. Robert seemed ill-at-ease at dining *en famille*, while the girls clearly were unsure how to react. When dinner was over and Eliza at last sought her bed, her head was aching. Drat Robert, anyway! Had he no idea of what his unexpected, whirlwind visits did to his family? It hadn't been so bad when the children were young; they had accepted that their father had to be away. Now, though, as they grew older they questioned his absences, and Eliza had no easy answers for them. Or for herself. Once she had sworn that her marriage would not be a typical *ton* marriage, like that of her parents' and of so many others she knew. Her marriage was going to be different. How young she'd been, and how wrong. And what could she do about it now?

Jessy, her maid, clucked at her as she helped her undress exclaiming over her ankles which had swollen in the heat. Eliza ignored her, but the truth was she felt heavy and uncomfortable, with all of summer and five months of pregnancy before her. It would be bearable, though, she thought as she slipped between the cool linen sheets, if only things were different between her and Robert.

Once, they had been. Drifting somewhere between sleep and wakefulness, Eliza relaxed the guard she usually kept on her mind and let herself drift back. Theirs had been a splendid wedding, the union of two aristocratic families. No one had consulted the bride and groom as to their wishes, but that had proven unnecessary. Eliza fell in love with her tall, blond fiancé at first sight, and he, though quieter and more self-contained, seemed to like her. Those first days together — well, there were memories that could still put her to the blush. They were besotted, and though Robert rarely spoke of his feelings, he demonstrated them vigorously enough. He could have left her alone at Stowcroft when she carried their first child, as even then he was already active in politics, but instead he was beside her when Delia was born. Eliza's happiness was complete.

, When had things begun to change? They were supremely happy that year, as summer mellowed into fall and winter followed. She had no intimation that they might not always be that way, until Robert mentioned going to London for the season. Of course he'd wish to go, to take his seat in Parliament. To her own surprise, however, Eliza didn't want to go. She enjoyed the balls and entertainments of the season, yet she also had the sense that she'd left them behind for more important things. There was another consideration. The journey from Devon would be too long for a child less than a year old, meaning that Delia would have to stay behind. Eliza couldn't bear it. She didn't want to leave her plump, blond-haired daughter. The child needed her, her mother, not a wet-nurse or a nanny. Robert, she felt certain, would understand.

· Robert didn't. Uncharacteristically he blew up, and their quarrel was bitter. Their reconciliation was as volatile as the quarrel had been, but both were aware that something had changed in their marriage. Something had been lost.

After that the quarrels were less frequent and soon ceased altogether. Robert seemed to be pleased with his growing family, to her delight not favoring his son over his daughters, and yet he continued to stay away for longer and longer intervals. Occasionally he asked her to come to London with him; occasionally she asked him to stay home. Neither took offense when the other refused. Their marriage drifted into a comfortable routine, and if each missed the joy of those first days, they didn't show it. Only rarely did the passion flare between them. The last time it happened had been Twelfth Night.

There was a soft snicking sound, as of a doorknob turning, and Eliza pushed herself up on her elbows. It had been a very long time since Robert had slept in the adjoining room, but she knew every creaking floorboard, every squeaky hinge, very well, indeed. "Robert?" she whispered.

He came closer, the hand that had been shielding a candle moving, so that she could see him. He was attired only in his

230

dressing gown, making her heart beat faster. "I thought perhaps you were asleep."

"No, not quite." She lay back against the pillows as he sat on the edge of her bed, placing the candle on the bedstand. He had come to her, in spite of the strain between them. Her spirits rose. Perhaps she was worrying about nothing. Perhaps this baby would bring them closer together.

"Are you tired?" he asked. "Shall I go?"

"No, of course not," she said, and opened her arms to him.

Chapter Three

Laura laid down the French primer from which she had been reading in a halting voice. "How long will Papa be here?"

"I don't know, Laura," Eliza said, looking up from her knitting. "We haven't discussed it. He did just arrive yesterday."

"It would be ever so nice if he stayed." Laura swung her legs back and forth, her eyes distant. "He doesn't spend much time with us."

"He's always believed that men aren't supposed to have much to do with their children. It's how he was raised."

"Was Grandfather like him? Was he always away, too?"

"Yes, I believe so." Eliza frowned over a dropped stitch. "So was his mother, I'm afraid."

"He must have been awfully lonely."

"I don't think he thinks so." Of course he had been, though it was something she'd never thought of him. Robert always seemed self-possessed and assured. Once, though, he too had been a child, left behind while his parents went jaunting off to London without him. As had she. It was why she was determined to be with the children, so that they wouldn't be brought up by strangers, so that they wouldn't feel so lost and rootless as she sometimes did, even now.

"I don't know why we're talking about it," Delia said. "He'll go back to London as soon as he can."

Eliza came out of her reverie. Delia sounded much too cynical for her age. "Perhaps not. Parliament will be ending its session soon. Clive will be home from school, too."

"Oh, Clive. Of course he'll stay home to see Clive."

Eliza looked up again in surprise. Was Delia jealous of her brother? "He's glad to see you, too, Delia."

"But we're not boys."

"And thank heavens for that! Laura, please continue reading." The girls glanced quickly at each other and, after a moment, Laura returned to the primer. Eliza paid her little mind, though, ignoring any and all errors. How long would Robert be home this time? They hadn't talked about it last night, but then, talking had been the furthest thing from their minds. To her chagrin that thought sent color surging into her face, making her lower her head to hide it. She was a married woman, not a green girl, to be embarrassed by such things. She had felt like a girl last night, though . . .

"Am I interrupting?" a voice said at the door, and Eliza jerked her head up, her eyes meeting Robert's. For a moment he returned her gaze, and she was caught, unable to look away, knowing he was remembering, too. A knowing little smile touched his lips, and she dropped her head again.

"Papa, I can speak French," Laura announced. "Do you want to hear?"

"Certainly. Do you always hear the girls' lessons?" he asked Eliza, coming to sit next to her.

"No. Miss Stevenson has the headache, poor thing, and so I told her to stay abed." She put her knitting down, pushing it aside, but not before she saw Robert's eyes fasten on it and sharpen. He had guessed what it was then, the fleecy white confection she would wrap around her new baby. And what he thought of that, she still didn't know. "Was there something you wanted, Robert?"

"I thought I'd see what you were doing," he said, almost diffidently, annoyed with himself. This was his house. He had slept in a bedroom down the hall and taken lessons in this very same room, yet he felt like an interloper. The girls were polite, and Eliza seemed to be on guard against him. Was it like this every time he came home? He quickly reviewed his memories of past homecomings and decided that this one was different. What was causing the constraint, however, was something he couldn't even guess.

The girls were looking at him so uncertainly that he couldn't bear it. Dashed if he were going to be pushed out of his own house. "I thought you'd like to hear about London," he said, and then held both girls transfixed with tales of what had happened in the city. Laura was enthralled by his story of the Laplanders who had come to England in the winter, bringing with them meat that had been frozen and was in a remarkable state of preservation. Whenever they went out in their outlandish coats of reindeer hide, he said, they attracted a tide of followers. Delia, disdaining such stories, was far more interested in hearing about Princess Charlotte's wedding to Prince Leopold of Coburg, which Robert had attended. The bride wore silver and white, he said, obligingly dredging up details from his memory, and old Queen Charlotte had been splendid in gold tissue. And everyone was wearing the new Kendal bonnet or Coburg hat . . .

"Papa." Laura had been shifting impatiently during this recital of current fashions. "Did you bring us any presents?"

"Laura!" Eliza exclaimed, looking up from her knitting.

"Of course I did." He smiled as he rose. "Have I ever forgotten?"

Laura dropped the primer, her face bright, and scrambled down from the table. "See, Delia? I told you he didn't forget. What did you bring me?"

"Laura," Eliza chided again, more forcefully this time, and the little girl subsided. "That was nice of you, Robert."

"You know I always bring something, Eliza. Since I don't get home as often as I'd like."

"Mm-hm." Eliza nodded, and he felt that little spurt of annoyance again. Damned if he were going to defend himself.

"I have something for you, too, Liza."

"Give the girls theirs first," she suggested, smiling, and after a moment he smiled back. Even Delia looked excited by the prospect of a gift.

"Very well." From the hallway he produced several lumpy, tissue-wrapped packages. "For you, Delia. And you, Laura."

"Oh! A doll!" Laura exclaimed, tearing open the paper. "Oh, look, Mama, her gown is like one of yours."

"Very pretty, Laura. Did you choose it yourself, Robert?"

"Of course I did. And wrapped them, too."

"Ah," Eliza replied, sounding amused, but this time he didn't mind.

"Oh," Delia said, her voice awed. She was more careful, more deliberate in unwrapping her package, but now she held up a fan of ivory and lace and gilt. "Oh, Daddy, it's so pretty!"

Daddy. She hadn't called him that in years. "I thought you'd like it, poppet."

234

"Oh, I do!" She held it before her face, peeping at him over it so coquettishly that he was startled. Delia was no longer the little girl he remembered. Once again he had the dismaying sense that his family were strangers.

"Your first grown-up fan, Delia," Eliza said, smiling. "That was thoughtful of you, Robert."

"Yes, well." He cleared his throat. "You've turned into a young lady, Delia."

"Where's Mama's present?" Laura demanded.

Robert smiled. "Here." From an inner pocket of his coat he withdrew a long, narrow box of midnight-blue velvet. "For you, Liza."

Eliza's heart sank. Slowly she took the box. Slowly, knowing her family was watching in anticipation, she opened it, dreading what she would find. Her gasp of surprise and pleasure, though, was genuine. "Oh, Robert," she said, her voice not quite steady. Inside the box was a magnificent necklace of sapphires and diamonds set in gold. Robert's taste in jewelry was exquisite, but this time he had outdone even himself. It was beautiful, and she hated it. "Oh, 'tis lovely."

"Do you like it?" he asked as the girls gathered 'round, their eyes as bright as any jewel.

"It's lovely," she repeated, and because she knew it was expected of her, clasped it around her neck.

"Oh, Mama," Delia said, sounding awed. "You'll need a new gown to wear with it."

"A London gown," Robert said and their eyes met. Anger flared within Eliza, anger she tamped down rather than display before the girls. How vexing of him! She liked jewels as much as anyone, yet he knew quite well that she had nowhere to wear them. Unless she went to London. Apparently he was going to reopen the old argument, about her staying in Devon with the children. It wouldn't be the first time he'd used a gift for such a purpose.

"I don't think I'll buy any new gowns quite yet," she said, rising and crossing the room to kiss Robert on the cheek. "Thank you, Robert, it is beautiful. I think I'd best put it away, though. It's not really suitable for a picnic."

"A picnic?" he asked, following her into the hall.

"Yes. I promised the girls that since Miss Stevenson is ill we could go down to the beach and picnic there."

235

He frowned. "Should you be doing that just now, Eliza?"

"Yes, I feel perfectly fine. It isn't a difficult walk."

"I'll come with you."

"What?" Eliza looked up, startled, as they reached her room. "You needn't, Robert. I know you dislike eating outside."

He smiled. "I'll survive this once. I don't think you should go down the cliff path alone."

"I can manage."

"I'd rather you didn't on your own. Besides, I want to. You're always asking me to spend more time with the girls."

"Of course," she said, after a moment, and turned away, reaching up to unclasp the necklace.

"You don't like it, do you," he said abruptly from the doorway, his back turned.

Eliza paused, her hands dropping. "I like the necklace, Robert. I just don't like what it represents."

"Aren't I allowed to give you a gift?"

"Of course you are, but what this means, and now—"

"I had no idea you were increasing, as you know," he snapped. "I'll leave you to get ready now."

"Robert—"

"We'll leave in half an hour," he said and strode away.

"Robert," she repeated, but he was gone. Ooh, he always did this to her! Whenever the conversation threatened to get too serious, too painful, he walked out, leaving her simmering with anger and unspoken words. Now, adding insult to injury, he had just taken command of their expedition to the beach. What else, she wondered, dragging a brush through her fine, wispy hair and bundling it into a knot at her neck, would he take charge of while he was here? It was almost enough to make her wish he'd return to London.

Almost. Eliza set down the brush and stared at her reflection, hesitantly touching the necklace that still lay at her throat. Another gift. It was the way Robert showed his affection, by giving extravagant presents, rather than gifts of the heart. When first they had been married that hadn't mattered, but now it did. Because he would leave again. Nothing she could do would stop it, and it hurt. No present, no matter how expensive, could salve that pain.

Eliza looked at herself in the mirror and then raised her chin. She would survive it; she always had no matter how bad things got. This time she had another reason to hold on, her child. In the meantime she would do all she could to protect herself and her children from the pain that would come with Robert's departure. If that meant holding a part of herself aloof from him, then that was what she would do. No matter how much it hurt.

With that, she pulled off the necklace and swept out of the room.

Chapter Four

Some time later they all assembled on the lawn, Robert carrying the picnic hamper and the girls running ahead. At the top of the cliff Robert stopped, his hand holding Eliza's elbow. "Are you sure this is safe?" he asked.

"Perfectly. 'Tis an easy climb and I rest when I'm tired. And, oh, look at the view, Robert."

"Yes." The view of the cove, formed by two protecting arms of the cliffs, with its dancing whitecaps was indeed spectacular, but at the moment all he wanted to look at was his wife. Her skin had a luminous quality that made her glow, her figure a lushness that was alluring. Lord, he wanted her, with an urgency that startled him. He thought he'd outgrown such impulses, but apparently it was possible to desire one's wife even when she was heavy with child.

In London, he stifled the normal urges a healthy male, separated for long periods from his wife, would feel. He had never kept a mistress and had never felt the lack. One night with Eliza, though, and he was as randy as a young boy. No matter his hurt over her rejection of his gift, so carefully chosen. His desire for her was as strong as it had been when they'd first married. Dangerous, this fierce, fiery passion. Such feelings had led to their current predicament. Another child. Good God.

"Papa," Laura said later, when they had nearly finished the meal of cold roast beef with bread and cheese, and early strawberries in thick clotted cream, "how long are you staying?"

Robert paused as he sipped at his lemonade, his eyes meeting Eliza's. "I'm not sure, Laura."

"You'll return to London, though, won't you?" Eliza said.

"I don't know. Parliament will be ending session soon, and

238

we're not accomplishing much this year in any event." He leaned back on his hands, looking up to the sky. "All we seem to be doing is arguing among ourselves. The radicals are talking revolution, which of course the government is determined to stop, and the rest of us are caught in the middle. In the meantime soldiers keep returning from the Continent and can't find work, rents are dropping, and no one's buying anything. No one's doing anything except pointing the blame at everyone else and everything's at a standstill. I don't remember ever feeling so frustrated, Liza." He lowered his head and looked at her, feeling as if a vast burden had been lifted from his shoulders. Talking with her had always had this effect. "I was glad to come home," he said, knowing in that moment that he spoke only the truth.

Eliza looked away. "Still, I've never known you to miss a minute of it."

He shrugged, but before he could answer, Delia rose. "Mama, may Laura and I look for shells?"

"Of course," Eliza said, and the girls set off, leaving silence behind, leaving Robert feeling vaguely guilty. There was no reason why he should. The way he and Eliza lived was the way most people in the *ton* lived. He liked his life in London. He felt he was doing important work, and he liked that feeling. No question, though, that London's grayness, its sooty air and misty weather often pressed in on him. Until this moment, sitting on a sandy blanket on a glorious spring day, he hadn't realized just how oppressed he'd felt. And yet, when the time came he'd be eager to leave.

Far down the beach, Delia and Laura bent to pick up shells and place them in baskets, their skirts carefully tucked up so that they wouldn't get wet. From this distance they looked like the children they were, and yet Robert couldn't deny the changes in them. "They've grown," he said.

"I know." She turned to smile at him. "Delia has a beau."

"What?" He sat up straight. "She's only a child."

"Sir Peter Slocum's oldest, Michael. It's really very sweet."

Robert snorted. "Sweet." He doubted that. Remembering what he had been like at that age, he doubted it very much. "She's too young for an entanglement."

Eliza laughed. "An entanglement! Oh, Robert."

"What?"

239

"You sound just like my father."

"I do not." He thought about it for a moment. "I suppose I do, at that. But, drat it, Eliza, I'm not ready for one of my children to start courting. I don't feel old enough."

"I know." Eliza smiled. "Nor do I. But they've grown, Robert. Perhaps you haven't been here to see it —"

"I won't come to daggers drawn with you on that, Eliza. Not when I've just got home."

Eliza stayed quiet for a moment and then sat up, hugging her knees. "How long do you plan to stay?" she asked finally, looking out to sea.

"I don't know." Until his child was born, perhaps. Until his daughters stopped looking at him as if he were a stranger. Until his wife trusted him again. "I left work undone in London."

"Then why did you come?"

"It matters not." He rose, apparently undisturbed by her waspish tone of voice. Why could he not just tell her that he'd been concerned for her, frightened of losing her? Why would the words not come? "I'm going to take a walk. Would you like to come?"

Eliza yawned, startling both of them. "I'm sorry. No, not just now, Robert. I do get sleepy these days."

He grinned down at her, looking so much like the young man she had married it made her heart ache. "And you didn't get much sleep last night, did you?"

"Robert."

"I didn't know the mother of three could still blush."

"Almost four," she retorted.

Robert's smile stiffened. "As you say," he said, and turned away.

Eliza watched him walk away, chewing at the inside of her lip. For a moment all had been as it once was between them, when she and Robert were young and in love. For he had loved her, of that she was certain, and she thought he still did. His love had changed, though. She supposed that was normal. People didn't stay the same, they changed, and so how they felt would change. Wouldn't it? Then why, she wondered, did she love him as much and as painfully as she had at eighteen?

A gull screeched overhead, jolting her out of memories that threatened to be both unbearably sweet and unbearably hurtful. Far down the beach Robert had reached the girls. Delia stood a little apart, her head bent, but Laura was chattering up at him excitedly and gesturing toward the water. Her babies had grown up. Suddenly she was very glad that there would soon be another, though until this moment her feelings on that had been mixed. Placing a protective hand on her stomach, she felt fierce love surge through her for this child. Robert had yet to show any interest in the new baby, and perhaps he wouldn't if she didn't somehow prod him into it. If she wanted to regain their old closeness, she would have to make an effort. Raising her chin, Eliza rose from the blanket and set off down the beach, toward her family.

"Oh, no, Papa's coming toward us. No, don't look," Delia said hastily as Laura's head swiveled. "He'll see you."

"So?" Laura watched her father approach, and then turned back to contemplating the sea-washed rocks, just beyond the water's edge. Both girls had been very aware of their father's presence on the beach, but neither were quite sure how to react. Papa didn't come on picnics and such. Papa was usually busy with estate business when he was home. What could he possibly want now?

"I wish we could reach that starfish," Laura said, staring at the rock where the starfish clung, in spite of the incoming tide. "Do you think, if I step on those rocks—"

"You'll fall," Delia said. "You'll get your dress wet and Mama will be mad."

"No, she won't. Not really." They both knew that when Mama got upset, it usually wasn't over something so silly as a wet dress. Climbing out on the rocks was nothing, she'd done it before. Still, Laura hesitated. Just now she didn't want to do anything wrong. There was something different about Mama lately. She cried at the oddest things and lost her temper at the oddest times. Both she and Delia had learned to be careful around her. "Maybe I will."

Delia looked out at the starfish and then shook her head, regretfully. "Better not. It's awfully far out. Though it would look quite nice on the frame Miss Stevenson said we could make, wouldn't it?"

"If Clive were here, he'd go out for it."

"If Clive were here, Papa wouldn't pay any attention to us."

"Yes, he would. Papa likes us."

"Then why does he always go away? Why doesn't he ever take us to London with him?"

Laura idly tossed a stone into the water. "Maybe he will, this time."

"No, he won't. Papa won't take us there."

"Where won't I take you?" a voice said behind them, and both girls whirled to see their father standing a few feet away, his hands resting on his hips.

The girls exchanged looks. "Nowhere."

He looked from one to the other, searching their faces. He hadn't missed their glances, nor was he unaware of the wariness in their eyes now. Was he such a monster, then, that they feared him? "What do you have there?" he asked, dismissing that thought.

"Shells, Papa." Laura came closer, the wariness leaving her face. "See? We've found so many different ones."

"I used to pick up shells on this very beach." He smiled down at her. "Had quite a collection, as a matter of fact. What do you plan to do with yours?"

"Miss Stevenson said if we found enough we could glue them onto a picture frame."

He nodded, enjoying this moment of closeness and trust with his daughter. "A fine idea."

"I just wish I could have the starfish."

"I told you, silly. It's too far out," Delia said.

"Maybe Daddy could get it." Laura turned large, confiding eyes on him, looking so like Eliza that something caught in his chest. "Please?"

"Where is it?" he asked.

"Out there."

Robert followed her pointing finger and saw the starfish, clinging to a rock that was nearly awash with the waves. Well, why couldn't he get it? he thought, suddenly feeling reckless. Often he had to disappoint his children. Not this time. He would do a great deal to keep Laura looking at him as she was now. "All right."

"Papa!" Delia gasped as he stepped onto a rock. "Papa, you'll fall!"

"No, he won't, silly," Laura said. "He can do anything."

Not quite. Robert crossed to the next stone, finding it unex-

242

pectedly slippery with water and seaweed. Damn, he should have taken off his boots before trying this, the salt water would ruin them. *Damn the boots,* he thought, and crossed to another rock.

"Papa, be careful," Delia called.

He took a moment to steady himself. "I won't drown, Delia," he said, though now he doubted the wisdom of this escapade. The rock with the starfish on it was farther away than it had looked on shore. He could reach it, but it would mean jumping and he might well fall. He'd come this far, though. He wasn't going to turn back.

There was nothing for it. Taking a deep breath, he jumped. From the shore he heard shrieks as he tottered on the slippery rock, his arms thrown out to keep his balance. Damn, but he'd done it! Grinning like a boy, he crouched down and dislodged the starfish, carefully placing it in his coat pocket. His valet would have something to say about that, as well as his boots, but he didn't care. He'd done it.

Standing, he turned. "I've got it!" he called to his daughters, just as a wave broke over the rock and sent him sliding off, into the surf.

Chapter Five

"Daddy!"

"Papa!" Delia cried at the same time, throwing out her hand to block Laura from dashing into the surf.

"Girls, it's all right," Eliza said from behind them, hurrying to put her hands on their shoulders. From down the beach she had monitored Robert's progress across the rocks, wondering what on earth he was doing. "Everything's fine."

"But, Papa —"

"Look." Eliza pointed, and they all looked out to sea. Robert, having slipped briefly under the waves, was now sitting next to the rock, in water that was obviously only a few inches deep. His hair was plastered to his head, and a piece of seaweed clung to the shoulder of his once-immaculate coat. Eliza choked back a laugh. He looked disgruntled and embarrassed, not at all in the mood to laugh at himself. "Are you all right?" she called.

"Perfectly." He looked up at her and grinned. "I must look a fool."

At that Eliza did laugh, startling the girls. "You do look rather funny."

"Daddy, there's seaweed on your shoulder," Laura called.

"Is there, now." Frowning down at his coat, he picked the offending piece of seaweed off with such a fastidious gesture that Eliza laughed again.

"Laugh all you want, madam." Robert surged to his feet, water coursing off him, and began trudging purposefully toward them. "Perhaps you'd like a seawater bath?"

Eliza abruptly pulled back from the girls. "Robert —"

"Hm." He stopped before her and touched a finger to her nose, making her jerk back in surprise. "You're starting to freckle."

"Am I?" She sounded as breathless as a young girl, she thought, dazedly. "I — my hat, I forgot it — Robert, what in the world were you doing?"

He grinned, and it transformed his face, making him again appear the young, approachable man she had once loved so. "Getting this," he said, and brandished the starfish aloft.

"Daddy! You got it!" Laura launched herself at him, and the strange moment of closeness between him and Eliza was gone. "Oh, thank you, thank you, thank you! It's the best gift ever!"

Robert looked startled. "You're quite welcome, muffin."

"Delia, look, we've got it!"

Delia looked at her scornfully. "You're all wet."

Robert abruptly reached out for her, pulling her close. "And so are you."

"Daddy!" Delia shrieked, and then laughed. "You're silly."

"Yes, well, I think you should all get out of those wet clothes," Eliza said, but she was smiling. Robert was hugging his daughters. There were miracles, after all.

"Oh?" Robert's eyes held a wicked gleam. "Do you not care to join us, Liza?"

"No, I do not!" She took a hasty step back. "Come, now, we should go home."

"Oh, Mama," both girls chorused.

"Oh, Eliza," Robert chimed in.

"Now, you stop that," she said, but she smiled. "You need to get out of those clothes before you take a chill."

"And then?"

Eliza felt the color rushing to her cheeks. "Come, girls," she said, briskly, putting her hands on their shoulders and turning them away from the beach. They grumbled, but obeyed. After a moment Robert caught up with them, slipping his hand through Eliza's arm. She smiled at him, and together they walked home, feeling more like a family than they had in many a year.

A week passed, and then two, and still Robert showed no signs of planning to leave. His mornings were spent in the book-room with his agent, or out on his estate, checking on how the new crops were faring or meeting with his tenants. In a break from past visits, though, he reserved most afternoons for his family. After the day on the beach he had asserted himself and forbidden Eliza to climb the cliff path, but they found other things to do. The girls quickly discarded their initial coolness, welcoming him into their lives, though Delia, like her father, was more naturally reserved. And there was Eliza. She smiled at him as she always had, and welcomed him warmly at night. Even on those nights when she told him frankly that she was tired she seemed glad that he stayed with her, nestling next to him and giving him an illusion of closeness. But there was no question she had changed. Once her emotions had all been on the surface. Now she was calm and placid and very polite, as if he were a stranger. He didn't like it at all. There had been love between them once, and passion. Where had it gone?

Eliza's emotions were mixed. She liked having Robert home, but it was unsettling, as well. In the past years she had taken over much of what had been his responsibilities. Though she had always consulted him by post, she was the one who had dealt with tenants' concerns, decided when farm buildings needed new roofs, purchased a new, hardier breed of sheep. She had made the decisions as to the girls' educations, and she had full responsibility for running the house. Though she hadn't been raised to do so much, she enjoyed it, thrived on it, glad she was more than just another bored society matron.

Robert's return had changed all that. With casual authority he had taken up the job of running the estate again. The tenants that had once turned to her now went to him, their relief at dealing with a man rather than a woman apparent. So did the estate agent. She blamed Robert for that, irrational though she knew it was. He had, for example, let the girls' governess go for her holiday earlier than usual, and for a longer time, leaving Eliza unexpectedly with the two girls on her hands. That Miss Stevenson would have been going on holiday soon hardly mollified her; it was her responsibility, and he had usurped it. He had sent for a builder to deal with the dry rot in the old section of the house, something Eliza would have done had not his return distracted her, and he had even spoken to Sir Peter about Delia's budding romance. That had embarrassed Delia and infuriated Eliza, and so she had confronted him.

When faced with her anger and frustration, though, Robert's reaction had been bafflement. Was he not relieving her of work she shouldn't have to do? And did it really matter who saw to such things, so long as they were done? In the face of such reasonableness Eliza fumed in helpless, impotent silence. When all was said and done, he *was* the marquess. The estate and all who lived on it were his responsibility, not hers. At least for as long as he intended to stay.

And that was the real problem. She had grown accustomed to her husband's brief visits home, though she had never liked them. The fact that this time he made no mention of going disconcerted her. For so long now her life had been orderly and predictable, and that was how she liked it. The pain of separation was manageable that way. If she knew when Robert planned to leave she'd be hurt, but she could live with it. Certainly it would be easier to deal with than this dreadful uncertainty. Someday he would go, and it would hurt the worse for her not having been prepared. And, worst of all, he had yet to mention the new baby.

"Well." Robert's voice at the door of the drawing room distracted her. It was late morning, and apparently he had finished his work for the day. Briefly she wondered what he had done today that would ordinarily have been her task and then dismissed the thought. Resenting his interference did no good. Soon he would be gone, and the responsibility would be all hers again. Lonely responsibility.

"Yes?" she answered, smiling, and looked up. Their gazes caught, holding them fast in a bond that was almost tangible in the hushed stillness of the room. In that moment she realized she could cope with anything, if only he would stay.

"What are you doing?"

"Writing letters." She looked down at her desk without seeing it. He wouldn't stay. That, she had best accustom herself to. "You're done early today."

"Not much to do." He crossed the room to sit in a chair near her, his legs stretched out. "You seem to be busy."

Eliza sealed the last envelope with a wafer and rose from her desk. "Will you frank these for me? I'm writing to employment agencies in London. We'll need a new teacher for the school in the village."

"Yes, I know, the vicar told me after church last week. Give me those and I'll take care of them for you." He reached across for the envelopes and their fingers touched, tip to tip. Again their gazes caught, and then Eliza pulled back. "Where are the girls?"

"Outside, in the garden." Eliza went to sit on the sofa facing him. "Robert, Michael Slocum rode over to see Delia. You won't make a fuss, will you?"

"I?" He looked innocent. "Why should I?"

She gave him a speaking look. "Don't you realize how embarrassed Delia was when you spoke to Sir Peter?"

He shrugged. "She's my daughter. I would be remiss in my duty if I didn't take care of her."

"When you're here," she retorted.

His eyes grew opaque. "As you say," he said, after a moment. "When I'm here."

Eliza turned away, biting her lip. She hadn't meant to say that. Things were going so well between them that she tried to avoid any mention of their circumstances. Their time together was so brief; what good was it to indulge in recriminations for something that couldn't be helped? "I'm sorry, Robert. I know you mean well."

"Damning with faint praise, Eliza."

"Well, do you expect me to be happy with the way things are?" she burst out.

"No." His voice was quiet. "I expect you to consider your husband's wishes."

Again she looked away. However had they got onto this topic? "It does no good to argue this. I am sorry, Robert. I know you care about the girls."

"Of course I do. You needn't be jealous about it."

Eliza's head whipped around. "Jealous! Of all the absurd things—"

"Aren't you?" He gazed steadily at her. "Don't you wish to keep them to yourself?"

"No!" Jealous! Of all the tangled emotions she had felt during his stay, jealousy was certainly not one of them. "I'm glad you're spending time with them, Robert. I only wish you could be with them more."

"Do you? Then why did you get so angry when I gave Miss Stevenson her holiday? And why does it bother you that I care about Delia's entanglement?"

She laughed. "Robert, Michael's only a boy!"

"Yes, well, I remember what I was like at that age," he said, not meeting her eyes.

He looked remarkably like a boy himself, so much so that affection flooded through her. He would never understand why she

248

resented his peremptory manner, and so she would not frustrate herself, or him, by trying to explain. Besides, knowing what motivated it made matters a little easier. He genuinely cared about their children. "I wish I had known you then," she said.

"We were young enough when we met. I, twenty-one, and you only eighteen." His eyes glinted with sudden mischief. "Of course, we were already betrothed."

"Yes, and didn't that make me angry when I found out!" She grinned at him. "I thought it would ruin my season beyond repair. How young I was."

"And how pretty." He returned the grin, the shared memory curling around them and drawing them closer. "Do you remember when we first met?"

"I remember." Her eyes were soft. "It was at my first real ball, after I was presented at court, and I was wearing a white muslin gown that I thought was daring. I was so young." She looked up at him. "And determined to enjoy myself, even if I was betrothed."

"Our parents should never have made that stupid contract and expected us to be bound by it," he said, leaning his head back against his linked hands, the very picture of lean, male arrogance.

"I expected to hate you, you know," she said, ruefully, as if she had never told him this before. When they had first been married they had delighted in telling each other the tale of their first meeting. They hadn't done so in a long time. "When Mama told me I'd been promised to you since childhood I was furious, and I decided I would never like you."

"And I told my father that if we didn't suit we wouldn't marry and hang the stupid contract." He smiled. "He wanted to take a strap to me, but I was taller than him."

"Your father would have let you have anything you wanted, and you know it."

"I do. He knew I'd want you."

Color surged into Eliza's face. "Your parents and mine wanted to join their bloodlines," she said tartly.

"As you wish." Robert's smile was knowing. "Regardless, I wouldn't have forced you into it, Eliza. But, as I recall, I didn't have to."

"No. But as I recall, I was very cross with you for a while, for not telling me who you were at that ball. I still think it was unfair of you, Robert, not to use your title when we were introduced."

"I don't." He grinned. "I knew you didn't want to marry the

249

Viscount Leigh, but I thought perhaps Robert Evans would have a chance."

"As he did."

"As I did," he agreed, smiling at her. She smiled back and they fell silent, remembering. It had been at that ball, the one Eliza hadn't really wanted to attend because she'd known her fiancé would be there. Since he'd just come up from the country she hadn't met him yet, but rumor had it he'd be at this ball. She really didn't want to marry him, not then. The thought of marrying someone she'd never met, someone her parents had chosen, for heaven's sake, was revolting. She was pleased when the tall, blond young man was introduced to her. Robert Evans. She looked up into his deep-set gray eyes, and fell completely, irrevocably in love.

"We went out into the garden," Robert said suddenly.

Eliza smiled, remembering that breach of propriety, how exciting it had been and how thunderous a scold she had received for it later. It hadn't mattered, though. There in the garden they'd kissed, Eliza's first real kiss ever. "And you told me who you were."

"You were furious." He grinned. " 'Twas the first time I realized you had a temper."

"Yes, and it hasn't improved, I fear."

"It doesn't matter," he said softly.

She looked up, startled. "Doesn't it?"

"No." Bending forward, he stretched out his hand to her. After a startled moment, Eliza reached out to take it. Their fingers touched, clasped, intertwined, joining them inexorably together. "After that I couldn't marry you fast enough."

Eliza turned pink again, but her eyes on him were steady. "I remember." Oh, she remembered, so well, her anger turning to delight, the anxious fear that he didn't feel the same, the wonder and passion of their few stolen moments together. Both had been impatient for marriage, certain their happiness would last forever. "What happened to us, Robert?"

Robert opened his mouth to answer, but at that moment the French windows from the terrace opened, and his daughters tumbled in, laughing and chattering. With them was Michael Slocum, tall and gangly, with large hands he didn't seem to know how to control. At sight of Robert he went quiet, and color surged into his face, burning to the tips of his ears. A few moments earlier Robert might have frowned in disapproval of the boisterous, easy relationship that obviously existed between Michael and Delia, but remembering his own past made him see things differently. Eliza was right. They were children. Childhood romances rarely lasted. "Good morning, Michael," he said mildly.

"Good morning, sir." Michael made a quick, awkward bow, visibly relaxing, to Robert's chagrin and amusement. Was he really such an ogre?

"Laura caught a frog," Delia said scornfully, "and Michael thought it was capital."

Robert and Eliza exchanged glances and then quickly looked away, for fear they would start laughing. "I do hope you didn't bring it in, Laura," Eliza said.

"No, Delia wouldn't let me. Cook gave Michael an empty jug and he's taking it home."

At that Robert did laugh, turning it quickly into a cough. "Are you all right, Papa?" Delia asked.

Robert cleared his throat. "Perfectly."

"He has a frog in his throat," Eliza said, and this time Robert didn't try to restrain his laughter. The children's puzzled faces only added to his mirth. "Well. Do go clean up, girls, nuncheon will be soon. Michael, will you stay?"

Michael looked at Robert, who had himself under control again, and nodded. "Yes, ma'am, I'd like that."

"Good. Shannon will show you where to wash up." She tugged on the bellpull, and after a moment the butler came in. As quickly as that, Eliza and Robert were alone again.

"And I was worried they were growing up too fast," Robert said, at length.

"They are still children." Eliza smiled briefly. "But you're right, there's more to it than simple friendship, and they may not know how to handle it." She stretched her hand out to him. "I'm glad you're here."

Robert took her hand, as he had just a few moments before, linking them together. "So am I," he said, and as he did so realized the deep, profound truth of that. There was, for the moment, no place else he'd rather be.

Chapter Six

"Good, you're home," Robert said, standing in the doorway of the book-room as Eliza and the girls came into the house, some days later. Behind them Shannon struggled in, his arms loaded with parcels.

Eliza looked up from tugging at the fingers of her gloves. "Yes. Did you want us for something?"

"I simply wondered where you were."

"Shopping in the village." Ignoring the impatient quirk of Robert's mouth, Eliza turned to the girls. "Get cleaned up for nuncheon now, there's not much time. Why?" she asked, turning to Robert.

"I finished work early today, and you weren't here."

If she hadn't been so tired Eliza might have been amused by the aggrieved note in his voice, like a little boy's, but it had been a difficult morning. "Am I supposed to be at your beck and call, Robert?"

He looked mildly surprised. "No, of course not, but—"

"But you expect me to be here when you want me, while you go as you please."

Robert followed her into the drawing room. "I merely said—"

"I know what you said!" she exclaimed, and then drew her arm across her forehead, her anger gone as quickly as it had come. "Forgive me, Robert. It was a beastly morning, but I didn't mean to cut up at you."

"Sit down." Taking her elbow, he led her to a chair and then tugged at the bellpull. "Tea," he said to Shannon. "You look tired. Are you doing too much?"

252

"No, it's this blasted heat. I do wish it were cooler." She looked up at him, thoughtful. It was the first time he'd referred to her condition, however obliquely, in a while. "The girls were a bit of a trial today. Especially Delia."

"Tell me about it," he invited, sitting down as the tea was served, and Eliza poured out the story of the morning's expedition. Delia was at a difficult age, no longer a child but not yet a woman, and she tended to want clothes that were unsuitable for her. This, of course, had led to disputes at the dressmaker's in the village. But as Eliza began to describe the outrageous gowns Delia had wanted, the scarlet silk and the truly horrible puce and pink, she began to see the humor in the situation. By the time she finished Robert was grinning broadly, and her own good spirits had returned.

"Ah, that was nice." She drained her tea and set the cup down on the table next to her. From somewhere had appeared a stool for her feet, and she sat back, comfortably tired. This felt so good. It had been a long time since someone had taken care of her. She was the caretaker, the one who managed things. To be pampered was a luxury. To share the trials and tribulations of the day with her husband meant even more. "We need to do this more often, Robert."

"There's no reason why we couldn't," he said, and though his voice was light there was an edge to it that roused Eliza from her lethargy.

"Don't let's quarrel, Robert," she said, lazily. She had no desire to raise the old argument again. "This is too nice."

"You brought it up." He rose to pour himself some more tea. "I'd like us to be together more, too, Eliza, but things aren't exactly as I expected."

Oh, unfair! She opened her mouth to protest, but at that moment Shannon came in, clearing his throat. "Ahem. Excuse me, me lord, but there's a Mister John Evans to see you."

"Oh? Send him in, Shannon."

Eliza gave him a questioning look. "Who?"

"A distant cousin. He wrote to me some time back asking if I could help him secure a position. I thought—ah, here he is. Welcome to Stowcroft." Robert rose as a tall, stoop-shouldered man came into the room. He resembled Robert, though his fair hair was already thinning on top, while his features, similar to Robert's finely sculpted ones, were blurred. Eliza distantly remembered him from family gatherings. Whatever was he doing here?

"Thank you, my lord. My lady." John Evans made a jerky bow, his spectacles slipping down his nose. "Thank you for inviting me here and for finding a position for me."

"Shannon, we'll need fresh tea," Eliza said. "And what position is that, sir?"

"You may remember that John is a scholar," Robert put in. "I've offered him the position of schoolmaster for the village."

Eliza went very still. "I see," she said, and rose. "Robert, might I speak with you a moment?"

"I can leave," John stammered.

"No need. Excuse us, please." She smiled mechanically at him and swished into the hall, Robert behind her.

"This is dashed rude, Eliza," he said, stopping just outside the door.

"Oh? Would you prefer we fight in front of your cousin?"

"Fight?" He raised his eyebrows. "We're not going to fight."

"Oh, yes, we are! You always do this to me, Robert! You come home as if you've never been away and take charge of everything. You send the girls' governess on a holiday —"

"Which was due her, anyway."

"— and make decisions about Clive's education without consulting me —"

"We settled that one years ago, Eliza."

"— and now this! It is the outside of enough, Robert, hiring a teacher for the village when that's my duty."

Robert frowned, looking mystified. "I told you, he wrote to me asking for a position, and it struck me he'd be perfect for it. What does it matter which of us hires him?"

"Because I wanted to do it! Oh, you won't understand." She spun away, her arms crossed on her chest. "You never do."

"I do understand. You're emotional because you're increasing."

"Oh, yes, so I must be wrong about this."

"Not wrong, exactly, but overreacting. Be sensible, Eliza."

"Oh, so now I'm foolish."

"I didn't say that. I'm sorry if I didn't consult you, but it's done, now. I thought it would make life easier for you." He smiled. "A gift to you, as it were."

"A gift! I'm tired of your gifts, Robert."

254

"What? What's wrong with gifts?"

"What's wrong? You try to buy me with them, and you can't. You can't expect to leave your family for months on end and then have us welcome you with open arms, just because you bring us gifts."

"Are you implying that that's what I do? Buy my family's love?"

"It is what you do, Robert."

"You really think that?" He glared at her and turned on his heel, striding into the book-room. "Then in that case, I might as well leave."

"Papa, no!" a childish voice cried out, and Eliza looked up to see Delia and Laura on the stairs, horrified witnesses to this fight.

"Oh, no," she muttered, and went into the book-room. "Don't threaten that weapon unless you intend to use it."

Robert, slamming books and papers together into piles on his desk, looked up, his eyes cool. "Who says I won't?"

"The girls heard us, Robert." She sank into a chair, suddenly weary. "They're innocent, but they'll be hurt by this."

Robert continued stacking books. "Is it my fault I'm not wanted in my own house?"

"You know that's not true." Tiredly she rubbed her hand over her face. "But the children are getting older, Robert. They're having a harder time accepting why you go away."

"And you?" He perched on the corner of his desk, his gaze penetrating. "Do you want me to stay, Eliza?"

"I—." Eliza looked down at her hands. Did she want him to stay? Of course she did, more than anything. Having him here these past weeks had reminded her of all she had once wanted, all she'd hoped her life would be. Laughing with him over some private joke, sleeping in his arms at night, sharing the day to day problems of raising a family—all that was precious beyond any gift he could give her. Oh, yes, she wanted him to stay. He wouldn't, though. She knew better even to ask.

"I see," Robert said after a moment, when Eliza continued looking down at her hands. "That's it, then, isn't it."

Eliza looked up. "I don't want you to go, Robert."

"Don't you?" With one sweeping gesture he knocked over the books he had piled so neatly, scattering them across the desk and to the floor, making Eliza jump from the noise. "If you

255

wish to be with me so much, then why do you not come to London with me?"

"You know why!" She stared at him. Robert in a temper was a rare sight, indeed. "The children—"

"That don't fadge. The children are old enough to travel. I ask you to come with me." He paced across the room. "You will not come, and there I am, miles away from you—"

"Whose fault is that?" she exclaimed. "This is your home, Robert! Why cannot you stay here?"

"My home," he said bitterly. "When my children look at me as if I'm a stranger and my wife resents whatever I try to do for her."

"What do you expect?" she retorted, her own anger roused now. "You're gone most of the time, and yet when you return you expect us to jump to your bidding, like that!" She snapped her fingers. "And you bring us gifts, as if that makes it all well. Well, it doesn't, Robert. I cannot take much more of this. The children don't know you, and it's no wonder if they treat you as a stranger. And do you think I like living my life alone?"

"You could come to London with me, damn it." His eyes flickered over her. "Or you could have, before you got yourself pregnant."

"Got myself—ooh!" She snatched up a book and threw it at him, and he dodged it neatly. "As if you had nothing to do with it."

"As far as you're concerned, I don't."

"What?"

He wheeled to face her, bracing his hands on the back of a chair. "You don't want me here, do you, Eliza? You have everything just as you want it, and I'm just in the way. No wonder there's another child on the way." He sank into the chair, drawing his hands over his face, looking tired and much older than he was. "Another reason for you to stay behind."

"Don't be putting all the blame on me, Robert Evans. I don't recall hearing you protest on Twelfth Night. But now it's just another reason for you to go, isn't it?" She pressed her hand to her stomach. "Something else to blame me for."

"I would like, Eliza, just once, to think that I matter to you at least as much as our children do."

Eliza opened her mouth to protest, and then stopped. They had never settled this argument before. She doubted they'd set-

256

tle it now. "They need me more than you do," she said finally.

Robert's lips curled. "Of course. They must come first, by all means."

"They're children, Robert. I don't want them to grow up without their parents near, the way we had to. They need me."

"They'll be grown someday. What then?"

"I—"

"Never mind." He crouched and began picking up the scattered books. "This does no good. I'll pack and return to London as soon as I can."

"Robert—"

"No. Don't say it." He looked up at her, and for a moment there was such exquisite pain in his eyes she wanted to cry out. "There's really nothing more to say, is there?"

"No," she said, and blindly stumbled out of the room.

In the hall Laura rushed up to her. "Mama? Is Papa leaving?"

"Yes, Laura." Eliza touched her hair. "I'm afraid so."

"Ahem. Me lady." Shannon cleared his throat. "About Mister Evans."

"Mister Evans?" Eliza said blankly, and then remembered. Robert's cousin, who would now be the village schoolmaster. She had forgotten about him, so much had happened, yet the bell hadn't even rung yet for nuncheon. "Ask his lordship about him. It's nothing to do with me."

"Mama." Laura followed beside her, clutching at her hand. "Why is Papa leaving? Why?"

"He has business in London, Laura. I'm sorry."

"Make him stay!" she begged, her voice high and tight. "Please, don't make him go."

"Laura, I can't stop him."

"But I want you to."

Clumsily Eliza crouched to embrace her. "I can't, dearest. He has to go—"

"No, he doesn't!" Laura pulled away and Eliza rocked back, throwing out her arm to keep her balance. "You're making him go. I hate you!"

"Laura—"

"Leave me alone!" Laura cried, and ran.

"Laura," Eliza called after her. She stepped forward and stopped. There was no reasoning with her when she got upset like this; in this, they were much alike. If only she could make the child see — but how could she, when she didn't understand, herself?

There had been no sound, but something made Eliza look up. Delia, very pale, stood on the stairs, her hands gripping the banister so hard the knuckles were white. "Delia?" The girl started. "Delia, I'm sorry," she began and Delia turned, running up the stairs.

Eliza stared after her, and then, her shoulders slumping, turned away, quite, quite alone. She had, she realized, sinking down onto the bottom stair and putting her head in her hands, made a mull of it this time. Now what was she going to do?

Chapter Seven

The traveling carriage had been ordered brought 'round, and in the marquess's chamber his valet was busily at work, packing for the long journey ahead. The servants went quietly about their routines. Arguments between the lord and lady were not uncommon, Lady Stowe having the temper she did, but there was something different about this one. Though no one knew exactly what had happened, a sense of foreboding filled the air. It seemed nothing would ever be the same again.

Eliza had passed a restless night, and now she sat alone in her sitting room, away from Robert, away from her daughters. Last night Laura had broken down and cried in her arms, but Eliza knew she hadn't quite been forgiven. When the girls were older they would understand that sometimes things happened that were no one's fault, and everyone's. Someday they would know that some problems had no solutions. For now, though, they were better off with Miss Stevenson, who had returned from her holiday, and her brisk, unsentimental caring.

When had things gone so wrong? The question returned again to torment her. Back when she had first refused to travel to London, when Delia was but a babe? When Robert had begun staying away for longer than Parliament's session, doing work he considered more important than his family? She didn't know. In all that time life had gone on, deceptively serene, each of them seeming to accept the pattern it had taken. Only yesterday had that deception been revealed, and only because of the child she carried.

Poor little mite. She laid her hand on her stomach, as if the child understood what had happened and needed comfort. She loved this baby with the same fierce protectiveness she felt for all her children, and until yesterday she'd thought that Robert would someday feel the same. No matter what else he was, he was a good father. Now she was no longer so certain. He would accept the child, of course, perhaps even feel some affection for it, but he would never love it. Never. The baby she had hoped might bring them closer together would, instead, be the wedge that drove them, finally and inexorably, apart. Yesterday Robert had repudiated the child, making it clear that he blamed her for it.

Dear God, that hurt. As if he had nothing to do with it! She hadn't known on Twelfth Night that she might conceive, not after nine childless years. Nor, remembering that mad moment, did she think she would have cared. It was only later, when she had realized that she was pregnant, that she had felt — what? Astonished, because she had thought her child-bearing days were behind her. A little frightened, as she always was at the awesome responsibility of raising a child, and deeply happy. And, somewhere deep inside, so deep that she hardly admitted it, relieved.

The sound of carriage wheels on the drive outside made her look up, and she drifted over to the window. There stood the traveling carriage, its paintwork of burgundy and gold gleaming in the faint sun. She didn't have to travel in it, and that thought brought with it a mixture of sorrow and that strange relief. Relief that Robert was leaving her? No, of course not. Relief, though, that she didn't have to go, that she could stay behind? Yes, and for that she should be ashamed of herself. It meant that everything Robert had said to her yesterday was true.

It was a lowering thought. Eliza sank down onto the edge of a chair, staring blankly ahead of her. She had no desire to go to London. It was high time she admitted that, if only to herself, and stopped using the children as an excuse. But, why? She had enjoyed London, had enjoyed her season. Well, most of it. Long since she had learned to ignore others' opinions of her, and yet there had been a time when they mattered. In London there were people who'd made her feel inadequate and plain as a girl, and even after she was married. There was her mother-in-law, looking at her with open disdain. The wives of party leaders and cabinet ministers, who had treated her with indulgent courtesy for her ignorance of political matters. And then there was Robert, so involved in his work that he hadn't seemed to see her anymore. She was nothing in that world, not even to herself, and so she had seized any excuse to stay in Devon. True enough it was that the children had needed stability, and that they had needed her. True it was, too, that she had been glad of a place to hide. Robert was right. All this time she had been lying to herself, and to him. She didn't want to go to London with him.

The admission reverberated inside her, stunning in its power, and yet it felt familiar, something she always known about herself. Until now she hadn't admitted it, though. Instead she had occupied herself with other matters, as if by not thinking about it she could absolve herself. She knew differently now. Her marriage was in serious trouble. Once Robert left, things would never be the same between them, and she would be to blame. Not completely, of course, but at least Robert had always been open about what he wanted. She was the one who had lied, to him and to herself. The problems in her marriage were partly her fault.

I can't let him go. Jumping to her feet, she nearly ran from the room. Though she wasn't certain what she would say, she knew that she couldn't let Robert go without talking to him about this. Surely if she admitted her feelings to him he would listen. He had to. If he left her now, with their marriage in shreds, they would never repair the damage.

Robert's valet was just closing the last of the trunks when she burst into the room. Both men turned to look at her. "Yes, Eliza?" Robert said, his voice mild.

"I—I need to talk to you, Robert."

"The carriage is waiting." His face was expressionless. "We've said all there is to say."

"No, we haven't! Please, Robert. This is important."

He stared at her for a moment and then turned toward his valet, who was watching them with undisguised interest. "Very well. Walters, leave us." He waited until the valet had gone before turning to her. "Well?"

"I—" Eliza began, and stopped, flushing as she looked away. Under the coolness of his gaze her courage evaporated. She felt young and gauche, as she often had in the early days of their marriage. Robert was steady and dependable and did things according to some inner plan. She, on the other hand, was a creature of impulse. There were times when that could be disastrous. "I've been thinking."

Robert's face was not encouraging. "Yes?"

"About what you said—it's true. I haven't wanted to go to London. But that doesn't mean I can't change!" she burst out as he abruptly turned away, his hand flicking out as if to ward off pain. "Oh, Robert, please, let's talk about this—"

"How would you feel if I told you I don't like coming home?" he accused, rounding on her.

She closed her eyes. "You don't mean that." But inside she knew how she'd feel. Exactly as she did now, hurt, abandoned, angry, bewildered. "Robert, it's not you. It's London I don't like."

He paused and then shook his head, bending to pick up a valise. "It's too late, Eliza."

"Don't go." She followed him out of the room, into the corridor. "Please. Stay so we can talk about this. One more day won't make a difference. Please."

"I can't, Eliza. I left work undone." He looked pointedly at her stomach. "And you won't come with me, will you."

"I can't," she whispered.

"Then I don't see we have anything more to talk about." He turned and headed down the stairs.

"Robert!" Eliza started after him, and then stopped. He was right. There was nothing more to say, nothing that hadn't already been said. There was too much between them, too much hurt, too much distance. She wouldn't beg. It was too late. "You'll take care of yourself?"

He looked up in surprise from the bottom of the stairs. "Of course. You, as well?"

"Yes." She came down a few more stairs, encouraged by the mildness of his voice. "Will you—will you be home for the new baby?"

He hesitated. "Yes. I'll be back around the end of August." They gazed at each other in silence, wanting to say so much; unable to say anything. "Well," Robert said and turned.

"Robert." She couldn't let him go, not like this. Nothing she could say would heal the breach between them, and yet she had to say something. She had to tell him how much she loved him. With eyes only for him she hurried down the stairs. "Wait!"

Robert turned. "What?"

262

It all happened so fast that later Eliza was able to reconstruct what had happened only with some difficulty. Intent on reaching her husband, on convincing him of her feelings, she forgot everything else. Forgot the hollows in the oak stairs, worn smooth by the passing of hundreds of years and thousands of feet. Forgot the slipperiness of the old wood boards; forgot, most of all, the change in her own sense of balance. As she rounded the turn of the stairs, she slipped. At another time she might have recovered and saved herself; at another time, the results might not have been so disastrous. As it was, her foot went out from under her. With a little cry, Eliza fell headlong down the last few stairs onto the polished flagstoned floor of the hall.

Chapter Eight

The doctor had arrived, and now there was nothing for Robert to do but wait. Pacing back and forth in the corridor outside his wife's room, he relived yet again that awful moment when he had seen her hurtle down the stairs, and he had been unable to save her. He remembered the dazed look in her eyes turning to panic, and his own sharp fear, thrust aside for the moment. He always had been good in a pinch, and this certainly was that. She was lighter than he'd expected her to be, he'd thought as he lifted her, and she clung to him with a mixture of desperation and trust that pierced his heart. In spite of the hurt between them Eliza had turned to him. He only wished there were some way he could make everything right.

"Papa?" a frightened young voice said behind him. He turned to see his daughters running down the corridor toward him. Laura's blue satin sash was twisted at the waist of her white muslin dress, and Delia looked both very adult and very young. Instinctively he opened his arms and they crashed into him, burrowing against him for safety and reassurance. His arms closed around them, and for the first time the weight of the burden Eliza carried struck him. In other circumstances they would turn to their mother for comfort. Instead, they'd come to him, and he hadn't the slightest idea what to do.

"Hush," he said, more out of a need to speak than in hope of quieting Laura's noisy sobs. "Come, let's sit down." Holding them close, he led them over to the stairs, the damned, treacherous staircase, and sat on the top one, a daughter on either side. "It'll be all right."

"Miss Stevenson said Mama's hurt," Delia said.

"She fell on the stairs." He sounded surprisingly normal. "Doctor Fuller is with her now."

"I'm scared, Daddy." Laura burrowed her head against his shoulder. "Are you going back to London?"

"No," he said, and then repeated it, his voice more definite. No, he was not going back to London. What was there for him, after all? The dearest things in the world to him were in his arms now, and behind the closed door just down the corridor. His family. Until this last month he hadn't realized quite what they meant to him. Now he did, and all because Eliza had unexpectedly gotten pregnant. Because he'd gotten her pregnant, he amended. Now the baby's life was in danger, and that filled him with a fierce grief that was stunning in its intensity.

"It's my fault," Laura sniffled, and he looked down at her in surprise.

"What is, muffin?"

"I was mad at Mama because she was making you go away. I made something bad happen to her."

"What?" It was Robert's first encounter with a child's irrational sense of power over the world. How did one respond to such a statement?

"Don't be silly," Delia said. "You weren't even there when Mama fell."

"But I was mad at her."

"Well, so was I, and mad at Papa, too, but we didn't make anything happen. We're just children."

"Laura. Delia. Enough," Robert said, intervening before the bickering escalated. He felt like yelling at something himself, but he couldn't. "What happened yesterday and today was between your mother and me. Is that clear?"

"Yes, Papa." Delia drew back to look at him. "Are you really staying?"

"Yes, I'm really staying."

"And you won't go away ever again?" Laura begged.

He hesitated, torn between the work that meant so much to him, and the love and purpose he had found where he least expected it, here in his home. Giving up his life in London would be hard, but he would do it, for his family's sake. He had to. "I think I might . . ." he began, and at that moment a door opened behind them. Forgetting everything else, he got to his feet and turned to face Dr. Fuller.

265

"All is well," the doctor said, nodding at them, and Laura let out a whoop of joy.

"Laura," Robert reproved, but he grinned at her, lightheaded with relief and hope. Thank God. Oh, thank God. Only now did he admit how scared he had been, not just for Eliza's sake, but for his own. Had something happened to the child Eliza would probably never have forgiven him. Nor would he have forgiven himself. Now, though, they had a second chance. He rather liked the idea of being a father again.

He rose, placing his hands on his daughters' shoulders. "Go along now. Everything's all right."

"But, Papa," Delia protested, still looking worried.

"Go on. I'll come talk with you later." He watched them go, Laura skipping, Delia looking back at him over her shoulder. He felt rather like skipping himself. That his life had changed was something he would think about when Eliza was well. Nothing else quite mattered, he thought, and turned to talk to the doctor.

Eliza could hear Robert's voice in the hall. He hadn't left then. Not that she'd expected him to, but likely he would, now. The crisis was over. She pressed her hand to her swelling abdomen. All was well, thank God. So why did she feel so like crying?

Robert's voice grew momentarily louder as the door to her room opened, and then it ceased. Opening her eyes to slits, she watched him speak in a low voice to her maid, dismissing her, and then cross the room. Quickly she closed her eyes again, postponing the evil moment when he would leave. "I know you're awake," he said, sitting on the side of the bed.

Eliza opened her eyes reluctantly. He was smiling, but there was a crease between his brows and his eyes were shadowed. "I'm sorry." She held out her hand to him, clinging to his warm fingers. "I didn't mean to do such a stupid thing."

"I'm sorry, too." He bent and kissed her hand, and then enfolded it in both of his. "If we hadn't been arguing—"

"Yes, well, that's past, and everything's fine."

"Except you have to stay abed for a week."

Her face twisted. "Yes, well, I shan't like that."

"And you were supposed to be careful, anyway."

266

"Well, I'm not as young as I used to be," she said, watching him warily. Now just what had Dr. Fuller told him?

"So I understand. You might very well have trouble this time."

"And I might not."

"Why didn't you tell me?" he demanded.

"It never came up. I felt fine, and I thought—"

"That I wouldn't care? Did you really believe that of me, Liza?"

"I never thought that," she protested. "Whatever else has happened, Robert, I know you care."

"What, then? Do you realize that since I've been home you've tried to shut me out of your life?"

"I haven't—"

"And for the life of me I don't know what I've done wrong."

"You're going to leave me again!" she cried, and fell back against the pillows, squeezing her eyes shut.

"Liza, don't. I'm sorry." He bent over her, laying his face against hers. With a sob she slid her arms around his neck, clinging to him and giving into weak, hateful tears. "Don't cry, darling."

"I hate crying," she sobbed. "I hate it, but if I yell I'll get upset, and I can't have that, but I'm just so damned mad at you, Robert Evans!"

Unforgivably he chuckled. "That sounds more like my Eliza."

"It's not funny." She nestled against him, loathe to move. She really was angry with him. She was. In a moment she would tell him so. For now though she just wanted to love him.

"I know it isn't, dear, and I've given you enough to be mad at, haven't I?" He drew back, looking down at her, his eyes serious. "I had a chance to do some thinking, Liza. I've been stupid, going off and leaving you."

"Robert—"

"It's high time I took a look at my life and made some changes. I won't be going back to London, Eliza. I'm staying here with you and our children."

Eliza pulled back. "No. That won't do."

"What? Of course it will." He frowned. "Damn it, Eliza, you're the most maddening person! I thought you'd be happy about this."

"I am, but—ooh! If this isn't just like you!" She pulled back, crossing her arms over her chest. "When I had just decided that I was wrong not to go to London so you wouldn't have to give up your work, now you're the one who makes the noble gesture! It's not fair."

"Does it matter, so long as we're together?"

"Yes! I want to go to London."

"You want what!"

"I said I want to go to London." At the sight of his thunderstruck face, she began to giggle. "Oh, if you could see yourself."

"This isn't funny, Liza. What the devil are you talking about?"

"You're not the only one who's been thinking." She gazed up at him. "You were right, you know. I did use the children as an excuse. There's no reason I couldn't have gone to town with you years ago. No, let me finish." She laid her fingers on his lips. "I was scared, Robert. I remembered all the beautiful women and the political wives and—well, I was scared."

"Of what?" he said, mystified.

"That you'd look at them and then wonder what you ever saw in me."

"Are you daft? Why the devil do you think I keep coming back to Stowcroft?"

"I don't know. Why the devil do you?"

"Because I love you, damn it! I'm sorry," he said, lowering his voice. "You could make a saint swear, Eliza. But I do love you. I always have."

"Truly?"

"Truly."

Eliza closed her eyes, and though she smiled, content and secure from what he had just said, she sighed. "We've made a mull of it, haven't we."

"It's not too late." He gazed down at her. "Did you mean what you said, about London?"

She opened her eyes. "Yes. I was thinking next spring, when the baby's old enough to travel. Well, Delia will be having her season in a few years, and she should grow accustomed to town before then."

"Is that the only reason?"

"No. I love you, Robert. I—oh!"

Instantly his gaze sharpened. "What is it? What's wrong?"

"The baby."

Robert jumped to his feet. "I'll call the doctor back."

"No, silly. Come here." She reached out for his hand. "The baby moved. Oh! There it is again." Grasping his hand, she pulled it to her abdomen. For a moment there was nothing, and then he felt it, a tiny ripple of motion. Just so had they shared the first movements of their other babies, and it was as special now as it was then.

His child. Robert looked down at his hand, absurdly large on Eliza's slight body, and felt the wonder of it sizzle through him. A precious gift of the heart from one to the other, and he had nearly refused it. "I don't want to be apart from you, Eliza," he said, his voice low. "I don't want to miss seeing this child grow, the way I did with the others." He raised his head and looked at her, his eyes clear and defenseless. "I want you with me in London, but this is our home, too." A home he had so nearly lost. "I want to be here."

"We don't have to stay here all the time, though. I wouldn't ask that of you."

"No, and I see no reason why we should live in London all the time, either." He reached out to tuck back a strand of hair from her forehead. "It doesn't matter, does it? As long as we're together."

"Yes. Oh, Robert." Her eyes were luminous. "Can we do it, do you think?"

He looked down at her hand in his, idly stroking her slender fingers. "Yesterday you accused me of trying to buy your love, yours and the girls. Maybe I did, but I didn't know what else to do. But I've learned. I think we both have."

"I think so, too. But, Robert, there are gifts you can give me."

"What?" he asked, eyeing her as she rose to her elbow and looped her arm around his neck.

"Gifts of the heart," she said, pressing her lips to his. "We'll give each other gifts of the heart."

And they did.

Reversal of Fortunes

by Nina Porter

Chapter One

"That settles it," Mama cried, shaking her blond curls in emphasis. "Since, Phillipa, *you* have failed so utterly, *I* shall have to do it myself. Tomorrow then I intend to begin the necessary steps to reverse our fortunes."

Since it was Mama's lamentable mismanagement of the said fortunes that had left the three of them in their present impecunious condition, Phillipa heard this decision with some trepidation. Across the room, Aunt Pitty heard it with even more. She gave a tremendous sigh, shook her graying head and, covering her mouth with her lacy handkerchief, whimpered softly.

Poor Aunt Pitty, Phillipa thought. All these years of keeping quiet, of bearing whatever Mama said in respectful silence. The life of a poor relation was not pleasant in any case, and in Aunt Pitty's case — and hers, too, though she didn't care so much for herself — Mama had been a heavy cross to bear.

The last five years had been difficult for them all, well, except perhaps Mama, who, after all, always had things her own way. How she was to accomplish that *this* time, Phillipa could not begin to imagine. But she did know that Mama was not to be thwarted. If Mama decided to do something, she did it. And if it was not in the highest taste, or not feasible financially, Mama simply ignored that. Mama was good at ignoring things she didn't like — very good.

Phillipa swallowed a sigh. Should she voice her objections to this horrible plan now or keep her counsel? Sometimes Mama took these spells, made dubious plans, and then the next day all was forgotten. Many times the best thing to do was to remain silent — and hope that whatever was driving Mama to such strange actions would disappear overnight.

Unfortunately this did not often happen. Mama, once she got her mind set on something, seldom changed course. However, at the moment silence still seemed like the best defense.

Aunt Pitty, however, must not have thought so, for with a tremulous sigh, she lowered her handkerchief and said carefully, "Felicity, my dear, do you really think it wise to—"

Mama swung around, dropping her needlepoint to the floor so sharply that it almost seemed thrown down. "What do you mean?" she demanded. "Of course I think it wise to—"

She broke off as Jimson appeared in the sitting room doorway. "Guests, Mrs. Pardonner. Lady Linden and Miss Martine Linden."

Phillipa, accidentally pricking her finger with the needle, stifled an exclamation of dismay. Of all the ladies who might come calling on Mama, Lady Linden was the one any reasonable person would wish least to see.

From her delicate lyre back chair, Aunt Pitty sent her niece a look of commiseration. "I do not feel quite well," she began. "Perhaps I should go up and—"

"Nonsense," snapped Mama, smoothing down her stylish gown. "A minute ago you felt perfectly fine." She twisted her face into a frown. "I cannot for the life of me understand why you don't like Lady Linden. She has been most kind to us."

Phillipa bit her bottom lip, determined to hold her peace. Kind hardly described Lady Linden, who was a deplorable gossipmonger, the most deplorable in all London. Why Mama should even like the woman was quite beyond her understanding, except that from Lady Linden Mama gathered all of the latest gossip about the *ton*. It was obvious to Phillipa that, even with her dowry, *they* did not belong in that elevated society. But as usual, Mama meant to have her way.

"Show them right in," Mama said, and Aunt Pitty sank back into her chair with another pitiful sigh.

Jimson left to do so and Mama sent Phillipa a quelling look. "And you will remain, too. Poor Martine needs some female friends."

Phillipa did not reply to this. Undoubtedly poor Martine needed friends of any type or kind, but she wasn't likely to find them, not as long as she persisted in carrying tales all about London.

Lady Linden came bustling into the room in a gown of satin

274

cerise the seams of which threatened to part with each step. Behind her came Martine, her gown of such a brilliant yellow that it seemed chosen precisely to make her complexion even more sallow than it was. Her thin nose quivered with the scent of fresh *on-dits*.

Unkind, Phillipa told herself, you are being quite unkind. But the truth of the matter was that Martine did look like a cat, its nose twitching on the trail of a mouse.

"Oh Felicity," Lady Linden cooed, rustling across the drawing room and coming to a halt in front of Mama. "How pleased I am that you are at home. We have had the most dreadful luck this afternoon. Can you imagine? Everywhere we went the people were out."

Aunt Pitty, meeting Phillipa's eyes, was suddenly overcome with a fit of coughing and Phillipa, smothering her own laughter, grabbed up her stitching and bestowed upon it her full attention.

But though she kept her eyes upon her design, her ears were alert and her heart palpitating. Would Mama disclose to Lady Linden this dreadful new plan of hers? If she did, all London would soon know that Felicity Pardonner had given up on her only daughter.

It was most unkind of Mama to set all of London talking about her spinsterhood, but Phillipa knew there was no point in expostulating with her maternal parent. She had tried it more than once in the five years since Papa had departed this life, but always to no avail.

"Sit down," Mama said to Lady Linden, waving her grandly to a nearby chair.

Phillipa heard Aunt Pitty's indrawn breath. The chair was old and not very substantial. And Lady Linden was — even in the kindest terms — extremely substantial. Lady Linden looked at the chair and, shaking her head of girlishly bouncing curls, moved to the settee to Phillipa's intense relief — and no doubt Aunt Pitty's, too. "Oh no, my dear," Lady Linden said with a girlish giggle. "That chair is far too delicate for a voluptuous form like mine." And the woman actually looked down at her vast front in approbation.

Aunt Pitty was taken with another fit of coughing and Phillipa knew she herself would have been laughing, too, except that from the look in Mama's green eyes, more trouble was coming, much more trouble.

"I have a serious problem," Mama said, leaning toward Lady Linden after she had distributed her bulk on the settee. "And you are just the person to help me."

Lady Linden preened. "I should think so, my dear. You can ask me anything, anything at all. I know everything there is to know about the *ton*. Tell me, what is it you wish to speak of?"

"Marriage," Mama said portentously.

Lady Linden straightened, her eyes gleaming. "Why there's not an eligible *parti* in all of London that I don't know every scrumptious detail about." She sent a commiserating look in Phillipa's direction, one that made her hackles rise. "Of course, your poor girl *is* a little long in the tooth already."

The nerve of the woman, Phillipa thought, bristling but keeping her tongue between her teeth. How dare Lady Linden say such things and with her stickish—and unmarried—daughter right there in the room.

Miss Linden, making a promenade of the room and examining each piece of furnishing, paused long enough to nod in agreement. "Indeed, yes, Mama says youth is all. Though of course beauty is important."

"That may well be," Mama said petulantly. "But it is not for Phillipa that I am seeking." She gave her daughter a look of complete disgust. "She has utterly failed in her duty to her family. At twenty she is on the shelf. No, since our fortunes are at a low, and she has not captured a husband to restore them, I have despaired of help from her."

Phillipa stiffened, but still managed to keep silent.

"She is certainly not a beauty," Lady Linden observed, for all the world as though Phillipa could not hear every insulting word. "Such dark hair is not the fashion this year. Nor are dark eyes. Now you, my dear Felicity, you have real beauty."

Mama straightened in her chair, her face glowing with a smile of delight. And Phillipa wondered for the thousandth time how she could have been the offspring of such a vain and uncaring parent. If it hadn't been for Aunt Pitty, she doubted that she would have reached adulthood. But Aunt Pitty had always been there for her, loving and caring, whispering that it would be all right. It was to Aunt Pitty she'd run with her childhood sorrows and it was for Aunt Pitty that she'd almost accepted one of the few suitors who had presented themselves.

But Aunt Pitty had given her their secret sign — the one that meant 'don't do it' — and later she'd told Phillipa to stand firm, not to marry except where she could love.

Yes, spinster Aunt Pitty had been much more a mother than Mama ever was. But Mama was Mama and long ago Phillipa had ceased to rail at her fate. She was too busy trying to make the best of matters.

"Thank you," Mama said to Lady Linden, leaning over to pat her hand. "You are most kind. Now I was thinking that perhaps you could tell me — in the strictest confidence of course —"

"Of course," muttered Lady Linden, her eyes flashing avidly.

"In strictest confidence," Mama repeated, clearing her throat, "that you might tell me if any suitable gentleman is looking for a wife."

"A suitable gentleman," Lady Linden echoed, her chins quivering with pleasure at this new *on-dit*. "A husband for you?"

"Of course for me," Mama replied. "Phillipa has no sense in these matters. She has turned down several eligible *partis* already. So," she pressed a hand dramatically to her bosom, "it appears I shall have to handle matters myself."

"Yourself," repeated Lady Linden, in obvious gratification. "Well now, let me think." She pulled at one of her false curls, twisting it around one pudgy beringed finger. "There is Major Hardesty, uncle to the Viscount Valdane."

Miss Linden turned from the mantel where she had been wrinkling her thin nose at a painting by an unknown artist, presumably because it was not very valuable. "Oh, the Viscount Valdane! He is the handsomest man!" She fastened her watery gaze on Phillipa. "Surely you have seen him. Tall and dark, with the most charming smile. They say he's the best catch of the season."

Phillipa knew that many men were given that title. Unfortunately, she also knew — by sight at least — the Viscount Valdane. And he was every bit as handsome as the stickish Miss Linden insisted. He also had about him that dark slightly sinister look that meant danger to the female heart. Her heart, of course, was quite untouched. The viscount had no idea that she even existed. And given Mama's present turn of mind, Phillipa could only hope to keep it that way.

"Oh yes!" cried Lady Linden, clapping her plump hands in glee. "I know the thing to do! I shall give a dinner party!"

"Capital!" cried Mama. "That is just the thing!"

"Yes, indeed," agreed Lady Linden. "I shall invite Major Hardesty, of course. And the viscount."

The look that Lady Linden sent her daughter then convinced Phillipa that it was not Mama's nuptials that were foremost in her ladyship's mind. No, Phillipa thought, unless she were greatly mistaken, the Viscount Valdane was destined to be Miss Linden's dinner partner — and, if her mama had her way, much, much more.

Chapter Two

"And so," Phillipa told her bosom bow Constance the next day, "I am doomed to watch Mama make eyes at this Major Hardesty — and Miss Linden" — she shuddered — "will no doubt throw herself at the viscount."

"How awful for you," Constance cried, her round face full of concern. "But they say the viscount —" She blushed prettily. "That is all the girls rave over him — that dangerous look, that dashing —"

Phillipa snorted, "It is *he* who is in danger! To have Lady Linden after him — and for such a daughter, should give any man pause."

Constance nodded. "Ah yes, still you are fortunate. I should like to be there just to see the man — up close."

Several nights later, looking around Lady Linden's ostentatiously appointed table, Phillipa recalled her conversation with her friend. But even the good-natured Constance would have found her spirits dampened by *this* assemblage. Baron Linden was absent — he never deigned to grace his own dinner table — or so his lady had announced. Perhaps he was too busy trying to find the money to keep it provided with food.

At any rate the setting was uneven: Mama, Lady Linden, Phillipa, and Martine, on the female side, and the major and the viscount on the male.

Since Lady Linden lacked male guests, she had contrived to put the viscount on one side of the table with Martine, and the major, flanked by Mama and Phillipa, on the other. The head of the table she reserved, quite naturally, for herself.

The meal began quite drearily with Lady Linden expostulating on the sad dearth of efficient servants, and the others agreeing with her wholeheartedly. Phillipa, to whom servants were of little concern, was, on the other hand, most dreadfully concerned with the nearness of the viscount. As the daughter of a mere merchant, albeit a wealthy one, she hadn't had much to do with the *ton*. She might have, of course, if Papa had not died as he had. If he were still alive, he would have provided her with a very substantial dowry, a dowry large enough to attract some lord whose funds had suffered loss. In fact, Papa had often spoken in glowing terms of the honor her eventual marriage would bring the family.

But that was before. After his death Mama, carried away by the kind of freedom she had never known before, had contrived to spend all that he had saved, including the dowry, so that when it was time for Phillipa to leave the schoolroom there were no funds left for the dowry or a come-out. After that Phillipa, though she knew she was of passable looks, was of little interest to a lord in need—or any other.

She had accepted this, she reminded herself sternly, as she glanced across the table at the viscount, accepted it because she had no other recourse. But she had not been much in the company of lords, and the viscount—well, Martine had certainly not exaggerated the charm of his smile. It was a smile to set a foolish girl's heart pounding—as witness the ridiculous glow on Martine's normally pasty face, the way her watery gaze returned so often to his face.

Phillipa frowned. She was not ordinarily so unkind in her thoughts about others, but this plan of Mama's had quite disquieted her. And the extreme proximity of the viscount did little to settle her already overwrought nerves.

Lady Linden leaned toward the others, so perilously far forward that the front of her gown, a creation in a rather bilious green, adorned in the very middle of the bodice with a large, similarly bilious, flower, was in imminent danger of dipping into her soup plate. "Oh yes, Major Hardesty, I am a firm believer in the institution of marriage. A very firm believer. Nothing is better for a man. Or a woman." She batted her lashes against her plump red cheeks and shifted in her chair, which, since it didn't protest, must have been reinforced to hold her bulk. Phillipa reminded herself again that it was ill advised to make unkind judgments on others.

So she turned her attention to her soup. But notwithstanding Lady Linden's encomiums on her French chef, the soup was not only unappetizing to the eyes, but so salty as to approach inedibility.

Phillipa shifted her gaze to the viscount. Perhaps her palate was simply not as aristocratic. The viscount tasted his soup and elevated his hawkish nose a trifle, quickly masking the glimmer of dislike that crossed his handsome features. So, she thought, his opinion agreed with hers. Now why should that make her feel triumphant?

"Isn't this soup the outside of enough?" Martine turned the full force of her damp eyes on the viscount.

"Indeed it is," he agreed dryly. And at that moment he raised his head, his eyes meeting Phillipa's. She caught her breath — surely she was mistaken. But his eyes were *twinkling*. And then, while she felt the color rising to her cheeks, he slowly lowered an eyelid in a conspiratorial wink!

"Milord," pouted Martine, actually having the temerity to pull at the man's coat sleeve. "Have you seen the learned pig?"

The viscount turned back to the woman at his side, but not before Phillipa saw his face which wore, though only momentarily, the look of a man much put upon.

"Of which learned pig do you speak?" he inquired. "The one at Bullock's or the one at Farrington's Folly?"

"Oh — ah — either," Martine stammered, evidently disconcerted by the direct gaze of his eyes.

They were quite attractive eyes, and Phillipa fell to considering their owner's charms. So deep was she in her contemplation of the viscount's physical perfection that she was startled to hear Mama say sharply, "Phillipa, for mercy's sake! Come down out of the clouds."

"Yes, Mama," Phillipa replied, dutifully turning toward her.

"Major Hardesty asked you a question," Mama said brusquely. "Kindly answer it."

The major smiled, showing several missing teeth — or rather the sockets where they had once been. He inched his considerable weight toward her and said, "I asked, hmmm, my dear, if you like the hunt."

"I'm afraid I have not had the opportunity to hunt," Phillipa said. "Papa did not keep hunting stock and —"

"Not keep hunting stock!" the major thundered. "How could the man live?"

"He managed quite well," Phillipa replied, trying not to bristle. "After all, his trade took quite—"

"Ah yes," the major proclaimed. "Trade."

Phillipa stiffened. With that tone he might as well have said "thievery." How could this sanctimonious creature put on such airs?

"Really, Uncle," the viscount said. "From your intonation one would think our family was composed entirely of sainted clergy. I know for a fact that our revered ancestors included some men of quite an unsavory reputation."

Phillipa's previous good will toward the viscount wavered. Did he, too, intend to cast aspersions on Papa's trade? She was about to enlighten him as to his mistake—for she quite well knew that Papa had been the most honest of men—when Martine put a hand most familiarly on the viscount's sleeve.

"Oh, Charles—you don't mind if I call you Charles?" she twittered, batting her lashes in a poor imitation of her mother.

The viscount inclined his head a scant half inch, but Martine took it for an affirmative. "Oh Charles, you are so right. These dreadful tradespeople can be—"

"I'm afraid you were not hearing me right," he interrupted, his tone almost scathing. "I cast no aspersions on those in trade." He looked across the table at Phillipa and allowed himself a small smile. "Indeed, I happen to have been acquainted with Miss Pardonner's father—in a business way—and no more decent man ever walked the face of the earth."

Phillipa felt such a rush of gratitude that it quite overwhelmed her, causing her to look at him in a much warmer fashion than was consistent with good breeding. Hastily she dropped her gaze to her plate.

"But Charles," Martine whined. "You said—"

"I *said* that my revered ancestors included some of unsavory reputation. I said nothing whatsoever concerning Miss Pardonner's. I assume them all to be men of the highest character." And he flashed Phillipa the smile that she'd heard had become famous in all fashionable London for its effect on the female gender.

"Quite right," Major Hardesty interrupted, screwing up his face in a way she supposed denoted thoughtfulness. "Hmmm, quite right. Nothing the matter with a little trade, especially when it brings in the funds."

"Oh, Major," Mama said, pressing closer to him. "You are so wise. I knew I should like you immensely."

The major looked pleased. So, Phillipa thought, perhaps she would have a new father. The major didn't seem a bad sort, in spite of his somewhat disreputable looks and a definite odor of dog that clung to his person. But to think that she might be related to the viscount, to Charles—

She let herself think his Christian name, but she would never impose as Martine did and say it aloud.

At the head of the table, Lady Linden laughed gaily. "Ah, you lucky young people. Just ready to embark on that great adventure—marriage. How I do envy you."

The viscount straightened. "You need not waste any envy on me," he said dryly. "I do not propose to put on the leg shackles—not in the foreseeable future."

Lady Linden chuckled, apparently not at all put out by this hitch in her plans. "Of course," she simpered. "Not until you have found the *right* woman." And she directed her gaze at Martine, who managed to look horribly embarrassed and happily enamored at the same time.

Phillipa tried to discern the viscount's feelings in the matter, but his face presented only a bland mask of politeness. Surely he could be taken at his word when he said he did not wish to marry. Still, Lady Linden was a formidable opponent. Like Mama, she allowed nothing to deflect her from her purpose.

"My dear," the major said, leaning toward Phillipa. "Tomorrow I shall come to call and—hmmm—perhaps you and your dear mama will grace my carriage with your—hmmm—loveliness."

Somewhat surprised, Phillipa hesitated. Surely the major didn't think *she* had anything to say about Mama's choice of a husband. "Yes," she assured him finally, "that sounds quite nice."

Chapter Three

But their ride in Hyde Park was definitely not nice. When the viscount didn't appear with his uncle, Phillipa suffered a sharp spasm of mortification. She had put on her best walking dress — not this year's fashion, since Mama had reserved this year's new gowns for herself — but still quite nice. And she'd had the dresser go to great pains with her hair, which she'd always been told was one of her better attributes. It was silly, of course. She meant nothing to the viscount, and she'd been telling herself all morning not to expect him with his uncle, but still she was disappointed.

Politeness must be served though, and she resigned herself to a boring ride as she let the major assist her into his curricle. He assisted Mama also and then to Phillipa's surprise instead of taking the seat opposite them, he put himself between them. Since the major was a man of some proportions as was Mama, this put them all at very close quarters, too close for Phillipa's comfort.

Mama didn't seem to mind at all though, and Phillipa swallowed a sigh. No doubt Mama thought close proximity to the man would further her ends. But however much Phillipa wished her mother success — and in a way she must because it was certainly true that the family fortunes needed repair and they did have to live — she didn't relish the prospect of having the major in the family.

He was such a coarse man, smelling of dogs again. Did they sleep with him? she wondered. But even worse was that slur he had cast upon Papa, who was a better man by far than any pretentious military major. After living with Papa how could Mama wish to live with such a man as the major? How could she wish to kiss him? Now the viscount—he was an entirely different matter. Kissing him—

"Nice day for a hunt," the major said with great heartiness. "Dogs'd love it. Hmmm. Good for a man's blood." And he dealt himself a resounding blow on the chest and looked around as though he himself were responsible for the lovely spring weather.

"Oh my," Mama simpered. "Major, dear, you're so terribly strong. And you know so much."

The major actually appeared to increase in size, puffing out his chest. "Well, hmmm, if it's about the hunt, hmmm, ain't no one knows more'n me."

He turned to Phillipa with his gap-toothed smile. "And this little lady here oughta let me give her a mount. Hmmm. Teach her to ride to hounds, I would. Hmmm. Make a first class horsewoman of her." And he actually reached over and patted her on the knee.

Phillipa swallowed and awaited the outburst. But Mama had either not seen, or what was more likely, had chosen not to notice, the major's reprehensible behavior.

"I'm afraid not, sir," Phillipa answered. "I don't care to ride." Horses were foreign creatures to her—good to draw carriages, but certainly not something on which she wished to climb. But it wasn't the prospect of learning to ride that caused her present distress. She simply could not understand how Mama could allow the major to take such liberties with her daughter's person.

If he felt inclined to pat knees, then let him pat Mama's. Mama had been married and knew firsthand what transpired between men and women. Phillipa sighed. It looked like *that* was something *she* would never know. But for the moment she found herself grateful for that very fact. She couldn't imagine kissing the major, couldn't imagine it at all. But Mama was different—especially where the family fortunes were concerned.

"Yes, sir," the major said heartily. "A beautiful day. Hmmm."

Sticking a none-too-clean glove under Phillipa's nose, he exclaimed, "Look! Over there in that carriage. The Prince Regent hisself."

Phillipa looked. She had seen the regent before, though not so close as this. He was certainly a portly man—not at all regal

285

in appearance despite his rich looking clothes. And as to the rumor that he wore stays — it looked like it might well be true.

"That woman with him," the major went on. "That skinny one. She won't last."

In spite of herself Phillipa was intrigued. "How do you know a thing like that?"

The major grinned. "I know Prinny, the old devil. He don't really like 'em so young. Hmmm. He likes his women older — and with more meat on their bones." He glanced at her bosom. "Hmmm. *If* you know what I mean."

Digesting this appalling piece of information, Phillipa reflected that perhaps the major had it the wrong way round. Perhaps young and beautiful ladies did not care for such an abundance of flesh as that sported by the Regent. But then if he did want a lovely young woman, the regent had the means wherewith to get her. Some women would do anything for money. She had only to think of Mama to know that.

"Yes, yes." Mama pressed even closer to the major, leaning her bosom on his arm. "But, my dear sir, tell us about your life. Serving in the military must have been so challenging. So terribly heroic."

"Indeed it was," he began, puffing out his chest again. "Why I remember once in—"

Phillipa stopped listening and let her thoughts drift to the viscount, to Charles. For some reason she had been calling him that in her thoughts ever since the dinner at Lady Linden's. And yet very little had passed between them that night, only that small exchange at the table when he had so ably defended Papa.

As soon as the meal ended, Charles had pleaded a previous engagement, disentangled himself from Martine's grasp, and taken his leave. Phillipa had been sorry to see him go, but she thought she could sense his eagerness to put the evening behind him. It must be difficult to keep a polite face with Martine clutching at him in that awfully possessive way. How could Lady Linden ever imagine that a man like Charles could have a *tendre* for a pasty-faced chit like Martine? Phillipa sighed again — she was being catty, but even at her best Martine was no great beauty. And Charles had a huge estate, he had no need to marry for funds. Besides, he would never do such a crass thing.

He was a wonderful man, Charles was, not at all as she had imagined him. Not cold and distant — at least not with her. And his concern for her, though it had probably been prompted by good breeding, had seemed genuine. Martine was right about one thing, though. All London's ladies must be buzzing about him. A man like that would have his pick.

Strange that he hadn't already married. There was hardly an unmarried woman in London who would have turned him away. Certainly she would not have.

Marriage to Charles . . . It would never happen, of course, but still it was pleasant to think about, pleasanter than listening to the major's pompous lies.

Early the next afternoon, Phillipa sat in the sitting room of Constance's mother, recounting the details of the dinner and the ride to her friend over a cup of tea.

"He actually said that!" Constance cried. "How kind of him to defend your papa. And right, of course," she hastened to add. "Your papa was a fine man."

She leaned forward eagerly. "But just think of Miss Linden. How can she throw herself at him like that? How can she behave in such a demeaning fashion?"

Phillipa shook her head. "I'm sure I don't know. Oh, Constance, whatever shall I do? This plan of Mama's is going to be the end of me. How can I hold up my head when all London is talking?" She lowered her cup. "Everyone will be whispering about me."

Constance's round face wrinkled in a frown. "Did she — did your mama speak of marriage in front of the viscount?"

"Oh no!" Phillipa cried. "Not yet. But I'm dreadfully afraid she will. If she accepts the major, Charles — that is, the viscount — will become family."

She sighed and continued in a quiet voice, "I am dreadfully worried. Sooner or later, it's bound to come out. And when it does I shall be absolutely mortified!"

Constance leaned forward to pat her hand. "Now, *now,* my dear. It can't be as bad as all that. Remember, Lady Linden had already known about your mama's plan for several days."

Phillipa straightened. "Merciful heavens! That's it! Everyone already knows! That's why people were looking at us so strangely in the park today. Not because we were all jammed together in the same seat, but because they've heard what Mama means to do." She put down her tea cup with a clatter. "And — and that's why *he* was so kind to me last night! From pity! Oh, dear, now I shall really die of shame!"

And nothing Constance could do or say could make her feel any better. When she left some time later, Phillipa held her head high, facing down whatever stares might come her way. But inside she was shriveling. If only she could find a corner and hide in it.

No corner was forthcoming, but by the time Phillipa reached home she had made her decision. None of this was her fault — and she simply would not act as though it were. She didn't intend to go creeping about the city like some criminal just because she had been cursed with a maternal parent possessed of very little sense, one who insisted on making a raree show of herself. But still, Phillipa could not help wishing that Charles — no, she had better call him by his more distant name — that the Viscount Valdane were not involved in this awful charade.

Chapter Four

That afternoon Phillipa, Aunt Pitty, and Mama sat at their stitching. Phillipa had had a good talk with Aunt Pitty, and that had helped to raise her spirits. She did not quite believe Aunt Pitty's affirmation that people had better things with which to occupy their minds than Mama's weird doings. Though she was not really a part of it, Phillipa had lived on the edge of the *ton* for a long time, hearing about its every whim and fancy from Mama who knew everything about everyone because she followed its doings most avidly. So Phillipa knew that scandal — scandal of any and every kind — was the food and drink of many of the elite. But in a way, Aunt Pitty was right. Certainly, the *ton* meant nothing to Phillipa — except the viscount she admitted honestly — and she wasn't likely to see him again.

After they had stitched in silence for some time, Jimson appeared in the doorway. "Major Hardesty to call, madame."

"Show him in!" Mama cried. "Immediately." And she fussed with her hair and adjusted her gown like a green girl just out of the schoolroom.

The major paused in the doorway and struck a pose. Phillipa supposed it was meant to show off his heroic figure — unfortunately what it showed most was the portion of his anatomy just below his waistcoat, a portion of rather large proportions. "Good day to you, lovely ladies," he almost bellowed, and crossed the room to stop in front of Mama. "I've come on business," he announced solemnly. "Hmmm. Serious business."

Mama fluttered her lashes. "Of course, Major dear. I shall send the others out."

The major shook his head and lowered his bulk into a nearby

chair. "Rather not," he said. "Rather, hmmm, let 'em hear."

Mama looked a trifle startled, then she rallied. "Of course, of course." She smiled at him sweetly, preening a little. "Now, Major, do tell us about this business you spoke of."

So, Phillipa thought, the major was really going to do it. He was going to propose to Mama.

"I've come about marriage," he said, puffing out his chest. "A man in my position needs a wife. My old one's been gone this twelvemonth. Hmmm. So I've been looking about. And I've decided I'd like to offer for—"

"Oh yes!" cried Mama, clapping her hands. "Yes, I accept! When shall we call the banns?"

The major looked somewhat startled. "Well, hmmm, shouldn't we ask the little lady?"

Mama shrugged. "Phillipa? Why? It's no concern of hers."

The major's face slowly turned pink. "No concern?" he blustered. "That's carrying it a bit far, ain't it? I don't hold—hmmm—with this newfangled idea of letting a girl choose just any man she wants. But if Phillipa's going to marry me—"

"Phillipa!" Mama's voice rose to an earsplitting shriek. "My God man, why should Phillipa marry you?"

The major's complexion darkened from pink to purple. "Because I offered for her!" he thundered. "And you, you just accepted my offer."

He got, somewhat heavily, to his feet and stood huffing and puffing. "What kind of havey-cavey game are you playing, madame?"

Mama sprang out of her chair to face him. "I! I am playing no games! You tendered me an offer of marriage. And I accepted it."

"You!" The major appeared almost taken with apoplexy. "I wouldn't be marrying a woman as old as you!"

"Well, I never—" Mama began, her face purpling as well. But the major turned his back on her and advanced to Phillipa who, hardly knowing what to think, was fully occupied in keeping her composure.

The major drew himself up to his full height. "Since your mother has plainly lost her wits," he said, "I'll make the offer to you direct. I know your dowry's—hmmm—gone. But I don't need it. I got my dogs and my horses. Hmmm. And I'll have you."

For a second Phillipa was tempted to accept him. If only she and Aunt Pitty had somewhere to go, somewhere to escape from Mama's considerable wrath. But across the room Aunt Pitty was coughing urgently, and Phillipa saw her give the "don't do it" sign.

"You're most thoughtful, Major," Phillipa told him. "To offer me this signal honor, but I'm afraid I must refuse. You see, I don't wish to leave my mama alone in her declining years" — she would pay for that later, she was sure — "and it's plain you and she don't deal well together."

The major's face slowly cleared. "You've a lot of wit for a mere chit," he observed, giving her what to him was clearly a compliment. "And you're right about *that* one. Hmmm. We wouldn't do at all. So I'll make my goodbyes." He bowed briefly to her and Aunt Pitty, and, without even glancing at Mama, stalked out.

Phillipa braced herself for Mama's explosion of rage — and it came. Phrases like "declining years, indeed," "stupid ungrateful girl," "never understand how you can be so witless," "ruined my whole plan," came hurtling out of Mama's mouth like rocks.

But Phillipa refused to be bruised by mere words. She had done nothing whatsoever to encourage the major, and Mama had no right to hold her responsible or to rail at her because of the failure of that ridiculous plan.

Phillipa sat silent, thanking the Lord that she had not given in to that moment of weakness and said yes. Marrying the major would only have given her an additional taskmaster, and Mama was quite enough.

Some minutes passed and Mama gave no sign of stopping her tirade, but suddenly Aunt Pitty moaned, leaned forward, and slowly slipped to the floor. Phillipa was on her feet in an instant. She rushed across the room calling for the butler as she went.

As usual, one of Aunt Pitty's spells had the effect of silencing Mama, who found all illness frightening. Mama scurried out and Jimson called a footman, who lifted Aunt Pitty's slight form and carried her up the stairs to her room.

Worriedly, Phillipa trailed behind. Aunt Pitty had been looking poorly lately. Pray God she wasn't ill.

Once the footman had put her down and left, Phillipa closed

the door after him and turned back to the great bed. Aunt Pitty looked so small, so fragile, lying there — and so still. If she ever lost her —

Phillipa pulled up a chair. Usually Aunt Pitty came out of a spell on her own and an hour or so later seemed none the worse for it.

Aunt Pitty opened one eye. "Are we alone?" she whispered.

Phillipa bent toward her anxiously. "Yes, dear, you just rest now. You've —"

To her astonishment, Aunt Pitty pushed herself to a sitting position and smiled. "I'm all right, my dear. Perfectly fine."

"But you just —"

Aunt Pitty looked a trifle embarrassed. "I suppose I shall have to tell you."

"Tell me what?"

Aunt Pitty leaned closer. "That my spells are not real."

Phillipa tried to absorb this. "Not real? But you've always —"

"Resorted to them when nothing else worked with Felicity." She sighed again. "At first I tried reason. That didn't work, as you well know, so I resorted to the only mode of persuasion I had left — her fear of illness. It works every time." She patted Phillipa's hand. "Of course I try not to use it too often. I'm sorry if I've worried you, dear, but I didn't feel I could tell you about it — till now."

Phillipa leaned forward, still trying to take this all in. "But why are you telling me now?"

Aunt Pitty took a lace-edged handkerchief from the table beside the bed and dabbed at her forehead. "Because there is something else I must tell you. I have debated over it long and hard. And I believe my reasons are not selfish ones."

What was Aunt Pitty talking about? None of this made sense. "Tell me what?" Phillipa asked.

Aunt Pitty frowned. "You're sure the door is shut tight?"

Phillipa nodded. "I closed it myself."

"Then pull your chair closer."

Phillipa did so. "Really, Aunt Pitty, I don't —"

"I am telling you this because I don't want you to let Felicity push you into some unfortunate marriage." Aunt Pitty swallowed hard and pressed the handkerchief to her trembling lips. "I thought for a moment down there that you were going to accept the major, just to remove yourself from here."

"I thought about it," Phillipa said truthfully. "But I couldn't go through with it."

"Good," Aunt Pitty said. "But I don't want you to be forced into such a position again. And I certainly don't want you to feel that you are beholden to Felicity."

This was very confusing. Always before Aunt Pitty had urged her to listen to Mama, to be a dutiful daughter. "But I *am* beholden," she said. "I know she's not much of a mother. But she did give me life and—"

"No," Aunt Pitty said.

"No what?" Phillipa asked, growing even more confused.

"Felicity did not give you life. She is not your mother."

"Not my mother, but—"

"She agreed to—raise—you." Aunt Pitty hesitated over the word raise. "But she never liked it. She did it only because Ernest insisted."

Phillipa's heart pounded. "Papa?"

"He was not your papa, but he loved you dearly."

She could not understand. "But if he was not—and Mama was not—"

Aunt Pitty took both of Phillipa's hands in hers. "My dear child, *I* am your mother."

Phillipa stared at the patient smiling face of the woman she'd always loved. "You, Aunt Pitty? You are my mother?"

"Yes," Aunt Pitty said. "You are mine. I loved a man—he was of noble blood, a second son—and he loved me dearly. But he was killed before he could marry me. And your papa—that is, your uncle—took me in. Felicity disapproved, saying she would never raise a bastard child, but Ernest insisted. And we told the world that you were hers."

"So that is why she never loved me," Phillipa said slowly. "And why you did."

Aunt Pitty raised the handkerchief to her lips. "I did the best I could, Phillipa dear, to protect you. I'm sorry about your father. But no one need ever know. Felicity will never tell because of the scandal."

She leaned closer. "I meant to take the secret to my grave with me. It was bad enough when she wasted your dowry, but this latest madness . . . I simply could not let her force you into marrying an awful man like the major. I could not remain silent."

As the truth at last sank in, joy flowed through Phillipa and she clasped Aunt Pitty to her in a tearful hug. "Oh, oh, I'm so glad you told me!"

Aunt Pitty patted her hand. Then she leaned back into her pillows. "When you were small and got hurt, you always used to run to me. And one day you said in your sweet childish voice, 'I wish *you* were my mama.' How my heart ached to tell you then." She wiped her eyes. "But I had nowhere to take you. And while Ernest lived, we were safe enough. Felicity wanted to please him and things were not so bad. But now —"

"Now it doesn't matter," Phillipa said. "I am grown and I can cope. And this, this is the most marvelous news! It makes me so very happy."

Aunt Pitty's smile was radiant. "So, now that you know, you must not let Felicity make you feel guilty. This money business is all her fault. She's a bitter, grasping woman, but at least she's no real relation of yours." She grabbed Phillipa's hands again. "But do remember, my dearest, only you and I must know about this."

"Of course," Phillipa said, giving her another hug. "Thank you, my real mama, oh thank you."

Chapter Five

Phillipa, hugging the joy of her secret to her, wondered that no one could see it on her face. She longed to tell someone — anyone — but Aunt Pitty was right. If this became general knowledge, Mama would toss them both out into the street.

She was still concerned over what Mama was going to do, but she knew now that no matter what transpired, her heart would go on singing with the newfound joy of having a real mother, a mother who loved and cherished her.

Later in the day, Aunt Pitty and Phillipa sat in the drawing room. Mama had withdrawn to her room in the sulks, announcing her intention of avoiding the company of such ungrateful creatures. The two of them kept silent, but the moment the door closed behind Mama, Phillipa turned to Aunt Pitty and saw that she, too, was smiling in relief.

They spent several pleasant hours, recalling little happy occasions from Phillipa's childhood. "I do so wish," Phillipa said, "that I could call you Mama."

Aunt Pitty shook her head. "I used to wish that, too, my dear. But you know, it was you who first called me Aunt Pitty because you couldn't pronounce Patricia. And I kept the name, encouraging you to use it as I felt closer to you every time you did."

She frowned. "You were such a good child. So beautiful. I don't understand why Felicity couldn't love you."

Phillipa laughed. "It doesn't matter now that I know the truth. Nothing she can say or do can really hurt me."

Aunt Pitty leaned closer. "I believe I was right to tell you, but my dear —"

A rap on the closed door jerked them both erect. "Yes?" Phillipa called.

Jimson opened the door. "A caller, Miss Pardonner."

Phillipa swallowed. Not the major again. "Who is it?"

Jimson's face remained bland. "The Viscount Valdane, miss."

Phillipa's stomach began a wild dance, but she kept her voice even. "Show him in."

"Yes, miss." Jimson's expression turned almost furtive. "And I won't bother madame. She left strict orders not to be disturbed." He hesitated. "If that's all right, miss."

"That's quite proper," Phillipa said, smiling at him. There had been so many times when Jimson and other members of the household staff had protected her from Mama's wrath. She wished she could do something to show her gratitude to—

And then the viscount stood in the doorway, an even finer figure of a man than she remembered, his boots shining, his coat fitting exquisitely. "Welcome, milord," she said, dropping her embroidery into its basket. "We're honored by your visit."

He crossed the room and after greeting her aunt, took a chair near her. "I'm surprised you even receive me," he said dryly.

Phillipa raised an eyebrow. "But, milord, why shouldn't we?"

He leaned back, crossing one long leg over the other. "From what my esteemed uncle told me, I assume that on his last visit here he did not carry himself with much courtesy."

Phillipa smiled. "No, I'm afraid he didn't. But then neither did Mama. She was much put out." She sighed. "Perhaps you wish to speak to her your—"

"No." The word was spoken quietly, but with much authority. "I came to see you."

"You did?" Phillipa blurted before she could control her tongue. "But why?"

He smiled, a smile of pure enchantment. No wonder all the eligible young women—

"As head of the family, I felt an apology was overdue. First my uncle maligned your father, a fine upright man. Then he proposed marriage, which I imagine was quite a shock to a young woman of your tender sensibilities. And then, if I understand correctly from his rather heated rendition of the facts, he more or less insulted your mother."

296

"That is essentially what happened," Aunt Pitty said with a little smile. "But Phillipa and I were not offended. Were we, my dear?"

"No . . . Aunt Pitty." Phillipa turned to the viscount. "It was most kind of you to come, however. And thank you for defending my father the other night at Lady Linden's dinner. I did take offense then, I'm afraid."

The viscount's dark eyes twinkled. "And rightly so. You are proud of your father."

"Yes." Phillipa's thoughts raced. What would the viscount think if he knew that she was illegitimate? That Papa was in reality her uncle?

"I am sorry if the major caused you grief," the viscount continued. "He is somewhat rough-hewn and a little given to demanding his own way."

Aunt Pitty coughed, but Phillipa allowed herself an outright laugh. "It seems many of us must learn to deal with relatives who are difficult."

The viscount's eyes surveyed her for so long that Phillipa felt a rush of anxiety. "Milord, is something wrong?"

He started. "No, no! My apologies. I was merely wondering how your mother could have had such a lovely creature as yourself." He stopped and smiled ruefully. "Now I've done it again. It seems to be the fate of our family to offer insults to yours."

"No insult was taken," Phillipa said quickly. "It's quite a natural question anyway. Mama is so fair and I am quite dark."

"I prefer dark beauties," said the viscount with a look that made her heart leap into her throat. "But it was not outward appearance to which I referred, but inward character. You are so very different in disposition that one wonders how *she* could have raised *you*."

"That's rather easily explained," Phillipa said. "You see Aunt Pitty had most of the task of my upbringing. So whatever is right about me is due to her."

The viscount directed his smile at Aunt Pitty. "May I say, madame, that you did an admirable job? You have brought up a young woman of great sense and good breeding."

Phillipa's heart swelled at the compliment and she saw tears of joy in Aunt Pitty's eyes.

"Thank you, milord," Aunt Pitty said. "I am proud of her."

Phillipa could feel the color staining her cheeks. No one had ever said such nice things about her before. It was pleasant, but rather embarrassing.

The viscount laughed, a deep hearty sound that struck someplace far within her and evoked a surge of joy that tingled through her whole being.

"We are bringing Miss Pardonner to the blush," he said, his eyes sparkling. Glancing at the clock on the mantel he added, "I'm afraid I must be going as I'm expected elsewhere. I just didn't want you to think of all of my family as boors."

"Oh, I could never—" Phillipa cried before propriety set in. "That is, you've been most kind, milord. Thank you for stopping by."

"The thanks should be mine," he returned, rising to his feet. He nodded toward Aunt Pitty, then turned the full force of his smile on Phillipa. "I trust I shall see you again, Miss Pardonner. Good day."

Phillipa sat in stunned silence. What could he mean by that? Where would he see her again? But before she could ask him—if she had dared ask him—he was gone, striding out in all his splendor. Only then did she have time to think of what she was wearing, and to wish she'd been more stylishly attired.

"What a thoughtful thing to do," she said finally.

"Very thoughtful," Aunt Pitty replied, her voice low. "The viscount has excellent manners. And a good heart." She smiled. "I really don't believe you need to worry about Miss Linden snaring him. Such a man would not look twice at so mercenary a girl."

"I think—" Phillipa began, but she got no further.

Mama appeared in the doorway, her face purpling. "Where is he?" she cried. "Where's the viscount? I mean to tell—"

"He's gone," Aunt Pitty said, in a tone Phillipa had never heard her use before. "He came to make apologies for his uncle's behavior. He made them and he left."

Mama stood, uncertainty written on her face. "Well, well, then that's good."

She came into the room and took her chair. "Tell me, what did the man—"

"Guests, Mrs. Pardonner," Jimson announced. "Lady Linden and Miss Martine Linden."

With a sigh, Phillipa composed her features and resumed

298

her stitching. At least this time the Lindens' visit might spare her more of Mama's invective.

"Felicity, my dear!" Lady Linden bustled in. "I came the moment I heard. How discouraging for you!"

"Very." Mama waved toward the settee. "The shock of it has unsettled my whole system."

"As well it might!" Lady Linden intoned, dropping dramatically to the sofa, which squeaked loudly at such an onslaught. "As well it might. Such a disappointment. And then to think that he offered for Phillipa." And she cast her a look of utter disdain.

But this time Phillipa didn't feel any hurt. Lady Linden meant nothing to her. Nor did the woman she still called Mama. She had a real mother now.

"It was most nerve-wracking," Mama whined, "to hear such a thing. And then after all that to have the ungrateful girl refuse to marry him. Can you imagine?"

"The major is such an upright man," Lady Linden declaimed. "Surely no right-thinking woman would refuse him."

"Perhaps Phillipa wished for a younger man," Martine interjected with a sly look. "A man like the viscount."

"Martine!" Lady Linden said sharply. "Don't be stupid. The viscount certainly has no use for the likes of Phillipa."

Phillipa kept on stitching. Once that would have hurt, but not now. Perhaps she had no chance with him, but he'd been very kind to her, very kind. And she knew that Martine had no chance with him either. He would marry a woman of breeding and accomplishments, someone far above them both. But she would always have the memory of his kindness to cherish.

"Oh dear?" Mama cried. "What shall I do? I'm quite unnerved by this awful situation. Still, I must do something. I must find someone."

Lady Linden shifted on the settee, causing it to protest again and smoothed her gown of wide blue and yellow stripes. "Give me a moment, my dear. I've a prodigious mind, you know. I'll come up with something. Never fear."

Phillipa kept her eyes on her stitching. She didn't see how the situation could be made more scandalous than it already was. But if Lady Linden could contrive to do so, she undoubtedly would.

They sat for some minutes in silence: Phillipa and Aunt Pitty stitching, Mama and Lady Linden staring into space, and Martine studying the room's furnishings.

Finally Lady Linden spoke. "I have it! I have the very thing!"

Mama leaned forward. "I knew you could help me. Tell me what I should do."

With deliberate effort Phillipa kept her tongue between her teeth. Whatever Lady Linden had in mind, it could not be good. But since Mama never listened to anyone in her family, it was best to keep quiet.

"I cannot come up with a man suitable to be your husband," Lady Linden said. "Major Hardesty was the only one I knew of." Mama wilted visibly. "But I have heard," Lady Linden went on, "there are whispers that the Prince Regent is at odds with his present favorite. And you know," her face actually glowed, "he seems to favor the grandmotherly type. Look at Lady Hertford. So your age and your looks are all to the good."

Mama contemplated this for some seconds while Phillipa's heart remained in her throat. Mama become mistress to the Prince Regent?

Surely even Mama would reject such a patently foolish notion. But Mama's face brightened. "That's it," she cried. "I am very good at pleasing a man. Ernest always said so." Her face fell. "But how shall I meet him? I don't travel in the regent's social circles."

"Do not despair," Lady Linden replied, her eyes agleam. "My friend, Lady Hepplewhite, is having a fete this week next — and the regent has promised to be there. I shall just get her to invite you." She cast another disparaging glance at Phillipa. "I suppose she'll invite her, too. It will look better."

"I can leave her at home," Mama said.

Lady Linden looked thoughtful. "No, no. It would look best to take her along. Everyone knows she's unwed and so they'll assume you're casting about to find a husband for her."

Mama nodded. "I see. Yes, you're right."

Phillipa, her eyes still on her stitching, smothered a smile. A fete, Lady Linden said, and one to be attended by the regent. So there was a good chance the viscount would be present. She might see Charles again — and soon.

Chapter Six

When the day of Lady Hepplewhite's fete arrived, Phillipa greeted it with mixed feelings. She hoped to see Charles, but she feared what Mama might do with the Prince Regent.

Still, pleasant anticipation won out over unpleasant. Though her gown was several years old, it was her favorite color, a soft pale rose, and she felt she looked her best in it. Charles — she had given up trying to force herself to think of him as the viscount — would probably not notice her, but she still wanted to look her best.

Just before they stepped into Lady Hepplewhite's mansion on Grosvenor Square, Mama turned to her. "You will be on your best behavior," she ordered.

"Yes, ma'am," Phillipa said dutifully. She could no longer bear to call the woman Mama, but if she were careful, perhaps the omission would go unnoticed.

Phillipa replied politely to Lady Hepplewhite's greeting and, trailing deferentially along behind, allowed herself to gaze around at the beauty of Lord and Lady Hepplewhite's rooms. She flushed a little when she realized that she was also searching the crowd for Charles. But for all her searching she was unable to find him.

"There!" Mama cried, grabbing Phillipa's wrist with iron fingers. "There's the regent!"

"I see him," Phillipa said. He looked no better than he had that day in the park. How any woman could wish to have such a portly man —

"Come," Mama said, tugging at her.

"But —"

"No buts. Come now." And Mama set off, pulling Phillipa along after her.

Phillipa composed her features, reminding herself that this woman was *not* her mother. Mama couldn't embarrass her because the important people, the only ones who mattered, were Aunt Pitty and—and Charles.

And so, her wrist still in Mama's iron grasp, she stood patiently, awaiting whatever humiliation lay in store for her.

"Your Royal Highness," Mama gushed, rushing right up to him and batting her lashes. "Such an honor to meet you!"

The Prince Regent, resplendent in garments of the latest fashion, his cravat a vast expanse of glittering white linen, raised his lorgnette and stared at Mama haughtily. But Mama was not to be put off. She dropped Phillipa's wrist and moved closer to the regent, smiling coyly.

Phillipa eased away, hoping to lose herself among the guests. Slowly, step by step, she backed off, until she could no longer hear the inane things Mama was saying. But somehow, much as she wished to ignore the whole dreadful affair, she could not tear her eyes away from the awful picture unfolding before her.

Mama cooed, Mama simpered, Mama giggled, Mama tittered. And through it all, Phillipa stood, transfixed.

Finally, wishing she could hide herself someplace, any place, she wrenched her eyes from the miserable scene and turned to remove herself from the sight as well as the sound. And then she saw him.

Charles stood not more than ten feet away. He looked so handsome in his corbeau breeches and coat, his intricately tied cravat as snowy as the regent's. But at his side stood a very beautiful woman, her jewels gleaming in the candlelight, her lovely face possessively close to his.

Phillipa swallowed hard. Charles was not looking at the beauty on his arm. He was intent on something across the room. When she turned to follow his gaze, she felt the blood rush to her cheeks. Oh no! He was staring at Mama, at Mama setting lures for the regent.

All Phillipa could think of was to get away, not to let Charles see her at all. She stepped backward, crashing into a portly gentleman behind her and almost spilling his lemon ice. The gentleman gave her a disdainful look and an affronted sniff.

"Excuse me," she murmured abjectly, now even more embarrassed. She searched the room trying to find a familiar face, but except for Charles they were all strangers. That should be no surprise. This world was completely foreign to her. She didn't have jewels and fine clothing. She didn't want them. She just wanted some peace, some quiet. A little cottage in the country where she and Aunt Pitty could live out their lives in harmony, without Mama's continual scolds.

She started for the buffet table — perhaps she could occupy herself with a plate of food.

"Surely there's no need to look so miserable."

Phillipa spun, almost falling into his arms. "Oh, milord, you — I —" She faltered into an embarrassed silence.

"Can't you call me Charles?" he asked plaintively. "You did before."

A great wave of giddiness washed over her. "Ch-Charles?"

"That's right. Charles." He smiled encouragingly. "I like the sound of it on your tongue."

This so stunned her that for a moment she stood speechless. She had wanted to see him, but she hadn't expected anything like this, to have him actually *talk* to her. Her heart skipped about madly as he took her hand, tucking her arm familiarly through his. "Come, Phillipa," he said. "Let's free ourselves from this press of people." And he led her to a secluded corner behind some palms.

He motioned to some chairs. "We'll sit here. And perhaps you'll tell me why you look so desolate." He smiled that enchanting smile which in her present agitated state completely dissolved any defenses she might have left.

"I —" she began again, but how could she tell him about Mama's scandalous plan?

Charles leaned closer. "Is it possible your forlorn expression has to do with your mama's plans to become the regent's next favorite?"

She stared at him. "However did you know about that?"

He chuckled, a rich warm sound. "Your mama is hardly subtle in her approach, so it would take no great wit to discern what she's about." He flicked a tiny speck of lint from his immaculate black sleeve. "As it happens, though, it took no wit at all. Lady Linden and her daughter came to call on me the other day, and so I was most thoroughly informed."

Phillipa felt herself blushing. "Oh dear, it's just as I feared. First the major and now this." She pressed a hand to her forehead. "We'll be the laughingstock of London. And all for nothing. Surely she can't hope to succeed."

He laughed. "Actually, she appears to be doing quite well. But since Prinny has been a little put out with the Hertford lately, this is probably just a diversion, a little charade to make his favorite toe the mark."

"Oh no!" Phillipa exclaimed, quite forgetting that she shouldn't be discussing family business with a stranger. "When she finds this out, she'll be in a towering rage."

When Charles took her hand in his, the strangest sensation drummed through her. "Don't distress yourself," he said softly in his deep voice. "It's true your mama is a little eccentric, but so is most of the *ton*. And surely she will not lay *this* failure at your door."

"Surely she will," Phillipa replied, aching to tell him that this woman was *not* her mother. "Aunt Pitty and I will be lectured endlessly." She sighed. "If only we had a place to go."

There was no rational reason for it, but it seemed natural to tell her troubles to Charles. And anyway, he was already privy to most of them. "If I could just obtain some kind of a position. As a companion perhaps, or even a governess. Papa saw to it that I was educated." She turned to him with growing excitement. "I think I could make enough to keep us in some comfort. We shouldn't need much. We're not fashionable, Aunt Pitty and I."

In her excitement she grasped his sleeve. "Oh, milord, would you help us? You have so many friends. Would you help me find a position?"

A look she couldn't decipher traveled over his handsome face. "I'll help you," he said, patting her hand. "You won't have to listen to your mama much longer. I promise."

"Oh thank you, milord, you are so—"

"But only if you call me Charles."

Phillipa managed a watery smile. "Yes, Charles. And thank—"

"Charles! My dear, dear Charles!"

Charles got to his feet as Martine burst into view, her thin nose quivering, her hand outstretched to grab his sleeve.

"Great galloping—" he murmured before he clamped his

304

mouth shut. Pulling free of Martine's grasp, he turned to help Phillipa to her feet, drawing her arm though his again.

She drew in a breath, her heart leaping about. That had sounded very much like a muffled curse. Did that mean Charles had no desire to see Martine as well? That he wanted to remain alone with Phillipa?

But before she could pursue this intriguing thought, Martine shook a skinny beringed finger in her face. "How rude of you, Phillipa, keeping dear Charles in the corner like this when everyone is eager to speak to him. Naughty, naughty!"

The muscles under Phillipa's hand quivered as Charles drew himself even more erect. "Miss Linden," he said, his voice heavy with disdain. "I appreciate your attention to my affairs. However, I have been managing them quite successfully for some years now. And though some people" — he paused and gave her a scornful look — "seem to think they can do a better job at it than I can, I prefer to keep on doing it myself. Furthermore, if I did not *wish* to be here with Miss Pardonner, I would certainly be elsewhere."

"I—" Martine stammered, her face turning first red and then white. "I'm sorry, milord."

He fixed her with an even fiercer stare. "And I believe you owe Miss Pardonner an apology."

Martine seemed to shrink. She paled so visibly and looked so distressed that Phillipa found herself feeling sorry for the girl. "I'm sure Martine meant no offense," she said.

"No, no. I didn't," Martine hastened to say. "But — but if Phillipa took offense, I'm most dreadfully sorry. Really I am."

Charles looked to Phillipa. "Is that a sufficient apology?"

"Yes, of course," Phillipa replied, wanting only to spare Martine more embarrassment.

Martine backed away, her face still pale, and hurried out of sight.

"That was most kind of you," Charles said. "She *did* mean to offend you, you know." He grinned down at her. "You know it very well."

His grin was even more engaging than his smile, and Phillipa found herself grinning in reply. "Yes, I know. But I'm afraid she can't help what she is. Really, can you imagine having Lady Linden for a mother? It's a wonder the poor girl turned out as well as she did."

Charles nodded in agreement. "You have a kind heart, Phillipa Pardonner. Your Aunt Pitty must be a fine woman."

"She is," Phillipa said, wishing she dared tell him the truth, wishing that all the world could know that Aunt Pitty was her real mother. But soon, at least, they would be able to lead a happy life together. "Do you think it will take long," she asked, "to find me a position?"

"You are very eager to leave your home," he said. "But I will do—"

"So! This is where you've been hiding!"

Phillipa kept from cringing, but she was sure Mama's strident cry had been heard by all, even over the babble around them. "I—" she began, but the viscount's words cut her explanation short.

"I asked your daughter to accompany me here, Mrs. Pardonner," he said. "To discuss a private matter."

Mama's eyes gleamed. "What private matter can you have with my daughter?"

"It is nothing to concern yourself with," he replied cheerfully. "Take my word on it."

Since he was a peer of the realm, Mama could hardly do anything else. She certainly could not challenge him. He had silenced her for now, but once they were home . . .

"I see you are ready to leave," he said courteously. "Allow me to escort you to your carriage."

Phillipa watched the play of emotions on Mama's face. Clearly she wasn't ready to leave the fete, but just as clearly she wanted to be seen in public with the viscount escorting her. Vanity finally won and Mama smiled her sweetest smile. "How kind of you, milord. I'm in fine fettle, but I'm afraid poor Phillipa *is* drooping." And she took the arm he offered her.

On his other arm Phillipa could think of little but his promise. Charles had promised to help her find a way to escape.

Chapter Seven

Two days passed, then another. Aflutter with eager anticipation, Phillipa knew it was too soon to expect Charles to have found her a position. But still every day she rose in happy expectation. He was a man of his word — he would do as he had promised. She had only to be patient and wait.

She tried to be patient. She suffered in silence Mama's reproofs, rebukes, and reprimands — consoling herself the while with her two wonderful secrets. Knowing that Aunt Pitty was really her mother and having Charles's promise made even Mama's vituperation bearable.

But as the days passed and Mama received no inviting message from Carlton House, her attacks grew even more vitriolic. She was delivering just such a stream of abuse one afternoon exactly a week after the fete when Jimson appeared in the sitting-room doorway.

When Mama paused to catch her breath, he said, "The Viscount Valdane to call, madame."

Mama stared, then rallied. "Whatever can he want? Well, send the man in."

Phillipa bent over her stitching, trying to control her pounding heart. Did his coming mean he was keeping his promise? Did it mean he had found her a position?

"Milord," Mama said. "How good to see you."

"And you, Mrs. Pardonner." He bowed slightly. "I have come to ask a favor of you."

"Of me?" Mama flushed. "Of course, milord, what is it?"

"I wish to borrow Miss Pardonner for a little while."

"Borrow?" Mama repeated.

"Yes. I have a matter in which I need her help."

"Yes, yes. Of course," Mama said. "We will come immediately."

No! Phillipa's heart threatened to stop. She clutched her embroidery. If Mama came she would spoil everything. He wouldn't be able to—

"I'm afraid that's not possible," Charles said smoothly.

Mama frowned. "My daughter cannot go out alone with a gentleman."

"Naturally," he replied, "I intend for her aunt to accompany her." He smiled. "I would have asked you, of course, Mrs. Pardonner, but such a menial task is far below your touch."

And while Mama sat in shock, trying to think of a reply, he shepherded Phillipa and Aunt Pitty into the hall, into their bonnets, and out to the carriage.

"What is this task, milord?" Aunt Pitty inquired as they set off.

Phillipa leaned closer. "I didn't tell you before because I wanted to be certain first. But his lordship has kindly promised to help me find a position, so we can get away."

A strange look crossed Aunt Pitty's face, but all she said was, "I see."

Phillipa turned to Charles. "That's it, isn't it? You've found me a place?"

"Yes," he replied. "But I want to show it to you."

"I'll be happy with anything," she said, almost giddy with relief at the idea of being out from under Mama's tongue. "As long as Aunt Pitty can come, too."

Charles nodded. "I quite understand that. I didn't think you would leave her behind."

The house was grand, quite the grandest Phillipa had ever seen. When they reached the foyer and gave the butler their bonnets, she swallowed hastily. "This is a very large place."

He nodded. "Large houses can be very lonely."

"Yes, I suppose so. But I will be very busy. Are there children? Am I to be a governess? Or—"

"The position is that of companion," he said. "It is a somewhat unusual position, but one appropriate to your capabilities."

"I see." She did not see, not really. But even if her prospective employer turned out to be a cranky old beldame, she surely could not be any worse than Mama.

"I find I'm very tired," Aunt Pitty said to the viscount. "If I could just sit some place and have a cup of tea?"

"Of course," Charles said. He nodded to the butler who went off immediately. "Use this sitting room. Starnes will bring tea."

Aunt Pitty sank into a chair. "Thank you."

"With your permission I'll show Phillipa the rest of the house."

"Of course."

As Charles guided her through the beautiful, richly appointed rooms, Phillipa tried to puzzle it out. Something was odd about this arrangement. Even though he showed her all the rooms, including a huge ballroom, an employer had yet to appear.

Finally, in a small upstairs sitting room, Phillipa turned to him. "Where is she?"

"Where is who?" he asked, his dark brows forming a frown line.

"My — my employer."

"I said nothing about a woman."

She didn't understand this. She didn't understand it at all. "But you said I am to be a companion. I cannot be companion to a man."

Instead of answering her, he led her to a settee. "Sit down, Phillipa, we must talk."

She sat, but it was with a sense of great unease. Why did he look at her so strangely? "Please, Charles," she began. "I don't understand."

He took one of her hands in his. "This house — it belongs to me."

"You? But —"

"And I am the man who wishes to have you for a companion. This house is mine — it will be yours."

She wrenched her hands from his and leaped, trembling, to her feet. So that was it! It was all a trick, a cruel sort of joke. He knew about Mama and he thought the daughter would be willing to — "I thought you were my friend," she cried. "And you have betrayed me like this! Aunt Pitty will be very disappointed in you!"

He looked genuinely surprised. Evidently he had expected an easy surrender from her.

"Phillipa," he said, rising and starting toward her, "Whatever are you—"

She turned quickly, hurrying to get out of the room before he could reach her, but she caught her toe in the hem of her gown and started to fall. He caught her just in time, pulling her against his chest.

"Phillipa, what is wrong? I know this isn't what you wanted. But it won't be hard work. I thought—I hoped—"

Held so tightly against his waistcoat that she could scarcely breathe, she tried to think. She couldn't accept his dishonorable offer. Though to be with him—But no—She eased herself out of his grasp and fixed him with a stern eye. "You have mistaken your prey, milord. I am not worldly, but there are—"

He stared down at her. "Prey? What is this talk of prey?"

"I suppose you gentlemen have other words for it, but I am unfamiliar with them. I thank you for whatever kindnesses you have already offered me, but I must refuse."

"Refuse!" he thundered. He was clearly a man used to getting his way. How could she have so mistaken his character? "What have I done wrong? I admit that I've no practice at this thing, but—"

"No practice? You mean I am the first young woman you have tried to seduce?"

"Seduce?" He threw his hands into the air. "Seduce? I have not even offered to kiss you—though you have the most enticing mouth."

Outraged as she was, his compliment still pleased her. But compliments would not get him his way. She drew herself up. "Pretty words may get you other women," she said. "They will not get you me."

And then, before she could move, he had grabbed her by the shoulders and was pressing his lips on hers. She had been kissed, a few times, by penniless suitors Mama had rejected. But never ever had she experienced anything like this. Everything inside her seemed to melt and flow toward him.

Perhaps she could accept him. Mama was in no position to stop her and she and Aunt Pitty could escape—Aunt Pitty! No, she couldn't do it. Her real mama would never countenance such a thing.

Charles released her so abruptly she almost fell and threw himself into a chair. Lowering his head into his hands, he sighed. "What a mess I've made of things. I thought to give you time to know me, but I so much wanted—My God, my first and only proposal of marriage and I have been refused."

Marriage? Her numb lips formed the word, but made no sound. He didn't want to set her up in keeping! He wanted to marry her!

How wonderful! She took a step toward him, another—and stopped dead. She couldn't marry Charles. He was evidently prepared for the gossip that would ensue if he married a commoner, a mere merchant's daughter, and dowerless at that. But she was not a merchant's daughter. She was a bastard. She could not bring that shame upon him.

Slowly she backed up. Better to let him believe she had refused him for other reasons. If he knew she had some secret, he would never let her rest till he got it out of her.

"I have heard enough," she said, putting all the ice she could into her voice. "Please take me home."

Chapter Eight

Phillipa kept silent during the entire ride home. Aunt Pitty and the viscount chatted together quietly, but Phillipa couldn't trust herself to speak. To think that he had wanted to marry her!

She swallowed a sigh. Perhaps she should have said yes. No one need know about the stain of her birth, and as a married woman she could care for Aunt Pitty. But she couldn't imagine Aunt Pitty lying to the man she loved.

Phillipa glanced across the brougham at him. She did love him. That only made matters worse, of course. If she hadn't loved him, she might have accept — But no, if she hadn't loved him, she still wouldn't have accepted him. She could never bear to live with a man she didn't care for.

When they reached her home, the viscount handed them down. "No doubt your mama will wish the particulars of our task," he said.

Phillipa shrugged, avoiding his eyes. "We'll tell her we went to help a sick child."

Aunt Pitty nodded. "Felicity has a fear of sickness, milord. She won't question us further."

He seemed satisfied by that. "Very well. Good day then." And he got back in his brougham and drove away.

"We have been with someone ill," Aunt Pitty told Jimson. "And we are going to our rooms to refresh ourselves."

"Very well, madame."

Phillipa wished desperately to be alone, to give vent to the tears threatening to choke her, but she dared not say so for fear they would escape her control.

Aunt Pitty accompanied her into her room and carefully

shut the door behind them. "Now," she said, leading Phillipa to the settee. "Tell me what happened."

And so Phillipa told her, and ended by saying, "Of course I told him no."

"You don't care for his person," Aunt Pitty said.

"Oh yes, I do. He's very handsome."

"Then it's his character you object to."

"Oh no! He's been most kind. And that — that about setting me up in keeping — that was all a misunderstanding on my part."

Aunt Pitty shook her head. "Then I fail to see what kept you from accepting him." She peered at Phillipa shrewdly. "It wasn't me, was it? You didn't insist on bringing me?"

"I would have," Phillipa replied stoutly. "But I didn't need to since he had already said you could come."

Aunt Pitty shook her head. "Surely you're not afraid of marriage."

"No, no. I don't think so." Phillipa tried to think of some excuse. She couldn't speak of the real reason, that she didn't want to saddle the man she loved with the scandal of a bastard wife. That might hurt this woman who meant so much to her. "I — I — I just don't believe we'd suit." She swallowed hard over the lie, holding back her tears with effort. "Please, I — I just want to lie down. I've got the most awful headache."

"Of course, my dear." Aunt Pitty patted her cheek. "You lie down and rest. We'll talk later."

"I — I really don't want to talk about it — not anymore."

Aunt Pitty nodded. "Very well, You rest now."

Phillipa took off her shoes and lay down upon the bed, but rest escaped her.

Joy and despair mingled in her heart. To think that Charles wanted to marry her. What joy that brought. But she'd been right to refuse him. Love would allow for nothing less. Love wouldn't bring disgrace on the loved one.

And then the awful truth hit her with full force — there would be no position for her. No escape. She and Aunt Pitty were doomed to live on, under the lash of Felicity's tongue. The tears came then, and she wept in earnest.

The knock on the door roused her from a heavy restless

313

sleep. "Yes? What?" She pushed the hair from her eyes and sat up.

"It's me," Aunt Pitty said. "May I come in?"

"Yes." Phillipa rubbed at her swollen eyes.

Aunt Pitty stepped into the room. "I hope you feel better, my dear. The viscount is below."

Phillipa clutched her sodden handkerchief. "He — Aunt Pitty, I cannot see him."

Aunt Pitty frowned. "I'm afraid you must. He says he will not leave until he has your explanation."

"But — but what shall I tell him?"

"Tell him the truth," Aunt Pitty said, looking at her sternly. "Tell him you won't marry him because you're a bastard. That's it, isn't it? That's your reason."

Phillipa cast about in her mind for another reason she could use, any reason.

"Phillipa," Aunt Pitty said. "Don't lie to me." She smiled sadly. "You know I can always tell when you are lying."

It was true — she could. Phillipa admitted defeat. "Yes. That's the reason. But I didn't want to say that to you. It was not your fault and —"

"I think you should tell him."

"But you said —"

"He's a man of discretion. He will keep our secret." Aunt Pitty looked even sterner. "Phillipa, you owe him the truth."

Phillipa shuddered. "Where is Ma — Felicity?"

"Felicity happens to be out making calls," Aunt Pitty said. "If you come right down, you will be finished before she returns."

"I — All right. Just let me wash my face."

Ten minutes later, with eyes that were still puffy, Phillipa entered the drawing room. The viscount stood up, his worried gaze on her face. Aunt Pitty rose, too, and, carrying her embroidery, went to the far side of the room.

Phillipa stepped in, shutting the door behind her. "You wished to see me?" she asked, hearing the tremble in her voice and hating it.

"I did," he said, coming toward her. "I feel I am owed an explanation. I thought — I felt — you seemed to welcome my attentions. But evidently I bungled the job." He frowned. "I wanted to show you what I would share with you, but perhaps that was too crass. And afterward I realized I had neglected to tell you the most important thing—that I love you."

Her knees threatened to give way and she swayed toward him. He was at her side instantly, putting an arm around her waist and leading her to a sofa.

"Now," he said when they were settled. "I insist on an explanation. I am sorry my love offended you, but—"

"It was not that," she said quickly. "Oh, at first I thought—well, you didn't mention marriage, and with Mama going after the regent the way she was, well, I thought you were thinking like mother like daughter—and that you were offering to set me up in keeping."

"My God!" he cried. "No wonder you were outraged." He squeezed her hand. "You should know I would never do such a thing. But, but I did mention marriage." He winced. "Eventually. And still you refused me."

"I didn't wish to," she said gently. Oh, this was so very difficult. She longed to throw herself into his arms, to wipe the dreadful secret from her mind and grab her happiness. But she couldn't do that. "I was about to say yes when I remembered something. I—I cannot marry you."

His dark eyebrows shot up. "For God's sake, Phillipa, why not?"

"I—" She hesitated, not sure how to go about it. "Then the secret was not mine to tell. But now—"

He took both her hands in his and gazed into her eyes. "Now tell me."

She wanted to look away, not to see his disgust when he heard the truth, but she forced herself to meet his gaze. Better to get it over with.

"I—I am not the daughter of Felicity and Ernest Pardonner," she said softly. "I am the daughter of Patricia Pardonner—of Aunt Pitty."

He stared at her, his eyes cloudy. "Aunt Pitty and—"

"I do not know my father's name," she replied, trying to hold onto her dignity. "He died before he could marry my mother. And so," she said, withdrawing her hands from his, "you see—I am illegitimate. I am—a bastard."

There, it was done. Now he would thank her politely and take his leave.

But still he sat there, his gaze probing her soul. "And—"

She shook her head. "That's all. There is no more."

"Thank God!" And he pulled her to him and kissed her even more thoroughly than before.

When he released her mouth, she could scarcely breathe and hardly think. Still she managed to say, "But, Charles, you cannot marry me."

"I can and I will," he said emphatically. "I thought your secret was something insurmountable."

"But I am—"

"I know, love." He kissed the tip of her nose. "It doesn't matter."

"But if it comes out?"

He kissed her ear. "I don't care. But, pray, who is to tell? Not you, not I, not Aunt Pitty."

"Mama," Phillipa said. "That is—Felicity. She knows."

"So she does," he said dryly. "But she has kept it secret all these years. And I daresay she will continue to do so. After all, she will have a peer for a son-in-law."

He kissed Phillipa again. "We shall take your real mama with us, of course. That's one reason I wanted you to see the house. To know that you would be comfortable there."

"Comfortable?" Phillipa smiled. "I should say so! But there is one other thing."

He looked a little startled, but he said, "Yes, my love, tell me and you shall have it."

She hesitated. "It might—it might be a little difficult."

He laughed. "Not for me. Unless it's something truly impossible—like silencing the Lindens."

Phillipa laughed. "No, nothing like that. It's just—the servants here have been so good to me. Since I was a little girl, they've been protecting me from Ma—Felicity—whenever they could. And I wish I could take them along, too. Of course, I know it's silly, but—"

He stopped her with another kiss, then he said, "It's not silly at all, my love. And as it happens Starnes has been talking about retiring to a cottage in the country. Jimson may have his position and we will find room for the others. As you saw, it is a very large house."

"Yes, it is!" She nestled further into his arms. "And you are a wonderful—" She came erect. "Oh dear!"

He chuckled. "Now what? Have you forgotten someone?"

"Mama—Felicity. She still has no income. And the regent doesn't seem to be interested in her."

"Thank goodness for that," Charles said. "But don't worry about your—about Mrs. Pardonner. I will engage a new staff for her. And pay them myself. I will also settle an income on her—modest but sufficient for her needs—to be managed by a steward of my choosing."

He raised Phillipa's hand to his mouth and kissed her palm. "There! Have we considered everyone? Have you no dog, or cat, or—"

"I wasn't allowed a pet," Phillipa said with a little giggle of joy. "But now that you mention it, I would like—"

"You shall have any animal you desire," he said. "You shall have anything—anything in this world that you want."

"That will be easy," she said, turning her face to him. "When I have you, Charles, I want for nothing else." And she put her arms about his neck and kissed *him*.

It was a most satisfying kiss, but it was interrupted midway by the crashing open of the drawing-room door.

"Scoundrel!" Felicity cried. "How dare you make advances toward my daughter?"

Phillipa drew back, confident that Charles would handle the matter. But from across the room, Aunt Pitty spoke sharply. "*My* daughter has just accepted the viscount's offer of marriage," she said. "They will be calling the banns immediately."

"They can't—" Felicity sputtered. "I won't allow—"

"We can and you will," Charles said firmly. "Aunt Pitty will explain it all to you." And while Felicity watched he drew Phillipa to him for one more kiss. "Soon, my love. Very soon."

Then, with a bow to Aunt Pitty and a smaller one to Felicity, he made his exit, leaving Phillipa and Aunt Pitty, hand in hand, to explain this latest reversal of their fortunes.

A Memorable Collection of Regency Romances

BY ANTHEA MALCOLM AND VALERIE KING

THE ROMANCES OF LORDS AND LADIES
IN JANIS LADEN'S REGENCIES

BEWITCHING MINX   (2532, $3.95)

From her first encounter with the Marquis of Penderleigh when he had mistaken her for a common trollop,
Penelope had been incensed with the darkly handsome
lord. Miss Penelope Larchmont was undoubtedly the most
outspoken young lady Penderleigh had ever known, and
the most tempting.

A NOBLE MISTRESS   (2169, $3.95)

Moriah Landon had always been a singularly practical
young lady. So when her father lost the family estate over a
game of picquet, she paid the winner, the notorious Viscount Roane, a visit. And when he suggested the means of
payment—that she become Roane's mistress—she agreed
without a blink of her eyes.

SAPPHIRE TEMPTATION   (3054, $3.95)

Lady Serena was commonly held to be an unusual young
girl—outspoken when she should have been reticent, lively
when she should have been demure. But there was one tra-
dition she had not been allowed to break: a Wexley must
marry a Gower. Richard Gower intended to teach his wife
her duties—in every way.

SCOTTISH ROSE   (2750, $3.95)

The Duke of Milburne returned to Milburne Hall trusting that the new governess, Miss Rose Beacham, had in-
stilled the fear of God into his harum-scarum brood of
siblings. But she romped with the children, refused to be
cowed by his stern admonitions, and was so pretty that he
had the devil of a time keeping his hands off her.